THE TRACK OF THE CAT

By WALTER VAN TILBURG CLARK

The Ox-Bow Incident

The City of Trembling Leaves

THE
TRACK
OF
THE
CAT

A novel by

WALTER VAN TILBURG CLARK

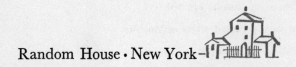

Random House · New York

CONTENTS

PART

1

1 -·-

Arthur was the first in the Bridges' ranch house to hear the far-away crying, like muted horns a little out of tune. The wind turned and came down over the shoulder of the Sierra against the house, shaking the log wall beside his bunk and hurling the snow across the window above him. It let go and slid away south, wailing under the eaves. The house relaxed and the snow whispered twice by itself, and then the faint, melancholy blowing came from the north.

Arthur rolled over to lie with his back to the wall, and curled his arm up over his head, as if to protect himself from an attack he couldn't fight against. The sound like horns sank away; the gale surged back over it, roaring through the pines on the mountain, and he didn't wake. In the shallower sleep that followed, however, the sound became a human voice crying out in despair.

It was the voice of someone he knew and loved, but the cry had come so unexpectedly, and he had been so deeply moved by the fear in it, that he couldn't remember who. He stood there listening, trying to close his mind against the continuous thunder of the wind, in order to hear that thin, plaintive cry if it came again. He had to know who it was.

He was standing in deep snow on the edge of a very high cliff, and the gale, laden with snow, was streaming across him out of the northwest. He was wearing the cowhide parka the mother had made him for winter riding, the one his brother Curt made the same old jokes about every winter, when he first put it on, calling him priest or monk because it had a deep, peaked hood, like a cowl, or old woman because, he said, the hood looked like a poke bonnet, or medicine man because the red-and-white hair of the

3

steer had been left on the hide. There was a heavy, lumberjack mitten on his right hand, but his left hand was bare. The bare hand was cold and he could feel the snow flakes driven against it. He wondered what he'd done with the mitten. He had drawn the hood of the parka as far forward as he could, to keep a breathing space between him and the flying snow. Only now and then a few flakes from the eddy about him turned in and touched him lightly and coldly upon his face above the beard. Within this sanctuary, he listened for the voice. He believed that if he heard the voice just once more, he would know who was calling, and could guess what the trouble was.

At the same time, he knew there was nothing he could do. He didn't dare move, for fear the wind should blow him off the edge of the cliff, or the snow and ice under him prove to be only an overhanging eave, and shear away at the shift of his weight. Even if he dared to move, it wouldn't do any good, because he didn't know where he was or which way to turn in order to get down off the cliff.

He believed that he stood above the western edge of the home valley, the Aspen Creek Valley, and not far south of the ranch. The voice had certainly called from below and north, and the ranch was the only place in the valley. There was nobody in the valley to call him except someone at the ranch, one of his family, or Joe Sam. But he knew he couldn't be on the edge of the valley. The only cliff in the mountains all around from which one could look out onto the valley was the one at the upper end of the Aspen Creek itself, and that was five or six miles north of the ranch, and not nearly so high and open as the one he was standing on.

He didn't know the mountain behind him, either. He could look at this mountain without turning his head or drawing back the hood, and he looked up at it through clear, thin air, too, although the abyss at his feet was filled with a river of snow pouring south in the wind. A vast, concave snowfield rose behind him from the edge of the cliff, and out of it reared the mountain, two lofty spires of pale stone together on the north, the northernmost slight, and carried like a child at the shoulder of the other, and a third peak, lower and blunter, a kind of half dome, apart from them on the south. There were glaciers between the peaks, the northern one narrow and pointing upward, the southern one wide and curved at the top, so that its point reached down and north into the snowfield. The mountain was thinly marked with snow in its crevices, and belted by a long, narrow cloud, which hid the summit of the blunt peak, but let the two spires rise through it and into the black sky.

4

This mountain moved Arthur profoundly, though he didn't know why. Also, it seemed to him in some way familiar, as the cliff he stood upon reminded him of the Aspen Creek cliff. Yet it wasn't a mountain a man would forget, once he'd seen it, and he couldn't remember ever having seen it before. It seemed to him to belong somewhere as far away as the Andes or the Himalayas or the moon.

He stopped thinking about the mountain, and his mind, with no purpose to work at, moved feebly against extinction. He wondered once more why his left hand was bare. He knew then that the hand was numb, and thrust it awkwardly into the pocket of the parka. There it encountered a small, familiar shape, one of the little figures he was always whittling because it pleased him to see them come out of the wood, and because whittling was the way he kept a hold on what was real while he was thinking. He'd been whittling, that was it. He was left-handed, and he'd taken off the mitten to whittle. He felt carefully over the little, wooden figure with his stiff fingers. It was a crouching mountain lion, and not quite finished. Of course. It was Joe Sam's black panther, the private, stalking god he had invented to mean the end of things. The first snow had begun, hadn't it? It was snowing now. And he was wearing the parka, wasn't he? He made a new black panther for Joe Sam every year, before the first snow came. The old Indian carried one on him all the time until the first storm was over, in a buckskin medicine pouch, decorated with porcupine quills and hung by a rawhide thong around his neck. Sometimes he wore it in later storms too. It was impossible to guess just what made Joe Sam decide the black panther was around again. Only it was always around in the first storm. So that was it. This was the first storm, but it was early this year, only October. He hadn't expected the first snow so early, and the cat wasn't finished. Joe Sam hadn't made his medicine against the cat, and it was still free to hunt where he was. That was the danger which threatened the one with the beloved voice. The black panther was stalking the beloved one down there. He must get down some way, and help, or at least give warning.

It came to him, in this urgent need, that if he turned north, he wouldn't have far to go to get off the cliff onto a slope of shale he could go down. He turned very carefully upon the doubtful edge, but even as he turned, the voice cried out again. His body, already cold and tense, jerked at the sound. He opened his mouth to call back that he was coming, but then made only a terrified wail like the one he wanted to answer. The snow eave had given way, a long, jagged crack opening as suddenly as lightning along the edge

5

of the granite, and he was falling helplessly into the abyss. It wasn't snow-
ing in the abyss now, and he could see in the clear darkness. He could see
the broken pieces of the ice edge swooping down after him like phantom
birds of prey. One of them was so close upon him that even as he fell, turn-
ing slowly in the air, he put out a hand to ward it off.

His bare left hand was touching something cold and smooth, but it wasn't ice. Extending his fingers, he moved them along the surface, and found it curved. He cupped his hand over the smooth curve, and smiled in the darkness, uncertainly mocking the remnants of the fear that still made him breathe like a man who has been running hard. It was an old test with him, this touching something real. He was awake now. His fingertips, exploring gently in above the peeled log, touched the flat, clay caulking. He felt the powdery surface of the clay rub off on his fingertips, soft as the dust off a moth's wing.

He was still listening for the cry, though. He was lying in his bunk against the west wall of the bunk-room, and Curt and young Hal were in there with him. He couldn't hear the cry now, but he could hear Curt and Hal breathing, and he could tell by their breathing that they were still asleep. Hal, across the room by the east wall, was breathing softly and evenly and slowly, and Curt, against the north wall, was snoring. Perhaps there hadn't really been any cry either.

While he listened, Curt snorted twice, and muttered angrily. The leather straps of his bunk creaked, and there was a soft thud as his knee or elbow struck through the quilts against the wall.

Arthur smiled a little, and thought, Always fighting some-thing, even in your sleep. Or did you hear something too?

He kept on listening, though, in spite of himself. The rest of the dream was letting go of him now, but the cry remained real, and he kept on listening for it. His hand moved farther along the log. It was icy cold. There was no sound of flame lap-ping in the old stove either. He turned his head on the pillow and saw only darkness, no lights shining in the cracks of the stove, or moving in their small, soft dance upon the floor. It must be very late, if the fire had burned out; it must be getting on toward morning.

The melancholy left by the dream was renewed, and the

6

feeling of time gone by without any good from it. He realized that he had been much younger when he stood on the cliff in the snow. His beard had been softer, and his body had felt full and powerful in the warm parka. Even his fear had been cleaner and more active, and that great love which he had sent out to the owner of the unknown voice had been a younger man's love. He had been about twenty in the dream, perhaps, about the age he had been when they came to the valley. He'd felt the life like that, in his body inside his garments, when he was twenty. Now he was twice that, and he felt long and thin and tired in his bunk, and the quilts weighed heavily upon him. The dream weighed heavily upon him too. He didn't come and go between the two worlds as confidently as he had when he was twenty, never confusing the events of one with the events of the other. Now he was still trying to remember who it was that had cried out like that in the dream. He kept listening, and he kept trying to remember. It seemed important to him that he should remember.

Perhaps it was Gwen Williams, he thought, and mocked himself with the faint smile in the dark. I forgot her. I thought of the family and Joe Sam, but I forgot she was here too, now. Wouldn't Hal like it if I told him I was dreaming about his girl already, when she only got here last night?

I don't know, though, he thought more seriously. Seems like it was a woman's voice, but then, it would be. And a voice sounds different when it screams. You can't tell.

The wind came down again, shaking the log wall and his bunk against it, beating under the eaves, and throwing the snow like sand across the window over him. He knew that it must have been snowing for a long time already. There was a cold, thick quiet in the bunk-room that could come only from deep snow outside. He wasn't surprised, though. He'd been out on the range since early the morning before, helping with the fall tally, and driving strays down out of the aspen canyons onto the yellowing meadows. He had felt the wind growing stronger and colder all morning, and in the afternoon, he had shivered in the saddle as the clouds, streaming southeastward out of the Sierra, had darkened the valley.

Then suddenly his attention came to a single point and he

7

was just listening, because that cry he had heard in his dream was in the wind again, and he was sure he was awake now. It came faintly within the deeper blowing of the storm, and it was like the faraway blowing of several horns not quite tuned together and not quite steady. Then the wind drew off, and the blowing departed with it. A few last flakes of snow scratched on the window, and the wind rose into its hollow roaring across the mountain, not touching the house.

Arthur knew what the sound was now. His mind came wholly over to the waking side of the border, and the unhappiness left in him by the dream became a foreboding, and also a disappointment. Slowly he turned back the quilts, and pushed himself upright, and swung around to sit on the edge of his bunk. A wide plank of the floor was cold under his feet. He stood up and moved slowly forward, holding his hands out ahead of him, until he felt the edge of the table. He groped over the top of the table and found the matches and struck one. Lifting the chimney off the lamp, he held the little flame to the wick. It took slowly. When the wick was burning clear across, he flipped out the match and tossed it toward the stove and set the chimney back on. The flame sank away, and then, as he turned the wick slowly up, it grew and brightened and became steady, and the shadows slunk back into their waiting places under the bunks and the table and behind the stove. Shining curves and points were picked out by the light, the silver conchas on Harold's dress chaps hanging at the head of his bunk, the nickel edge of the stove top, the big buckle of Curt's old leather bat-wings on their peg by the kitchen door, and the butt of his six-gun, and the row of little brass discs in his cartridge belt. The shining points winked like observing eyes around Arthur, and a tiny lamp burned mysteriously in space outside the window over his bunk.

His face showed clearly at the center of the light, thin, with a high, narrow forehead and high cheekbones and a thin, dark beard with a narrow gray streak going down through it from each corner of his mouth. He straightened up slowly, and the one color the close lamp had given his face became two colors, weathered darkness to just above his eyebrows, and then white forehead his hat had bleached all summer. He looked at his brothers. Hal was sleeping with his head on his arm and

8

his face turned toward the light. His arm was out straight on the pillow, and his big hand hung limply over the edge of the bunk. His wide, beardless face was calm, and his tousled hair shone gold in the light. Curt, sleeping with his face to the wall, was only a thick shape under the red-and-white quilt, and a dark head on the pillow.

Arthur moved away from the light toward Curt's bunk. He was a grotesque figure, with his long hair thick at the back, and his wrists and long, narrow hands protruding from the sleeves of the winter underwear he slept in. His shadow loomed over Curt, and then, as he advanced, grew shorter and narrower. He moved slowly, and as if still in a dream. His shadow came down off the rafters onto the wall, and dwindled there, and finally, when he stood beside Curt's bunk, lay only across Curt's head and shoulders. The shadow darkened Curt's sleep, or the near presence oppressed him. He stirred uneasily, and muttered thick words of protest. Arthur waited, looking down at him. He didn't know that he was waiting. He was thinking about the mountain in his dream. It still seemed to him that he should remember where he had seen that mountain before.

The wind turned down from the Sierra again and leaned heavily upon the house and pummeled it for a moment, and then failed, and beat off south under the eaves, and once more the faint, melancholy blowing came after it. Arthur lifted his head to listen, and then drew a deep breath and sighed and leaned over and put his hand gently on Curt's shoulder.

"Curt," he said softly. "Curt, wake up."

Harold, with the light shining in his face, heard the voice like a whispering, and woke up. He didn't move, but only opened his eyes and looked at once at Arthur bending over Curt, and after a moment asked quietly, "What's up, Art?"

The wind was beginning to play under the eaves again. Arthur, still with his hand on Curt's shoulder, looked around and grinned. "Awake already? Thought you'd need your sleep this morning."

Harold grinned too. "Slept plenty. The old man wouldn't go to bed till we did. What's wrong?"

"Maybe I'm just hearing things," Arthur said. "You listen."

9

He raised his left hand from the wrist without raising his arm and pointed to the west wall. "When the wind shifts."

Harold raised himself onto his elbow and lay listening. He was going to speak once, but Arthur hushed him with the shy left hand. At last the wind swelled out of its fluttering, and thundered across the house. It spent itself and retreated south, and came again, less violently and almost straight from the north. The sound like faraway horns was in it, swelling and shrinking in the gusts.

"Something's at 'em up there," Harold said quickly, and swung out from under his covers and stood up.

Arthur nodded and turned back to Curt, saying, "Curt, wake up," and rocking him gently by the shoulder.

Harold was pulling on his shirt already. He grinned and said, "Look out you don't get a fist in the teeth."

Arthur nodded without looking around. "He was fighting the wall when I woke up," he said, and went on rocking Curt, and said, more loudly, "Curt."

Curt muttered, and struck loosely at the hand on his shoulder. Then he turned over suddenly and lifted himself on both elbows and stared up at Arthur. The down-curved wings of his big, dark moustache made an enormous, grim mouth in the shadow.

"Huh?" he asked loudly. "What the hell now?"

Arthur straightened up and made the little, left-hand sign to him to listen, but Harold, sitting on the edge of his bunk to pull on his socks, said, "Cows are bawlin'. Something's at 'em."

But the wind turned up without losing strength this time, lifting into the pines with a roar like a heavy surf, and the creaking in the walls died away and there was nothing else after it.

Curt squinted his eyes as if he could see the sound, and when there was only the gentle sliding of snow at the window, said, "For God's sake, do you have to wake me up to hear your dreams? Go back to bed," and rolled under the covers with his face to the wall again.

"It's no dream," Harold said.

"You only hear it when the wind's right," Arthur said.

Curt twisted over onto one elbow and stared up at him again. There was no sleep in his eyes now; they were wide and unsteady with rage.

"Look," he said, growling in the thick column of his throat, "all I want is a little sleep. If you have to hold somebody's hand, hold Hal's. He's hearing things too."

The wind turned down toward the house and deepened again, and Arthur, with his head bent to listen, so that he smiled at nothing between himself and Curt, once more made the little sign with his left hand.

Harold said, "Listen now," and sat motionless with one boot in his hands.

The long, melancholy blowing came down behind the wind.

Curt was out of his bunk and standing before the wind had lifted onto the mountain again.

"How long's that been going on?" he asked, accusing them both with the question.

Arthur, still smiling, shrugged his shoulders a little, but Harold said quickly, "We've only been awake a minute."

"And doing what?"

"I thought you'd want to know," Arthur said.

"You thought," Curt said. "The hell you did, ever." He pushed past Arthur, saying, "Why the hell wouldn't I?" and took his clothes off the wall and threw them onto the bunk and began to dress.

"Get your clothes on," he told Arthur. "Do you think it'll wait for us?"

Arthur stood there with his head turned away, as if he were still listening, but for something farther away than the bawling of the cattle now. He was close to remembering whose voice it was that had called to him out of the chasm below the cliff.

Curt had his shirt and pants on already. He sat down on the edge of his bunk and pulled his boots on, and stood up and began to pound the heels against the floor to get them clear on. He saw Arthur still standing there listening, and asked sharply, "What ails you now? Gettin' Joe Sam's second sight?" He picked up the scarred bat-wing chaps, and, when Arthur didn't reply, stood holding them and staring at him.

Finally he said softly, "I bet it's that black cat, eh? That awful

11

black painter, big as a horse, and you can see through it? Sure," he murmured. "What the hell's the use of hunting a cat as big as a horse, especially when it hates men worse than anything, and lives forever, and a slug just goes through it and it keeps a-comin'? That it?"

He pulled on the chaps, wrenching angrily at them when they caught. "Do you see the black cat out there, medicine man?" he asked, his voice louder. He jerked the big nickel buckle of the chaps to lock it. "So you'd like to go back to bed?"

Arthur looked at him then, still smiling, but as if at something else. "I had a dream," he said. "I was just trying to remember . . ."

"You had a dream," Curt said. "He had a dream," he told Harold. "Look, dreamer," he said to Arthur, "I know what really ails you, if you don't. You know damn well it's a cat, and no dream cat either, and you're afraid dear pussy'll get hurt. By God, if I don't believe you'd give 'em our best beef, and bottle-feed the cubs too, if you could."

Arthur smiled, and studied him with his eyes in the way Curt couldn't stand. "I might at that," he said. "Slaughter for the joy of it is a thing comes back on you, in time. It's a matter of numbers. The cats were here when we came, and still there were more deer than there are now."

Curt made a short laugh, and would have answered, but again the wind turned down and struck the house like a slide of earth, and the three men looked away from one another and listened. The flame of the lamp shook and dwindled in an errant draft, and their three shadows danced in changing shapes on the walls. The wind went off crying under the eaves. The flame rose again, and the three shadows became steady, but this time no sound of the bawling followed.

Curt said suddenly and loudly, "Yeah, and the Indians was here first too, preacher, and they're goin'. What's left of 'em in these parts? Joe Sam. One crazy old Piute that thinks he's a hundred, and chuck full of kid's lies, that's what's left. And good riddance, I say. What the hell good are they? And the same for your cats. You and your dreams," he said contemptuously. "Yes, and the old man and his wonderful Comstock; the good old days. You're both the same kind now. Can't see what's

12

in front of your nose, but, oh, the good, old days. Well, once I'm out of here, you can have your good, old days; you can hand-feed your cats, if you want to, yes, and your Joe Sams too. You can marry your goddam dreams. Lay 'em every night and see what it gets you, besides weak knees and whining in the morning. And don't worry, once I get a stake big enough to work on, I'll get out of here, too, so fast you won't even see me goin'.

"But until then, by Christ," he said more heavily, making each word count, "we'll raise cattle, not dreams, and we'll kill whatever kills cattle. Get that, and don't FORGET it. You can breed your dreams later, and welcome. I'll have better things to do."

"Meaning if one Comstock's used up, there'll be another?" Arthur asked softly. "A bigger and better one?"

"You goddam right there will," Curt said, "for the guy that knows it when he sees it, and has the cartwheels to buck it. Is 1900 the end of the world, old whisker-face?"

"It'll do for the end of one, anyway," Arthur said, and then, smiling, and as if to stop the quarrel, "Well, a life's a life, and you can't buy more than one, no matter how many Comstocks you own. I'll stick to ranching the dreams then, and thanks."

"You think there won't be more, eh?"

"One kind or another, one man at a time, or in little gangs, sure, plenty, I guess," Arthur said slowly, as if thinking it out for himself, and seeing it as it would be. "But for everybody? No. That was a kind of dream too, a big, fat one, and it's over. We've gone from ocean to ocean, Curt, burning and butchering and cutting down and plowing under and digging out, and now we're at the end of it. Virginia City's where the fat dream winked out. Now we turn back."

"So there's nothing left now, you think?" Curt asked.

Arthur shook his head. "There's us," he said. "We can start digging into ourselves now; we can plow each other under. But not so many men will like that for a hope. Even a good dream, backed up, turns nightmare, and this wasn't a very good one to start with. A belly dream."

"It isn't all like that, Art," Harold said.

"You're damned shootin' it isn't," Curt said.

"No," Arthur said, looking down, and speaking as if to himself again. "Or it wasn't, anyway. There were good dreams too, little ones that got swallowed up by the fat one. And even the fat one made some good lives, before it got backed up."

"You'll eat air from now on, I suppose," Curt said.

"Somebody's going to have to," Arthur said, "and I'm built for it, I guess." He grinned and pulled out the slack of his underwear from his flat stomach.

Curt made the short laugh. "I'll leave you the air then. That's a divvy I'd like fine."

Arthur let the slack of his underwear back slowly, and peered at Curt from under his eyebrows, still grinning. "And the dreams, Curt? Not the fat one. All the little ones?"

"And all the dear little dreams," Curt said. "I don't want anybody sayin' I'm close-fisted with my own brother."

Arthur nodded. "Thanks. They're going to multiply."

Curt laughed again. "Well, you should know," he said. "I told you he'd breed 'em," he said to Harold. "Every night he's at it, and most days too. His own herd bull. I don't see how he stands it. But for now . . ." he began, looking at Arthur again, but the wind returned, thundering, and he broke off, and they listened. The wind gave way to the lull they were waiting for, but there was no blowing of the sad horns.

"I'm gettin' as bad as you are," Curt said to Arthur, and turned to the pegs by the door and took down his mackinaw, a bright red one with a wide, black stripe around the middle and on the sleeves. He took down his scarf and his big hat with the rattlesnake skin band on it too.

"Get your clothes on, will you?" he said, with his hand on the latch of the kitchen door. "You've laid enough dreams tonight to . . ." He stopped there and stood listening. In the kitchen, someone was moving the stove lids.

"Kee-rist," Curt said, but not loudly. "We've woke the old lady up. Now there'll be two of you, and we'll never get out of here. Get a move on, will you?"

"I'll go," Harold said. "I'm all set."

Curt had opened the door a crack, but now he closed it again, grinning, and shook his head. He watched Arthur cross slowly

14

to his bunk and take his blue flannel shirt from the wall, and then he looked at Harold.

"I gotta have Art," he said, "in case the cat's black, and big as a horse. I wouldn't know what to do with a cat that was black and big as a horse. And Joe Sam won't be any good this mornin'. He was already talkin' to himself last night, before the snow'd even started. Besides," he added, looking back at Arthur, and still grinning, "he'd be for the cat."

"You can't blame him," Arthur said mildly.

"Don't even know as I can trust Art, for that matter. He's gettin' awful fond of that black painter himself."

"I am at that," Arthur said. "I was just dreaming it was loose."

"Gee," Curt said, making the big eyes of a child in awe. "No wonder you're in no hurry. I'll tell you what, Art," he said confidentially, "I'll make me a special bullet. I'll melt up some of your dreams—they're plenty heavy enough—and make a magic bullet, and you can put the medicine on it, huh? Only," he finished sharply, "do it some time this week, will you?"

He opened the door again, and through the opening they could see the mother standing at the stove in her old gray flannel bathrobe, with her gray hair still hanging loose down her back. The light from the lamp was on her back, but her face was toward the stove and in the dark.

Harold looked at her out there, and said, "I'll go, Curt." He grinned. "It's a hundred to one anyway it's not black."

"I don't know, kid," Curt said seriously, still mocking Arthur. "It's the first snowstorm, and you remember how upset Joe Sam was last night. No, kid," he said, grinning back at him, "you gotta stay here and tend to the future. You're the white hope of the Bridges. You don't think she wants to talk to Arthur, do you?" He laughed, and went into the kitchen, leaving the door open.

Arthur sat down on the edge of his bunk to pull his boots on. "He's right about that, Hal," he said. "You better break Gwen in to the rest of us kind of gradual, and you better do it yourself."

In the kitchen Curt was saying, "Something's at the stock, Ma."

"I heard 'em," the mother said.

"I'm goin' up there."

The two in the bunk-room could see him taking the lantern down from the shelf behind the stove. Then he went out of sight toward the table with it.

"By yourself?" the mother asked.

Curt's voice, half laughing, and muffled by the wall, answered, "No, ma'am. I'm takin' Art with me. We got a notion it might be the black painter."

The mother set the stove lids back on and pulled the big iron skillet over onto them, and without looking around said, scornfully, "Black painter." She moved away toward the sink in the far corner, saying, "It might as well be, though, for all you'll ever find, goin' out there now."

Harold said, "He'll be like that all the way, if you go."

Arthur stood up and stamped his heels down into his boots and crossed to the big pine chest in the corner beyond his bunk.

"I'm used to it," he said. "After about so long, you don't hear it."

He lifted the lid of the chest and began to search down through the blankets and clothes packed in it.

In the kitchen the mother's voice was saying, the little Arkansas drag in it, slow and flat, "You'll put some food in your stomach before you go," and then, after Curt had answered something they couldn't understand, "It won't even be daylight for an hour yet. Shut that door, will you? There's a draft comin' in here like out of an ice-house."

Curt's boots sounded across the kitchen floor and the bunk-room door was closed.

Arthur let down the lid on the chest and straightened up with the cowhide parka in his hands. He held it up and sniffed at it.

"Mother goes a little heavy on the camphor," he said. He took the camphor bag out of one pocket, and poked it back under the lid of the chest. There was more than a camphor bag in the other pocket, though, and when he had emptied it, he stood there looking at what he held on his hand.

"Got some unfinished whittling," he said. "This one's an Indian skinning something, you can see that. But this one," he said, smiling and holding it up between his thumb and fore-finger for Harold to see. Only the first cuts had been made on it, many small, stubborn cuts, like ripples on a wave, but all going with the grain and the shape of the wood.

"Might as well be God, for all I can make of it now," he said. "Mountain mahogany," he added, letting the piece down into his hand again and staring at it a moment longer, trying to remember. "Probably I just got worn out tryin' to whittle it."

He dropped the two pieces of wood back into the pocket of the parka and poked the camphor that had come out with them into the chest. He remained there, bent over and holding the lid of the chest up, as the wind returned, wrestling the house and chafing the window with snow, and then rose roaring into the steep of pines. There was no other sound behind it, and he let the lid down and straightened up. He looked at Harold and smiled and shook his head.

"There won't be many tracks left in that," Harold agreed.

"It's not the little dreamers that hunt black painters," Arthur said softly. He crossed to the table, carrying the parka over his arm, and turned the lamp down.

"Get the door, will you, Hal?"

Harold went to the kitchen door and took hold of the latch, and Arthur curved a hand around the far side of the lamp chimney and leaned over and blew against it. For a moment the huge shadow angel his shoulders made across the beams of the ceiling fluttered wildly, and all the tiny, watchful, metal eyes winked rapidly, and then the room was dark.

"Curt generally gets what he goes after, though," Harold said.

"He generally does," Arthur said, and his boots sounded, coming slowly toward the door. "But he likes a few tracks to go on," he added.

"They help, all right," Harold said, and opened the door and held it, watching Arthur come up the shaft of light it let in.

2

The kitchen was already full of the sound and smell of the bacon on the hot pan. The mother was standing at the stove, cutting chunks of potato into the pan with the bacon, and she didn't look around when Arthur, and then Harold behind him, came in.

Curt was sitting facing her at the round table in the middle of the room, with the big east window full of darkness behind him. He had his red coat on, and the old black sombrero was on the back of his head. The lighted lantern stood on the floor beside his chair. Its flame appeared small and smoky in there, making only a little pool of orange light in the shadow under the table.

The ceiling of the kitchen was very high, to make room for the stairs that went up against the north wall to a small landing with one closed door on it, and there was only one lamp, with a china bowl and a big china shade, hanging from a long, spring-chain over the center of the table. The walls and the ceiling were whitewashed though, and all the doors, the outside one in the corner behind Curt, and the one on the landing, and the two in the north wall, one under the landing and the other at the foot of the stairs, were painted white, so the room seemed full of light after the bunk-room. There were small, hand-painted flowers scattered over the shade of the lamp that made separate, fluttering shadows, like moths, on the walls and ceiling, and the bowl of the lamp made a circle of shadow on the table. Curt peered across through the shadow of the bowl when Arthur came out, and saw him stop for a moment to get used to the change from the bunk-room. He looked at the cowhide parka over Arthur's arm and grinned.

"My God," he said. "I ask for a medicine man, and what do I get? A priest again. A damned monk. Well, that's next best, I guess, ain't it? Not too much difference. Especially when the monk's a prophet too. Did you know your monk was a prophet too, now, Ma?"

"Don't blaspheme," the mother said, but she spoke flatly, as if only out of habit, and she didn't look around this time either. "You may as well set down," she told Arthur and Harold. "There's nothing to hurry for, that I can see, and I'll be a few minutes yet with your breakfast."

Harold closed the bunk-room door and went around the table and sat down with his back to the stairs. Arthur, moving more slowly, came to the chair on the near side and hung the parka over the back of it and sat down. He leaned both elbows on the table and rubbed his eyes slowly with his long hands, and then sat there with his eyes still covered by his hands.

"He really is, though," Curt said. "He had a dream that showed him it was the black painter out there. That's why I gotta take him along."

"I had a dream of my own," the mother said, "and it ain't left me much in the mood for jokes."

"More dreams," Curt said, chuckling. "And Joe Sam was at his before he went to bed even. The place is crawling with 'em. Did you have bad dreams too, young 'un?" he asked Harold.

Harold smiled a little and shook his head.

"Good ones, eh? By Chrimus, so would I, if I was you. I wouldn't want to ever wake up. If I had a girl like . . ."

"Watch your mouth," the mother said sharply.

"Now, what did I say to make you go jumpin' on me like that?" He winked at Harold. "It's not as if Hal, here, hadn't ever heard of such things. Or Gwen either, as far as that goes," he added judiciously. "Now I have a notion, just to look at her, that . . ."

The mother turned around with the knife and a potato still in her hands and looked at Curt. Her face was like Arthur's, long and narrow and tired-looking, with deep hollows at the temples and under the cheek-bones, and her eyes set back in deep hollows. The lines across her forehead and beside her mouth were much deeper and less broken than Arthur's, though, and her tired look wasn't gentle or quiet. It wasn't the look that comes from lack of sleep, or from too much work, or from struggling against someone else's will. It was the look that

19

comes from war inside which is never ended, but never lost, either. When the will that sustained her in this war was turned outward, free of the enemy it had inside, it became like the threat of a weapon. No matter who she was looking at, everyone there would feel that she was looking at him, and that a weapon was pointed at him.

It was like that now. She was looking at Curt, but Harold, seeing her face, laid his big fingers over the edge of the table and looked down at them, and Arthur, almost at once, looked away from her and watched the shadows like moths on the wall.

"I told you to watch your mouth," the mother said.

Curt tried to keep it a joke still. "Now, Mother," he said, too loudly, "it's not Hal that's the monk. He's pretty near twenty, and he . . ."

"Did you hear me, Curtis?"

The anger gathered suddenly in Curt's face, and his eyes began a little, blinding dance. "Look," he said, "I'm no kid either. I'm thirty-seven years old. Arthur here's forty," he said to make an ally. "The old man, for Christ's sake, is over seventy. And you go bossing the whole bunch of us like we was kids. We can't even make a little joke, for God's sake. Well, we ain't kids, even if you never . . ."

"You don't have to shout," the mother said. "My hearing's as good as it ever was, and the girls is already awake in there. Do you want Gwen Williams to hear the names you're callin' her?"

"Jesus," Curt said, not so loudly, but as if he would burst. He doubled his hands into fists and pressed them down on the table hard enough to lift his shoulders. "What did I call her? Just tell me one thing I called her. " He looked at Arthur, and then at Harold. "Did you hear me call her anything?"

"It didn't take any fancy guessing to know what you meant."

"Look," Curt said, "if we're going to start guessing, then what I've thought about Gwen Williams is goddamned brotherly love compared to what you . . ."

Harold said, "Let it go, Curt, will you?"

Curt turned on him. "You stickin' up for her now? You know as well as I do what she thinks of your . . ."

"I think what I think," the mother said sharply, "and I'll

keep it to myself till there's some use to say it. If you're in such a tearin' hurry to get out there and see what you can see in pitch dark and a blizzard, you better be gettin' them ponies saddled while I'm puttin' the breakfast on."

The veins began to bulge on Curt's throat and forehead, and he stared at her back with the little, mad dance in his eyes. "By Jesus," he began finally, but got no further before the mother said, turning over the potatoes with a fork as she spoke, "And there's no need that I can see for your takin' holy names in vain every time you open your mouth."

Curt stood up suddenly, pushing his chair back with a loud, scraping noise, but keeping his fists on the table. Arthur waved a hand at him slowly and shook his head in time to the waving, like a man taking his side but saying it had gone far enough for now. Curt turned his head to stare at him, and Arthur pointed at the closed door at the foot of the stairs. Curt set his mouth, but listened, and heard the murmur of women's voices behind the door. While he listened one voice made a quick, excited laugh. Then the other voice laughed too, a lower sound, full of soft, easy amusement. Curt flushed as if the women had seen through the door how he was checked like a small boy and were laughing at him.

"To hell with 'em," he said. "If a man . . ." but his voice was only a mutter, and he didn't finish. He straightened up slowly, and then stood there staring at the other three, one at a time. None of them said anything, or even looked at him. The mother, with her back turned, went on stirring the sizzling potatoes in the pan. Slowly he made a small, angry smile, and looked around at them again, but now as if they were enemies already cowed, and not worth even that much attention. He picked up the lantern and set it on the table and turned the flame a little higher to stop the smoking.

"That's not a bad idea at that," he said. "At least, if horses have dreams, they don't get up sour and talk about 'em."

He picked up the lantern and went to the outside door, but stopped there again, and said, "And when I get back, we're leavin' pronto. Get me?"

"I'll have your breakfast on," the mother said. "It'll be an hour yet before there's light enough to see what you're doing anyway."

"We don't need any light to get to the creek," Curt said, "and that's where it come from."

He opened the door. The roaring of the pines deepened and a gust of cold wind came in, driving a thin serpent of snow across the floor and nearly blowing the lamp out, so the shadow moths fluttered wildly on the walls.

"When I get back," he yelled, to be heard over the wind, and went out, slamming the door behind him. The flame of the lamp steadied and rose again, and the moths danced small and gentle in their places. Slowly the fine, white powder on the floor vanished. The high woman's voice spoke in the north bedroom again.

Arthur took a jack-knife and the unfinished mountain lion out of his pants pocket. He opened the knife slowly, thinking of something else, and felt along the edge of the blade with his thumb. The blade was worn narrow as a dagger with long use and many sharpenings. He began to cut slowly and carefully at the shoulder of the lion, holding the knife in his left hand and pushing the back of the blade with the thumb of his right hand, curling off small, neat shavings.

Harold watched him, smiling a little. "No wonder Joe Sam was in such a stew," he said.

Arthur nodded. "Behind in my whittling."

The mother set two plates on the lid of the water tank on the end of the stove, and lifted two fried eggs onto each plate and began to scrape the potato and bacon onto them. In the bedroom the high voice said something quickly and gayly, and the other made a short answer and then the soft, easy laughter. Harold turned his head to listen and smiled. "They're having a good time in there," he said.

"Aren't they," the mother said dryly. She drew the boiling coffee pot off the fire, and poured coffee, still hissing and bubbling, into two cups beside the plates.

"It's good for Grace, having someone new to talk to for a while," Arthur said.

"It's precious little but talk I'll get out of her, too," the mother said. She brought the two filled plates to the table and

22

set them down in front of Arthur and Harold and laid a knife, spoon and fork beside each plate. She stood there for a moment, staring down at the plates, and then she looked at Harold and said, "Harold, it'd be better if you'd go instead of Arthur, the way Curt's takin' on this morning."

"No, Mother, it's all right," Arthur said. "He can't very well go off with Gwen just come, and her first visit, too."

"There'll be time enough to see her," the mother said. She went to the stove and picked up the two heavy coffee mugs and brought them back and set them down beside the plates. "He wouldn't be gone a lifetime," she said to Arthur. "Either they'll find something at the creek, or they won't. They'll be back before noon."

Arthur looked up at her, holding the knife still, and smiled and shook his head. "You know Curt better than that, Mother," he said.

He looked across at Harold. Harold was staring at the shadow in the middle of the table. His face was quiet, but set. Arthur looked down, and began his careful whittling again.

"No, I'm going," he said. "Anyway," he added, smiling, "Curt needs me, in case the cat is black."

He held the little wooden lion up and away from him and studied it, still smiling, and then brought it back into his lap again.

"That heathen nonsense," the mother said.

"I'm not so sure," Arthur said. "Joe Sam just likes a god he can see."

"A god," the mother said. "Well, I'm sure, if you're not. Stupid, childish nonsense."

"And a black panther," Arthur went on, as if she hadn't spoken, "is as good a god as any to mean the end of things."

"You're worse than Curt and his swearing," the mother said. "Your godless jokes. If you keep it up, you'll be believing them, next thing you know."

"Not godless," Arthur said. "Full of gods, like Joe Sam."

"Humph," the mother said, and went back to the stove and took up the coffee pot again. The wind returned against the house, and she stood with the coffee pot in her hand and listened to it. The wind pressed briefly and without thunder,

23

only making that hollow beating of big wings under the eaves. Before it let the dry snow off the little window over the sink, Grace and Gwen laughed together again in the north bedroom, and Grace said something after the laughter, with that same high gayety in her voice.

"If I'd had my way," the mother said angrily, "I'd of turned that no-good old Indian off the place the day he come. Him and his creeping ways and his crazy notions. But no, your father had to be smart. He had to get him a hired hand for nothing but his keep. Hired hand," she said scornfully. "Less use than nigger help, and dirtier too. I'd ruther have a fool nigger around. They're mostly cheerful anyway."

Harold looked across at Arthur, and then pulled his chair in closer and began slowly to eat his breakfast. Arthur stopped the knife again, and looked at the mother from under his eyebrows. The mother took a deep breath and stood there for a moment, as if to steady herself against her own anger, and then let the breath out and poured coffee into a third mug. Arthur looked down and began to whittle again.

"Joe Sam has his own jokes," he said.

"Jokes," the mother said, coming to the table. "We'll be lucky if one of his jokes don't wind up with us all layin' in our beds with our throats cut." She sat down and set her coffee mug on the table in front of her.

"He's planning it pretty carefully," Arthur said, holding the wooden lion out again to study it, and smiling at what he was thinking. "It's about eighteen years he's been here now, isn't it?"

"Do you know what he's thinking when he gets this way?" the mother asked. "No more'n I do, for all your gossipin' with him. Or all your heathenish readin' either." She spoke quietly, but the little fury was dancing in her eyes the way it did in Curt's.

Arthur went on carefully whittling at the lion, and didn't answer. Finally the mother looked away from him, and sighed and put her hands up to the sides of her face and pressed hard at her temples with her fingertips.

"Was it a bad dream you had, Mother?" Arthur asked.

"Never you mind my dreams," the mother said, but not angrily. "I don't take no stock in them either." She took her

24

hands down from her face and laid one in her lap, limply, palm up, and lifted her coffee mug with the other. She blew slowly across the coffee twice, and then sipped at it twice.

"If you're going hunting painters," she said to Arthur, "even black ones, you'd better get some breakfast in you."

Arthur made four more careful little cuts on the shoulder of the lion, and then reached around back of him and slipped it into the pocket of the cowhide parka, with the other two carvings. He closed the knife and put it in his pants pocket and drew his chair in. He picked up his fork, but then just held it while he looked at the mother's face. She was staring down across the mug into the center of the shadow on the table.

"Only coffee again?" Arthur asked gently.

She turned her head finally, and looked at him and smiled a little. "I have to get waked up some way," she said. "You know how it is if you have a bad dream last thing before you wake up."

Arthur nodded, and they were quiet for a time, Harold eating and Arthur picking at his food with the fork and the mother blowing on her coffee and sipping it. The quick, cheerful conversation of the two voices went on in the north bedroom.

The mother put her coffee cup down finally, and looked into it, and said, "Harold, have you thought any how you'll live when you get married?"

Harold glanced at her, but she kept studying her coffee, and he looked back at his plate. "It hasn't gone that far," he said.

"It's what you want, isn't it?" the mother asked. "It's for sure what them Williams think you want, all the time you've spent sittin' in their kitchen, with more'n twenty miles of ridin' to get there."

Harold's neck grew red, and the color rose slowly into his cheeks. Without looking up, he got himself ready to say something but then didn't say it after all, but just closed his mouth again.

"Isn't it what you want?"

"I guess it is," Harold said slowly. "If she does."

"You needn't to worry too much about that," the mother said. "Not with the money this ranch can make, and that gopher hole the Williams is livin' in."

Harold lifted his head quickly and stared at her this time.

25

Arthur peered at her too, squinting as if he were trying to see something a long way off, or through a blinding light. The mother didn't look up. Harold drew a short breath and worked the muscles of his jaws three or four times, and then looked down again. "She's not that kind," he said.

"Maybe not," the mother said, "but whether she is or not, it's high time you thought what you're going to do. Was you expecting to bring her here, into this house?"

"No," Harold said, "I wouldn't think so."

"No, I wouldn't think so either." She looked at him for the first time, and studied him for a moment as he sat bent over his plate but not eating. "What was you figurin' on doin' then?" she asked.

Arthur said softly, "It doesn't have to be settled right now, does it, Mother?"

"Now's as good a time as any. I don't see there's anything to be gained puttin' it off."

"It'll work out," Arthur said. "Just give it time."

"Things won't be any different a year from now, or ten years from now, for that matter. Nothin' works out by itself, that I ever see."

"They do when they matter enough," Arthur said.

"Even if they did, what's to be hurt talkin' them over sensible beforehand?"

"Some times are better than others," Arthur said.

"It's not me that's hurryin' things," the mother said. "It don't seem likely to me that Gwen Williams thinks she's been asked over just to keep an old maid like Grace company. I'd be glad enough to let it wait if it would. Harold's too young to be gettin' married. Nineteen's too young to get married. And to an older woman at that."

"You talk as if she was fifty," Harold said. "She's not two years older'n I am."

"She's a woman," the mother said, "and that's as good as ten years extra any time. You're a child comparin' to Gwen Williams. And them Welsh minin' people grows old ahead of their time anyway. I know. I've seen a-plenty of 'em, from Hangtown to Virginia City."

"That's not the people; it's the work," Arthur said. "And

26

the Williams aren't mining now. They're living the same way we do."

"I wouldn't say so," the mother said. "In that little black shack, and runnin' a handful of half-starved stock."

Arthur didn't reply this time, and Harold began to eat again.

"But the matter's out of my hands now," the mother said. "If it was ever in 'em, which I didn't notice it was. All I'm askin' is, do you have any sensible plan made?"

"We'll work it out," Harold said stubbornly.

"Not without some notion how, you won't. You wasn't plannin' on movin' in with the Williams, was you?"

"I can take care of myself. I'm no kid."

"I don't know what else you are. You was born in this valley, in that very room where they're so busy chatterin' now, and you never been out of it, more'n to drive stock to Reno or sit in the Williams' kitchen. You don't know nothing but ranchin' this valley. What would you do anywhere else?"

"This isn't the only ranch in the world," Harold said.

"It's the only one you're ever likely to see, though. Or was you figurin' on keepin' a wife on a cow hand's wage?"

"I wouldn't be the first that started that way."

"I know," the mother said. "It was simple once. All they had to do was make 'em an iron with the right curves to fit over somebody else's brand, and they was set. But the country you could do that on's all took up now, all that's any use for anything. And the open range has got outfits runnin' on it that ain't exactly honin' to share it with rustlers, not that I've heard tell of."

Harold sat staring at his plate and didn't answer.

"It's practical facts I'm tryin' to get straight," the mother said, "not dreams."

Still Harold didn't say anything, and finally, before the mother could speak again, Arthur said, "This is a big valley. It could carry a lot more stock than we've ever run on it."

The mother looked at him, and smiled tightly, and the triumph was already in her eyes. "I had a notion that's where we was headin'," she said.

"Well, why not?" Arthur asked mildly. "We could all help with a house-raising, like old times."

27

"And divide up the valley, maybe?" the mother asked, before he could go on.

Arthur smiled, seeing how she followed her planned line, and shook his head. "We wouldn't any of us like to see the valley fenced, I guess. There's no need of it. We could have one round-up and one drive, the same as ever, only let Hal take his share out, that's all."

"Like you been takin' yours out the last twenty years," the mother said.

"It doesn't matter to me," Arthur said. "I'd just as soon see mine in the kitty. But it does matter to Hal now, and Dad owes him the start."

"It's some time since your pa's had anything to say about it," the mother said dryly. "Or cared anything about it either, for that matter." She finished her coffee and set the cup down. "He never did care, far as that goes," she said. "The money don't come sudden enough in ranchin' to suit him. Not around here, anyway. Your pa's a man to think in big figures. But if he did have any say," she concluded, "he wouldn't be for splittin' up the holdin's. Nor I wouldn't neither. Once the splittin' up starts, there's no end to it."

"There's no need to split, Mother," Arthur said. "Hal takes his share of every sale separate; that's all the change there'd be."

The mother made the thin, concluding smile again. "Have you spoke to Curt about that yet?" she asked.

Harold spoke suddenly and angrily. "Sure, that's where it sticks, all right. That's where it always sticks. Everything."

"Curt has big ambitions," Arthur said softly. He stood up. "More coffee, Mother?" he asked.

The mother nodded. "Thank you," she said. She looked at his plate. "You ain't ate hardly anything," she said.

Arthur grinned down at her. "Look at your plate," he countered.

"It's this wakin' up so early," she said. "I ain't ready to eat yet."

Arthur shook his head at her. "When did you last have anything but coffee for breakfast?" he asked.

"Go on with you," she said, smiling in spite of herself.

"You see," he said. "You can't remember yourself." He went

28

to the stove and came back with the coffee pot and poured the mother's cup full, and said, "Hal?" Harold pushed his cup toward him and Arthur filled it too, and looked down at Harold, smiling, and said, "Some day, boy."

"That's our motto here," Harold said. "Some day."

Arthur crossed behind the mother and filled his own cup. "It happens," he said softly, and nodding. "It happens in anything. It can go on one way just so long, and then it happens. Curt will see that too, when the time comes." He carried the coffee pot back to the stove and set it just off the firelids to keep hot.

"Curt will see it when he's made to see it and not before," Harold said. "That's one place where I agree with Mother anyway. And if that's what you mean," he added, doubling one big hand into a fist on the table, but not moving the fist, "I agree with you too. It'll happen."

"You wouldn't want to see it broke up yourself, would you, son?" the mother asked.

In the north room Grace laughed shrilly, and upstairs the floor boards creaked, and then slow, heavy footsteps crossed the room and paused and crossed back, as if the laughter had started the moving up there. Arthur returned to his place and sat down.

Harold sat staring at his coffee for a time. Then he picked up the mug and emptied it without pausing and set it down hard and stood up. "If that's the only way to do it, yes," he said. "Curt's had his way around here too damn long. And he don't give a damn about the ranch, either. Only what he can get out of it for himself. If he got an offer he liked, he'd sell it right out from under us, and not ask anybody about it either."

"No," the mother said, shaking her head at him. "No, he wouldn't, son. He talks that way sometimes, but he wouldn't. You know that."

"I know he won't," Harold said softly. "I know he won't, but it isn't because he wouldn't like to."

"It's just talk," the mother said. "He loves the place."

Harold shook his head. "No," he said. "There's only two things Curt loves: money and his own way. Well," he said, "talking about it's not gonna do any good. I'd better get at the chores, I guess." He started around the table.

"You ain't goin' to say anything to Curt now?" the mother asked quickly.

"No. I'll wait till Gwen's gone. But we're gonna settle it then. One way or another, we're gonna settle it then." He crossed to the pegs by the outside door and took down a green plaid mackinaw that hung there, and put it on.

"If Joe Sam's out there, bring him in when you're done," the mother said. "I'd sooner not have him around when he's like this, but I can't let him sit out there and starve. He never touched his supper last night. There's gotta be somebody there to make him eat."

"All right," Harold said. He pulled a fur cap with ear flaps out of his pocket and put it on and went out, letting in the sound and the cold of the wind for a moment, and then closing it off.

Arthur had both his hands around his coffee mug on the table, as if to warm them. "Sounds like the storm's letting up some," he said.

"It ain't done yet, by a long ways," the mother said. "If Curt had the sense he was born with," she said angrily.

"Harold won't start anything now," Arthur said. "He's . . ."

"I ain't worrying myself none about that," the mother said sharply. "Curt can take care of anything that young one'll start for a long while yet. It's this fool goin' out in the dark in a blizzard."

"Oh," Arthur said softly, as if he saw more than she meant in what she said. He looked at her with that squint to his eyes again, and smiling a little. "I wouldn't worry myself any about that, Mother. We'll be all right."

The mother shook her head. "I don't know," she said. "It's that dream, I guess. I can't get it out of my head somethin's gonna happen."

"You'd better go back to bed, Mother. We're all fixed up now."

The mother shook her head again. "It ain't that," she said. "I can feel in my bones somethin's gonna happen, like I felt this snow comin' two days ago."

30

The floor boards upstairs creaked again under the heavy tread.

"Dad's getting up too," Arthur said.

"He was awake when I got up," the mother said, and added dryly, "He's fixin' himself up in front of the lookin' glass."

Arthur grinned. "Having Gwen here cheers him up a lot."

"Don't it," the mother said.

The heavy tread stopped, and the door on the high landing creaked. The mother began to sip at her coffee, but Arthur looked up and saw the big figure in the shadow on the landing, against the lamplight in the bedroom.

"Have the girls come out yet?" the father asked.

"Not yet," Arthur said.

"They're gettin' dressed, though," the mother said. "They'll be out any minute." She didn't look up.

"Then I'd better have my hot water up here," the father said. "And bring up my shaving things too, will you, Lettie?"

The mother lifted her cup slowly, and sipped slowly at the coffee, and slowly set the cup down again, and didn't say anything.

"Lettie," the father said, "I asked you . . ."

"I heard you. I don't see no reason to change our regular ways. Gwen's seen a man shave before this, I guess. She has a father and three grown brothers, and they don't keep up heat except in the kitchen, I don't imagine."

"As if it weren't enough to be roused out at this hour," the father said angrily. "Now a man must shave in the midst of a flock of women."

"Who are we this morning?" the mother asked, looking up at him. "John Mackay seeing Paris? Or Leland Stanford on a private train? There's no law says you have to shave at all, that I've heard tell of. It was long enough since you had, up to yesterday, goodness knows."

"It seems to me," the father said, "that with company in the house, it would do no harm for one member of the family to make a decent appearance."

Arthur sighed softly, and pushed his chair back and stood up. "I'll bring your things up, Dad."

"Thank you, son, thank you," said the big voice in the upper shadow. "It is gratifying to receive some consideration in one's own home."

The father went back into the bedroom, only partly closing the door behind him, and they could hear him clearing his throat repeatedly, like a man about to begin a public address.

"And him seventy-one years old this last summer," the mother said.

Arthur didn't answer, but took the shaving mug and brush and razor from the shelves by the sink, and made lather in the mug with hot water from the kettle.

The mother, still sitting at the table, with her back to him, said, "There's no call you should wait on him either. He's not helpless yet."

"I don't mind," Arthur said.

He dipped hot water from the reservoir of the stove into a white enameled pitcher, and started up the stairs with the pitcher in one hand and the shaving things in the other.

"You'd better take him up a towel too," the mother said, rising, "or he'll be bellerin' for that, next thing."

She went around the table to the big oak chest under the front window, and took a towel out of it, and brought it back to Arthur on the stairs.

"It's wonderful how little it takes to put some people in mind of their pride," she said, tossing the towel over his arm.

Arthur grinned down at her, but didn't answer. He went on up slowly into the shadow on the landing, and knocked twice with the toe of his boot against the door frame, and pushed the door open with his shoulder and went in. The father's oratorical thanks rolled out through the open doorway.

- - 3

Old Bridges sat in his place at the table, with darkness still in the big window behind him. He scraped together the last forkful of egg and potato on his plate and raised it and took it into his mouth quickly, his head reaching for it like a turtle's. Then he laid the fork down and leaned back, chewing, and tugged at the corners of his worn, brocaded vest, trying to smooth it over his paunch, and looked across the table at the mother. She was sitting with her head between her hands over a big, leather-covered Bible. It was open to the gospel by Matthew, with the words of Jesus printed in red, and she was reading slowly, shaping each word silently with her lips. Her gray hair was still hanging loose and she still had on the old gray bathrobe. The father's pale eyes, watering a little in the light and from the pleasure of his meal, examined her attentively, as if they hadn't seen her for a long time, and then his eyebrows rose slightly. They were impressive brows, thick, black and peaked, and the lifting gave them the appearance of leading independent lives on the big, sagging face, which was otherwise dull and heavy. With the black brows still raised, the old man smoothed first one wing and then the other of his long, white moustache. Still the mother didn't feel his attention, but went on reading silently with her lips. The old man glanced sideways at Arthur, but Arthur wasn't paying any attention either. He was sitting there, his chair drawn back from the table now, whittling slowly on the wooden lion.

The father looked back at the mother and cleared his throat. It was a loud sound in the room where for some time there had been only the fluttering of the fire, the slow ticking of the big pendulum clock on the wall behind Arthur, and the faint chipping of Arthur's knife, but neither Arthur nor the mother looked up. The old man cleared his throat again.

Grace spoke in the north bedroom, near the door and in a high, happy voice, so the words were quite distinct. "I hope it snows for a week then."

The father glanced at the door and changed his mind about speaking. After a moment, he drew a cigar out of his upper vest pocket and clipped the end off it with a little silver knife that hung with a lodge emblem on his watch chain. He closed the knife, returned it to his pocket, and lit the cigar. When it was drawing well, he leaned back in his chair and blew a great cloud of smoke up around the lamp.

"Those young ladies are certainly taking their time this morning," he said to the lamp.

Neither Arthur nor the mother looked at him or said anything.

"But then," said the old man, genially, "I suppose they must be hungry for women's talk. Certainly Gwendolyn must be, living month after month all alone in that family of sour Welshmen."

The mother took one hand from her forehead, and began to follow the words with her finger as well as her mouth.

"Though there's little enough sociability to be found in this house, for that matter," the father said more loudly, staring across at her.

The mother's finger went on moving a word at a time across the page.

"Lettie," the father said.

"Yes?" the mother asked, without looking up.

"If I might have another cup of coffee, please."

"It's on the stove," the mother said, and her mouth moved silently again.

Arthur laid the knife and the wooden lion on the table and stood up.

"For one who pretends to be a wife and a housekeeper," the father began loudly.

"I'm getting it, Dad," Arthur said, and picked up the old man's coffee mug.

The old man paid no attention to him, but kept staring at the mother while his jowls grew red and began to tremble. "Lettie, what's got into you this morning?" he demanded finally.

The mother stopped her finger under a word, but didn't look up. " 'What's got into you?' you'd better ask."

"And since when has it become a misdemeanor to ask for a cup of coffee?"

"I'm getting it, Dad," Arthur said.

"That is not the point," the old man said, pressing himself back in his chair with one hand against the edge of the table and the other, with the cigar in it, lifted at the mother. "This life, which you seem to resent so bitterly," he said to her, "was

34

not, if you will kindly keep that fact in mind, of my choosing. On the contrary . . ."

This time the mother looked across at him when her finger stopped. The will like a weapon was in her thin face again. "Don't you come playing any of your bonanza kings on me this morning, Harold," she said with soft, quick fury.

The old man withdrew the accusing hand, but began, "As the nominal head of this family, if nothing more, I deem it . . ."

"Don't, I tell you."

Arthur came back with the filled coffee mug and set it down at the old man's place.

"Thank you," the old man said stiffly. Looking back at the mother again, he added, "And now, if you please, my bottle and a glass."

The mother returned his stare for a moment, but then only set her mouth and looked down at her book again.

Arthur went to the big sideboard that stood against the wall under the clock and opened the cabinet door at the end. There were three whisky bottles in it, one partly empty and the other two with unbroken seals. Arthur took out the opened bottle, closed the cabinet with his knee, and took a glass from the row that stood upside down on the marble top of the sideboard. He brought the bottle and glass back to the table and set them down in front of the father.

The old man slowly, making a defiant ceremony of it, uncorked the bottle, poured the glass a third full of whisky, corked the bottle again and set it aside. He raised the glass as if to make a toast, and squinted at the light coming through the whisky in it.

"With storms indoors as well as out, a man deserves a little cheer. To better days," he said, looking at Arthur, and then looked at the mother and added, with sudden fury, "and a life somewhere out of this Godforsaken hole," and drank off half the whisky and set the glass down sharply.

"Virginia City, maybe?" the mother asked, without looking up.

"I can tell you one thing," the father began, hoarsely, leaning forward and pointing at her again. "If the life we are leading at present is the best your . . ." but broke off and looked around,

35

hearing voices outside and the hollow knocking of a boot against the sill.

Curt came in first, seeming to fill the doorway, and then the room, because of his purpose and activity. He pulled off his mittens and said, loudly and cheerfully, "Just a cup of coffee, Ma, and we'll be all set. You ready, old dream-monk?"

"Any time," Arthur said.

"That's the first break this morning, then. We had a hell of a time with the horses. All spooked up."

Harold came in with the lantern and closed the door, and stayed there, leaning against it.

The mother got up and went to the stove. "Horses is quick to sense things," she said.

Curt laughed. "You too now? Does it take second-sight to know it's snowing and something's wrong with cattle when they beller?"

He saw Arthur's knife and the unfinished lion lying on the table. He came over beside Arthur and picked up the lion and looked at it, turning it over two or three times in his hand.

"Not bad," he said, "not bad. But a long way from done yet. No wonder Joe Sam's raising hell. All this snow and no medicine puss. Well," he said, tossing the carving back onto the table so that it turned over twice and slid out into the shadow in the middle, "he'll have to sweat it out a while longer yet. We have to finish the real one first." He chuckled. "So get your gown on, priest."

"You eat some breakfast first," the mother said. "It's all ready for you." She brought a filled plate and a mug of coffee to the table and set them down in front of Curt.

"Make way for an ordinary cat-killer, priest," Curt said, pushing aside the knife.

Arthur stood up, and Curt pulled the chair in and started to sit down, but then took the cowhide parka off the back of the chair and held it out to Arthur.

"And take your gown too," he said. "I can't sit easy with a thing like that behind me."

Arthur took the parka, and Curt sat down and pulled the chair in and began to eat at once, taking huge mouthfuls and swallowing them half chewed.

"There's no need to choke yourself," the mother said.

"Storm's letting up," Curt said thickly, through the food in his mouth. "If we get out there by daylight, there's a chance we can catch him at it."

The mother sat down in her place again, and asked him, "What makes you so certain sure it's a painter that's at 'em?"

"What else would they yell for? I killed every wolf in this neck of the woods ten years ago. And I lost two damn good dogs last spring too, if you remember, and there wasn't much question what got 'em, was there? Or those calves we found down the south end." He took another mouthful and chewed for a moment, and said, "No, sir, one of them bastards has been workin' this section for four or five months now, and this is him, all right. He's took over here, and I'll get him this time if I have to chase him to Placerville."

"Could be a bear," the mother said.

Curt chuckled. "The only kind of bears I've ever seen around here," he said, "was rugs before they was shot. Sheep, maybe, if they could get close enough to 'em, but not a steer."

"Could be just the snow worries 'em," the mother said.

"You're just tryin' to talk me out of it," Curt said, grinning at her. "You know as well as I do that ass to the wind and their eyes closed is all any snow ever got out of 'em. Nope, it's that cat, and I'll nail the bastard's hide to the wall this time. I owe him that for them two dogs." He took another mouthful, and drank some coffee through it, and added, "I only wish I had 'em now. I should of got me another right away. But the snow's next best."

"There's no arguin' with fools," the mother said. "Especially when they've got used to bein' boss ahead of their time."

"No use," Curt agreed, grinning at her.

"Well, there's one thing I can tell you," the mother said. "You don't nail the next hide up on the house."

"Not even if it's black?"

"Not if it was red, white and blue," the mother said. "Such a stink every time that door was opened."

Curt swallowed and leaned back and laughed and slapped his thigh. Then he sat forward again and said, still chuckling, and pointing his fork at the mother, "I remember you was afraid to

37

touch it to take it down yourself, on account of that smell. But a black one," he said, suddenly solemn, "would be good luck for the house. Wouldn't it, medicine man?" he asked, half turning to Arthur.

"I'll take less luck, if it'll make less stink," the mother said. "If you bring anything back you haven't just imagined, you'll spread it on the shed, not the house, and on the back side too."

"All right, all right," Curt said, grinning, and took another large mouthful of egg and potato. "Anyway," he said thickly, "the way it's been growin' lately, if we was to get the black one, his hide would cover the whole house. We'll have to peg it out on the meadows, eh, preacher?"

"There's nothing to worry about there," Arthur said. "If we ever get that one, it won't be with bullets."

"Nonsense," the father said. "Utter nonsense. If . . ."

Curt pointed the fork at him now. "No, by God. For once I agree with old whiskers, absolutely. If we ever get that one, it won't be with bullets." Bending his head toward the plate again, he looked at the mother, grinning. "Which is why I have to take old whiskers along."

"This whole performance is ridiculous," said the father angrily. "In such weather as this. If there was a grain of sense in the pair of you, you'd stay in the house and make use of this opportunity for a little sociable . . ."

"But," Curt said, still grinning at the mother, "I'll take a gun along too, just in case it turns out to be my kind of a cat. You know, an ordinary, yellow cattle-thief."

He scraped together the rest of the food on his plate, but then raised only a small forkful of it to his mouth. Chewing on it, he peered through the shadow of the lamp at the door of the north bedroom. The father was staring angrily, but Curt paid no attention, and after a moment the old man muttered something no one could understand, drank off the rest of the whisky in his glass in two swallows, set the glass down again, and once more filled it a third of the way with the same slow, ceremonious defiance.

Arthur began to put the parka on.

From the north bedroom there came another little chorus of the two laughters.

"By golly," Curt said, "you'd think it was a party in there, or something. Here I am, just waiting around to pay my respects, and they go on gabbling in there like they had all the affairs of the world to settle. What on earth do women find to talk so much about, Ma?"

Harold stirred restlessly against the door, and then stood away from it. The mother looked at him, and then back at Curt.

"They're still on Gwen's trip to San Francisco, I expect," she said. She smiled a little, a tight, downward grimace, and looked sideways at the father, not moving her head, but only her eyes. "They didn't much more than get started on it last night."

The father's jowls grew red again, but he pretended not to understand, and fixed his attention on relighting his cigar, which had gone out while he listened to Curt's teasing.

"You'd think," Curt said, "they could get all about frills and bustles that was any use to 'em in this place settled pretty quick."

"Frills and bustles is a long subject," the mother said dryly. "I wouldn't figure on waitin' it out, if I was you."

Arthur came beside Curt, and picked up the unfinished lion, and the knife, and put the lion in the pocket of his parka, with the other two pieces, and closed the knife and slipped it into his pants pocket.

"Well, now," Curt said, grinning again, "I just don't like to go off without even a good mornin'. We gotta be real careful nothin' slips up just on account of bad manners. Weddin's are pretty rare things in this family."

Arthur moved off toward the gun rack made of deer legs bent up and fastened to a long panel that hung beside the bunkroom door.

"And Harold himself bein' just a mite green at this sort of thing," Curt went on. "I thought that . . ."

"Which gun do you want to take?" Arthur asked him.

"Everybody's rushin' me all of a sudden," Curt said, and laughed. He looked around at Arthur. "My Winchester," he said. "The carbine. And you better borrow Hal's. That old Sharp's of yours is about as much use as throwin' rocks."

"You forget," Arthur said. "There's no use taking a gun for my kind of cat."

He lifted down the topmost of the five guns that lay across the

39

deer legs and took a handful of cartridges out of the open box on the shelf under the rack.

"How about the snowshoes and some grub?" he asked.

"I'll fix you something right away," the mother said, putting her hand on the table to help herself up.

Curt had the last of his food in his mouth, and waved his hand at her to sit still, and after a moment swallowed and said, "Never mind. We won't be out long enough to need it."

"If we have to track him," Arthur began.

"We'll get him there, if we get him at all. If he's up in the creek canyon, it's a regular box, and if you don't start singin' hymns to warn him, we'll have him in there like in a trap."

The mother moved her hand over onto her Bible, as if she hadn't meant to rise at all, and said, "First you're certain sure it's a painter, though how you can tell by the way a cow bellers five miles off, what's at it, passes me, and now you're just as set it's the creek canyon."

"It can't be any place else," Curt said. "The bellerin' come from the north; wind's that way. And it was from a good ways off. It's all open this side of the creek, no wind-break for 'em to head for, and if it was the other side, we couldn't hear it. North side of the canyon's too high. There's always some of 'em head up in there in a blow, and the echo off that north wall would carry good. It's gotta be in there. They water up in there a lot," he added.

"Well," the mother said, "if it's in there, there'll be tracks too. I'll just fix you up a snack to take along."

She started to rise again, but then Grace laughed, and the door of the north bedroom opened, letting her laughter into the kitchen clearly, and a small, dark woman in a yellow, satiny blouse and a black skirt came in with the laughter behind her. The mother sat back, looking at her. They were all looking at her, as if she were making an entrance onto a stage, and she stopped a few feet inside the door, still smiling about the joke, and looked at the waiting group. Her smile changed a little, and she said, "Good morning."

Grace came out right behind her, still laughing, though softly now, as if the joke mustn't be brought in where the others were. Then, when she saw over Gwen's shoulder her brothers

40

with their coats on, and Harold by the door with the lighted lantern, and Arthur with the carbine in his hands, she stopped laughing suddenly and her white face at once looked much older and thinner.

The mother and Arthur said good morning where they were, but the father rose hurriedly and made a little bow and gestured sweepingly at the empty chair opposite Curt.

"Good morning, my dear, good morning," he said loudly. "Sit here, won't you? There'll be some breakfast for you in no time at all. And a cup of coffee. It's a pity we've got you up at such an hour. Hardly the way to treat one's guest, and the very first morning, at that. But since it's done, the coffee will help."

"Thank you," Gwen said, just glancing at him, and then away, and came slowly toward the chair.

He moved around to draw the chair for her. The mother watched him attentively for an instant, but then looked away as Gwen had, and stood up and went to the stove.

Curt sat where he was and watched Gwen come into the circle of the lamplight. He was half grinning all the while, and he looked first at her high, full breasts pressing up the yellow cloth of the blouse, and then at the brown, round throat where the blouse opened, and at last at her brown face with the eyes set wide apart and the low, wide forehead with the crown of heavy braid above it. Then he slowly stood up too, still watching her.

"Well, well," he said. "The sleeping beauty. You must have pretty near too good a conscience, to sleep through all that's been goin' on in here." He spoke more slowly and deeply than he'd been speaking before, making his words with a drawl almost as long as the mother's.

Gwen came behind the chair and stood there, because everybody else was standing, and the father had to wait beside her. Gwen smiled at Curt, but no more than she had been, not really meeting his look or accepting his opening.

"I sure hate to break up the party just when it's gettin' good," Curt said. "But we got a little call to make, Arthur and me."

"A call?" Gwen asked politely.

"Well, it's more like we gotta receive a call. Only it's a kind of bashful guest, and we gotta go out and make sure he don't run off on us. It's an old friend of Arthur's, a black one." He chuckled.

Gwen looked at him and waited, not understanding, and too shy, with everyone watching her, to guess.

"It's only a foolish joke of his, my dear," the father said. "And a worn-out one, at that."

"You haven't heard about it yet?" Curt asked her.

Gwen shook her head. "I heard the cattle," she said.

"Well, we're in a kind of a hurry," Curt said, "so I guess we'll just have to leave Hal to explain it the best he can."

He picked up his coffee cup, and emptied it, and set the cup down again, and said, "Which is kind of too bad, in a way, because only Arthur here can really explain it. He talks to the thing."

"Come on, Curt," Arthur said.

Curt grinned but didn't look at him. He jerked his head back a little at Arthur and spoke to Gwen, still in that slow, fixing drawl that wouldn't let her break away from his look.

"He's bashful with strange women, but just the same, he's the only one can really give you the fine points of this business. You'll have to work on him a little when he gets back."

Grace came up to the table beside Gwen. "You're going out there now?" she asked. "In this snow?"

"Take it easy," Curt said, turning the grin at her.

"You're not going, Arthur?" Grace asked.

"Here we go again," Curt said, shaking his head, and making the sad face of a man pleading for reason without much hope of getting it. "What could I do with a black painter all by myself?" he asked. "An ordinary yellow one, maybe, but . . ."

"Oh, stop it," Grace said sharply. "You make me sick."

She went around the table quickly, and past him, not even looking at him. She stopped in front of Arthur, and stood staring up into his face.

"You don't have to go," she told him, speaking quickly, her voice rising a little. "There's no sense in it. It's dark out there, and it's snowing. What on earth could you do? If he's so set on going, let him go alone. Does it take two men to shoot a shadow?"

The mother was cracking more eggs over the edge of the

pan and spreading the shells to let the insides drop into the hissing grease.

"You're gettin' yourself all worked up, Grace," she said, without looking around. "Set down, now, you and Gwen, and I'll have some breakfast for you in a minute."

Grace clutched a fold of the cowhide parka in each hand and stared up at Arthur.

"You don't have to go," she said. "You don't. Why do you let him make you? Why do you always let him make you? That's all he does it for. Don't you know that?"

"It's all right," Arthur said, smiling down at her, turning awkward before the others watching. "The storm's letting up now."

Grace felt the others watching her too, then, the stiff silence in the room around her excitement. She let go of the coat and turned away abruptly.

"It's not that," she said. "It's foolish, that's all. It's so foolish. Let him do his own foolish showing off."

Curt, half turned to watch her, said, "I'll bring your darling Arthur back safe and sound, Gracie."

Grace had started to pass him, coming back to the table, but now she turned swiftly to face him, her eyes very bright and her hands clenched into fists at her sides.

"If it was only you, I'd wish it was a black panther. You and your cheap sneering, and your self-importance, and your always judging others by yourself."

"Grace," the mother said sharply.

"He does," Grace cried. "He always does. A cheap dirty-mouthed bully, always . . ."

"Grace, did you hear me?" the mother said more loudly, and moved toward her from the stove. But Grace's voice broke, and not even seeing the mother, she turned and half ran toward the open bedroom door, crying out through her tears, "Oh, you fool, you fool," though not saying who she meant, and ran into the bedroom and slammed the door behind her.

Gwen looked at the mother and turned as if to go in after Grace.

"No, let her be," the mother said. She went back to the stove and picked up a peeled potato and began to cut it into

43

the pan with the eggs, saying, "She'll be all right. Just give her time."

Gwen stopped, and stood undecided, halfway between the table and the closed door.

The father cleared his throat. "Grace is a high-strung girl. All this excitement at this hour has upset her."

Curt laughed, but before he could say what he meant to, the mother said, "Now you get along, you that's in such a lather to be out there."

"We'll be back before too long," Curt said to Gwen, saying more with his grinning stare. "Then Art here can explain it all to you. He's good at talk, Art is. He gets it out of all them books he's always readin'."

Harold spoke from the door. "Joe Sam will freeze out there, waiting for you to finish your joking."

Curt turned a little and looked at him, and he wasn't grinning now. "Any time you catch me rushin' myself for that old bastard," he said. "Let him freeze. Spookin' the horses with his crazy antics."

"They were spooky enough already," Harold said.

"And how long had he been out there in the middle of 'em? Half the night, for all we know. If . . ."

He stopped because Arthur brushed against him going past to the door. Harold stood aside to let him by, but didn't look away from Curt.

"He's only got that shirt on," he said.

Arthur opened the door and went out, carrying the Winchester.

"Hey," Curt called, and strode after him. "Better let me have that, padré, before you hurt yourself."

After that they could hear, through the open door, his pleased voice saying loudly, "Just the same, you old heathen, I bet you a pint of the old man's best it's yellow."

"I'll be back in a minute," Harold told Gwen, and went out with the lantern and closed the door. The lamp steadied again, and gradually the warmth of the stove came back where the cold had drawn in along the floor. Outside they could hear Curt's voice still baiting the old Indian.

"Sit down, my dear, sit down," the father said once more,

44

and, when Gwen moved aside, drew out the chair for her. Gwen sat down, smiling up quickly at him, but then looking away quickly too, keeping herself secret against the admiration in his voice and eyes.

Outside there was a muffled, turning trample of hoofs in the snow. Harold's voice called, "Well, get him, whatever color he is," and Curt's voice made some short and laughing answer. The hoofbeats quickened suddenly into a multiple drumming, and then were lost at once, without fading, as the wind turned and roared down across the trees on the mountain. The door opened, letting in another serpent of snow along the floor. Harold entered, carrying the lantern, waited for Joe Sam to pass him, and closed the door.

4

The old Indian stood there, trying to hide his shivering, and squinting against the light in the white kitchen. Harold, standing behind him, took off his cap, so his fine, bright hair shone like gold in the light. The cold had brought high color under the tan of his face too, and the old man looked dark and wooden and slight as a young boy, standing in front of him. His body was so flat there seemed to be nothing under his blue work shirt, and the black canvas pants he wore were as flat behind as they were in front.

Gwen thought, looking curiously at his face and hands, and two short, tight braids with strips of red-and-blue cloth woven into them that hung down before his shoulders, He's like one of those dolls with only the head and hands and feet made to look real and all the rest just cloth to hold them together.

Joe Sam turned his head and looked at her then, as if he had heard her thinking, and after a moment she had to look down. His face didn't change.

It really is like a face carved out of wood, she thought. It can't change. It's like Arthur had made it with his whittling

45

Harold's always talking about; deep wrinkles, like Mrs. Bridges, only all broken up with little ones too, like dried-out earth or old leather, on his forehead and cheeks and chin, and by the puckering at the corners of his eyes and around his mouth.

She wanted to look at the face for a long time, but she couldn't because of the eyes. It wasn't that he looked at her, but rather that he didn't look at her, although his eyes were turned at her face, and that only his right eye seemed to be watching whatever it was he saw behind her. His right eye was surprisingly young and liquid and alive in the old, dry face, but the left eye was turned a very little out and up from it, so they didn't appear to be looking together. The lid drooped over it more too, as if from an old injury that had made him unable to lift it.

Harold said, "It's all right, Joe Sam. Go on in," and the mother turned from the stove with Gwen's plate in her hand and saw the old Indian standing there. Even the father stopped watching Gwen and, turning his glass on the table between his thumb and fingers, looked around too.

"Go ahead, Joe Sam, go ahead," he said impatiently.

The mother brought Gwen's plate to the table and set it down in front of her as if there were no one sitting there yet.

"Get over by the stove and warm yourself," she said. "It's a wonder you don't take your death of cold, wandering around in your shirt sleeves."

Joe Sam didn't answer, or even show in his face that he'd heard her. Appearing to start only by his own wish, he walked slowly, very upright and very softly in his buckskin moccasins, dark and shiny with use, over to the wood box in the shadow by the stove. He turned around in front of the wood box and crossed his ankles and let himself down slowly and without a sound and then sat there, as upright as he'd walked, his hands lying limp and palms up in his lap. His face almost disappeared in the shadow, only tiny points of reflected light showing where his eyes were.

Harold followed him across, his boots clumping. Standing in front of him, he blew out the lantern and reached across him and set it on the shelf behind the stove. Then he went back to the pegs by the door and stuffed his cap into the pocket of his mackinaw and took the mackinaw off and hung it up in the row of coats. He turned, trying to comb his hair back with his big hand, and came to the table and sat down in Arthur's chair, across from Gwen. He leaned on the table, and locked his big hands in front of him and looked at Gwen, smiling a little, and when she smiled back at him, looked down at his hands.

The father spoke loudly and importantly. "What was all that Curt was talking about? Joe Sam been up to something with the horses?"

"Oh, nothing," Harold said. "He was already out there when Curt got there, and the horses were kind of spooky, so Curt blamed him. He wasn't doing anything."

"Was he in the corral?"

"Yes, he was, but he was just standing there by the fence. He wasn't doing anything. It was the snow spooked the horses."

"The old fool's going to get himself killed some time," the father said, "wandering around without the slightest notion where he is."

"I wouldn't worry about it," the mother said. "He'll look out for himself. Another cup of coffee, Harold?"

"Please."

The mother filled a mug and brought it over and set it down in front of him.

"Curt might be able to hunt at that," he told her. "It's just about stopped snowing."

"It wouldn't make no difference anyway," she said. "Curt would hunt anything, once he got started, if he had to make the tracks himself."

"And he'd get it too," the father declared. "Curt's about the best hunter I've ever known," he told Gwen. "He has a gift for it. He knows right away, without giving it a thought, what other men can't even figure out. He knows what a cat will do; he knows what a deer will do, better than they know it themselves. He'll outguess them every time. He doesn't need tracks. Just a start, and he knows what they'll do. He's a remarkable shot, too, remarkable, one in a thousand, one in ten thousand. Why, I remember once . . ."

"I don't guess Gwendolyn cares about Curt's fancy shooting enough to listen to all that," the mother said.

47

The father stared at her, the whisky slowness showing in his eyes already.

Before he could speak, Gwen smiled at him, and said, "Harold told me about it. He must really be a wonderful shot," and looked back at her plate.

After a moment the father said, "He's all of that, and then some. I'll tell you about a couple of the things I've seen him do, some time when it's possible to have a little conversation without these constant interruptions."

Gwen smiled at him again, and nodded. He was encouraged.

"Go ahead and eat, my dear," he said expansively. "We should have waited for you, but sometimes it seems to me we've lost even the most ordinary consideration in this wilderness, all sense of the amenities of civilization. You have no idea the pleasure it is, if only for that reason, to have you under this roof. It may remind us of ourselves a little, and heaven knows we need to be reminded."

He leaned toward her and smiled at her and raised his glass. "A most left-handed compliment, I fear, but not intended as such. The true pleasure, of course, is your presence."

Gwen flushed and made the quick, little smile again, and looked back at her plate.

"Thank you," she said.

"No, no; thank *you*," the father said, and flourished the glass at her, and drank from it, and sat back with it in his hand and smiled at her.

Gwen picked up her fork, but then, to loosen the close hold of his attention, looked away and watched the mother set a plate of potato and bacon on the floor in front of Joe Sam, and a mug of coffee beside it. The old Indian, so upright, and with his eyes gleaming, appeared unnaturally alert, as if he saw and heard something none of the rest of them could, and had become their sentry against what was waiting outside the door he stared at.

This black panther they all joke about, she thought. He isn't really seeing anything, though, she thought uneasily. Mrs. Bridges is right in front of him now, but he's staring at her the same way he was at the door. He doesn't even know she's there.

48

"There's your breakfast, Joe Sam," the mother said, raising her voice as if the old Indian were deaf. After a moment she said, "Joe Sam," still more loudly. Joe Sam didn't move or look at her.

The father stirred uneasily in his chair and set his glass down. "The old fool," he said, laughing a little. "He's seeing things again. The first snow always upsets him," he explained to Gwen. "Sometimes it puts him into a regular trance. He can't sleep, and he forgets to eat unless we make him. But there's no reason to be alarmed," he added quickly. "He's perfectly harmless. When he's himself," he went on, "he's not at all bad help, either, as Indians go. We just have to put up with these little spells now and again. But he's all right, really. Gentle as a lamb. There isn't a mean streak in the old codger."

Gwen made the difficult smile again, but clenched her left hand in her lap, and thought passionately, Oh, stop it, stop it. Stop talking about the poor old man as if he wasn't even here.

The mother was prodding Joe Sam's knee with her foot. At last he looked up at her slowly and asked, "What do?"

"He's as old as the hills, to hear him tell it," the father said, laughing. "He can't remember exactly how old, though. Too old to remember, even, I guess."

Gwen looked at Harold for help, but he was staring at his hands folded together on the table, and seemed to be thinking of something else.

"Eat," the mother told Joe Sam. "Drink your coffee. It'll warm you."

"Not cold," he said.

His voice was deep, surprisingly deep out of such a small, flat, old man, and with a heavy, male resonance in it that was stirring. Yet he spoke small too, reluctant to make a sound, as if, being compelled to speak, he was robbed of a power he stored for greater uses, as if he were violated by the presence of another.

"Go on, drink it," the mother said. "You're shaking like a leaf still."

"Coffee good," he said politely, although he hadn't yet touched the mug.

The mother waited, looking down at him, bearing her

presence down heavily upon him. Finally Joe Sam took up the mug in both hands and sipped at the coffee, holding the mug against his mouth between sips. He appeared to test the coffee in his mouth like an unfamiliar wine, and to be thinking about the way its warmth spread out in him. He didn't look at the mother again, or speak to her.

"And eat something too, do you hear me?" the mother said. She turned, drawing the bathrobe closer about her, and came back to her place at the table and sat down.

"Him and his black painters," she said, to no one in particular. "Every winter we have to go through all this nonsense all over again."

Having said that, she put herself apart from the others. The separation could be felt as much as if she'd gone into another room. She closed her eyes and set one thumb against the edge of the Bible, and opened the Bible where her thumbnail went between the pages. She moved a finger down the page and stopped it, and opened her eyes, and began to read where her finger pointed. She moved her finger along under the words, and shaped each word slowly and distinctly with her lips.

"Oh, that I were as in the months of old, as in the days when God watched over me; when his lamp shined upon my head, and by his light I walked through darkness." She pointed out the words for herself with her left hand, and with her right hand she held the dressing gown closed tightly at her throat, as if she were threatened, or as if it were cold in the room.

"It's really quite all right, my dear," the father's voice was saying. "It happens to him every year, although, to be sure, he seems to be taken harder with it this time than most." He chuckled.

"This black painter Curt was teasing you about invariably arrives with the first snow, arrives in Joe Sam's mind, that is, and apparently it requires strong medicine to get rid of it. That's all he's doing now, making his spells against the black painter. Actually a mountain lion, we gather. He took Mrs. Bridges' word for it, calls it a painter. Mrs. Bridges' family is Southern, you know. For a good many years now, Arthur has whittled him a little model of a lion each fall, so he could have it when the snow came. No idea what it really means to

50

him, of course, but apparently it's a comfort. He carries it around with him, in a little sack under his shirt, as a sort of charm against the real lion, I suppose. Only this year, with this unexpectedly early snow, Arthur doesn't have his charm finished, which aggravates his condition, I suppose. Sometimes he recovers in an hour or so, but it looks as if we might be in for a long spell this time. He's gone as much as two or three days, sometimes. But there's nothing whatever to worry about. Only have to keep an eye on him to see he doesn't wander off or sit down somewhere outside and freeze to death. He's never violent; never known him to lift a hand against anyone."

Gwen looked across at Harold again, and this time he was watching her and understood.

"It's all right," he said. "Joe Sam doesn't hear a word we're saying when he's like this. I don't think he ever listens to us much anyway. He doesn't know enough English to guess what we're talking about usually, so he doesn't pay any attention."

"You never told me very much about him," Gwen said, keeping her voice low.

"Well, now," said the father, "when a young man has to ride all that way to get in a little courting, you'd hardly expect him to spend many of his words on the hired help, would you, my dear? Especially when he has as few as Harold has. Or want him to, eh?"

"There's not much to tell about him," Harold said slowly, and looking at his hands again. "We don't any of us know much about him, except maybe Arthur."

"Arthur," the father said, and snorted. "I'd hesitate to put my faith in anything Arthur thinks he knows."

"Arthur knows quite a bit about him, I guess," Harold said to Gwen. "But he doesn't talk much about it. That's why Joe Sam trusts him, I guess. He talks to Arthur a lot."

After a moment, when Harold didn't go on, Gwen said, "He must be terribly old."

"Well, now, as to that," the father said, smiling at her, and then worked his lower lip up over his moustache and down again, smiling at the same time. "I wouldn't believe all I see, my dear, if I were you. He's no child, to be sure, but he's nowhere near as old as he thinks he is, either. They have no real

51

means of keeping track of their age, you know, and they grow old much faster than white men."

He left the statement in the air, as clearly only an introduction, and lighted his cigar again. When the smoke came full and easy, he blew a long, slow cloud of it up into the lamp, and went on.

"We had one once, did odd jobs for us in Virginia City. A woman. The men wouldn't work at all, if they could help it. Beneath their dignity. They preferred to beg for food and whisky and cast-off clothes. She was a sight, this one. Rose, we called her, in order that there should be something sweet about her."

He chuckled and looked at Gwen to be sure she understood the joke. Gwen made the little smile, and looked from the corners of her eyes at Harold. His face was expressionless and he was working one hand slowly back and forth over the other, which he had made into a fist on the table.

"And also," the father went on, "because we had to call her something. She was unbelievably fat and dirty, and had bad eyes, like most of them, and her hair down in bangs so long it half covered them. She wore a bedspread with huge red flowers on it for a shawl. That's actually what suggested the name Rose to us. And an old pair of men's shoes, three sizes too large for her, and never tied up. She was honest enough, as Indians go," he said, chuckling, and inviting Gwen, with a look, to enjoy this joke too. "Never stole anything unless we left it around in the open, or weren't there to watch her.

"Well, to get to the point, I always took it for granted that Rose was forty-five or fifty at least. Her face was heavily lined, and she'd had something like twelve children, though there didn't seem to be more than three or four of them left alive. They have no idea how to take care of a child, or any interest in doing so. Once they're off those boards the women carry them around on, they either survive or they don't, pretty much by accident, like any other little animals. But then I chanced to meet a man who'd known her before she came to Virginia City. He was a hunter or trapper or some such. At any rate, he was a squaw-man. He'd lived with Indians more than with whites, and wore his own hair clear down over his shoulders, like a

52

buck. Joel Blaine, I believe his name was. Ever happen to meet him up there?"

Gwen shook her head.

"No, you wouldn't be likely to, I guess. Probably before your time, and a secretive cuss anyway. Got that from the Indians too, I suppose. At any rate, he'd known Rose when she was a kid, and guess how old he said she was?"

He asked the question happily, and sat back smiling widely at Gwen and waiting to astound her with the answer.

"I wouldn't have any idea," Gwen said, trying to smile.

"Twenty-six or seven, not more," the old man announced triumphantly. "And it's the same with Joe Sam here," he went on, after allowing her time to understand him fully. "You couldn't possibly guess his age by looking at him, and he himself hasn't any real idea of it, either. He claims he's over a hundred, but I'll wager bourbon to sump water he's not much over half that."

"He's older than that," Harold said. "He was already a brave when Fremont camped at Pyramid Lake, and that was pretty near sixty years ago. Remember, he told Arthur about a brass cannon they had?"

"He's like any other child," the father said. "He don't know the difference now between what he saw and what somebody told him, maybe thirty years later."

"I don't know," Harold said. "He remembers a lot of little things, too, like about the kind of buttons Fremont had on his coat. And he was a war chief of some sort, when they had that fight on the Truckee. He spoke in the last council they had before the fight. He had four children too, and one of them, the oldest girl, was in her teens already. And they were all by his second wife. His first children were already grown up and had families of their own. He says two of the boys were killed in the battle. And that was in sixty."

Before the father could speak, he went on to Gwen, "It was right after that the black painter got started. The Indians took an awful lickin' in the second battle, when they had troops from California and everything in against them, and they scattered all over the country north of the lake. When the reservation was laid out, their chief, Winnemucca, called 'em all back, but there was quite a few wouldn't come. Thought it was a trap, I guess, or just didn't like the idea of being fenced in when they'd had the whole country to themselves."

"About the way the jack-rabbits had it," the father said.

"Maybe," Harold said. "Anyway, they'd been getting along on it for a sight longer than there'd been white men anywhere in America, and the country was still as fit to live in as it ever had been. Our kind wrecked it worse in ten years than they had in lord knows how many hundreds, maybe thousands."

"Ignorance and poor tools," the father said.

"We got a long ways to go in some things then, before we catch up with their ignorance."

"You sound like Arthur," the father said. "Arthur and that sour-faced newspaper friend of his in Virginia City that got him started reading all that useless trash; what was his name? Bates. Jim Bates. Back to nature, and it's a sin to make an honest dollar, and so on."

"Not an honest one," Harold said, and looked quickly at Gwen again.

"Anyway, Joe Sam was one of them that wouldn't come back. He took his family and traveled clear up into the mountains somewhere northwest of us here, up around Shasta somewhere, near as we can make out. Arthur thinks the black cat got started up there, in some extra bad winter. He thinks it's kind of Jo Sam's personal evil spirit, not a regular one for the Piutes. Either way, it's got so, in his mind, it kind of stands for the whole business of being run out by the white man, the end of things, you might say. Like the ghost dance was for the ones that stayed together."

"Wasn't there a real one?" Gwen asked.

"I don't know," Harold said. "I never saw a black one myself, or heard of anybody that did, for that matter. But there might have been one—a freak, dark enough to call black. There was something, that's sure."

"A dream," the father said. "The old fool can't tell dreams and facts apart any more."

"No," Harold said, shaking his head. "It comes out too often. Little things about it. Whatever he's added to it since, he remembers something."

54

"He can't remember anything," the father said. "He couldn't even remember his own name. 'Sam' he said, when we asked him," he told Gwen. "He'd heard it somewhere, and that was all he could think of. So we called him Joe Sam, because Curt was already calling him Joe."

"He knows his real name, all right," Harold said. "He won't tell us, that's all. Indians keep them secret. They think it gives anybody a power over them to know their real names."

"Rubbish," the father said, "pure, romantic rubbish. The notions Arthur digs up," he said to Gwen, "are enough to make a reasonable man weary. It's all this useles stuff he reads." He waved a hand loosely at the bookshelves in the corner behind him. "Novels and poetry and fairy stories about the ancient Greeks and the Chinese and the Lord only knows what. Not a dependable fact or a piece of usable information in the whole lot. Now it has him manufacturing the same sort of nonsense. He's as completely a dreamer as Joe Sam himself, only it isn't just by spells."

"He does a little thinking of his own," Harold said, as softly as Arthur might have said it.

The father snorted. "Precious little I'd call thinking."

"About all that's done around here, though."

"If somebody around here wasn't doing more thinking than Arthur," the father began loudly, but then stopped, pounding a fist softly on the table and muttering, "When a man can't even finish a sentence in his own house," because the door of the north bedroom had opened, and Grace was coming in. The rims of her eyes were red from crying, and she didn't look toward the table.

The mother said, still watching the lines of her Bible, "You'll have to put the pan on again, Grace. I didn't keep anything for you, not knowing when you'd want it."

"All I want is some coffee," Grace said.

She went to the sink, in the corner between the stove and the north bedroom, where her back was to the rest of them, and took a white wash basin down from the wall and filled it with cold water from the noisy pump. Then she leaned over the basin and began to douse her face with the cold water, lifting it with both hands and rubbing hard and quickly.

55

The mother got up and filled a coffee mug at the stove and brought it back to the table. Then she picked up her Bible and went around the table behind Gwen and sat down in the big, leather platform rocker by the front window. She worked the rocker around to one side, to get it out of the father's shadow, and leaned forward to put the light on the pages, and began to read again.

Grace emptied the basin, and wiped her face hard in the rough roller towel. She stood for a moment, just holding the towel over her face with both hands. Then she lifted her head, wiped her hands quickly, and came to the table, and sat down where her mother had been sitting.

"I'm sorry I made such a scene," she said.

"It's all been one big scene this morning, as far as I can see," the father said. "There's no need to apologize for any particular part of it. It seems to me," he said, smiling at Gwen, "that all the beds in the house, except Gwendolyn's and mine, had two bad sides this morning."

Gwen made her quick smile for him.

"Grace," he said, more cheerfully, "let me pour you a little drink. Best thing in the world for the nerves, and for this unseasonable cold as well."

"No, thank you, Father. The coffee's all I need."

"Well, I shall have one, I think," the father said. "Such a turmoil about nothing."

He poured his glass a third full again, corked the bottle with careful dignity, and raised the glass a little at Gwen.

Gwen made the smile for him once more, and then, after a moment, looked at Grace and asked, "You feel better now?"

"I'm all right, thanks," Grace said. "I shouldn't let Curt make me so mad. Goodness knows his teasing's nothing new."

She smiled at Gwen, though not easily, and lifted the mug and began to sip the coffee.

"Harold was telling me about Joe Sam's black panther."

Grace stiffened her shoulders and shivered. "The poor old man," she said. "No wonder he has these spells."

"We don't have to talk about it now, though," Gwen said.

"Oh, it won't bother me," Grace said. "Curt jokes about it all the time. Go ahead, Harold."

"Well," Harold said, rubbing his hand slowly over his fist on the table again, "there isn't much to it really. I mean to tell about. Near as we can make out, they were camped by some creek or other, and one day, about sunset it was, he heard his wife scream down by the creek. He got down there as fast as he could, but he just got a glimpse of this big cat sneaking off through the willows on the other side, and there was his wife and his oldest daughter, dead by the creek. His wife was dragged half into the water and her neck was broken, and the girl was farther up the bank, and pretty much torn up, I guess. He says the cat was black, and its tracks were a lot the biggest he'd ever seen. It happened in the first snowstorm that year. It was snowing when he found them. Now he always thinks the black cat's around again when the first snow comes."

Gwen made a little grimace of pain and looked from the corners of her eyes into Joe Sam's corner by the stove. Then she turned her head and looked there directly.

"Where did he go?" she asked quickly.

Harold was still studying his hands on the table. "He stayed up there for quite a while, hunting for that cat."

"No, I mean now," Gwen said. "He's gone."

The others looked at the corner too. The coffee mug and the plate, with all the food still on it, were there on the floor, and there was the wood-box, with the white, split, pine sticks piled high in it, but that was all.

"He went out while you was squabbling about Arthur," the mother said.

"I didn't hear a thing," Gwen said.

"It's those moccasins he wears," Harold said. "He won't wear anything else, even when there's snow down. In the summer he goes barefoot half the time."

"It scared me," Gwen said, laughing a little. "He'd been there all the time, and then I looked, and he just wasn't, and I hadn't heard a thing. I thought for a minute I'd only imagined him in the first place."

"He probably went back to the bunk-house," Grace said. "He sleeps out there, and he stays there most of the time, when he isn't outside. He doesn't like it in here with us."

"He didn't eat anything," Gwen said.

The mother looked up from her book. "You have to spoon feed him like a baby when he gets took with one of these spells. But I wouldn't worry my head about him any, if I was you. He's lasted a good while on his own system. You better go out and see he's got a fire, though, Harold. He's just as like as not to set there all day beside that stove with no fire in it."

Harold stood up. "I didn't get the chores finished anyway," he said. "I had to help Curt with the horses."

"He never got the black panther then?" Gwen asked.

"No," Harold said. "And he didn't shake his bad luck, either. He saw the cat once more that winter, and right after that another of his kids died. It was pneumonia, I guess, from what he told Arthur about it, but by that time he was blaming everything on the black panther, and it wasn't just an ordinary cat any more. And the next winter one of his sons died, starvation, probably; it was a tough winter. Long snow, as he says. But he'd seen the cat's tracks only a day or two before, and right close to his camp."

"*A* cat's," the father said.

"All right, *a* cat's. Though Joe Sam would know if he'd seen them before."

"I don't believe it," the father said. "By then it was as big as a horse." He laughed. The laugh was too long and too loud for his joke. "So he gave up hunting it, and moved out. What happened to the number-four papoose we don't know. He was all alone when he got here, and half starved to death. But he's kept the black painter, and it keeps getting bigger, too. It would probably be as big as an elephant by now, if he'd ever seen an elephant. And no doubt it's out this morning."

"He told me it was." Harold said, taking down his coat. While he put the coat on, he said to Gwen, "He thinks it's trying to clear everybody out of this country."

"Especially white men now," the father said, and laughed.

"Especially white men now," Harold agreed.

He opened the outside door and stood in the doorway, looking at the sky over the valley. "No stars," he said. "We're in for more snow at that, I guess," and went out, closing the door behind him.

Grace got herself another cup of coffee, and the father poured his glass a third full of whisky again. The mother remained in the big chair, bent forward over Matthew, following the words with her finger and shaping them with her lips. The wind moved only occasionally outside, and then with a soft and faraway hollowness. In the room only the fire and the lamp and the slow clock spoke.

Finally the father looked at Gwen again and cleared his throat.

"So you've been in San Francisco recently, young lady?"

Gwen made the little smile and nodded.

"We talked all about it before we got up this morning," Grace said quickly, but it didn't help.

"Ah," said the father, leaning back and looking up at the small, bright circle of light in the middle of the whitewashed ceiling, and drawing another cigar from his vest. "Ah," he said again, "there is a wonderful city."

He spoke briefly about the beauty of San Francisco on its hills, and with the blue bay inside it, and the green, soft mountains across the bay.

"However," he said, after a meditative pause during which he stared at the ceiling, "it's not the place it used to be."

Grace sighed, gripped the handle of her mug tightly, and sat staring down into the coffee. The father clipped the end off the cigar, set it between his teeth, and lit it, slowly and ceremoniously, allowing them to wait for the words to come.

"There is a spirit gone out of it," he said, with round solemnity, when the air about the lamp was full of slowly turning, blue smoke. "Something vital is missing now, a hopefulness, an enterprise that was in its very atmosphere once, as heady as champagne. You should have known San Francisco in the sixties and seventies, my dear," he said, bringing his gaze down out of the smoke clouds and looking at Gwen.

"It must have been exciting then," Gwen said, making the little smile.

"Ah, yes," the father said slowly, and as if turning the word over and over and considering its every possibility. "It was that at times, to be sure. But it was also more than that, much more. Excitement, after all, is a matter of moments, and what the old city had then was no such brief and periodic thing. It was going to be the Babylon of the world, the new Jerusalem, the capital of the Pacific, the very shrine of wealth and beauty and fashion. In short, it had a soul, for it had faith, and what, after all, is a soul, save the product of such a faith. Why, I can remember . . ."

He went on happily describing for Gwen the soul of San Francisco in its good days. He spoke proudly and in detail, as one who was himself, in part at least, responsible for the magnificence and the activity and the promise. In one tale of gigantic manipulation, he spoke of Ralston. The name reminded him of his own meeting with Ralston. He had met him at a bar. He described the bar, and the meeting, and spoke the words Ralston had spoken to him about the stock of the Savage Mine in Virginia City as the words of a prophet are repeated at a safe interval after his death. The quotation took him to Virginia City for a time, but the water problem of Virginia City carried him back to San Francisco, where there had been some most enlivening speculation in water also. The water problem reminded him of a race horse of Ralston's. The race horse reminded him of a famous dancer. Because of some stocks on which the famous dancer had profited abundantly, he was drawn back to Virginia City and what President Grant had said about the heat in the lower levels of the mines. He quoted President Grant also with the care and awe of a disciple. He continued to branch intricately and happily into this near past until the twenty or thirty years since the events he spoke of seemed five thousand.

Gwen looked at him when she had to, and smiled and nodded and made little sounds of agreement. Grace sat there with them, but after a little while she wasn't listening.

Gray daylight appeared faintly and at a distance in the front window. It increased until the lamplight on the table turned yellow. The mother sat back in her chair then and read by the light from the window.

5 ◦ – ◦ –

When daylight began to spread under the clouds, Curt and Arthur were north almost to the foothill that hid the creek. The snow covered its long whale shape smoothly, only the sagebrush, and the few, small, lonely pines farther up, showing dark on it. A fine, thinned-out snow was still falling. As the light increased, Curt pressed his pony, a small, nervous red, and in his mind cursed Gwen and then used her violently, with anger, not pleasure, making a whole quick story of it, because he had wasted time waiting for her. When he came onto the whaleback, he turned the red out toward the nose of it, and only a little up, and heeled him to a lope, meaning to circle wide and come into the canyon mouth. He turned in his saddle and angrily signaled Arthur after him, sweeping his right arm forward twice. Arthur pressed his gray mustang mare up to the red's pace, but shook his head and pointed up and west toward the high ridge of the whaleback where it joined the mountain.

Curt said softly, fiercely, "Now what crazy notion, priest?" but pulled in the red and turned him and waited.

Arthur came alongside, so the horses stood tail to nose, and said, "You could see pretty near the whole ravine from up there. Get a good shot without starting him, if he's still in there. He'll be jumpy, now it's daylight. He'd hear us long before we got up to him."

Curt stared at him, and smiled with one side of his mouth and said, "You'd just as soon not meet him coming down, eh, priest?" but looked up at the ridge and thought about it. "If you'd ever shoot a gun," he said angrily, "if you'd brought a gun too, we could cover both sides. Well, we'll take a look," he said, making it his decision, not Arthur's.

He spun the red back again, forcing Arthur's mustang to shy off, and rode up on the whaleback at a slant out toward the valley, weaving through the brush. Arthur waited to steady the gray, stroking its shoulder, and saying softly, "Easy, Smudge, easy," and then turned up after him. The unshod hoofs of the two ponies, slicked with soap to keep the snow from balling in the frogs, made a soft, muffled counterpoint. Before they would show over the taper of the whaleback, Curt reined the red sharply back and climbed along the upper slope toward the mountain. The angle was steeper, and the ponies began to labor. At the first dwarf pine, Curt let the red down to a walk, signaling Arthur angrily, with an open, mittened hand beating rapidly on the air, to come slowly too, and keep quiet. The creaking of the saddles and the blowing of the ponies sounded too loud. Their breath made little jets of quickly vanishing steam in the cold air.

Up ahead only the broken base of the mountain, where the trees were taller and began to fill ranks, showed clearly. Above that, the trees became spired shadows, dimming as they rose, until there were no trees, but only one great, uncertain shadow of mountain, and then only the gray snow mist, in which the mountain could be imagined reaching any height into the sky. Arthur was pleased with this mountain that couldn't be seen, feeling it revive the dream that was not worked out of him yet. He watched the drifting mist, trying to see into it to rocks and trees until Curt, up ahead, swung down from his saddle. They were close under the crest of the reach, and nearly onto the mountain too. The small pines were more numerous around them, and there was a feeling of being watched, as if the trees had eyes, or creatures with eyes were hidden among them. Arthur swung down too, and they climbed a little farther on foot, one behind the other, leading the ponies, until a little fort of broken rock stood over them on the north. There Curt halted, and imperiously signed Arthur up to him, and when he came alongside said quickly, but keeping his voice low, "Hold them while I take a look."

Arthur nodded and took the red's bridle and stood between the two horses, smiling a little in his beard in the shadow of the cowhide hood.

"And hang on, will you," Curt said, "or you'll lose them when I shoot."

He drew the mitten off his right hand and stuffed it into his pocket, and began to climb by short switchbacks, jerking impatiently when he slipped in the snow or on the broken rocks moving under it. Arthur stood below, watching him grow smaller until, like a tiny, jerking toy, he clambered into a break in the rock fort, stooping already, so he wouldn't show over the top. There the miniature figure lay forward, the red coat making a bright spot on the stone and snow, and crawled up, a little on its side, to keep the carbine free, and lay still, with spread legs, looking through the notch into the canyon beyond. There was no shot. The tiny red figure lay motionless up there for two or three minutes, searching the canyon carefully, and then stood up, and after looking down a moment longer, turned and began its descent. It came slowly at first, on the rock of the ridge, and then with long strides straight down the slope, growing rapidly larger, until the shape of the sombrero became clear, and then until the face showed in the black circle of the scarf bound around the head, and the fierce moustache stretched across it like small, black wings.

When he had come down to Arthur, Curt said, still breathing hard from his almost running, "Damn your advice. I should have known. He's in there, all right, but you can't see him. He's clear up at the head, in the box canyon. The cliff hangs over there, hides him. But he's in there. There's a little bunch of steers down in the bottom by the willows; all headed up-canyon, taking the wind right in their faces. We'd of had him by now, if we'd gone on in, goddamit. If only he don't run out . . ."

He took the red's bridle from Arthur and swung up into the saddle, turning the pony in the same move, and led off upslope and toward the valley, commencing the top stroke of the great, uptilted Z their tracks made on the flank of the hill. Arthur turned the gray, mounted more slowly, and followed. Ahead of him Curt's back bent forward eagerly to the climb. The thin, dark line of the carbine across the saddle in front of him was like a spear through him that he carried in his body, Arthur thought, and then thought, smiling in the hood, Them that live by the rifle.

Curt turned the red still more steeply up, and crossed the ridge, well below the rock fort, but almost as far above their first turn. Arthur saw him and the red show dark against the milky sky for a moment, and then, turning west again, sink behind the ridge.

The gray came onto the ridge blowing, and of her own accord turned down after Curt's pony. Arthur felt the wind that moved up there, not strong, but cold and heavy with the promise of more snow, and saw the base of the north wall sloping up white to a greater height than he rode on, and then crowned with the long, dark fort of the rimrock. Curt was already far down the slope ahead of him. Arthur saw him look back up, and then point down with his bare right hand. He looked where the hand pointed, and saw the tiny steers in the bottom, out against the screen of red willows that hid the creek. There were five steers, standing in half a circle, with their rumps in the willows and their faces out and turned up-canyon. Two of them had their heads raised now, testing the air. Most of the yellow leaves still clung on the willows behind them.

Curt was putting the red down the slope recklessly, but kept his arm pointing, and swung it along the course of the willows. Looking there, Arthur saw, like a faint, dotted line in the snow, the tracks climbing the bottom beside the willows and then beside the aspens. The aspen leaves were bright even under the clouded sky and in the ravine, and danced with a fine, continuous shivering in the cold down-draft along the creek. The trail went up into the broken rock under the platform of the box canyon, and was lost there, where the creek came down over terraces of ice.

Out on the bottom, and nearly up to the aspens, Curt drew rein and turned back in the saddle, holding the nervous red to half-wheeling within a small circle. He didn't wait for Arthur to come all the way, but when he was closer, pointed into the snow near the willows, and led on up along the track.

Coming past the spot he had pointed at, Arthur saw the snow churned and mud spattered over it, and bits of torn sod with the yellow grass still rooted in them. There were many clear-cut prints of hoofs, like split hearts, most of them pointing down along the willows toward the little bunch that was on guard down there, or out toward the south wall and then down. A few, however, four, he thought, singling them out, led on up into the

64

rock canyon, and among these, when he was past the torn-up patch where nothing was clear, he saw the other track, the one like an incomplete flower, its four petals only half enclosing the center. All the tracks were dusted over lightly with new snow.

A cat after all, and one that makes tracks too, he thought, smiling. And big, he thought, leaning down from the saddle to look at the prints. Not so big as a horse, though, after all. . . . Curt can use his noisy toy.

He straightened up and looked ahead along the trail of flower prints. They came close together in irregular clusters of four, with several feet of unmarked snow between the clusters.

Moving fast, he thought.

He peered across the snow toward the south wall, which was drawing in closer now, but saw no tracks.

And he's up there still.

The little mustang lifted her head, and would have stopped if he hadn't pressed her forward. She went on up, then, but half dancing and making a soft nickering protest.

"You think so too, girl, don't you?" Arthur said, and patted her shoulder in front of the saddle.

A cat in a box, he thought, and only this way out. Keep your eyes open up there, Curt. A bold butcher, too, to jump a bunch like that, and run half of them. The god's had about enough of us, he thought, and smiled in the darkness of the hood, but at the same time kept watch ahead, from side to side of the ravine, as much as the aspens would let him.

In the loose rock under the platform, Curt's horse reared, trying to turn. He smells it fresh now, poor brute, Arthur thought, and felt his breath tighten, and something in him dance quickly, like the leaves of the aspens beside him. Steadying the gray, holding her up-canyon, he watched Curt wrench the red back again and try to drive it up onto the loose rock with his heels. It half-spun and reared again, refusing, its hoofs stumbling and clattering in the rock. Arthur heard Curt cursing it, and saw him swing down and put his weight on the reins, nearly at the bit, to stop the plunging, and make a heavy, upward signal with the carbine for Arthur to hurry.

No cat by now, he thought, if there's any way out of the trap. There'll be tracking to do, and not on a horse either, or I miss my guess.

He urged the gray up, but then the red plunged again, dragging Curt, and trumpeted wildly, a shrill sound that flew back and forth between the rock walls of the ravine above, and Smudge reared and spun too, and Arthur let himself down into the snow and dragged her on up by the reins.

"The goddam horses," Curt said, when he wouldn't have to shout. He drew the red down toward Arthur, and held the reins out to him. "Hold 'em," he said, "and by God, hold 'em. I don't want to walk six miles in these goddam boots."

Arthur took both horses again, standing between them and checking their tossing with the drag of his weight only, and making a low, slow patter of talk for them. Curt started up into the tumbled rock, the carbine held ready in both hands. After two or three steps, he stopped and turned, though.

"Did you see those tracks?" he asked quickly, exulting. "It's as big as a horse, at that; twice as big as the bastard got my dogs; but you won't see through the cat that made those tracks." He turned and went on up warily, scanning the width of the canyon ahead of him, and working back and forth to find sure footing. Toward the top of the rocks, fifty or sixty yards above, he let himself down and crept up, a small, moving red patch on the jumble of dark rock faced with snow. The black walls of the canyon rose high above him on each side and at the back. Above the back wall, there was a patch of open snow in the timber, with the black line of the creek coming crookedly down it into the ice-bearded chimney. At the top of the shale Curt lay still, but only for a moment. Then he stood up and climbed over the edge and disappeared back onto the platform. After perhaps a minute, he returned to the edge and called down, his voice enormous and unclear in the hollow.

"Bring 'em up. Make the bastards come up."

Arthur, smiling, shook his head a very little within the hood, and moved up tugging the lines gently and steadily, and talking aloud to the horses. With Curt standing in sight, to show the place had been looked at, they let themselves be led now, though with the reins stretched tight and their necks reaching. A nar-

66

row trail made by the cattle went to the south corner of the platform, against the cliff, and Arthur coaxed them up there. They scrambled on the last steep pitch to the ledge, dragging him this way and that between them. Curt went back from the edge ahead of them. On the platform, however, before Arthur had seen more than Curt's red coat down beside a darkness on the snow farther in, the red pony reared and plunged again. Smudge nickered tremulously and swung away on the other side, and they stretched Arthur between them. Curt stood up quickly, dropping the carbine against the fallen steer, and came running. He caught the red down with both hands, cursing him, and then held him close at the bit with his bare fist and struck him over the nose twice with his mittened hand. Then Arthur had to wrestle the mare down again too.

When both horses stood, though trembling, and Curt's rolling his eyes so the whites showed, Curt cried, "Gone, goddam him. But his trail's as clear as print on a page. And look what the bastard's done, will you?"

"Did you see him?"

"No. Bring her in," Curt ordered, dragging the red across the snow-covered rock shelf toward the steer. Arthur followed him, coaxing the gray. Half way to the steer, the red refused again, plunging, and then the gray lifted a little too, and spun.

"It's the steer," Arthur said. "They don't like the blood."

"*The* steer," Curt cried. "*The* steer; the son-of-a-bitch. Take a look," and jerked his head toward the dark bulge of the south wall. Across the platform the snow was trampled and marked by jets of blood, and another steer lay there, its head bent up queerly onto the fallen rock at the base of the cliff.

"And another hurt," Curt said, jerking his head again, and Arthur saw the third, a young bull, backed into a niche beyond, its front legs spread stiffly to brace it and its head still lowered, on guard against nothing. Its eyes were dull and staring, and blood dripped slowly from the cup of one nostril.

"Killing for fun, the bastard," Curt said. "And running them like he was a wolf. He's a devil or crazy. And he picks 'em, too," he said bitterly. "Three of my best; two year olds and the cross, and one the bull I'd been counting on. And finished, by the look of him."

67

Arthur, seeing the dark coat with red glowing under it, like a banked fire of coals, of the steer on the platform, and the short up-curve of the horn, and then the curly, white foreheads of the two against the wall, nodded. He knew how Curt had figured ahead on the Hereford strain he was breeding into the lanky range cattle.

"He can't have gone far," Curt said. "His stink's in the air still, that's a cinch. Here, take this idiot again, will you? He'll stand now."

Arthur took the red's lines again, but said, "You can't track in those boots, Curt. And it's going to snow again before long."

"Won't have to track," Curt said. "Not far enough to matter. His trail's fresh as a daisy. There's no new snow in it at all. We must have just scared him off coming up here."

He went back to the fallen steer and picked up the carbine from against it, saying, "There's blood in it too. One of them got to him; the bull, chances are. And he's fed," he said, pointing with the carbine at the shoulder of the steer on the platform. The hide was ripped back, and a shallow hole gouged out with the white of bone and tendon glistening in it, and new blood still welling out.

"If he's that bold, he'll be too bold. His trail goes down the other side of the creek, and money says he's holed up in the willows."

He turned across the platform toward the creek.

"It's a big cat," Arthur said slowly, staring at the gouged steer. "He didn't more than get started on that. He must have had a long scrap with the bull, or been licking his wounds before he fed. He'll be plenty cranky, if he's waited. And it's no ordinary cat," he added, looking at the bull, and the steer fallen against the wall, "to break a bunch like that, and run three of them. They're no calves."

Curt stopped and turned. He was grinning, but his eyes were narrowed. "I could half believe your black devil myself, medicine man," he said. "Only it makes track, and it bleeds. So I'll took a look, I think."

Arthur shook his head slowly. "But for all that, I don't think he'd wait that close. If he's gone down-creek, it'll only be till he can get up over the side of the canyon. Then he'll head for high places. We made too much racket. You'd better let him go, Curt. Or wait for him here. He might circle back. You can't go a mile in those boots."

"Is he a friend of yours, mister?" Curt asked. "Sorry, then, but I'm still gonna look."

"Well, drag a deep track, in case it starts to snow again, or the wind comes up. I'll go back and fetch the stuff you need, and pick you up."

"You'd like that, wouldn't you?" Curt asked, still grinning. " 'I told you so,' " he said in a high, whining voice. "To say nothing of Hal's girl to play the loving priest with," he said in his own voice, and chuckled. "No, you wait here. I want to see, anyway. Then, if there's any going home to do, I'll do it myself. So I'll get what I need, and get it some time this week. And don't get dreaming about her here," he added, and chuckled again. "I still don't want to walk home."

Arthur stared at him soberly out of the shadow of the hood. Finally, when Curt's grin was gone, he said, "I'll watch them, don't worry. Get along, if you have to."

For a moment Curt stared back at him, with the little flicker beginning in his eyes, but then he made the one-sided grin.

"Just see you do," he said, and turned and went to the edge above the creek, and let himself down. He crossed the creek carefully, rock to rock, breaking the ice armor with his heel before each step, and went down on the other side out of sight behind the aspens.

Arthur turned the horses and led them to the edge of the platform so he could watch below, and stood there, talking to them softly, and sometimes looking among the aspens or along the north wall farther down, and sometimes out through the huge V of the canyon onto the white meadows. There was no snow falling in the canyon now, but the mist still hung over the valley, hiding the hills on the other side, so the part of the meadow he could see was like the beginning of a plain. The long, thin trace of the creek went onto it, bending south, and at last in the edge of the snow mist, spread into the dark, map-shapes of the tule marshes. Tiny black cattle were drifting slowly southward in small clusters on the plain. Slow clouds of white, like steam, blew across them sometimes, dimming them out, and then fell away and let them show dark again. There was still some wind out there then, though it was quiet in the canyon.

The horses waited easily now, making only little motions of impatience, but he kept himself ready to wrestle them down. The report of the carbine would be loud between those high walls.

The minutes passed, and no report came, though. There was only the soft blowing and shaking of the horses, and, when they were quiet, the faint, continuous talk of the creek under the ice and the even softer whispering of the aspens. Finally he heard the sound of Curt's boots. It grew louder, and then Curt's head and shoulders came up from below.

He saw Arthur standing at the edge, watching him, and called from the other side of the creek, "Well, you were right for once, whiskers; the son-of-a-bitch is gone."

He clambered up onto the platform, breathing hard, his eyes challenging against what Arthur didn't say. "You can see where he got out, without going all the way down to it. He just cleared the rim-rock and went up the north side."

Arthur nodded. "He'll be back, sooner or later," he said. "We could take the horses over on the side toward the ranch, where he wouldn't get wind of them, and come back up and wait for him."

"You could sit till the end of time, couldn't you?" Curt said. "He won't come back before dark now, if he ever does, and it'll snow again before then. Not for me, thanks. It's early yet. It can't be much more than six o'clock. I'm gonna track him."

Arthur opened his mouth to speak, and Curt said quickly, with the hard grin, "And you'll hold the trail till I get back with my stuff."

That yellow blouse is strong magic, to take you off the trail yourself, Arthur thought, studying Curt from the shadow of the hood, and said, "Either way."

"No," Curt said sharply, "not either way; that way," and fished the loose cartridges out of his pocket and gave them to Arthur. He took the red's bridle, and handed Arthur the carbine, saying, "It's loaded now," and hoisted himself into the saddle. Staring down at Arthur, he said, "And don't get to moon-

70

ing, for God's sake. He won't run far, I tell you, and you'd better see him first."

Arthur smiled up at him, the smile widening slowly until his teeth showed white in the dark beard, and nodded, but didn't say anything. Curt swung the red and put him to the lower edge of the platform, heeled him over, and, below the rock fall, lashed him into a scurrying run. For some time after he was out of sight the running still went on in the cliffs, and then it blurred and faded there too, and the aspens and the creek were the voice of the canyon again, and overhead, for a moment, a soft, hollow beating of wind.

6 ◗— —◗

For a minute Arthur continued to stand there gazing down the canyon at the place where Curt and the red had disappeared. Then he slowly turned the little mare so she could watch what he was doing, and dropped the reins into the snow, saying, "You wait here, Smudge. It's all right now. There's nothing can hurt you. It's all right," and crossed to the torn steer and bent over it, leaning on the carbine.

The steer lay on its side, with its neck too far extended, and twisted over so the lower jaw was half in the snow. A little blood, clotted by the cold, lay in the black cup of the upper nostril and the eye he could see stared up, open and already dry. A few flakes of snow lay unmelted on the long, winter pelt. Arthur looked at the great wound on the shoulder, and then at the neck. There were deep tooth marks over the ridge of the neck, and long parallel talon rips up the side of it. Yes, a very big cat, by the spacing, and a heavy one, to make a killing attack from the ground against a full-grown steer.

He drew off his left mitten and laid his bare hand on the bulge of the steer's belly. He smiled a little then, remembering the dream of himself on the edge of the cliff, and mocked softly, "So this is where I left it." Under the hair, the steer was not hard or even quite cold yet. A dew of melted flakes among the roots of the hair wet his hand.

He stood up again slowly, and slowly worked his mitten down into the pocket of his parka, on top of the unfinished carvings. His fingers touched the whittled edges, and he was faintly pleased by the feel of the wood and the thought of the whittling that remained to be done, and then troubled that he hadn't finished the cat for Joe Sam.

Finally he turned and walked across to the fallen steer under the south cliff, and stood looking down at it. Its neck was broken, too. The painful angle of the head, turning both horns down into the rock, showed that. The neck wasn't marked though. There were no marks of claws or teeth anywhere on the steer.

Broke its own neck, he thought, running blind, and in the dark, most likely.

He looked up and across the big body at the bull, standing spread-legged in his shallow refuge. The bull hadn't moved, unless the wide head had drooped a little nearer to the snow. It didn't see him. Its stupid, round, innocent eyes were half lidded and dull. All its slackening consciousness was centered on staying on its feet and keeping its horns turned out against the danger that wasn't there any longer. Walking carefully, his boot-heels making him slip and stumble among the tumbled rocks masked with snow, Arthur went around the steer and approached the bull. The bull swung its head a little more toward him, very slowly and without lifting it at all, but otherwise didn't move. When he was close enough to have touched it with the carbine, Arthur stopped and stood looking at it. He felt the creature's weakness and dull fear as in himself, and for a moment he couldn't see it, his eyes glazing over, turning their vision inward, as his mind shied from what he had to do. Then he saw again.

"Well, friend?" he asked, hardly knowing he spoke.

At the sound of his voice the bull shifted a little in the rock, nearly falling. Then it braced itself again, and the dripping of blood from its nostril freshened for a moment into a thin stream. The blood was thick and dark, almost purple on the snow. The snow around it was flecked with a brighter blood also. Outside the shelter of the niche, where the snow was trampled in a wide semi-circle, the scarlet streaks were dimmed by new snow. The bull's thick shoulder was torn as if by three heavy-bladed knives that had ripped together, and in one place four. Its throat was deeply torn too, and the blood was still welling out there, running in a thin, faintly shining trickle down over the bulging red shoulder and spreading like arteries on the white brisket. There were even long, open wounds, dug in deeply at the ends, like dagger thrusts, down the slowly heaving barrel. The polished white of ribs showed in two of them.

"A long fight, friend," Arthur said softly. "I'm sorry. It's only to make it quicker."

The first finger of his bare left hand tried the trigger of the carbine gently. It held rigid against his touch, and he felt, like an animal force, the charged power waiting to be sprung.

Hair trigger, he thought off the top of his mind. No slack at all. The way Curt likes it, I guess. No chance not to, once you've started.

He lifted the carbine until the muzzle, only a few inches from the bull's head, pointed just between the ear and the eye. The barrel wavered for an instant then, but steadied, and he drew, and the butt struck in his shoulder violently. The report was a deafening slam, at once deepened, enlarged and multiplied into a confused booming between the high walls of the canyon. The gray mustang started convulsively and wheeled and broke toward the edge of the platform, but snubbed herself twice on the trailing reins and wheeled back, swinging her rump about the pivot of her braced forelegs The echoes diminished, rolling faintly in the canyon below, and she saw Arthur standing there still, and she stood also, though trembling and staring.

The bull jerked as if stung, and then sank slowly forward and a little to one side, its knees buckling, its muzzle plowing out into the stained snow. Only small, unknowing panics of life moved it a few moments longer, the short, thick-shouldered forelegs stiffening and shaking, single tremors running swiftly here and there in the great muscles of the body. Then the last breath sighed out gustily, spraying the snow with blood, and the chattering dance of the hoofs in the broken rock slowed and stopped. The huge body sank away a little, relaxed, and lay still.

Arthur stood looking down at it, almost in the attitude of a man praying, except for the carbine held across him and still smoking faintly at the muzzle. A trickle of earth and pebbles spilled suddenly down the cliff onto the bull's shoulder. Arthur started, as if the quick, small touches might waken the bull and bring him lurching to his feet. He saw then that the dark horn that curved into the air now was gummy with blood, with a scattering of short pale hairs stuck in it. His closed mind made nothing of this, however, only seeing and storing it.

He turned, smiling inside his cowl, but fixedly, like a man asleep and dreaming strangely. Bearing the carbine across him in both hands still, and with the empty shell left in the breach, he worked his way out of the broken rock and moved slowly across the platform to the waiting horse. She started at the first touch of his hand but then turned her head to him and nudged his shoulder. He took the reins in his mittened hand, carrying the carbine in the other, and led her down to the creek and slowly through the shallow turmoil of water among stones and ice, turned her down-canyon on the other side, and mounted. He saw Curt's wavering boot trail, and the evener arc of widely spaced clusters on the slope, where the cat's speed had forced it up after the crossing. The clusters straightened out below and went down beside the aspens. Sometimes there were little jets of blood stretched between them, and less often, in snow that had drifted deeper against a boulder or the brush, a long serpent curve where the heavy tail had dragged. The mare went down slowly along the marks of the cat, afraid for her footing. Arthur didn't press her, but just sat the saddle, not looking around, his bare left hand braced against the horn, his right, in the mitten, holding the carbine across his thighs.

The aspens drifted by, making their soft, nervous fluttering, and the red willows began. Where the rim-rock ended against the sky above and the canyon walls became rounded hills sloping steeply into the valley, the tracks turned up. The blood marks between them were heavier for a few jumps, and then faint again, and finally as the tracks became single, there were none. Going at a steep angle, only a little with the length of the hill, they vanished north over the crest.

74

The mare passed their turning and went on down unchecked. She was almost out from between the wings of the canyon before Arthur missed the tracks.

"Dreaming again, Curt would say," he said aloud, smiling a little. He reined the mare in, and, twisting clear about in the saddle to see out of his hood, scanned the slope above him. After a moment, in one place only, high up on the shoulder, he saw the marks of the crossing.

"Dreams are all kinds, though, eh?" he said to the mare or the quiet canyon. "Some we wouldn't miss too much," and gently urged her down once more.

When he judged the north slope easy enough for her, he stopped her again, dismounted and, leaving her with the reins hanging, shuffled down through the knee-deep snow to the willows and then down-canyon along them to a place where they thinned at the edge of a sandy ford so a horse might pass through them. Here he crossed and went up on the other side onto the open meadow strip between the south reach and the creek. He saw the tracks of steers there, moving close together down toward the valley, and looking that way saw the little bunch, already down on the edge of the meadow. He looked up at the south slope, at the cut the horses had made coming into the canyon. Then he dragged across the steer tracks, with the sides of his boots, a wide, deep mark half the width of the strip of meadow, and on the creek end of it, scraping and stamping, made an arrow head longer than a man. After that he went back across the creek and up to the waiting mare, mounted, and turned her up onto the slope.

On the other side of the spur, a wide draw opened beneath them. The pines came clear down to the grassland in it, though thinning their ranks a little toward the lower edge. The wind had swept them clean, and they showed black against the snow. He turned the mare in toward the mountain and downward only a little. Where the spur became the mountain itself, and the slope of the draw grew steeper, he came on the flower track again. He pulled up to let the mare breathe before the new climb, and looked along the cat's trail as far as he could see it. It went up northwest, weaving no more than the trees made it, and the rosettes were still single and closely spaced. There was one much larger, blurred impression in sight, where the cat had sat down to rest, and perhaps to lick its wound. The wound was doing all right, though, he thought, seeing no blood now anywhere in the line of tracks.

After a minute he turned the mare onto the trail and they climbed along it, slanting north and upward among the trees. Once, well up in the quiet grove, a jay flashed suddenly over them, screaming, its blue brilliant even in that gray light. It perched on a high limb over the trail ahead of them, and kept scolding as they came nearer.

Arthur looked up at it and grinned, thinking, It's no secret now that the master killer has come out. Everything on the mountain will hole up and keep watch. They passed under the jay, and it flew ahead and perched again. Four times it preceded them, screaming as it flew, and scolding profanely from each perch. Then it was satisfied, and from the last perch, dropped away down-slope, still scolding.

The pitch of the mountain increased and even going across it the mare was forced to stand and blow often, reaching with her head to loosen the lines and breathe easier. Arthur didn't hurry her. His mind was still resting after what he'd done in the canyon. Notions moved in him idly, by their own small power, all frail and a little unhappy. They made passive overtures to what was around him, the pines, the gray boulders where the mountain itself began to show through the snow, the delicate writing of small tracks on the white slope, the sentinel jay, a chipmunk making its pebbly chittering somewhere out of sight, even the storm filling again, far up among the peaks. He couldn't complete this slow penance, however, for the full knowledge of his act was still trapped within him, as in a fist, so that he felt it, but couldn't see it. With that fist closed in him he remained apart from the life of the mountain.

Where another creek, smaller than the Aspen, and the willows thinner along it, went down to the northeast, the cat's track turned straight up the mountain. As Arthur on the mare came to the turn, there was a sudden crashing in the willows below them. Arthur swung the carbine over to put his left forefinger to the trigger, but then he saw the two young deer, last spring's fawns, he thought, going up in long bounds on the steep slope beyond the willows, the head of one against the haunch of the other. He reined in the mare and watched until the two came against the sky between dark pines, and vaulted airily, almost in one curve, two bodies long, over a manzanita thicket on the ridge, and vanished.

I smell strong of the curse on my breed right now, he thought, and turned the mare up on the trail beside the creek, but after a few yards had to swing down out of the saddle and lead her, the pitch was so steep.

Just below the crest of the first ridge the pines opened about a pile of great, rounded boulders, hedged along the base by manzanita. The trail turned south there and leveled out. Arthur's boot heels and the mare's hoofs made faint, stunted echoes among the boulders, and then only their own sounds again. They came to the edge of a short, deep ravine. There once more the cat had rested, sitting so it could look back down the slope. Arthur stood for a moment staring at the many overlapping flower tracks, the circle of the haunches and the wide sweep of its tail. Then he turned up again around the boulders and beside the ravine. The trail became so steep here that the mare behind him scrambled and slipped and he had to wait every time for her to catch herself and make a new start. Above the boulders it became easier again up a slope of sand under the snow, and along the edge of a rising thicket of manzanita nearly drifted under. Out of the manzanita there rose abruptly another formation of rock, the true peak of the foothill. This one wasn't rounded, but tilted up and weathered sharply into three edges, like spires when seen from below, two on the north end, close together, but the northermost much smaller, like a child at its mother's shoulder, and one, lower and apart from them, and bulkier, almost a half-dome, swelling over the trail and the edge of the ravine. The new snow marked their sides in gothic fretwork and lay in a narrow triangle, point up, between the two close spires and in a wide, inverted triangle between the highest spire and the half-dome.

Arthur stopped, looked up at the rock, and smiled a little. It was the formation they called Cathedral Rock. He had come there a good many times to sit alone and whittle, and once in a while with Grace, making it a goal for their ride. It was a good place to sit. The rock rose clear of the trees and the whole valley was spread out below. It was high enough to look over the hills on the other side too, and show the desert mountains rolling range beyond range into the east. The mind opened and grew quiet and solitary with that reach before it. Even as he looked up at the rock, though, a shadowy, less happy meaning, even a little fearful, stirred beneath the clear memories. But then he saw the cat's track going up under the half-dome, and the brief darkness passed from his mind while he remembered the shapes of the mountain above the rock.

A nervy brute, for a fact, he thought. Going back already; maybe in at the head of the canyon. He could make it down that creek chimney, maybe, if he couldn't get up it. Or going to keep an eye on his kill, from the edge.

Standing to breathe and let the mare breathe, he looked up at the rock again, and thought of the hours he'd spent there, his mind exploring while the little wooden figures took shape under his knife. In the summer the smell of hot granite, faint and clean, mingled with cooler airs from above, full of pine and cedar. The small, quick sounds of birds and chipmunks busy around him, like notes from an instrument plucked in drowsy inattention, became part of the warmth and sweet air. And everything came together, became bigger and easier and more durable, when he glanced down from his carving into the valley, where tiny, white-marked cattle moved slowly on the meadow stretches, and the tule marshes shone like metal in the sun. Then, always, he was led by the shape of the valley to look away into the northeast too, through the pass to the black, shimmering wall of the first desert mountain, where the road turned south for Reno, and beyond the black wall, farther and wider over the sea of desert hills flowing in the heat, to the narrow white rim on the eastern horizon, that might have been a rear guard of departing clouds, but was really a snow-capped range way out toward the middle of the state.

The extent of the view was great enough to show the curve of the horizon, and give the feeling that the world was floating in space, and sometimes, under its influence, his mind would sweep together, as the hand sweeps together scattered cards on a table, the many troublesome, fragmentary thoughts of weeks, or even months, into the one big answer they had all been looking for, the answer that, like all good answers, was only a beginning of a bigger question. When that happened, so that he finally rode home moving happily, for the time being, in a new and larger realm, he would always keep a particular fondness for the figure he had been carving then. To get that figure out during some closed-in evening of a winter, and finger it, and set it on the kitchen table in the rim of light beyond the shadow of the lamp bowl, like a little idol in the deliberate light of a temple, would be enough to bring the whole afternoon back to him, its near, clean smells and little, plucking sounds, its space and shining, its questions and answer and the new question. He could have made a gallery from among his whittlings that were scattered around everywhere in the house, especially in Grace's room and on top of the bookcase in the kitchen, that would remind him of fifteen or twenty such afternoons. They were a kind of secret diary, those whittlings, a notebook of his private living and all that was important to him. If he were to set them up in a row, in the order in which they'd been made, they would furnish an encouraging evidence, a proof that he could touch, that he was moving, however erratically and with whatever troubled intervals. The question that went with the last piece mattered more than those before it, as the piece itself was better cut, simpler and meaning more. He never would set them up like that, of course, except in his mind, but he could have.

Those gains had come more often in the fall than in the summer, he thought. The best time of all on the rock was in the Indian summer of late September, or of a better October than this was turning out to be. The mild warmth and the stillness that came then opened him more gently and more widely, without any effort on his part. It removed the last strain of anguish and contest from his thinking, and let his findings assume proportion and perspective almost by themselves. Then was the season of big answers and of resigned, late-afternoon wonder, when the mote-filled roads of light came straight down through the passes onto the yellowing meadows, and the pines and golden aspens stood under them in motionless, smoky blue shadow, and a single hawk, perhaps, wrote his attentive silence widely upon space below.

Looking up at the rock and remembering, he wanted, as a

79

kind of token thanks for these hours, to go up and sit against it now, and maybe finish Joe Sam's cat for him. He smiled a little at the notion, and shook his head gently within the hood, thinking what Curt would say if he came hurrying up here with his snowshoes and his food and found him sitting on a rock with snow on it, whittling and looking at the valley.

"Well, come up, Smudge," he said, and tugged gently at the reins. The little mare heaved forward and began to move up behind him, and he put the reins over his right shoulder and led her, the carbine in his left hand almost touching the snow as the pitch steepened again. He realized then that just the memories of the rock had served him almost as well as if he had gone up there and sat for a while. The painful fist within him had opened, as if his thought had balanced out the killing, or nearly.

I must tell Hal to bring Gwen up here before she goes home, he thought, and smiling a little added, They'll have to get out of that kitchen, anyway.

He was under the half-dome rock, though not there at all in his thoughts, when suddenly the mare neighed shrilly, in extreme terror, and wheeled toward the ravine. Before he could let go of the reins, he was dragged over backwards and to the side. He fell into the stiff springing hedge of brush at the edge, and half entangled there saw the big cat above him, crouched on a slanting ledge of the rock, its hind quarters gathering under it, like pressed springs, for the leap, and its long, heavy tail lifted a little for balance and curling and uncurling slowly at the tip, as if separately alive.

His body, after an instant, struggled fiercely to get free onto the solid trail, and to pull the carbine up out of the tangle of branches into which its weight had drawn his left arm and shoulder. His mind, though, quite independently and scarcely disconcerted, mocked him gently, saying, The shell in the chamber's empty, my friend. Dreaming again, Curt would say.

He let go of the gun and tried to roll in the breaking and clinging of the brush, but the panther leapt, spread like a launching bird, and he froze under it, staring up at the great, nervously grinning head bent toward him, fangs bared, between the reaching forelegs, the pale, enormous eyes, lambent within, fixing his own as their target. Even then his mind made one more little jest against him, saying quickly, Not even a black one; not the belly, at least, and then he saw on the pale belly the long, blackened wound the bull had dug. He felt it torn in his own flesh, and made one more convulsive effort to roll free, but got only one hand, the bare one, and one knee onto the trail, and then, with a small moan of surrender, squeezed out of his body without his knowing it, had only time to brace himself and turn his face down from the darkening fall.

Far away, separated from him by the distance between the living and the dead, he heard the terrified mare crash in the thickets below and cry wildly.

7 ⬗

Curt sat by the table, working the last of the hot beef fat into the buckskin pacs that had dried hard and wrinkled during the summer.

He looked across the table at Gwen again, and said, "Well, if it's a black one, and that big, we'll make it into a blanket for your wedding bed. You'll need it, with a hard winter coming up, and a bashful kid for a husband. And think how peaceful you'd sleep under it, when you got around to sleeping. Why, he's the cause of all the trouble in the world, that black painter. Joe Sam says so. Arthur says so. Grace says so, though that don't count so much, because she always says what Arthur says. Even young Hal there, though he don't spread his opinions quite so easy yet, is beginning to think so. There must be something in it, if all our thinkers think so. Imagine how easy you could rest, with the end of all the troubles in the world right there over you to prove there wasn't anything could go wrong."

He grinned and stared into Gwen's eyes with the hawk look that made her defend what he ridiculed. It didn't work any better now than it had from the start. Gwen just sat there across from him, with her chin in her hands, smiled a little, and looked

81

at him out of her dark eyes, with their slight, Oriental tilt, and said, "That would be fine," without showing anything she really thought.

Because she repulsed him so easily, and because there wasn't much time left, he was suddenly angry. He stopped kneading the greasy pac, and stared at her, and the little fluttering of rage was in his eyes, so she had to look away from them, but by now he knew this didn't mean a gain. When the fury in his mind thinned enough to let him think words, he looked down at the pac and rubbed the grease twice more into the creases of the instep and tossed the bit that was left over into the wood-box.

Goddam, superior bitch, he thought. He began to work the pac fiercely between his hands to seem busy and in control of himself. A black mucker's daughter, for Christ's sake, he thought, playing the superior bitch with me. A whore, ten to one. They all are, at heart. And play-acting a dumb virgin. Saving herself for her puppy love. By God, just let a man get hold of her once, and . . .

Grace came out of the storeroom under the landing, closed the door, came across to the table and put on it an oilskin packet that bulged with what it held.

"There's your lunch," she said. "I put in just what you asked for, but I still think you ought to take more."

"Thanks, that'll be plenty," he said, not looking up.

He pulled on the pacs and began lacing them over the blue woolen pants he'd put on instead of his jeans and chaps.

Or if this Grace would quit poking her long nose in, he thought. If I could just get the little bitch alone for an hour once. What the hell can you do in here, with Grace always poking her nose in, and the old man falling asleep over his liquor already, and the old lady there . . .

Grace said, from the front window, where she stood looking out into the yard, "Hal's bringing Kentuck out now."

Such a hell of a hurry to get me out of here, Curt thought, like I was going to ruin her right here in front of 'em, or something. Does she think Mother's ever going to let her baby marry the little tart? What does she think the old lady's been sitting there all this time for then, and not even paying any attention to things I been saying she'd jump down my throat for most times? And did, before they come out, for that matter.

He jerked the laces of the second pac tight and wound them twice around the ankle and knotted them.

"He's been long enough at it. Let him wait," he said.

He stood up and began working his feet forward into the toes of the pacs, to loosen them.

After a moment he looked down at Gwen again, grinned and said, "If it turns out to be just an ordinary-sized, yellow cat, though, one I could skin with this," and he picked up a bone-handled hunting knife in its sheath from the table and danced it on his hand to make her watch it, "it won't hardly do for a blanket. It would be all my present, too. Arthur, he won't have anything to do with ordinary yellow cats. You know what I think then?" he asked, slipping the knife into the left pocket of the red coat, and then the oilskin packet, and the little metal container full of matches that had stood on the table beside the knife.

"No. What?" Gwen asked, but not as if she cared whether he told her or not.

"We'll make you a costume out of it. You know," and he outlined the shape of the costume on himself with his hands. "One of those Hercules kind of rigs, like the Greeks wore, only for a lady, of course, higher in front, and maybe with black lace on it. And then you can give us a special wedding dance."

This time, when Gwen looked down, it wasn't because his eyes were unsteady. The red flush rising on her throat showed even under her brown skin. Curt's grin widened and became easier.

"I'm not much of a dancer," Gwen said.

Curt laughed. "I'll teach you," he said. "I'll give you as many lessons as you want, free of charge, and do the catching while you practice, too. You know, one of those dances where you come running across the stage and jump and land right in my arms on one knee."

He held his arms out in a circle, to show how he would catch her, and then drew them slowly toward his body, at the same time making a mocking show of breathless tenderness.

"You'd learn in no time," he said, straightening up and grinning at her again.

"Hal's got him all saddled," Grace said sharply. "He's bringing him over."

Curt was feeling better. "You don't say. The times that kid can be fast and the times he can't is a puzzle. Arthur, now," he said, crossing to the gun rack and taking another handful of cartridges for the carbine, "you can depend on him. He just don't ever move."

He dropped the cartridges into the right pocket of his coat and picked up the bear-paw snow-shoes he had strapped together and set against the wall, and the coiled lariat that lay against them. He started toward the outside door, but stopped opposite the table and looked at Gwen again.

"Darned if I don't hope it's just an ordinary yellow one, at that. Not much of a prize, maybe, nothing like a black one the size of a horse's, but it would really go good with your complexion."

But Gwen stood up and pushed in her chair and looked back at him easily now. "Thank you," she said. "It's not much in my style. I'd a lot rather have the black one."

Curt laughed. "Don't tell me you're going to be like all the rest of them around here," he said, "a-scared to try anything new. Now I'd of thought, to look at you, you'd have more spirit than that."

He laughed again, and went to the door and opened it, not waiting to give her time to answer him.

The mother marked her place with her finger and looked up for the first time.

"Don't you go playing the fool, Curtis," she said. "If it starts snowing again, you get yourself back here as fast as you can."

Curt stepped outside, grinning now to see the trouble Harold was having bringing Kentuck across. The black stallion hadn't been used for nearly a week, and he was dancing and sidling and tossing all the way. Joe Sam was coming across too, by himself, and safely behind Harold and the stallion. Curt looked up at the pale shroud of snow mist on the mountain. It was lifting some, he was sure. The newly frosted pines showed farther up than they had when he came in. He believed it was thinning out overhead, too. There was even a little color of sunlight spreading in it.

"It'll hold off some time yet," he said, loudly enough for the mother to hear him inside. He thought that really the storm

84

was breaking up, and even the snow on the ground would be gone in a few hours. The sun was still warm this time of year, if it got a chance. He wouldn't say anything as definite as that, though, not with weather to deal with. It was too much like making a dare.

The father had lifted his head and blinked suddenly, at the sound of the mother's voice. Now he rose and moved with heavy, dignified care to the door, and stepped down carefully into the snow beside Curt. He stood there, with his left arm behind him, his right hand fingering the lodge emblem on his watch chain, and squinted up at the snow mist too.

"I should judge it might even clear up," he said, as if that were the result of a long, careful consideration.

Curt was angry that the old man had made the foolish dare after all, but there wasn't anything he could say about it.

The old bastard, he thought fiercely, always blabbing about something is none of his business. Sure, all he's got to do is sit on his big behind in the kitchen and guzzle. What does he care if it snows? He probably even wants it to. Then he can have everybody in there and play cards all afternoon and make eyes at the little Welshy like he could still do something about it.

He moved forward a step, as if, being right there beside him, the old man could guess his thoughts, but then waited and made Harold come the rest of the way.

When he stopped, still being jerked about by the big stallion's tossing, Curt asked sharply, "Did you soap his hoofs?"

Harold stared back at him for a moment, but finally only said, "They're soaped," but wouldn't look away from him.

The mother called from inside, "Close that door, Curt, will you? Do we have to lose all our heat, just because you got a notion to chase your own shadow?"

Grinning inside, Curt thought, The kid's mad enough to chew nails.

"Little frisky, was he?" he asked, and turned back, but then saw Grace and Gwen coming out, and stopped, and grinned at them openly, thinking, No wonder the kid's mad, with her watching him. Well, it's not the only stallion you got to look out for, kid.

Gwen closed the door, and she and Grace stood there together in front of it, a little apart from the old man, and watched the stallion dancing. Curt turned and came alongside the animal, but still left Harold holding it while he tied the lariat on at the bow of the saddle, and then hung the bear-paws over it by their carry-strap around the horn. Across the saddle he saw Joe Sam standing there alone, safely beyond Harold, his face turned to the stallion, but that intent look of not seeing in his good eye, and he grinned and looked at Harold.

"You tell our old medicine man there what I found?"

"Yes," Harold said. "He asked me."

Curt took the reins from Harold, and with the same hand took hold of the saddle horn. "And what did he say?" he asked.

This time Harold grinned back at him a little too. "All he wanted to know was why Arthur didn't come back with you."

Curt's grin became hard to keep.

"Poor old Arthur," he said. "Doesn't anybody think he can take care of himself? Even the half-wit worrying."

He swung up into the saddle, carefully making it an easy-looking mount, slow and all in one move, his back very straight and his right leg, bent at the knee, just sliding over the cantle.

"What you think now, Joe Sam?" he called, reining the stallion to dance sideways. "Still a black painter?"

The old Indian appeared to be looking up at him, but didn't answer, only stood there very straight, with his arms down straight at his sides.

Curt stopped grinning and prodded Kentuck with his heels and danced him on a tight rein, sidling a little, toward Joe Sam.

"You hear me?" he asked.

Joe Sam looked up at his face, seeing him for the first time.

"What say?" he asked quickly.

Curt kept pressing Kentuck forward slowly until the old man was compelled to take three or four steps backward and to the side, away from the lifting forehoofs, and to raise one arm as far as his waist in spite of his wish not to. Then Curt checked the stallion, pulling him across the old man and letting him rear a little before him, but not wheel or move away. Looking down, making the small, tight smile, he said easily, almost indiffer-

86

ently, "That's better. Speak up quick when you're spoke to. Now, what do you say?"

Harold started toward them, calling, "Let him be now, will you, Curt? He don't know what you're talking about."

"What, another squaw-man?" Curt said. "He will," he promised. "Now what do you say, Joe Sam?"

"What say?" the old man asked, trying to smile.

"I asked you do you still think your painter's black? Do you still think it's no good to hunt it, after what we found out there?"

"No good hunt," Joe Sam said seriously, and shook his head slowly and just once.

Curt laughed, and Harold stopped a few feet from him, watching, not any surer now than Joe Sam was where the bullying would stop, and not wanting to make trouble about it if Curt was done.

"Why not, Joe Sam?" Curt asked, chuckling like a man humoring a not very bright child.

"Snow," the old man said. "Much snow." His good eye remained watchful.

Curt laughed again. "You hear that, young one?" he called over his shoulder to Harold. "It's just plain, ordinary snow now. There's sense in the old fool yet. You just have to know how to get it out of him, that's all."

He swung Kentuck and took him back, dancing again, in front of the father and Grace and Gwen. Going by slowly that way, straight in the saddle, with one arm loose at his side, he grinned down at Gwen, and said, "I'll hold you to it," as if she'd made the promise to match his. "And I'll shoot him through the eye, too, so there won't even be a hole to spoil it."

He let Kentuck out and heeled him up to a jumping start, but quickly eased him off to a lope and rode north into the plowed tracks the red and Arthur's mustang had made before daylight. He didn't look back. The five stood there silently, watching him grow smaller on the snow, Harold and Joe Sam together out on the trampled yard, and the old man and Grace and Gwen in a row in front of the door.

8

They were almost out to the whaleback again, when Kentuck stumbled twice and dropped out of his run. Curt, angry in his mind because he couldn't get rid of the feeling that he'd been foolish in his little sport in the yard, yanked him up and drummed savagely with his heels. Kentuck leaped forward, but at once stumbled again, nearly falling. Curt swore and pulled him in, and let himself down into the snow, growling. "What the hell now?"

He found the stallion's right forefoot balled with snow and sand.

"The lazy son-of-a-bitch," he muttered. "Too damn busy working on his little tart to even soap a hoof."

He lifted the clogged hoof onto his knees and pulled off a mitten and tugged at the ball, but could only scrape shallow, white grooves into the surface of it. He let the hoof down and straightened up and looked around, but couldn't find anything handy to pry with. After a moment he thought of the skinning knife, and drew it out of his pocket and then out of its sheath. The rough bone haft felt good in his hand.

He set his jaw and narrowed his eyes, made two grunting stabs in the air with it, and then stood there, holding the knife easily, a smile of contempt on his mouth, and said, "Try to shove me around, will you?"

Then, as if a quieter self stood watching him, he thought how he would look if anyone saw him, standing there in the snow, with only a horse and the sagebrush to watch him taking revenge on the air.

He laughed a little and let the knife down, and said aloud, "You'll be crazy yourself, if you keep that up. Save it for the black painter. It won't get you anywhere with the kind that makes tracks."

He was eased by the stabbing, though, and having made it all right by the short joke after it, was quieted. He slipped the sheath into his pocket, and lifted the clogged hoof onto his lap again and began to dig and pry carefully with the point of the knife, trying to spring the pack out in one lump. The ball was only beginning to stir, though, when Kentuck nickered over him and swung away, making him drop his hold and stagger aside to keep from falling. The stallion nickered again, and then blew shrilly. The sound was shocking as a trumpet blast in the silence, and after an instant came back in a high, whining echo from the mountain. Curt straightened and leaped and caught the reins. Half circling him, with raised head, Kentuck trumpeted again, and again the mountain answered, but also there was a second, fainter reply, as if the valley echoed too. Clinging high under the bit, Curt looked down where Kentuck was looking, and saw the horse far out on the white meadow and standing to watch them. For a moment he only wondered to see a horse out there, but then, as it began to turn, half minded to start up toward them, he saw the swing of the tiny, empty stirrup, and knew the horse too.

"By God, the little broomtail," he said aloud.

A score of quick tales of doom went unfinished across his mind. There were familiar phantoms in some of them that sprang up out of recesses where he'd buried them, as Indians were sometimes buried, with stones piled on the graves, partly to keep the coyotes out, but partly to hold the dead down too. He turned on the ghosts.

"For Christ's sake," he said aloud, "the damn fool's gone to sleep again. Whittling again while his horse runs home."

He thought of riding down and catching the mare and looking her over to see if there were marks on her that would tell him anything. But the spoken contempt had not wholly cured his fear. The ghosts kept stirring, though small and one at a time now. He felt hurried. The mare could wait. He'd find the tracks, and follow them out and they'd tell him what he had to know. He lifted Kentuck's hoof again, dragging his head down by the bridle and twisting the lines around the raised leg, and slashed off the ball of snow flush with the hoof and began to dig with the point of the knife again. Kentuck blew for the mare twice more while he worked, but he only cursed him softly and put his weight more heavily against the leg. At the fifth careful try, the pack in the frog stirred in one piece.

He pried deeper and slowly and it sprang out, making a little thud on the ground snow. Dropping the knife into his pocket as it was, he freed the reins, spun Kentuck half way round, and mounted. When Kentuck turned, even against his pull, rearing a little, and crying once more at the mare, he put him down hard, cursing, reined him hard around to the north, and drummed and lashed him up into a run. Looking back as they swung onto the reach, he saw the mare trip on her dragging reins and stand, looking after them. Turning again, as they topped the crest, he saw her moving away toward the ranch, very small at that distance, and carrying her head to the side to drag the reins free.

He turned back and looked down into the creek canyon as Kentuck started the descent. At first he saw only the thin column of willows filing down onto the meadows, but then, distinct from that height, once he saw what it was, the big arrow Arthur had made to point at the crossing.

"Not asleep up to here, anyway," he said aloud, and for a moment the fears were many and quick in him again. He pulled Kentuck off the sloping track they had made at daybreak, and put him straight down at the arrow, so that often his haunches buckled under him and he slid. Thinking the cat might be in the canyon again, Curt raged that he hadn't brought a second rifle. When he imagined accidentally flushing the lion in the willows with nothing but the knife for a weapon, it seemed no better than being empty-handed.

He followed the muddied arrow across the strip of meadow, and put the black slowly down and through the creek, splashing and rattling. Coming up out of the water, he searched the north wing of the canyon and found where the mare had gone out on the long slant, and pressed Kentuck straight up the slope and turned him into her track. At the crest, he drew rein and looked along the trail on the north side as far as he could see it, and then quickly over the wide hollow, among the pines. He saw nothing moving anywhere, and started Kentuck down. The trail was distinct, even far up and across among the shadows of the trees, because Arthur's mare had tossed red needles and black mould up onto the snow. The phantoms quickened again when the cat's track came in, making a V with the hoof marks and then running with them.

"Still not asleep, old medicine man," he said.

The two tracks running together made him feel that what-ever had happened must have happened close ahead. He watched about him constantly among the trees and then among the first boulders, and twice he reached into his pocket to make sure the knife was haft up and easy to get hold of. He felt more than ever empty-handed without a rifle, but he was cold about it now. He didn't blame Arthur, either. It was his own fault. He should have made Arthur bring a rifle when they first came out, even knowing he wouldn't use it. Not having done that, he should have thought of bringing another with him this trip, instead of making whoring lies in his head about Gwen, and then working on her as if they were the truth. No use thinking about that either, now.

"Don't think at all; it makes you blind. Just keep your eyes open."

Where the double track turned straight up beside the little north creek and then became a triple track, the deep incisions of Arthur's boot heels showing clearest of all, he was forced to dismount too, and lead Kentuck. He climbed easily in the soft, flat pacs, going up step by step in the mare's prints, and the drag of the laboring stallion irritated him, but he kept a close watch just the same. He would be an easy prey on foot. There was no doubt in his mind by now, that the lion, besides being a giant, was crazy, a killer without reason. He thought of Arthur standing beside the dead steer in the box canyon, look-ing at him solemnly and curiously, and speaking of how bold the cat was. The warning had a power now that it had lacked then. Each time it made him remember Arthur's quiet reluc-tance in the bunk-room while they were getting dressed, and then many different times back through eighteen years, when they had joked about the black panther, but Arthur always with the little serious undertone, never really making fun of the notion as much as he did of Curt. The chain of quick, small memories passing through his mind, like black birds flying over him again and again in identical formation, began to impress him in spite of his scornful denials. After all, Arthur didn't really believe in the black panther any more than he did, cer-tainly not in one as big as a horse and transparent as a shadow, that started roaming the Sierra every year just when the first snow came. Because each memory returned embodied, and framed in familiar reality, himseif speaking, Arthur speaking, Joe Sam watching, Harold listening, at breakfast or supper in the kitchen or out in the sun by the corral fence, it had the strength in his mind of something that had happened.

When the trail turned south across the mountain and passed under a thicket of manzanita with a heap of rounded, half-joined boulders standing up out of it, Curt thought, Going back already, sure as hell. Going in from the top, and for a moment felt what was as bad as fear, that Arthur, for all his dreamy hanging back, had made the better guess about what the cat would do.

"Just what the old monk thought," he said aloud.

He was up in the edge of the waiting clouds now. The air about him was full of a fine suspended snow, like fog, with a pale shining beginning to spread in it. Objects near him were clear enough, but the ravine ahead of him showed only as a great milky blue shadow, except when a cold breath from the mountain above whirled the snow into long serpents that swam in the chasm, and let the rocks and pines and clumps of brush on the far wall show through dark and clear for a minute or two. He went very carefully in this mist, pausing often to be sure what made some shadow he thought for an instant had moved.

He came to where the cat had rested at the turn on the edge of the ravine, and stood there to read the record.

Watching its own back-trail, he thought. Already got half a mind to do the hunting itself. It took its time, too. Had a long lead. It just sat here and watched him coming up.

He was shaken even more than before, so that even his breathing changed a little, by the belief that whatever had happened couldn't have happened far from there. He could feel how the cat had hated the retreat, growing nettled, wanting to stop it.

When he went around the castle of boulders to climb beside the ravine, Kentuck dragging at the end of the reins behind him again, the wind swung down at him strongly for a moment, so he had to stop and turn away from the snow in it. He wanted to duck his head and shield his face with a raised arm too, but held himself against the wish, and only narrowed his eyes. The wind roared in the pines above, and then below him, and made a soft, hollow singing in the boulders beside him, and fell away again, bearing the curtain of snow aside with it. The Cathedral Rock stood up big and clear above him, and he scanned it carefully, especially the half-dome rock that stood over the trail. There was nothing moving except here and there the brush that jerked as if alive in the brief after-gusts. He tugged at the reins to start Kentuck again and went on up. The mist settled slowly around him once more, with the first sunlight spreading in it. It made an unreal place of the mountainside, a region that hung in space and unworldly silence, and Curt set his teeth against the sudden, loud sounds the stallion made scrambling up behind him as they came off the sand onto the granite shelves below the rocks.

Another gust halted them, and then, as it sighed away down the ravine, he saw, and all at once, as if it had just that instant fallen there, the spread form, like a dark, irregular star, lying on the incline under the half-dome rock. The white patches of the parka looked like snow, but even so, the ghosts gathered in him at once, making a single, big fear that filled him and shut off his breath. The flight of dark birds started over him again, but he stopped it, and looked warily all around over the rocks and brush with attentive eyes and an empty mind. After a moment he scrambled on up, jerking and cursing at Kentuck without knowing it. Then the stallion nickered softly and swung back, almost upsetting him, and wouldn't go up any farther for anything he could do.

But you won't run out on me, damn you, Curt thought, and took the rope from the saddle and looped it around Kentuck's neck, high behind the ears, and knotted the other end around a thick manzanita stem. While he worked at the rope, he glanced up often at the spread figure on the trail and quickly about among the brush and up at the pinnacles of the rock. Once or twice, tricked by a movement of the snow veil in the wind, he believed that the star-shaped figure stirred.

He yanked the knot tight against the manzanita and tested it twice, and then went up the slope half running, telling himself, The mare threw him; she spooked and threw him and he got knocked out on the rock. But even while he hoped, he didn't believe it. The mare had been gone too long, for one thing, showing up way out on the meadow there.

When he was close enough to see Arthur's bare left hand clutching at the rock in the snow, he also saw the carbine gleaming in the brush beyond. He didn't even pause beside Arthur then, but peering once more up at the half-veiled rock above, stepped over him and worked into the brush and drew the carbine up out of it, and examined it, first one side and then the other. It wasn't damaged to matter, a few sliding scratches, no more. He felt much better with it in his hands. He came up to the edge of the track again, trying the trigger, ejecting the empty shell, and feeling the newly tightened trigger with pleasure.

At the same time he thought, He saw something, though. He got one shot at something.

When he stood where his soft boot could have touched Arthur, he looked quickly up over the shadowy rocks once more, at the ghostly edge of forest farther above, and then knelt and gripped the right shoulder in its stiff, cowhide sleeve, and drew at it gently, as one might start to waken a sleeper. More than the shoulder moved to his tug, but not even one finger of the bare, left hand by itself. The outstretched arm slipped suddenly across the rock. He let the shoulder back down, and the arm slid out again. He withdrew his hand and gripped his own knee with it. Squatting there, using the carbine as a prop, he saw that the bare hand reaching onto the rock was blue, and that a thin sifting of the little snow flakes lay unmelted on it, and on the hood and back of the cowhide coat. He saw also what his hand had told him first, that there was a wide, ragged tear in the shoulder of the parka. There were three parallel marks below it, scraped through the red hair and into fine grooves in the leather underneath. For a moment the panther in his mind, possessed of purpose and malice and cunning like a man's, was an enormous black one in spite of him.

Then he stood up slowly to do what he should have done first thing. There were many of the great flower prints in a confused circle around the body. Then they went up from it along the base of the half-dome rock, two sets of tracks, but both

94

clearly made by the same cat. He followed them up, constantly watching around and over him as he went. Beyond the rock, where the open path turned back slightly from the edge of the ravine, the two patterns changed. One went on by single prints at regular intervals, an unhurried walk. The other gathered suddenly into the clusters with wide spaces between that meant running leaps. The two trails still lay together though, and he followed them on up until, ten or fifteen yards above the rock, they separated. There he stopped and peered along the leisurely track which continued upslope, but bending a little north now, away from the ravine, and vanished finally in the fog of snow at the edge of timber. Then he turned and traced the leaping tracks. They curved back into the upper side of the rock, and there took on the slower pattern again, and showed only here and there, a print or two at a time in the snow in the crevices. The scattered signs were enough, though. They led back around to the down-slope face of the big boulder that stood over the trail.

Jumped him from the rock, Curt thought.

He felt an unwilling awe of the cat that would conceive this trick before he was on the rock and then use it. There passed through his mind, quick and incomplete, like the bird fears again, many tales he'd heard of the cunning and treachery of mountain lions. They were better stories now, more real, things to remember and think about and learn from.

Looking once more up along the climbing track that vanished in the mist and woods he said aloud, "But he changed his mind about going back for breakfast, the murdering bastard," and turned and went down again to Arthur's body.

Propping the carbine carefully against the base of the big rock, he knelt and drew the body over toward him. It turned stiffly at first, all in one piece, but then loosened a little, the right arm giving, and turned against the stretched left arm as against a pivot. Tightening his mouth a little, making a faint grimace of distaste, Curt forced the left arm down, put his own arm under the head, and turned the body onto its back. As it turned the legs twined on one another and the head fell limply back and to one side over the crotch of his elbow, and stopped his breath. When he let the shoulders down into the snow, the head remained bent back and turned that way. The hood was pulled off the face, and the dark beard, stiffened with ice, jutted sideways at the sky, with beads of earth and sand frozen into it and the mouth in it a little and rigidly open.

It was as if this first glimpse of the face made real what had happened.

Jesus, Curt thought, half outside himself, and with something of the nature of prayer in the word too, Jesus, it even got him. He conceived Arthur, for the moment, as a creature made up of his dreams, and beyond any hazards of flesh.

He straightened the head from the shoulders, so that the face looked up directly out of the shelter of the hood. Then, kneeling there, carefully not looking at the mouth, he gazed at the face above the beard. It was quiet and unchanging. The shadowed lids were closed over the eyes, and the long, black lashes, like a woman's, lay curved on the high cheek bones. The lines of time and thought had grown a little fainter already, the weathered cheeks and bleached forehead smoother. It seemed, looking at that face, that even violent death must have entered slowly and easily, like a pleasant dream or a long, engrossing thought for which there was plenty of time. Grains of fine quartz sand, shallowly sunk in the skin along the left side of the nose and up onto the cheek, and the faint red scrapings they'd made were the only visible blemish. Curt reached down his bare hand and gently brushed out the sand. The daze that guarded him was broken by the act, and all at once he was filled by a rush of love and pity for the face. A few tears came, and he was no longer able to see the features clearly. He stood up slowly, and at this movement, anger rose to help him against the weakness.

"The goddam cat," he said aloud. He wiped at his eyes quickly with the back of his bare hand. "The goddam, son-of-a-bitchin' cat."

He was a little relieved, and saw the face clearly again, and knelt and carefully worked the beads of sand and dirt out of the beard. He tried gently to close the mouth, but the jaw was set, and he couldn't. He knelt a moment longer, just looking at the face, with nothing for his hand to do.

"Don't you worry, Art," he said. "I'll get the son-of-a-bitch if I have to chase him to the Pacific."

This oath, and the thought of the deed it promised, released him. He lifted the body, propping the head in the hollow of his shoulder, and staggered to his feet, and went slowly down toward the tethered stallion. Kentuck nickered softly and swung away on the end of the rope as he saw the strange shape coming, and perhaps already felt the death in it. Curt stopped and spoke to him, but still he pulled away, watching with his head high, and the white showing above the dark center of his eyes. Curt spoke again, a little longer, and then once more began to approach. Each time the stallion strained away, he waited again, holding the long body across both arms. At last Kentuck let him come alongside, although he trembled and kept his head high and turned to watch.

Curt lifted the body and slid it onto the saddle slowly. Holding it there with one arm, he patted Kentuck's shoulder with his free hand. But when he judged it safe, and drew his arm from under the cowhide hood, the dead man's head swung down within it as if it had come loose. Curt's lips writhed back from his teeth, and quickly he propped the head again with his arm.

After a moment he lifted the whole body down, moving as carefully as if it had been a living man badly hurt, and laid it on the ground. He removed his other mitten and stuffed it into his pocket with the first. Then he carefully worked the cowhide parka off the body, so Arthur lay in his dark blue shirt, with his long hair spread on the snow. He removed his own red mackinaw, and took the mittens and food packet and matches, and the cartridges and the knife and its sheath, out of the pockets, and made a neat little pile of them to one side. Slowly he worked the mackinaw onto Arthur, and took off his own sombrero and unwound the long black scarf from around his head, and raising the stiff collar of the mackinaw till it stood up about Arthur's head, bound it in place with the scarf, to make a supporting sling.

He lifted the body onto the saddle again, talking to Kentuck all the time he worked. The stallion, having stood for it once, stirred only a little. Balancing the body across the saddle so it hung there without his holding it, he began to work down the

97

tether rope to the knot, watching the body all the time, prepared to leap and catch it if the horse jerked, and talking steadily to Kentuck, though only with his mouth. When he got to the knot, he untied it hastily, tugging and muttering, and came back up to the stallion quickly. He felt much better when he could hold the body again with one hand, while the other loosened the slip-knot and lifted the loop over Kentuck's head. He bound the body securely to the saddle with the rope. Once he lessened the indignity he felt in the position of the body and in the act of binding it, by promising again, out loud, "I'll get the son-of-a-bitch, Art, if I have to chase him to the Pacific."

He knotted the end of the rope in the cinch ring, took the bear-paws off the saddle horn and dropped them beside the cowhide parka in the snow, and tied the reins to the horn, leaving them loose enough to give the stallion head-room. Then he stood there, holding the reins at the bit, trying to think of something to do or say that would make the trifle of ceremony he needed for the parting. The wind came down, bugling in the rocks and whirling the floating snow about him and the burdened stallion.

Finally he said, "If I'm out all winter, I will, so help me God."

That wasn't enough; it didn't fill the bill. There was a long past it didn't make up for, and a lonely journey home. Nothing else came, though. He hadn't got close to this man while he was alive, and he couldn't now.

He picked up his sombrero, but didn't put it on, and led Kentuck down the track to the place where the panther had sat to look back, and a little over the edge. There he released him, slapping him sharply over the rump with the hat, crying, "Get home now; get home with you."

The big stallion plunged at the blow, but slipped in the snow and sand and old pine needles, and catching himself, went on down slowly, picking his way among the trees. The body lay firm in its ties, head down on one side and feet on the other, moving only with the roll of the saddle. Far below, the black stallion came into a bar of clear sunlight, and for a moment the red coat made a spot of bright color on the snow.

PART

2 ⬩⬩ ⬩⬩ ⬩⬩

9

The noon meal was late because the mother kept it for a long time on the back of the stove, waiting for Arthur.

Finally she said, "We better eat, I guess. Everything's dryin' out," and served the plates and handed them around.

They ate with the empty place still set at the table, but nobody said anything about it until they were nearly finished. Then Grace, who had eaten very little, and hadn't spoken at all before, said abruptly, "I wish Arthur would get back. It's going to snow again."

She interrupted a story the father was telling, and for a moment he held his fork still and glared at her. She didn't even look at him, though, so at last he spoke.

"For heaven sakes, girl, stop your fretting. Did you ever know him to get anywhere on time?" and as an afterthought, "And there's no telling when Curt'll be back, either, if he's found something to hunt."

He couldn't get his story started again, after that, and the meal was finished in silence, except for his muttering to himself, now and then, as if someone were arguing the matter against him, about the state things had come to when the head of a house couldn't even finish a sentence at his own table.

At last the mother rose and picked up her plate and Harold's and carried them to the sink. She came back and picked up the father's and Gwen's, and paused there, holding them.

"I'll fix up a plate for Joe Sam, and you can take it out to him," she said to Harold.

"He's asleep," Harold said. He didn't want to say it, and he put his hands on the edge of the table and looked at them instead of at her.

The mother didn't say anything, but remained where she was, holding the plates and waiting for him to go on.

"Already?" Grace asked.

Harold nodded. "I went up to see if his fire was all right, before I came in, and he was asleep."

"Well," the father said loudly, "that's a good sign. Must be the storm's about over. There you are, Grace, all that fretting for nothing."

The mother began to move again. She carried the plates to the sink, and spoke from there, with her back turned.

"You can wake him up, can't you? He has to eat something. You take it out, and stay there, and see he gets it down him."

"I don't much like to wake him up," Harold said.

"Don't you worry. He'll go back to sleep fast enough," the mother said. She came back and picked up the last things from the table. "In fact, he ain't likely to do much *but* sleep for a week now."

"I don't know," Harold said. "He looks bad. He looks sick to me. I've never seen him look so bad before."

"That's because Curt bullied him," Grace said. "Showing off this morning."

The father snorted. "Don't be a fool, Grace. The boy didn't touch him."

"Don't you think he has any feelings?" Grace asked. "Just because he's an Indian, don't you think he has feelings?"

"Stop it, Grace," the mother said. "How do you mean, he looks bad?" she asked Harold.

"I don't know," he said uneasily. "He was sleeping all curled up, like a little kid would, with his arms around his knees."

"Did he have any covers over him?"

"No, but . . ."

"Then he was cold, that's all. Why wouldn't he be, lally-gaggin' around out there in his shirt-sleeves half the night?"

"No, his fire was still going good enough. It was good and warm in there. He don't look right to me. His face looks kind of too old, some way, even for him. Kind of all caved in. And he was breathing hard and sort of moaning to himself, or talking to himself, maybe."

"Could be he ain't over his spell yet," the mother said. "Just went to sleep with it still on him."

"He never has before," Grace said sharply. "Did he say anything you could understand?" she asked Harold.

Harold made a fist out of his right hand on the table, and slowly rubbed the other hand over it, and said, "He was dreaming about Arthur, I guess. He said his name two or three times, but that was all I could get."

Grace sat staring across the table at him, with the white, old look on her face again, but the father made a short, impatient laugh.

"There's nothing in that to get all worked up about that I can see," he said. "He always looks for Arthur, if he's in any kind of trouble. Arthur's the only one will take the old fool seriously. Birds of a feather," he said, and laughed again.

Grace turned her face at him, and for a moment it had almost the sharpness of the mother's when she was angry. "Joe Sam is no fool," she said. "He knows a lot of things that . . ."

"He knows a lot of things that never was, in this world or the next," the mother said. "Did you wake him up?" she asked Harold. "Maybe it would stop his dreaming."

"I tried to, but I couldn't without getting pretty rough, so I just covered him up and fixed his fire."

"Well, that's probably as good as anything," the mother said, and started toward the sink with the dishes she was holding. "Let him sleep it off, then. He can eat when he wakes up."

"Good lord, such a fuss about nothing," the father said. "Can't we talk about anything but Joe Sam and black panthers today? After one of those spells, the old fool always sleeps as if he'd been on a three-day drunk."

Grace stood up and pushed her chair in. "Harold's seen that before," she said.

"Now where are you going?" the father asked quickly. "I thought we were going to have our little game of cards now."

Grace sighed and made a thin mouth of patience. "When the dishes are done, Father."

"You get on with your card game," the mother said. "I'll take care of the dishes."

The father was excited by the idea of the card game. He pushed himself to his feet hurriedly, almost falling.

"You just sit down, Grace. I'll get the cards," he said quickly and cheerfully.

He shuffled over to the bookcase in the corner and bent down and began to fumble in a black box at the end of the lowest shelf. He kept talking cheerfully while he hunted in the box, and didn't hear Grace, who went to the outside door and opened it, and stepped out into the snow, and stood there with her hands together in front of her, looking north. From his place at the table, Harold could see her out there, with the long, low sheds of gray sapling poles across the yard behind her, with the dark entrance to the corral between them, like a tunnel, and beyond the sheds the tall black V of the hay derrick against the lowering mist of the snow.

The old man, still hunting in the corner, was saying cheerfully, "A good lively game is just what we all need to cheer us up. Gwendolyn, you sit in Mrs. Bridges' place there. You're my partner. I wouldn't want you to have any but the best. Those two think they're a pair of pretty smart hands with the cardboards. Vanity of youth, that's all; vanity of youth. We'll show them a thing or two about how it's done, you and I." He chuckled. "Confound it," he muttered, "how all this trash— ah, here they are."

He straightened up, helping himself with one hand on a bookshelf, and half turned toward the table again, and stood there counting the cards, slipping them rapidly off the top of the deck from one hand into the other, and wetting his thumb every few cards, to draw them.

Finally he said happily, "Disgraceful condition, disgraceful. But they're all here, and you can read the spots still."

He hunted out a piece of paper and a stub of pencil from among the litter on the lower shelves, and came back to the table. He saw Gwen still sitting in her own place, and nodded across at the mother's chair.

"Over there, right across from me," he said. "And not too far around, either," he added, chuckling. "Leave a good safe space between you and Harold. Holding each other's hands is one thing; looking at them's another."

He watched her until she was seated across from him, and then nodded his approval and laid the cards and paper and pencil down at his own place, and went across to the sideboard in that same busy, slightly stooping walk, and came back with his bottle and a glass. He sat down and drew out a cigar, clipped it carefully with the silver knife, and lit it. Then he poured himself a third of a glass of whisky, corked the bottle and set it aside. After taking a sip of the whisky, he sat back and drew deeply at the cigar, and blew the cloud of smoke slowly up around the lamp. Then he was ready. He laid the cigar carefully on the edge of the table, picked up the cards, and began to shuffle them. They bent limply under the pressure of his big thumbs and knuckles, and made a soft, cushiony fluttering as they fell together.

He winked at Harold, and asked in a loud, serious voice, "Well, what shall we play, Black-Jack or poker?"

The mother was rattling the plates in the dishpan in the sink, but without looking around or stopping her work, she said, "Not in my house, you won't. Neither of 'em."

The father chuckled, and winked at Gwen this time.

"Well, it'll have to be just Hearts, then, I guess," he said mournfully. "It's a poor, female kind of a game, but still, it's cards, and better than nothing. Where did Grace get to now?" he asked, holding the cards ready to deal. He looked around, and couldn't find Grace, and muttering, "Where on earth did she get to now?" he turned in his chair, and saw the door open, and Grace standing outside in the snow.

"Grace," he called. "Come on. We're waiting for you."

Grace came back in and closed the door. She went around behind the father, and sat down opposite Harold.

"For goodness' sakes, girl, stop your fidgeting," the father said. "Arthur knows this valley like the back of his hand, and he always takes his time. And if he didn't, Curt would bring him back. Maybe he's gone with Curt. Besides," he added, "he is without a doubt the world's worst card player. The sky's the limit," he said happily to all of them, and began to deal the cards.

He kept on talking while they played, but it was easy to talk with him now. There were no old stories, and no self-importance to be careful of. Gwen began to laugh when he did, and to joke back at him. Even Harold grinned at him, and defended himself sharply when the old man belittled him as an opponent. They quarreled cheerfully and loudly about the score, and accused each other of cheating. Only Grace didn't seem to be really in the game. Each time the father thumped a losing heart down on a trick, with a loud, triumphant, "Ha," she started and looked at him. Often she was slow to play her card, so that he became impatient and rebuked her, though always making a joke of it. When the cards were being dealt, or the old man was laboriously calculating the score and writing it down with the stub of pencil, she would look around to see what the mother was doing, or stare out the window behind him at the deepening gray pall of the snow clouds in the valley, and he would have to call her back to pick up her cards.

The mother paid no attention to the game. When the dishes were done, she sat down in the platform rocker with her big Bible, but read in it for only a few minutes. Then she rose and laid it in the chair, took a dust cloth, a broom and a dustpan and went upstairs into the big bedroom. They could hear her up there, moving the bureau and the bed, and opening and closing drawers, and advancing slowly and heavily across the floor with her broom. When she came down again, she went into the bunk-room. After a while she came out and put more wood into the kitchen stove, and then carried wood and paper back into the bunk-room. They could hear the sounds of her laying a fresh fire in there too.

When she returned to the kitchen after that, the father said, "In the name of sanity, woman, rest yourself for a while."

"I got all rested out this morning," she said sharply. "You stick to your game, and let me please myself." She carried the broom and cloth and dustpan into the north bedroom, where Grace and Gwen had slept, and closed the door.

The door was still closed a dozen hands later, and Grace stood up while the father was recording the score.

"She'll freeze to death in there, with the door closed," she said.

"Now, don't you get to popping around too," the father said. "You might light the lamp while you're up, though. It's getting so dark in here I can't tell the black lady when I have her."

"It needs filling," Grace said.

Harold got up, brought the kerosene can from its place beside the woodbox, and drew the lamp down. Grace held it for him while he filled the bowl, and then he held it while she removed the chimney and trimmed the wick and lit it. When the flame was around the wick, she set the chimney back on, adjusted the wick to an even burning height, and Harold let the lamp back up.

Gwen began to deal the cards out of the rim of light and across the shadow of the bowl. Harold returned the kerosene can to its corner and came back and sat down again, but Grace went to the door of the north bedroom and opened it. Harold, pulling his cards to him one by one, looked past her into the bedroom, and saw the mother standing at the north window, looking out.

"You'll freeze, Mother," Grace said. "Are you done in here?"

The mother turned. "Yes, I'm all done, I guess," she said. She picked up the broom and pan and cloth, and came back into the kitchen. Grace stood there for a moment still, looking out the north window herself, and then closed the door.

"It's snowing again," the mother said.

The others looked at the east window, even the father turning in his chair to look too, and saw the big flakes coming down slowly but steadily in the gray light outside. The father turned back, shaded his eyes from the lamp with the hand that held his cards, and peered at the clock. Two of the moth shadows made by the roses on the lamp shade were fluttering on the face of the clock, and a streak of light shone across the glass between them, but at last he found the hands.

"It's only four-thirty, Mother," he said. "There's a good hour of daylight still; hour and a half, more likely."

"I know," the mother said.

She put away her cleaning things, and came over and sat down in the big chair again with the Bible on her lap. She didn't open the Bible, though, but only sat holding it with both hands.

"What in the name of God do you suppose those two fools are doing out there so long?" the father asked suddenly and angrily.

"I'm sure I don't know," the mother said.

The father took a drink of his whisky, set the glass down, and answered himself. "Curt found a trail he could follow, I expect," he said, "and he must have taken Arthur with him."

"I suppose so," the mother said.

"Well, don't sound so like they were lost forever. They're both grown men."

"I know."

The father muttered something, and then said clearly, "Whose lead is it?"

After a few tricks had been played, he was as cheerful as ever. The others kept looking out through the window, though, at the snow coming down softly and slowly onto the yard and the sheds, and after a little while, when she thought no one would notice, the mother turned her chair so that she could watch through the window all the time.

At five-thirty it was too dark to see the snow from the lighted room, except for the flakes that drifted down right next to the window. The father gave Grace the queen of spades on the last trick of a hand, and he slapped it down with a triumphant roar. His voice was deep and resonant now, as it was after he had been talking for some time about politics or stock manipulation.

"Gwen," he declared, loudly and happily, beginning to add the score, "Gwen, there's no use their even trying against us, what with you having all the luck, and me all the skill." He laughed uproariously. "They're so far in the hole now, it would take them a lifetime to pay it off."

Grace suddenly stood up and turned her back to the table.

"What's this? What's this?" the old man asked, looking up from the score. "Giving up already?"

"We're letting the fire go out," Grace said.

She went to the stove and put wood in, and poked it about to let the flames up through.

"I'll be back in a moment. Go ahead and deal," she said.

The father began to shuffle the cards. "She wants more,

Gwen," he said happily. "She thinks they can turn the tables. Some people never learn."

Grace set the lids back on the stove, moved across the room to the outside door, and opened it. At the sound of the latch, the mother looked around from the window, and watched her.

The father began to deal. While he flipped the cards out, he said to Harold, "You'd better get up and walk around your chair, or spit and make a cross."

After each four cards, he licked his thumb.

He was still chuckling, and had his thumb to his tongue when Grace said, "Harold." She spoke quietly, but with the suddenness and intensity of a cry. The mother glanced out the window, and then stood up, forgetting her Bible, so that it fell heavily to the floor.

"No, Mother," Grace cried, and then, again, "Harold," and disappeared from the room.

Harold jumped up and ran heavily after her. Gwen stood up too, and put her hands to her cheeks without knowing it.

The mother said, half moaning, "Oh, I knew it; I knew it."

"What's all this? What's the matter?" the father asked.

Harold had stopped in the doorway, and was peering across the yard. "No, Mother," he said quickly and sharply. "You stay here. Gwen, you stay with her, will you, please? Maybe it isn't anything," he said thickly, peering out again. "This light. You can't really tell."

He went out after Grace.

Gwen came around the table to the door.

"What is it? What the devil's the matter?" the old man asked loudly. He was struggling to rise, hoisting himself up between the table and the chair.

In the gray light, in the even, almost straight falling of snow, Gwen saw Harold running toward the sheds, and Grace running ahead of him, and stumbling weakly as she ran. Then, beyond them, she saw the horse, a dark, blurred silhouette against the poles of the shed, with no one riding him, but queerly bulky where the saddle should have been, and in spite of herself cried softly, "Oh, no, no."

Grace cried out twice. The cry was shrill and hawk-like in the silence under the looming, veiled shadow of the mountain.

The burdened horse started at the sound, and began to trot toward the mouth of the tunnel between the sheds. In the kitchen the mother moved too, coming slowly, as if in a trance, to the door, and pressing sideways to get past Gwen.

Gwen held her arm with both hands, pleading, "Please, Mrs. Bridges, Harold said stay here. We'd better stay here, Mrs. Bridges."

The father came behind them, still asking, "What's wrong? What . . ." but then, weaving slightly where he stood, and peering out between them, squinting against the fumes in his mind and the gloom outside after the lamp over him, said "It's Kentuck. It's Curt's horse."

The stallion turned into the tunnel and vanished in the darkness, and Harold called, "Grace, Grace, wait."

The mother said evenly, "Let me get by, please," but when Gwen started to plead again, murmuring, "Harold doesn't . . ." said sharply, "Take your hands off me," and Gwen let go of her and flattened herself back against the doorframe.

"It's Curt's horse," the father mumbled. "Something's happened to Curt. What was that on him? Could you see?"

The mother didn't answer, but stepped down into the snow and began to walk steadily, with long strides like a man's across the yard toward the tunnel. Her arms hung down at her sides, hardly swinging at all, as if she carried something heavy in each hand. Ahead of her, Grace disappeared between the sheds, and then Harold after her.

Gwen hung for a moment in the doorway, but then glanced at the old man leaning beside her and said, more to herself than to him, "Oh, she mustn't," and ran out, calling, "Mother, Mother," though not loudly, but as if fearing that unfriendly listeners would hear her. The mother didn't slow her walk, or hasten it, or turn.

The father suddenly became afraid, waiting alone in the doorway.

"They're crazy," he said quaveringly. "They've all gone plumb crazy."

He stepped down and started across the yard too, leaving the door open behind him. A first, easy return of the wind whirled the falling snow around him, and stirred his thin hair. His shadow went before him in the pale oblong of light that reached out from the lamp shining in the empty kitchen.

10 - -- -

Harold caught up with Grace just inside the mouth of the tunnel. In the glimmering twilight at the other end, they could see the big black standing at the corral gate, his back faintly frosted with snow, and a whiter snow on the bundle that lay across him. Joe Sam was there too, but standing back away from Kentuck, against the corral fence, looking at him and not moving. Kentuck was restless. He turned, trampling the snow at the gate, nickered softly, and was answered by some horse in the corral.

Harold took Grace's arm and said, "Don't go in there, Grace. Go on back to the house and keep Mother company. I'll see to this."

Grace didn't answer, but only whimpered like an animal confused by great fear, and stumbled on toward the corral.

He caught her by the shoulder then, saying, "Grace, listen to me," but she wrenched away from him, pushing at him and crying wildly, "Let me alone, let me alone," as if she didn't know him and was afraid of him.

He let her go and followed her, not running now, but only striding quickly. He saw her put her hands on the bundle, not to do anything, but only to make sure it was real, and heard her cry, "Oh, it's Curt," and was a little stung by shame, as if guilty of the same unkindness, at the relief, almost joy, in her voice.

"It's not Arthur, Hal," she cried back at him. "It's not Arthur."

"Grace, let him alone," he called sharply, seeing the black sidle and turn with its head up at the shrill excitement in her voice. "Get back. You'll get hurt."

He came up and shouldered her aside, and felt the stiff body with his own hands, and half guessed the truth as Curt's coat sank in about the narrower back. He spoke to Kentuck to quiet him, a meaningless patter of endearments, and among them said to Grace, "Is that anything to celebrate? Go on back now. You won't do anything here but get in the way."

Grace wouldn't go, though, but only backed away toward Joe Sam, to be clear of the nervous stallion, and kept staring at the bundle on the saddle, while Harold tugged at the frozen knot in the lariat. She spoke with each out-breath, saying over and over again, like a meaningless, rote prayer, "Oh, my God; Oh, my God; Oh, my God," but still half in relief.

The mother came up then, with Gwen close behind her. She was breathing steadily, but very deeply, so that each breath was like a quiet sigh.

"It's not Arthur, Mother," Grace cried at her.

The mother didn't look at her, but said in a deep voice, almost a man's, "It's Arthur, all right. Be quiet, will you?"

She came beside Harold's shoulder. "It's Arthur, isn't it, Harold?"

"No," Grace cried. "Look at the coat, Mother. It's Curt's red coat."

Harold said, trying to keep the temper out of his voice, "I don't know, Mother. Now go back to the house, will you, please, and take Grace with you. She frightens the horse with that squealing. Joe Sam," he said sharply, "hold the horse."

The old Indian didn't move or answer, but stayed there against the fence, watching as if these were the troubles of people he didn't know. It was the mother who took the reins, close to the bit, and when the father came up, and Grace would have cried out her hope again, said, "Grace, you keep still."

The knot gave, and Harold drew the end through, and pushed at the stiff rope, and at last slipped the coil loose. He drew the body down carefully, feeling sickness rise as against a stopper in his throat, when it came stiffly, and keeping the curve the saddle had given it. Breathing hard, he laid it on its side in the snow. He saw the beard in the wrapping of the black scarf, and tried to kneel between Grace and the head, but she saw, or guessed, and pushed past him, crying, "Oh, oh, oh," and saw clearly the deep caverns of the eyes, and the narrow nose and bearded cheek. She wailed, so the others stiffened and held their breath at the sound, and threw herself down and laid her breast against the rigid shoulder of the body, creeping against it, her knees working in the snow, as a kitten or puppy struggles in against the mother to feed. She murmured Arthur's name again and again, the pent anguish breaking out more loudly at moments, her cheek against the dead cheek, her hands playing with aimless fluttering and stroking about the black scarf.

Harold was the first to break out of the trance her grief made. He knelt beside her and tried gently, speaking her name gently and repeatedly, to draw her away from the dead man. She stopped her chattering and wailing then, but only to cling to the body, trying to burrow into it when he pulled at her.

It was the mother who broke the frenzy, saying in the deep, man's voice, "Gwen, hold the horse, will you?" and when Gwen had taken the reins, coming to the three on the ground and pulling Grace up fiercely by the shoulder.

"Stop it, you little fool," she said clearly. "Do you think you can make him hear you by screaming? Get up."

When Grace still struggled to escape her hand, she jerked her back onto her knees, and, breathing hard, her eyes staring wide, struck her across the face, once on each cheek, not even hearing Harold's quick protest. Grace went limp and, still kneeling, buried her stung face in her hands and began to weep aloud.

The mother straightened up, lifting her chin a little, and took a deep, quivering breath. "Pa," she said, "take her in now, will you? She only makes it worse."

The old man was standing there, staring down at Arthur, his mouth working soundlessly under the big moustache, and he didn't turn to her or make any reply.

"Has everybody lost their wits?" the mother asked. "Gwen, you seem to have some sense still. Take her back to the house, will you, and keep her there. Joe Sam, unsaddle Kentuck and turn him in and give him some hay."

The old Indian came forward slowly and stiffly, and took the reins. Gwen and Harold lifted Grace to her feet. Her grief broke out more loudly for a moment, but she didn't resist them. Gwen put an arm around her, holding her closely, and began to lead her along the tunnel toward the yard, speaking to her softly as they went, trying to reach her mind with words that might have been used to a frightened child. She had to stop when Grace's knees weakened and gave, and hold her up until she could move ahead again herself.

"Harold," the mother said, "help Joe Sam. He don't know what he's doing."

He turned to her. "Mother, you go in too, please."

"What help would you have out of these two, walking in their sleep?" the mother said. "Turn the horse in."

Harold would have replied, but was cut off by Grace's voice suddenly screaming, so the big stallion swerved away again, "No, let go of me, let go of me," and Gwen's voice, low and pleading, broken by her struggles.

Then the mother called, still in the hollow voice that had power, but no life, "I'm coming, Gwen," and said to Harold, "I'll go in with them, I guess. Grace is too much for her alone. I'll fix the bed for him. Make Joe Sam help you."

She turned, saying, "Come, Pa," to the old man, and taking hold of his elbow.

"Eh! What?" the old man asked.

"Come on in. You'll catch your death of cold out here."

"Yes, yes, I'm coming. It's getting dark anyway, and there's nothing I can do out here. Do you need any help, son?"

"No, we'll manage all right," Harold said.

"Well, I'll go in then. If there's nothing I can do out here, I might as well go in. Get out of your way, at least."

After a few steps, following the mother, he stopped and turned back. "Why didn't Curt come?" he asked plaintively. "It's getting late and it's snowing."

"Curt can take care of himself, Dad. Don't worry about Curt."

"Of course," the old man said, nodding. "Curt can take care of himself. Curt won't make a fool of himself."

He nodded slowly, as if he had summed the situation up and was leaving it in good order, and turned and went on after the women. They were going out into the yard now, Grace bowed between the other two, half carried in their arms.

Harold looked after them, the three women together ahead and the old man following them, asleep in his mind, all going toward the open door of the house, with the lamp showing white inside, like a big star, and its faded light reaching toward them in a path. He felt the snow coming down on him softly, beating against him with gentle tappings when the night breathed, and looked down at Arthur's long, narrow body lying on its side, curved and dark on the snow, with the new snow gathering along it as it would along the top rail of a fence. Then, for a few seconds, the dusk seemed to him sadly and enormously charged with meaning.

The impression passed, though, without leaving anything clear for his mind to keep, except that he was a little eased by the bigness of the moment, and he turned to Joe Sam and Kentuck.

The old Indian was holding the reins, but doing nothing else. The saddle was still on, and the tangled rope still hung from it, dragging on the snow. Harold coiled the rope and tied it onto the saddle and took the saddle off, and slung it upside down against the wall of the tunnel, with the blanket over it.

"Let the bars down, Joe Sam," he said, taking the reins.

Slowly, and as if they were very heavy, Joe Sam slid back the three poles of the gate and let their ends down to make a narrow opening. Harold led Kentuck through, and took off his bridle, and was about to come back out, when he saw the two pale horses among the dark ones against the fence on the other side. He went across toward them until he was sure what they were, seeing the dark mane and tail of his own buckskin, Kit, and the near whiteness of the other horse.

It's his, all right, he thought, and turned and came back out and set the bars into their slots again. He dropped the bridle over the saddle and blanket, and returned to the gate, where Joe Sam was standing. It was almost dark now, so there wasn't much difference when he came out from under the roof of the tunnel. Joe Sam's face was only a darkness against the high, gray post of the gate.

"When did the Smudge come in?" Harold asked him.

Joe Sam didn't move or answer him.

"Joe Sam," he said sharply.

After a moment he thought the dark face was turned toward him.

"Did you see the little gray mare come in? Arthur's?"

Joe Sam was a long time answering, but finally said, "Me feed."

"That's good," Harold said. "When did she come in? What time?"

"Long time," Joe Sam said. "Not dark. Arthur's horse. Feed."

"Sure," Harold said. "That's right. That's good."

Curt's out there without a horse, he thought. He must be tracking, then. That's more news for . . . but he let it go unfinished, thinking. Well, that's not getting this done.

He went over and stood at Arthur's head and looked down at him. Finally he took a deep breath, and let only part of it out.

"Give me a hand, Joe Sam," he said, but had to say again, "Joe Sam."

The old man came slowly across then, and stood on the other side of the body from him, looking down at it too.

"We have to carry him in the house," Harold said. "You take the legs."

Joe Sam bent over and touched the body as he might, in electrical weather, have touched some metal before taking hold of it, and straightened up again.

"Dead now," he said.

Harold nodded. "We have to take him in, Joe Sam."

"Know all time," Joe Sam said. "Know all time, but not tell Arthur. Me tell other one. He go. No good."

"You told them," Harold said.

"Think me not know," the old Indian said, almost triumphantly. Then he said again, slowly, sadly, "Not tell Arthur."

"You couldn't help it, Joe Sam," Harold said. "He knew. He heard you tell Curt."

The old Indian stared through the tunnel at the yellow light in the window of the kitchen, and seemed to be thinking about that. While he was looking, the kitchen door opened, and the

116

mother's figure appeared in the doorway, black in the rectangle of light.

"Yes," Joe Sam said, but whether to prevent the mother, or to agree with Harold, or to finish some argument with himself, there was no way to guess.

The mother didn't call, but stepped down out of the doorway, and closed the door behind her, so the light was shut off and she disappeared.

"We take him in now, Joe Sam."

"Arthur dead. Black painter no dead," Joe Sam said, and bent to gather the stiff legs into his arms. Harold could make nothing certain of these words either, and, after a moment, raised Arthur by the shoulders, which were unbending as wood in his hands, and hard to keep his hold on.

The mother met them as they came out into the yard, and, without a word, turned and walked back ahead of them. She opened the kitchen door and stood aside, holding it open for them.

"I fixed up the bed in the north room," she said. "Lay him in there."

The father was alone in the kitchen, sitting in his place at the table, with a glass of whisky in front of him, and a new bottle beside his right hand. He didn't look around, or even seem to hear them, as they carried Arthur past him, and around the table and into the north bedroom. The lamp on the dresser in there was lighted, so their shadows came in behind them, and then beside them, the two forward-bending figures, and the sagging one between them. The eagle with his wings spread that perched on the false crest on the head of the bed cast a greater shadow eagle up onto the whitewashed wall. The mother's finest spread, a heavy, dark blue one, covered with curving, interlaced figures of fabulous beasts and long-tailed birds in a woven jungle of leaves and stems and flowers, with a unicorn looking out of the center, was on the bed and pulled up over the pillows. Harold had seen that spread only twice a year, when it was taken out of the chest and hung on a line in the sun. He'd never seen it used before. It gave to the room, and to the big, walnut bed, and even to the crest and the eagle, a new and heavy dignity.

Carefully, breathing hard, and not altogether from the weight of their burden, either, Harold and Joe Sam laid Arthur on the bed on his side. Then they stood there, looking down at him. The mother brought the lamp from the dresser and placed it on the small, round table in front of the north window. For a moment, then, the melted snow on Harold's face, and Joe Sam's, shone like sweat in the lamplight, and the shadow of the eagle grew enormous and stretched away toward the west wall. Then the mother straightened up and stood there looking down at Arthur also, and her shadow reached over Harold and Joe Sam, putting their faces in darkness. The light, streaming toward the bed from beyond her, showed clearly the part of the thin face there that wasn't hidden by the encircling black scarf.

After a moment the mother said, "I'll set in here with him tonight. You go along now. I have to lay him out proper."

"You'd better let me help you, Mother."

"Later on. You go along now."

When they were at the door, she said, "The girls'll have to sleep in the bunk-room tonight. Gwen's keeping Grace company in there now, till she gets to sleep. Harold, you'll have to move out to the shack with Joe Sam."

"I'll be in the kitchen, Mother, in case you need me."

"I'm all right," the mother said. "There's no need more'n one should set up, that I can see, and there'll be things to do tomorrow. You'll have to make the coffin, for one thing. You get your sleep. Gwen'll put some supper on for you and Pa, and you see to it that Joe Sam eats something this time, too."

Her words were clear and steady, but not full, as if her mind had arranged them a long time before, and her mouth was only repeating them now.

"And Harold," she added, as he turned away again, "take the rest of that whisky in the sideboard out with you when you go."

"Yes, Mother."

The mother bent over and began to untie the knot in the black scarf.

She's holding up all right, at that, Harold thought. It won't do any good; the old man always has plenty more stowed away, one place and another. No matter how drunk he gets, that's the one thing he never forgets, where he put the rest of his whisky. But if she can still play that game, she's all right.

"We'll get at the chores now, Joe Sam," he said.

The old Indian didn't say anything, but turned and went out into the kitchen ahead of him, and Harold looked once more at the mother, busy over the bed, and then followed him.

In the kitchen he crossed to the sideboard and opened the cabinet and took out the two bottles of whisky that were left. When he turned back with them in his arm, the father was watching him. The glaze of dull seeing was over his eyes already, but he saw well enough to know what Harold was doing. He held his glass up at Harold, as if making a toast, and laughed feebly, and put back his head and drained off the whisky, and at once set the glass down and half-filled it slowly and carefully. Then he looked at Harold again, and grinned and winked. It wasn't easy to grin back at him now. It put the old man way apart from the others in the house, that he had already forgotten what was lying in the north room. It made it so one could almost feel with his hand the separate, dead world he built around himself when he was drinking.

"Gwen'll get you some supper pretty quick, Dad."

"No hurry," said the old man. "No hurry 'tall. Very 'tractive young woman, your Gwen. Lucky boy, get such a woman. Welsh, though," he added, shaking his head. "Father nothing but three-dollar-day mucker. Good man, but only mucker. No ambition, those Welsh."

Harold thought of Gwen's father, the bent, wiry little man with the black moustache and the grizzled hair, sitting beside the stove in his kitchen, with his big, knuckly hands spread over his knees, like the claw-and-ball feet of an old chair, and the hurt, mystified look in his eyes that always came when he went into his own mind. As if they sat together, he thought of this big, flushed man being with him, talking loosely of success, and Mr. Williams not answering, but that look coming into his eyes to prove he wasn't listening, or, if he was, the look of separateness, of distance, that came into Gwen's eyes when Curt began to prod at her. The comparison made him angry and ashamed.

"He's a rancher now," he said stiffly, and added, "Which is

119

what we are, I think," and went to the bunk-room door and rapped on it gently.

"Yes? Come in," Gwen's voice said, but very quietly, as if Grace were already asleep. He opened the door and poked his head in.

The fire the mother had laid in the stove was burning now, and already the room had warmed up a good deal. Gwen was sitting on a stool beside Arthur's bunk, and Grace was lying on the bunk, with her face down on her arms, and a blanket over her. She was still weeping, but no longer with loud sobs, or with cries breaking out, but softly and more slowly. Gwen was keeping one hand on her shoulder. Her eyes were red from crying too, but she wasn't crying now. She smiled at Harold, and nodded to show that things were going better. Harold wanted to enter the room and go across to her and touch her. He was deeply moved by the signs of weeping that were on her face still, and by the gentle weariness that had come after the weeping. He was disturbed by the strength and warmness that came back into him, just from seeing her sitting there. He hadn't realized before that he was feeling so cold and strained and apart by himself. He wanted to be filled by the strength and active warmth she had, to go in and take her in his arms as much to comfort himself as to change the look on her face.

She's the only one really alive in the whole house now, he thought.

He couldn't go through the door, though. It was impossible to enter against Gwen's quiet and the privacy of Grace's weeping. He only smiled back a little at Gwen, and nodded too, but then, because he couldn't touch her, he was suddenly weakened by that small, silent exchange of their love. At once he felt that a great hollow had been eaten inside his strength because Arthur wasn't there any more. It came to him for the first time as real, that Arthur wasn't there any more, and wouldn't ever be there again. He thought clearly, making it a picture in his mind, of waking up in the morning and looking across the bunk-room and seeing Arthur already awake, lying there with his fingers laced under his head and gazing up at the rafters with that silence and distance on his face that showed he'd been awake and thinking for a long time already. Arthur was always the first one awake, and he always lay like that, staring up at something between him and the rafters, and thinking. Then there came the little custom they had between them. Very slowly and carefully, so Arthur wouldn't catch the movement out of the corner of his eye, Harold would reach down and get hold of one of his boots, and then he would rap softly with the boot against the plank side of his bunk. Arthur would turn his head slowly on his hands and look at him, and they would grin at each other, and make a silent greeting with their lips, just the shapes of the words, so as not to wake Curt.

Now he would still be waking up every morning in here, but Arthur wouldn't be there across the room. There'd be only the empty bunk, and perhaps not even that, but only the logs of the wall where it had been. It might even be better not to have the bunk there. Just the same, it seemed to him that he would still see Arthur's face when he looked across, the long nose and the up-jutting beard and the high-boned cheek, and the one big, deep-sunken eye staring up at whatever it was it watched there in the shadows above the rafters. He'd still see that, even if he saw the logs through it.

He felt the first tears coming up hot inside his lids, and nodded again quickly at Gwen, feeling starved because he had to turn away without touching her, and withdrew his head and closed the door.

"Where's Curt? Where in hell is Curt?" the father asked suddenly. "It's dark now, pitch dark. Why doesn't the young fool come home?"

Harold was restored by the small, useful anger he felt against this question, after what he'd been remembering.

"I don't know, Dad, but he'll be all right. He wouldn't try to come back after dark, not with it snowing. He's probably holed up somewhere, and'll come in in the morning. Trust Curt to look out for himself," he couldn't help adding.

"He should've brought Arthur back," the old man argued, as if Harold had said he shouldn't. "He should've come back with Arthur, not sent him alone. Would've made things easier for his mother. Now she's gonna worry 'bout him too."

Harold felt the quarrelsome reply coming up in himself, but took his mind past it, and thought of saying the other horse was

121

back, and Curt wouldn't walk it after dark, and decided against that too. He looked away from the old man's indignant, flushed face, into the north bedroom, and saw the mother standing in the middle of the room, holding up Arthur's good black suit on its hanger, and brushing off the shoulders of the coat.

He looked back and said, "He'll be all right, Dad. He knows all the tricks, and the snow can't last long this time of year."

He set the bottles down on the sideboard and put on his coat and cap and came back and reached the lantern down from behind the stove and lit it. He took the two bottles of whisky in his arm again, and went to the door and opened it. He stood there holding the door and looking at Joe Sam, and waited. When Joe Sam had gone out past him, he stepped down into the snow and closed the door, and they went around the corner of the house and up the slope toward the bunk-house. Joe Sam walked ahead, and both of them leaned a little against the slope and against the falling snow. The wind was moving more often and more strongly now, pouring the flakes in a white stream across the lantern light, and making a vast, muffled sighing in the pines on the mountain.

— — 11

When Harold came in, the father was already eating, his heavy face bent down close to his food, his eyes red-rimmed and vacant. He was holding a whisky glass out in his left hand, and every once in a while he would straighten up and chew his food a little longer before he swallowed it, and then take a sip of the whisky.

"Grace got to sleep finally," Gwen said. "I couldn't get her to eat a thing, though. Or your mother either," she added.

Harold nodded, set the lantern down by the table, and went to the door of the north bedroom.

Arthur's body still lay on its side in the clothes it had come back in. The black suit was hanging against the wall, and on the back of the chair under it was a clean, white shirt, with a black tie lying across the collar. There were clean, summer underclothes and a pair of black socks on the seat of the chair. Arthur's black dress boots, with the silver thread leaves on them, stood together in front of the chair. They were newly polished, and gleamed in the lamplight.

The mother was kneeling beside the bed, with her hands together on the edge of it and her forehead laid against her thumbs. The light showed Arthur's face above her, lying very quiet in the pillow, with the mouth still a little open, as if he were asleep and about to speak out of his dreams.

"Mother," Harold said softly.

The mother raised her head slowly, and turned it to look at him. She wasn't crying, but her look made a much greater distance between them than the length of the room.

"Won't you try and eat a little supper, Mother?"

The mother shook her head slowly, twice. "You might bring me a cup of coffee when you're done eating, though," she said, and bent down to her praying again.

After a moment, Harold turned and went back into the kitchen. Gwen was at the stove, filling his plate, and she looked at him, asking the question silently. He shook his head and went on past her to the pegs by the outside door, where he took off his cap and mackinaw and hung them up. Then he came back to the table and sat down in Arthur's place. He saw the lantern still burning on the floor beside him. He picked it up, and blew it out, and set it down again slowly. Gwen brought his plate, and he smiled at her. She smiled back at him, the quick, far-away smile, and sat down in the mother's place with her own plate.

She took one small mouthful, and then said, "Oh, I forgot the coffee," and stood up again. She poured coffee for them both, and brought it back.

They didn't try to talk. Only the father spoke up once in a while. He took it personally that Curt hadn't come back. He also took it personally that Arthur had let himself be killed. He remembered a great many earlier misfortunes too, and saw himself as the chief victim of them all. He wept a little because fate had picked him out for so much undeserved bad luck. With his mouth full of tears and whisky, he complained, "A man works hard all his life, and what does it get him? Does it all for his family; tries to give them the best there is, and what happens?" Neither Harold nor Gwen had to speak, because he answered all his own questions. He was by himself anyway, sitting there breathing hard through his big nose and staring down into his whisky glass.

Harold couldn't even look at Gwen, and finally he stood up abruptly, leaving most of his supper on the plate, and took a mug from the corner shelf and filled it with coffee. Then he stood there holding the mug and looking down at Gwen. She was sitting with her hands in her lap, staring at nothing in the shadow of the lamp bowl. Most of her food was still on the plate too. Only the father's plate had been cleaned up and pushed aside.

"Gwen," Harold said softly.

She looked up at him.

"Fix me a plate for Joe Sam, would you?"

She nodded and stood up slowly, using the table to help her, like an old person.

Harold went into the bedroom with the coffee. The mother was still on her knees by the bed, but this time she looked up when she heard him, and then labored to her feet. Harold drew the old straight-backed rocker from the corner to a place beside the table, and she let herself down into it. He gave her the mug of coffee. The room was still cold, and the hot coffee made a column of steam above the mug. The mother blew on the coffee long and slowly, staring over the mug at the depression in the edge of the bed where she had rested her hands and head. Finally she took a sip of the coffee, and a second sip, and then sat there with the mug between her hands, still staring at the edge of the bed.

"He was a good man, lots of ways, though," she said. "He had a good heart." All the masculine depth was gone from her voice now.

"Yes," Harold said. He glanced at the face on the pillow, and then closed his hand into a fist in front of him and looked down at it.

"I knowed it would be him," the mother said. "The mark was

on him. You can most always tell the ones that'll go early. They ain't got the hold on things that most of us has."

What does she know about it? Harold thought. Just because they never spoke the same language. But it disturbed him to find her thinking that way about Arthur. He couldn't think of anything to say that would help, though, so he only nodded, and stood there waiting.

"It makes a body think," the mother went on at last. "I didn't think too much about him when he was with us, I guess. He used to talk such foolishness. Hardly ever say right out what he meant, either. I guess I just got to takin' it for granted he was makin' light of whatever was spoke of, and sort of let his talk go in one ear and out the other. Like you have to Curt's cussin' all the time, knowin' it don't mean nothin'. But I guess he most always really meant somethin', didn't he? In his own way?"

"I guess he did," Harold said finally.

"Deep down I knowed he did, of course. Only I wouldn't give it no heed." She sipped at the coffee and lowered it into her lap again.

"He was always botherin' himself with a lot of fool questions, though," she said.

Who doesn't? Harold thought defiantly. And if you look at it big enough, what question isn't a fool question? At least he didn't get all his answers out of some old book, and then take 'em for the word of God.

"But it don't seem like he really meant to mock," the mother said.

"No," Harold said.

"It was mostly just a way of talkin' he got into," the mother said. "What with the rest of us thinkin' different, mostly. Except maybe Grace."

"I guess it was."

Finally the mother said, "It's a lonesome place, this valley, and sometimes I wonder now wasn't he the lonesomest one of the lot of us."

She looked up at him, and her eyes made him afraid of the question she was going to ask. She was studying his face as if she'd never really seen it before, and now she wanted to figure out what kind of a man he was.

125

She's takin' it hard, he thought. She's takin' it all on herself, and looked down at his knuckles again.

"You was the only one he ever really talked to," the mother said. "Was he really so terrible lonesome, do you think?"

Harold wanted to give her a real answer, but with the question straight out like that, and the mother looking at him and waiting, it wouldn't come together in his mind. He only felt how much older Arthur had been than he was himself, and couldn't trust the things he remembered. It put him off just to feel how much older Arthur had been, for that matter. He'd never thought of Arthur as being any particular age before. He spoke carefully.

"I guess he would have been pretty much alone any place, Mother. It wasn't anything about us."

The mother looked back at the edge of the bed. "I guess he would of," she said.

After a long time she said, "He was a queer son for your pa and me to have. Like there was somethin' the Lord put in him that wasn't in either of us. Or the devil," she added, almost whispering. "Sometimes I ain't too sure which."

Harold set his jaw and closed his fist tighter. You and your devils, he thought. Less devil than any of us; that was his trouble. Why don't you let him alone?

"Seems like he suffered in his mind so," the mother said.

Harold's anger thinned away. "It wasn't so bad for him, Mother."

Again the mother looked at him with her eyes awake and searching. "You don't think it was?"

Harold shook his head. "He liked it here more than any of us, lots of ways."

The mother kept studying his face until he could feel her look as if she touched him. At last she looked away again, and said, "Maybe so. I'd like to think it was so." She took two sips of her coffee and lowered the mug once more.

"He give some real thought to the ways of God, though, didn't he? Times he was so quiet?"

"Pretty near all the time, I'd say. One way or another."

"I'd like to think so," the mother said again. "And I guess it was so, pretty much."

126

For a minute both of them were as quiet as the figure on the bed. The flame of the lamp and the snow against the window made important sounds in the room.

Then the mother said, "There was times I used to think it wouldn't make a heap of difference if Arthur was to go, it was so like he wasn't here anyway. He'd set right there at the table in the kitchen, and I'd forget he was there. God forgive me," she said slowly. "There was even times, when he'd get on one of them heathen streaks of his, I'd think it might be better if he was to go. I could see his notions sproutin' out in you, and comin' out rank in Grace, she bein' the next oldest to him, and so foolish fond of him too. Now I ain't so sure. Seems like maybe he was the most here of any of us, even when he'd just set there whittlin' and never sayin' a word."

"Yes," Harold said, thinking of the ghost in the bunk across from his.

"Still I can't seem to pray right for him, some way," the mother said. "Not from the heart. I start in to pray, and then I get to thinkin' of somethin' he said, near enough blasphemy to burn for, and I see how he could of meant different than I took it, maybe, and the next thing, there I am just puzzlin' my head about it, instead of askin' the Lord to forgive him.

"Well," she said more strongly, "if I can see that much, the Lord can see a heap more, that's certain sure." She drank the rest of the coffee without stopping, and gave the mug to Harold.

"You go along and keep Gwen company now," she said. "This is a lonesome business for her to get into, and none of it hers."

Harold started to put a hand out toward her shoulder, but then couldn't touch her, and let the hand down.

"Why don't you let me take over for a while, Mother? And you go get a little rest in the bunk-room?"

"It's no good trying to rest the body till you can get some rest in the mind," the mother said. "Go along and leave me be now."

Harold still waited, though, trying to think of a good way to ask the question that was bothering him. He looked at Arthur's body in the red coat with the black stripe around it.

"You'll need some help changing his clothes, won't you?"

"I can't do it for a while yet, anyway," the mother said. "If I need any help, I'll call you."

So there was nothing to do but ask straight out.

"Was there anything to show how it happened?"

The mother closed her hands tightly over the arms of the chair, but she spoke quietly enough. "His neck's broke," she said, "and there's claw marks on his shoulder."

"So it was the painter."

"It looks like it was. You go along now."

"It's still pretty cold in here, Mother. You better let me get you your shawl."

"I ain't none too warm at that," the mother admitted. "Maybe you could bring me my coat; I ain't just sure where that shawl's got to. And fetch me my Bible too, while you're about it, would you?"

"You couldn't eat a little something?"

"I can't even stand to think about it. I could do with more coffee, though."

Gwen wasn't in the kitchen now. He filled the mug himself, and left it standing on the water tank of the stove while he went over to get the coat. The father heard his boots on the floor, and pushed himself slowly upright and looked at him, squinting to see beyond the light.

"Is she going to stay in there all night?" he asked.

Harold found the old black dress coat of the father's that she wore in cold weather. It was faded nearly green now, and the velvet collar was worn down to nothing at the edges. He took it down and folded it across his arm.

"I guess she is," he said.

"There's no sense in her wearing herself out like that. You could sit for her yourself, if you'd think of somebody else for one minute."

Harold went across and got the Bible from the big chair and took it in his arm with the coat. Then he could speak evenly. "I tried to take over, Dad, but she wouldn't let me."

"So she's going to leave me to sleep by myself," the father said angrily. "She thinks more of the dead than she does of the living, that woman; her and her getting into heaven."

Harold went back to the stove and picked up the mug of coffee.

"Well, I won't," the father declared loudly. "I'll stay right here and get drunk, that's what I'll do, good and goddam drunk. Won't freeze to death, then, anyway," he muttered.

Harold went back into the bedroom and set the mug of coffee on the table and laid the Bible beside it.

"Here's your coat, Mother."

"Oh, yes," she said, coming back from wherever she'd been in her mind. She stood up and held her arms back so he could put the coat on her. "It was all that fool reading that done it," she said.

"Did what?"

"Give him such outlandish notions."

"I guess so," Harold said, pulling the coat up. And he learned more about God from the most heathen Greek of the bunch of them, he thought, letting the anger go that he'd held onto in the kitchen, than you . . . but then, seeing her standing there, thin and tired in the big, worn-out coat, couldn't finish it that way. Than all your hell-fire, camp-meeting preachers could find in a million Bibles, he thought instead.

Through the white light in the bedroom and the yellow light in the kitchen, he saw the bunk-room door open, and Gwen come out and close it softly behind her. The mother saw too.

"How's Grace now?" she asked.

"She's asleep, Mother. Don't you worry about her. Gwen's keeping an eye on her."

"Curt ain't come in yet?"

"He wouldn't try to, in this snow, Mother. He's holed up somewhere till daylight."

"He must of got a long ways out," the mother said. She folded the slack of the big coat around her, and let herself down into the rocker again.

"Anything else you want, Mother?"

"Nothing else now, thanks."

When he came out, Gwen was putting meat and potato on a plate for Joe Sam.

"How is she doing now?" she asked in a low voice.

"Pretty good, I guess," he said. "She got to talking about him some; quite a lot for her."

"Well, that'll do her good."

"It ought to, I guess. Only she can't seem to let it be. She

129

keeps remembering things . . ." But then he stopped, and stood there thinking. "Well," he said finally, "I better take Joe Sam his supper, I guess."

He put on his coat and cap and lit the lantern, and came back for the plate.

"Maybe I'd better go with you," Gwen said. "There's the coffee too, and you'll need a free hand."

Harold glanced at the father. The old man's elbows were spread wide on the table, and he was holding the whisky glass between his two hands, with his face down close to it. Harold looked back at Gwen and smiled and touched her face with the tips of his fingers.

"Since when did you start making excuses to go some place with me?"

Gwen moved closer to him and looked up into his face, smiling a little. "I never did," she whispered. "And don't you get to thinking I ever will," she added, with mock severity. But then her mouth trembled, and the tears started up in her eyes. She turned away quickly, saying, "Grace is still asleep, but I don't dare leave her alone too long."

She went quickly over to the pegs and took down her cloak and swung it over her shoulders. She was drawing the hood up as she came back. It was a dark blue woolen cloak with a red silk lining. When the hood was up, her forehead and eyes were in shadow, and all Harold could see clearly was her mouth, still smiling for him.

Curt'd call her a priestess now, he thought. Or medicine woman. And she is, too, he thought. She wants what Arthur wanted. She couldn't say it in words, the way he could, maybe, but it's the same thing. She doesn't like the God that's in there with Mother now any more than he did. It's a God for the dead. Dad was right about that much, anyway.

And hers is for life, he thought, looking down at the blue hood. It's the God of Life against the God of Death, that's what it is, he thought, and for a moment felt that he was almost into the big secret, the secret that was quiet in the middle of everything, and that if it only wouldn't go too fast, he'd really see what Arthur had meant. He was tremendously hopeful. Everything seemed to be getting more beautiful and more important around him, and for the first time since Kentuck had come in, the despair was letting go of him.

But his mind said, with its old, stubborn resentment, That God in there wants us all dead. He's a mean old clerk of a God; He'd rather have us dead, so there'd be nothing more coming in, so He could add it all up and put his book away for keeps. That's what she's doing in there now, going over Arthur's bills with Him, counting the pennies.

The big feeling was gone then, and the despair came back even tighter than before. The wonder that had been in every-thing for a moment, wasn't in anything now, but just hang-ing in the air and getting fainter all the time, and he couldn't stop it. It was like waking from a dream in which he'd worked his way out of a bad trouble, and finding the trouble was still there, and bad as ever.

Gwen was standing close beside him, pouring coffee for Joe Sam. All he could see out from under the cloak was her two thin brown hands holding the mug and tilting the coffee pot. They were enough, though. He suddenly felt that if he took her in his arms now, he'd get back into the bigness he'd lost by quar-reling with the mother's God, and have it so he'd never lose it again. It was as if something had come out of Gwen to him and made the big moment in the first place. He put out his hand to touch the small shoulder under the blue cloak, but then he thought of the old man at the table, and the open bedroom door behind him. He didn't touch Gwen, but just reached past her and picked up Joe Sam's plate. Then he turned back to the table and picked up the lantern. He felt that he had been de-feated twice. No, it was worse than that. He had defeated him-self twice. The whole weight of what was in the house came down on him again while he stood there waiting for Gwen to put sugar into the coffee and get a knife and fork and spoon. He let her go ahead of him to the door.

At the sound of the two of them walking together, the father roused himself again and peered slowly around through half open eyes until he found them.

"Where you going this tima night?" he asked thickly.

"Just taking Joe Sam's supper up, Dad."

131

"Let him come and get it, the old fool," the father said, and his head swung back and down again by its own weight.

At the sound of the door opening, though, he drew a deep, sighing breath, pushed himself slowly upright in his chair, and peered around at them again.

"That fool Curt gonna stay out there all night?" he asked. "Hasn't even had his supper. Tell him come in, get his supper."

His head drooped back toward the table. "Didn' even eat his supper," he said drowsily.

Harold motioned to Gwen to go on out. He followed her and closed the door, and they went around the house and slowly up to the bunk-house, side by side and bowed against the thickening snow.

Joe Sam was sitting huddled on a box next to the stove. The lantern coming in made his shadow move hugely behind him. His moccasins were set side by side under the edge of the stove, and his broad bare feet were smooth as a young man's. They didn't seem to belong to the same body as the old hands that were clutching his elbows. His head was turned to look at the two coming in, and the lantern made his good eye gleam like metal.

"Here's your supper, Joe Sam," Harold said, and held the plate out and waited until Joe Sam had to take it. "And coffee," he said, and took the cup from Gwen and set it on the floor beside the box. Then he went to the far end of the room, took the lamp down from its high shelf and set it beside the wash basin.

Gwen moved closer to Joe Sam and said, "Here's your knife and fork."

The old man took them without a word, and sat holding them upright in one hand, with the plate on his knees.

"Are you warm enough?" Gwen asked.

"Warm. Good."

"Please. You eat something this time. And drink your coffee. That'll really warm you up."

"Warm. Good," Joe Sam said again.

Gwen leaned over and put the spoon into his coffee mug, and stirred three or four times around before she left it there.

Harold set the lighted lamp back up on its shelf, making the piece of broken mirror, that was fastened to the wall over the wash basin, flash its shape in light across Gwen and Joe Sam and the pile of stove wood behind them. Then he saw by the lamp that one of the whisky bottles he had set on the shelf with it was gone. He turned back, and finally saw the bottle on the floor in the shadow behind Joe Sam. The seal was torn off and the cork was out. Harold came over and stood beside Gwen and looked down at the old man.

"Joe Sam," he said.

After a moment Joe Sam looked at him, but at his shoulder, not at his face.

"Did you get any sleep at all?"

"Sleep," the old man said finally.

Harold sighed. "Well, eat now, anyway. You have to eat something."

"Eat," Joe Sam said. He looked down at the plate, and after a moment poked gently at the potato with his fork. Harold waited until he had taken the first mouthful, and then said, "I'll be right back. We got to get some sleep, you and me. The way it's snowing now, we'll have to take the drag out tomorrow."

"Much snow," Joe Sam said.

When Gwen and Harold were at the door with the lantern, he began to speak again, and they stopped.

"All time much snow," he said slowly. "Have much brother one time. All go now. Have much friend. They go now. My woman go, my boy, my girl. All go now. Much old." He said something soft and unhappy in Piute, letting it trail off faintly at the end.

"I'll be right back, Joe Sam," Harold said again. "I'm going to sleep up here too."

Joe Sam didn't answer. He sat there looking through them and out the open door at something they couldn't see.

When he and Gwen were half way down to the house again, Harold said, "He's gone and got drunk now, on top of the rest. I'll have to get right back up there."

"Yes," Gwen said, and he felt her hand fumbling for the belt of his coat. When she found it, she hooked two fingers over it and gave it a little tug, and then just left her hand there to be

133

touching him. He stopped and put his arm around her shoulder and drew her close against him. She pressed her cheek to his coat and held him tightly with both arms. He could feel her shoulders beginning to shake, and held her even closer, with his head down against the hood of the blue cloak. He held her that way for a long time, until her shoulders stopped shaking and loosened in his arm, and they began to feel the snow coming down on them. Then he turned her face up to him with a knuckle under her chin and kissed her wet mouth softly, twice.

When he lifted his head again, and was just looking down at her, she asked, "Would it make things any better if I went home, Hal? Do you want me to go home?"

"I don't ever want you to go," he said softly. "You know that. But this is Bridges' trouble, honey, not yours. Don't you want to go?"

She shook her head quickly, three or four times, and then held her face up to him again, with her eyes closed. This time, after a moment, their bodies began to hunt for each other through the thick winter clothes. Yet even then the light the lantern cast around them made it seem all the time that they were being watched from the darkness beyond, or from the lighted north window below. Gwen turned her mouth from under his, and he let go of her, just holding one of her hands.

"You couldn't send me home now anyway," she said quickly. "Not in all this snow."

"No," he said, and smiled a little, and kept watching her. "I'll come down with you," he said at last.

She shook her head at him. "You better not," she said, and hugged him hard once more, and then pushed him away.

"Well, take the lantern anyway," he said, and gave it to her.

He waited there, feeling the soft pelting of the snow he couldn't see, until the lantern and the small, hooded shadow it made in its circle of light had disappeared around the corner of the house. Then he turned and climbed back up to the bunkhouse and went in.

12 ⬤ ⬟ ⬟

He was in a deep ravine, and Gwen was with him. They were stand-
ing still, listening and not touching each other, because they had just heard
a faint, excited cry from far above. The ravine was familiar, but Harold
couldn't think where it was now, the voice troubled him so. It was the
voice of someone they knew and loved, and it was either trying to warn
them, or calling for help. There was nothing to do but wait, though, until
they knew what he wanted. They were in a bad place themselves, out in
the middle of a small clearing part way up the north slope. There was a
foot or more of new snow down around them, so that even with the gray
light in the ravine, they stood out like a bull's-eye on the white. When he
realized that, Harold was sure that the enemy, whether he was hidden
behind one of the big pines above, or among the aspens or the willows along
the creek below, had a heavy rifle and was a very good shot. For a moment
he was even convinced that there were enemies all around them, so that his
knees became weak, a cold sweat broke out on his forehead, and his mind
leapt from one useless notion to another like an encircled rabbit darting
from bush to bush. He got over that, though, when he realized that nobody
would try to call a warning about an encirclement. It would be no use, and
it might start things all the quicker. It had to be a single enemy then.
That was better, but not much better, unless they could discover where he
was. Neither he nor Gwen had a gun, and if the enemy gave himself away
by shooting one of them, the other one still wouldn't be able to do anything
but wait for his turn.

There was something else that troubled him too, though it was only a
kind of puzzle on the edge of his fear. They were standing in the center of
the clearing, but there weren't any tracks in the snow to show how they'd
got there. Gradually, as they kept on just standing there, and nothing
happened, this puzzle of the trackless snow distracted him. It was then,
while his attention was divided, that he recognized the ravine. It was the
Aspen Creek Canyon. He could look down along the serpent of leafless
aspens and willows and see its last turns, far out and narrow as a thread,
and then the black shapes of the tule marshes. Yet it wasn't quite right for

135

the Aspen Creek Canyon either. Having discovered this, he saw, almost at once, what the difference was. The sides of the canyon were much higher than he remembered. The rim-rock was so far above them that its top was lost in the gray sky. Also it was much farther down out of this canyon than it was out of the Aspen Creek. The black marshes out there in the snow fields looked no farther away than the valley marshes, but when he glanced down along the gigantic cliffs, he saw that this was because they were actually very big lakes lying miles out on a plain too wide to see across. He still knew the canyon perfectly well, but now it was such a huge trap that it would take hours to get out of it, and they didn't have hours.

There was another difference too. He should have noticed this difference at once, and it worried him that he hadn't. The sides of the gigantic canyon were thickly timbered clear up to the base of the rim-rock. The real Aspen Creek Canyon had only a few stunted pines standing up out of the sand. It was the trees, of course, that made it so easy for the enemy to move around without being seen. He knew where they were, and they didn't know where he was, and he could keep it that way if he wanted to. If they started down the canyon, and that was the only way out now, he could trail along beside them as far as he liked, and never be seen. Maybe that was why he was waiting. Maybe he liked playing cat and mouse. Once he had thought of it, it became a fact that the invisible enemy liked to play cat and mouse.

He understood all this very quickly, and once he did, the first paralysis of his will passed off. At once he touched Gwen, and motioned to her to throw herself down into the snow. She didn't look at him, but she understood when he touched her, and obeyed him promptly. He threw himself down beside her. Even as they dropped, as if their falling had started it, they heard the voice again. Because they were moving then, and not really listening, they still didn't know who it was, but they were relieved about their own situation anyway. Whoever was calling was much farther away this time than when he'd first called. If he was calling to them at all, he was certainly calling for help. It no longer seemed that the enemy was a man, either. No one trying to get away from a man with a rifle would keep yelling like that. He'd yell only if he thought it might frighten the enemy off.

"It's the black painter," Harold cried.

Gwen didn't answer him, but he knew she thought so too.

Then he was on his feet and running heavily, laboring to run faster, toward the place farther into the canyon and up the north side, from which he believed the voice had last cried out. He became desperate because he was running so slowly. His legs weighed like stone, yet he floated a little at each stride and could never take the next step soon enough. The snow, which had appeared dry and light on the clearing, turned out to be heavy and wet and slippery, and that made it even worse trying to hurry. When he did reach ground firmly, he always slipped back, and the harder he tried, the more he slipped.

The next thing he knew, Gwen ran past him. He couldn't understand how she could run so fast and easily, and he was frightened to see her rushing toward the danger ahead of him. He tried to call to her to wait for him, but he had no voice. He wasn't breathless or choked; he just didn't have any voice. He kept trying to shout, but he couldn't make a sound. Gwen got farther and farther ahead of him up the slope. He could still see her plainly, because they had come into a long climbing avenue through the trees. It was free of growth of any sort, and perfectly straight, like a road through a park. Far up this avenue she continued to move away with amazing speed and ease, and he saw that she was leaving no tracks behind her. Her cloak, flapping as she ran, made her look like a small, fluttering bird, and then like a tiny insect on a white wall, barely moving its wings, perhaps just cleaning them. At any moment she would arrive at the place where the black painter was waiting, but he couldn't do a thing about it. He still couldn't run any faster, or make a sound. He stopped trying to call.

At once, when he stopped trying to call, he wasn't running either. He was just standing there staring up the long avenue ahead of him. The black figure of the cat was creeping out of the woods on the left side, and Gwen, as if she didn't see it at all, was rushing right toward it. Harold wanted to cover his eyes, but he couldn't; he had to watch. The sweat broke out on him again, as it had during the first moment in the clearing. He heard a voice mumbling in fear or in crazy monologue. Either it was his own voice, or the cat up there was mumbling. Maybe the cat was purring. He became sure that the cat was purring, and then he was much closer, only a few yards behind Gwen, and could see that the crawling creature wasn't a cat at all, but a man. It was Curt, in the red mackinaw with the black stripe around it. But there was something terrible the matter with him. He was crawling on his hands and knees, and mumbling continuously, without sense. Every few feet, he stopped crawling and mumbling, and retched, and then vomited a great gush of blood. It seemed impossible that he could still be alive after even one such outpouring, yet every time he would begin to mumble again, and then to crawl ahead. He wasn't attacking Gwen, and he wasn't going to. He was only trying to get across the avenue and into the woods on the other side before the enemy caught up with him again.

Suddenly another figure appeared at the very top of the avenue. He was

137

tiny up there, but Harold could see that he was wearing the red and white parka, and that he was taking aim down the avenue with a rifle. Probably he was aiming at Curt in his red coat. It was impossible to be sure at that distance, and it didn't matter anyway. The tiny, mocking figure up there, taking such slow and deliberate aim, meant to kill all three of them, and he'd have time to do it, too.

All at once the whole situation became clear to Harold. He found his voice and cried out a loud warning to the figure in the red coat. It turned its face at him, and he was right. It was Arthur's face, bearded, and very thin, white and quiet. The eyes were closed too, and the big lids were blue.

Harold wasn't standing in the avenue through the trees at all; he was standing in the north bedroom. The lamp on the table was making great shadows of the eagle that perched on the bed and of the mother on the white wall. The mother was looking down at the white, bearded face on the pillow, at the face with the closed, blue-lidded eyes, and she was smiling grimly. Harold had his arm around Gwen now, and they were both staring at the mother. He was trying to draw Gwen away, because he believed that the mother was crazy. But then he saw that the mother had on a handsome, new, black overcoat with a velvet collar, and realized that he had been mistaken. The gloating figure was the father, and his satisfaction wasn't nearly as evil, because he was so drunk he couldn't really know what he was looking at. He was the one who was making that sound now. He was talking to himself. When Harold heard the sound, he remembered, or perhaps saw through the wall at the head of the bed, the tiny figure taking aim from the top of the white avenue through the trees. He was still aiming at Arthur, too, although Arthur was already quite dead. Harold was going to cry out, but before he could make a sound there appeared, as silently as if it had come out from inside, a neat, dark, round hole, perhaps large enough to put the end of a little finger into, right between the eyebrows of Arthur's face on the pillow. The report came long after the hole had appeared, but it was much too loud, stunningly loud, as if the rifle had been fired inside the room. But it would be impossible, if the rifle were fired inside the room, for the hole to appear so long before the report was heard. The entire time and order of events became terribly confused, and Gwen vanished. She wasn't in his arm, and he couldn't see her anywhere. It was as if the shot had carried her off too.

He was up on his elbow, staring and breathing hard. He saw that he wasn't in the north bedroom, and for a moment everything was more mixed up than ever. Then he came slowly over to the waking side and was greatly relieved. Everything in the dream receded and became a little less than real, except the report of the rifle. He remained convinced of the report.

He saw Joe Sam by the light that flickered through the little window in the door of the stove, and faintly by the first glimmer of daylight in the bunk-house window. The two lights made him two colors where he showed, red up his back, and pale, almost blue in front. He was standing close in front of the stove, but facing the door. He was naked, and he was shaking both fists above his head in fierce triumph. He was talking constantly in Piute too, a low, excited chattering.

That's the purring anyway, Harold thought. That's the noise Arthur was making, and then the old man in the bedroom. This didn't set the dream back farther, though. It made it more real again instead. It made it seem as if the dream was alive in the room again, and Joe Sam had something to do with it.

There was a strong smell of whisky in the room. There was something in Joe Sam's right fist that gleamed in the stove light when he moved it just right, too.

That bottle again, Harold thought angrily. The old fool must have got that bottle again in the night. However much he's got in him, he must have spilled a lot of it to make it stink so. He must have been up all night, he thought. He's kept the fire going.

"Joe Sam," he said sharply.

At once the old Indian stopped chattering, and then he slowly let his arms down. Finally he turned to face Harold's bunk, so he was standing with his side to the stove, and what he was holding in his right hand showed clearly. It wasn't the whole whisky bottle, but just the neck, with long, jagged points of the shoulders still on it. Joe Sam wasn't threatening anything, though. He just stood there by the stove, silent, and with all the excitement gone out of him, and held the bottle neck loosely in his hand. He looked very tired, and older than ever.

"What's the matter, Joe Sam?" Harold asked.

"Bottle break," Joe Sam said. He was very sad. He was lamenting an accident.

I'll bet it did, Harold thought. No bottle ever broke that way by accident. You broke it, you old faker.

139

The wind came down heavily against the bunk-house, making it creak and tremble, and then fell away again along the mountain. The fire it had beaten down leapt up again roaring, and Harold saw the glittering fragments of the bottle on the floor.

"Stand still, Joe Sam," he said, "or you'll cut your feet."

Joe Sam looked down slowly and curiously, as if just remembering that he had feet, but stood where he was. Harold rolled up onto the edge of his bunk, tried the floor lightly with his own feet, to make sure none of the chips had come that far, and stood up. He crossed to the shelves and lighted the lamp. The second bottle was still there and still sealed. He took the old stub of broom from the corner and swept the glass around Joe Sam's feet into a little pile in front of him.

"Better put that in too," he said, pointing to the bottle neck.

Joe Sam looked down at it the way he had looked at his feet. Then he leaned over and laid it gently on the pile of broken glass. Harold brought the nail keg that was the bunk-house waste basket from its corner by the front window, and swept the glass into it. He swept the last dust of glass that wouldn't go in, under the stove, and put the broom and the keg back in the corner. When he turned around, Joe Sam was still standing there in front of the stove.

"All right, Joe Sam. It's all gone."

The old Indian walked slowly over to his bunk and sat down. He laid his hands one over the other between his legs, so they covered his crotch, and sat staring at the worms and fluttering wings of light the fire made on the floor.

Harold came back to his bunk and began to dress.

"Did you get any sleep, Joe Sam?" he asked.

After a long time, Joe Sam said drowsily, "No sleep. All time snow. Much snow. Painter hunt."

Harold stood still the way he was, with his pants only half pulled up, and looked at the old man. So that was it, he thought finally. But he was plenty happy about it, that's a cinch. He was celebrating something.

"Did you get him?" he asked.

"No get," Joe Sam said. He sounded very unhappy about it, and he didn't say anything more.

Harold pulled his pants on up and buttoned them and fastened his belt. Then he sat down on the edge of his bunk and began to pull on his socks. Joe Sam said something in a very low voice.

"What?" Harold asked.

"No hunt painter," Joe Sam said.

After a moment Harold said, "No, it's no use, I guess."

"Painter get," Joe Sam said more clearly. "Painter get now. He know."

He's getting worked up again, Harold thought.

"Get who, Joe Sam?"

But Joe Sam just said sadly, in the going-away voice again, "No get now."

After a minute Harold gave up trying to straighten it out. He finished dressing and came over and stood in front of the old man. Joe Sam didn't even seem to know he was there.

"Maybe you can get some sleep now, Joe Sam," Harold said finally. "The painter won't hunt in the daylight. You better get under the covers, though."

Joe Sam didn't answer, and for some time didn't move. Finally he began to tug awkwardly at his blankets, trying to get them out from under himself. When he got them out, he just lay down on his side on top of them, with his knees drawn up. Harold worked the blankets out again, and pulled them up over him. Then he put on his mackinaw and cap, and picked up Joe Sam's plate and mug from the box. The mug was empty, but only the meat was gone from the plate. He stood holding the mug and plate and looking down at Joe Sam. Even under the blankets, the old man was still lying drawn up like a cold child. His eyes were closed now, and his breathing was slow and regular.

Harold turned away, saying softly, but out loud, "Old as time, and nothing but bones. I don't know what keeps him alive when he has these spells."

Joe Sam's voice said, "Much 'live, all right. Pretty quick get."

Harold turned back and stared at him. Joe Sam was looking at him, and grinning a little. Slowly Harold realized that he had spoken aloud himself. The old man was making a joke about it, and about the hunting that was going on in his mind too.

Harold didn't understand the last part, but finally he grinned too.

"Get what?" he asked.

Joe Sam's grin faded slowly, but only as if he were falling asleep in spite of himself. Before his eyes were quite closed, though, Harold thought the good one looked at him the way Joe Sam looked when he wasn't saying what he meant. The good eye was amused about the joke Joe Sam was keeping to himself. Then the dark, heavy lids came all the way down.

"Much whisky. Much 'live," Joe Sam muttered drowsily.

Harold thought, That's no answer, you old fraud. And you're not sleepy either; you're not a damn bit sleepy. But alive or not, there won't be any more whisky. I can take care of that much, anyway, and went over and blew out the lamp, and took down the bottle of whisky from beside it.

With the lamp out, the blue window turned gray, and through it he could see the snow still falling outside. The flakes were very big, but they were coming down slower and farther apart than they had been the night before. Standing there in the dim light and watching the snow fall, he was again seized by the emptiness and the wish to be asleep or even to be dead that came every time he remembered that Arthur was gone. He waited there, only bending his head a little, until the despair weakened into the bearable unhappiness that came after it. Then he said in his mind, Keep moving, boy. You can't lick it standing still, and crossed to the door. As he went out, he believed he heard a soft chuckle behind him, but when he looked, Joe Sam's eyes were closed and there was no smile on the sunken, melancholy old face. He pulled the door shut, and stood there in the quietly falling snow for a minute or two, just listening. There was no sound he could hear except the occasional passage of wind through the laden pines, and the soft whispering and thumping of their burdens falling.

He's up to something for sure, he thought, but Lord knows what. Well, I can't stay here all day, he thought finally.

"But I'll be right back, you old possum," he said very quietly, and started down, plowing his way through the fall of new snow that was nearly knee deep now. There was light showing in three windows of the house below. The small kitchen window

was a shadowy orange, but the white lamp itself showed in the
north window of the bedroom, and the clear light it made let
him see into the room through the west window. He could see
the tall, dark wardrobe in the corner, and one post of the foot
of the bed, and somebody's shadow, probably the mother's,
moving on the white wall beside the wardrobe. From up there
it was like seeing into one corner of a little stage. He was moved
by the glimpse, as he had been moved when he stood beside
Arthur's body and watched, through the tunnel, the three
women together, and then the old man alone behind them,
moving slowly away toward the lamp like a star in the kitchen
door.

He looked on out across the roof of the house. The mist of
snow still hid the valley, and the hay derrick stood up too near
and big in it, like the mast of a vessel appearing unexpectedly
out of a heavy fog.

13 - - -

When Harold opened the kitchen door, he saw the father
still there, asleep on his arms on the table. He looked at the big
head in the circle of light, the gray hair twisted up into little,
wry locks, the shape of flames, and then at the two whisky bottles beyond the old man's right arm, one of them empty, and
the other still half full.

All night, he thought. That must have been nice. He came
in and closed the door quietly. Then the smell of whisky and
stale cigar smoke was thick in the warm room. There were new
smells too, though, coffee, and the ham he could hear sizzling
in the pan. He peered across the table, through the shadow of
the lamp, and saw Gwen. She was standing by the stove with
a long fork in her hand. The whiter light from the bedroom
door reached her, making her face pale and her eyes too big
and dark.

"Hello," he said softly.

Gwen raised one hand a little, in a way that reminded him of Arthur, and turned back to the stove. He stood there looking at her for a moment, and wondering why she was so short with him. Then he put the whisky bottle into the cabinet under the clock, and came over beside her, and set Joe Sam's dishes on the sink shelf.

"I see you had company, anyway," he said.

Gwen nodded twice, quickly, but didn't answer. She began to break eggs into the pan with the ham. She did that too quickly also, and a little too hard. Harold moved closer to her, but, because of the bedroom light behind him, only put his hand gently against the small of her back. His own body would hide that.

"Did he keep you up all night too?" he asked.

Gwen shook her head and began to turn the ham over with the long fork.

After a moment Harold asked, "What's the matter, honey?" and slid his hand along so that he was almost holding her in his arm.

"Nothing," Gwen said, still keeping her head down. She was holding herself stiff as wood in his arm, and he had to make up his mind not to let go of her.

"Something is," he said. "Tell me."

"Let me alone, please, will you?" she said sharply, and at the same time glanced around at him. She looked down again at once, but he had seen the white anger of her face and the faint glitter of tears in her eyes. He let go of her slowly.

"It's nothing, really," Gwen said. "I'm just kind of tired, I guess."

He understood that this was an apology, but it wasn't one that made things any easier.

Finally he said, "It was Dad, wasn't it?"

"Please, Harold," she said again, but then added, "It wasn't anything, really. I just don't want to talk about it."

Harold turned part way, and looked at the father sleeping on the table. He was snoring heavily, and at every out-breath his big moustache shivered and his lips burbled softly under it. Harold set his jaw and turned back and took hold of Gwen's shoulders with his two hands.

"You better tell me about it, though," he said.

She shook her head. "It was my fault. I tried to get him to go to bed, that's all, and he didn't . . ." Her voice broke, and she bent her head down stiffly, fighting against crying.

"What did he do?"

She shook her head again. "Nothing."

"What did he say, then?"

"It doesn't matter, Harold."

"It does to me," he said. "What did he say?"

At first he thought she was going to flare out at him again, but that moment passed, and finally she said, "He's worried about Curt. That's all it was really. He didn't even know who I was, I don't think."

"Would you be crying about that?" he asked, and started to turn her around to face him.

She twisted free, and said quickly and fiercely, though almost whispering, "I'm not crying."

"Look, honey," he said, taking hold of her again. This time she turned to him suddenly, and buried her face against him.

"Oh, Hal," she cried softly, "he thinks I'm to blame."

He held her closely for a moment, and then kissed the top of her head, and asked, "To blame for what?" as if it were a joke that anybody should blame her for anything.

"All of it. For Arthur, and Curt not coming back."

"And just how does he figure that?"

"No, Hal, he meant it. That's what . . ." She buried her face and held herself tight against the sobs. "I don't care what he calls me," she said, the words muffled in his coat. "But he meant that, Hal. He thinks . . ."

"So he called you things too?"

Gwen nodded against him.

"Such as?"

Gwen shook her head. Then he could feel her stiffen, not just to stop the crying, but to free herself a little too. "I don't care about that," she said more clearly. "It's only because he really thinks . . ." but then gave up again.

"Listen, honey," Harold said. "He didn't think anything. He's drunk. He always gets drunk when there's trouble, and when he's drunk, he doesn't think. Like you said, he probably

145

didn't even know who you were. He probably thought you were somebody from forty years back. He likes you, honey; really, he does. He was all perked up, having you here."

"He knew who I was," Gwen said. "He called me a . . ."

Harold waited, but then she said again, "I don't care. But he really blames me. He thinks Arthur . . . He said none of it would have happened if I hadn't—if I hadn't made eyes at Curt."

"Oh," Harold said.

"He kept saying Curt would be back now if he hadn't sworn he'd get the hide for me, the painter skin."

"That's nonsense, honey," Harold said, and kissed the top of her head again. "Don't you pay any attention to such nonsense. He knows who was making the eyes. And what's more, once Curt got started after that cat, he couldn't have quit for anything, and it would be just the same if he'd never even seen you. You know that. And if you don't, we all do, and Dad the most of all, when he knows anything. He boasts about it; you've heard him."

Gwen nodded against his coat.

"Curt would stay out there till he got that cat if there was only him and it left in the whole world. He was just showing off a little for you, and that wasn't your fault. Nobody blames you for that."

"But if I . . ."

"But if you hadn't been here at all, it wouldn't have been any different. Not once that painter killed a steer. You remember that."

Gwen nodded against him. Then suddenly she pushed away from him and turned hastily back to the stove and slid the frying pan off the fire lids.

"Here I am letting everything burn up while I act the cry-baby," she said, laughing shakily. "I'll have your breakfast ready in a minute. Only these eggs. I'm afraid the eggs are ruined."

"They look fine to me," Harold said. He started to say something else, and then didn't. Finally he asked, "How's Grace this morning?"

Gwen spread a wire toaster on the fire lids and laid four slices

146

of bread on it. She didn't answer for so long he began to think she hadn't heard him. Then she said, "She's all right, I guess. She's asleep now."

"Meaning she didn't sleep last night?"

There was another long wait before Gwen said, "Not much, I guess," and at last added, very low, "She went in there once," and raised her hand a little from her side to point at the north bedroom.

"Oh, Lordy," Harold said softly. "Not like last night again?" he asked.

Gwen nodded, and then, before he could speak, said, "I'm scared for her, Hal. She just can't seem to let up any at all."

"No," Harold said. "No, it's tough on her, all right. Well," he said, "I'll stay down here tonight. Joe Sam'll have to look out for himself."

Gwen glanced at the plate on the sink shelf. "He didn't eat much this time either, did he?"

"No," Harold said, "just the meat."

Gwen asked, "Should we wake your father up to eat?"

Harold looked at the old man. "Better let him sleep, I guess. I'll see if Mother wants something."

He went to the bedroom door and looked in. The mother was sitting in the rocking chair by the bed, with the Bible in her lap. She had on her good black dress now, a heavy, stiff one with a big skirt and a tight bodice, that made her look like the old pictures she kept in the trunk upstairs. It had white lace at the throat and the wrists. She was sitting up straight, away from the back of the chair, with one hand laid out flat upon each half of the Bible. The lace of the cuffs looked very white on her brown hands on the stained, yellow pages. She had a black shawl over her shoulders, and her hair was drawn up tight, with no loose strands or wisps.

Arthur's body was dressed in the black clothes she'd laid out for it too. It was lying straight on its back now, the shiny boots together, the wrists crossed upon the breast, the face pointed at the ceiling and bound around with the black scarf again, to hold the mouth shut. It was like the body of a stranger lying where Arthur had been. That, and the mother dressed up the way she was, made the whole room strange.

147

He went in. The mother heard his boots, hard on the bare floor and then heavy on the piece of old carpet that did for a rug, and looked up at him. The little erasures her first pain and doubts had made in her face, the way death had made them in Arthur's, were gone now, and so was the inturned, half blind look in her eyes. They were her own eyes again, sharp and challenging, only more sunken than ever.

She and the Lord have made up their mind, Harold thought. Or did she see me hugging Gwen?

"You look tired, Mother," he said. "You've got everything done now. Why don't you try to eat a little something, and then get some sleep?"

"I'm all right," she said. She looked away from him, across the bed and out the west window, so that he looked too. There was only the snow piled on the sill and along the bottoms of the panes, and the big flakes still slowly falling.

"Is the snow going to stop, do you think?" she asked.

"Hard to tell. It's let up, but it doesn't feel like it's done yet, some way."

"Well, you better get at making the coffin, just the same. When you've had some breakfast."

"All right. Will you have breakfast with us?"

"I'm not hungry yet. You just bring me some coffee."

He knew better than to argue, when her face was like that. He nodded and returned to the kitchen.

"Just coffee again," he told Gwen.

"I'm fixing her some scrambled eggs," Gwen said. "They might go better than the fried."

"They might," Harold said.

He felt quiet and indifferent after standing there beside the strange Arthur, and feeling the mother keeping things to herself. He waited by the stove, not thinking about anything, but just watching Gwen stir the eggs and then scrape them onto a plate and fill a mug with coffee. At the sound of the fork scraping the pan, the father stirred and muttered, but then sighed and was quiet again.

Harold picked up the plate and mug and went back into the bedroom.

"Gwen thought maybe scrambled eggs would go pretty good," he said.

The mother stared at the plate of eggs for a moment, and then, without a word, took it and set it on the table. She kept the mug of coffee in her hands.

"Is there enough boards for the coffin?" she asked.

"I think so. There's a lot of wood in the shed, left over from the bunk-house. And there's the lumber Curt got for a tack room."

"Them's new boards, ain't they?"

"He just got 'em last month."

"You better use some of them, then, if they're good enough wood."

"They're as good as anything we've got."

"Well, they'll have to do, then. You better get at it as quick as you can. I got a feelin' the snow's about done, and there's the grave to dig yet."

Harold hesitated for a moment, but then said, "All right," and went back into the kitchen.

The father was awake and sitting up now, holding himself up with his hands against the edge of the table. He was looking around slowly out of bloodshot eyes and the world of sleep that was still more real to him than what he saw. When Harold sat down at the table, he turned his big face at him slowly, screwing it up to see him better.

"Oh," he said. He looked away into the shadow on the table. "I thought maybe Curt was back," he said. "I told him what I thought of him, the young fool, chasing out after black painters in a blizzard." He uncorked the bottle with whisky in it and very slowly and carefully poured his glass half full.

"Would you like your breakfast now, Mr. Bridges?" Gwen asked.

"Breakfast?" the old man said. "In the middle of the . . ." but then cautiously pried himself around in his chair far enough to see part of the front window, and said, after a moment, "Well, it is, at that."

He turned back and drank the whisky at one hoist, and set the glass down again.

"Very well, then, young woman, I will have some breakfast."

He leaned farther over the table and peered at Gwen through the shadow. "And just how did you get here, young woman?" he asked. "Curt," he said, turning his head ponderously to look at Harold, "who is this young woman, and how did she come here?"

"It's just Gwen, Dad. She's been here a couple of days."

"Gwen? Gwen? And who on earth, may I ask, is Gwen?" He spoke as if Harold were an audience of many people.

"Gwendolyn Williams, Dad. You remember her."

"I do not remember her," the old man said. He swung his head back and stared at her again. "Gwendolyn Williams," he muttered.

Gwen had a filled plate in each hand, but she waited there by the stove while he stared at her.

"Oh," the father said finally. "Of course. Harold's intended. Old Lew Williams' girl. Charming girl too, charming," he added. "Curt," he said, turning his head slowly to look at Harold again, and grinning a little, "Curt, I'm surprised at you, letting a young whippersnapper like . . ." He stopped speaking and stared at Harold, and his grin faded. "No," he said. He closed his eyes and sat there for some time with them closed, breathing loudly and frowning.

Gwen came to the table then, and set the plates down, one in front of each of the men.

The father opened his eyes again. "Where's Curt?"

"He'll be back today, Dad."

"Back today? I should hope so."

He thought about the matter, and then rolled his eyes to look at Harold without moving his head. He made a sly, knowing grin, and slowly, triumphantly, raised one hand and pointed at him.

"Out hunting," he announced. "That's where he is. And he'll get it too. He don't ever give up till he gets what he's after, Curt don't. He's a great shot, too, Curt is," he went on happily, "a great shot. Why, I remember once," he began, addressing his greater audience again, "and when he was only a youngster too, thirteen or fourteen, or somewhere around there, he won a turkey shoot down at old Jake Haley's ranch on the Carson River. Jake called the place a ranch, anyway. Half a dozen dry washes full of sagebrush, three scrawny cottonwood trees, and a litter of rags and old shoes and broken-down wagons is about what it amounted to. Jake used to say himself, when he had enough rot-gut in him to be half-way human, that rags was his chief crop. Grew old shirts about three to the bush, he did, though pants was rarer. But he did have turkeys. An old scoundrel, Jake Haley was," he said, chuckling. "He cleaned up on those birds, though there wasn't a thing to 'em but legs and feathers. They were more like buzzards than turkeys. In his more sociable moods he used to admit they were a cross, and that with the natural advantages of his place, the buzzard strain was getting a little the best of it. He couldn't have sold one of the critturs for a thin dime. So he used 'em all for turkey shoots. Four bits for three shots; plain highway robbery. And there couldn't anybody hit 'em, even at that price, the way he had it rigged. Buried 'em in a barrel in the ground, with only the head sticking out. Hundred yards, if it was an inch, and uphill, and enough neck room so the turkey could dodge all around. Made a mint out of that system, old Jake did. But he got one good scare, anyway, and Curt gave it to him. Knocked one off on the second shot."

He laughed a thin, gleeful whinny, startling after his deep voice speaking.

"Should have seen old Jake's face. Only the third man to shoot, and he got one. Nothing in the rules to say he couldn't keep on shooting all day, either. Old Jake thought he was ruined." He cackled happily.

Gwen pushed aside the bottles and the glass to make room for his coffee. She did it very slowly, to avoid catching his attention, but he saw the bottles moving and looked up at her. The pleasure died out of his face.

"Young woman," he said heavily, "I beg your pardon. Inexcusable of me. Inexcusable."

"It's all right, Mr. Bridges," Gwen said, flushing.

"It's all right," the father repeated. "You hear that, Curt?" he asked Harold. "Your intended, and I forget her name. Inexcusable. But she says it's all right. You're a lucky boy, Curt, very lucky."

Gwen sat down quickly in the mother's place, and she and

Harold began to eat. They couldn't look at the father or at each other.

. After a time the old man turned his head slowly and stared at Harold. "No, Harold's girl," he said. "Curt's out hunting, the young fool. But he'll get what he's gone after, just the same. He don't ever give up till he gets what he's after, Curt don't. Why I remember once," he began, changing to his public voice, but then thought about it, and stopped there. He began to eat, taking huge mouthfuls, but chewing them slowly. Once he put his fork down and sat staring at the shadow of the lamp while he chewed.

"It killed Arthur, just the same," he argued.

Harold looked at him quickly. "What did?"

"That damned black painter. Only I thought it was Curt. He was wearing Curt's coat. Wasn't, though; was Arthur. Saw his beard. Arthur took Curt's coat."

He considered that, sitting perfectly still. "Why'd he take Curt's coat?" he demanded. He stared at Harold angrily. "Keeping things from me," he accused. "Everybody keeps things from me. In my own house."

Harold sighed. "Nobody's keeping anything from you, Dad."

"Yes, they are. Can't even have an opinion around here any more. Can't fool me, though," he said craftily. "I know what's going on. Saw him on the bed in there. I know. Black painter killed him."

"Maybe a painter, Dad, but not likely black."

The old man stared at him angrily, but then gradually the anger weakened into confusion, and after a minute he turned back to his plate. When he had finished his food, Gwen brought him a second cup of coffee. He sat there trying to drink it, but kept nodding and sagging forward.

"There's nothing you can do now, Dad," Harold said. "Why don't you go up and lie down for a while?"

"Nothing anybody can do in this infernal snow," the old man muttered. "Might as well all go to bed." He hoisted himself to his feet and stood there, swaying and holding onto the back of his chair. "Waited up all night," he said. "Very tired. You will excuse me, my dear," he said to Gwen. "Have to step outside for a moment," he said to Harold.

He swung around slowly, keeping his hands on the chair, and looked out the window again. Then he swung back, and leaned over. Carefully extending one hand, he poured his glass half full of whisky again, and lifted it.

"Drop to warm myself first," he explained. "Cold out. Too early for winter. Always feel the cold more when winter's too early." He drank the whisky off without stopping, set the glass down, and straightened up. When he had his balance behind the chair, he turned and lurched toward the outside door.

Harold got up quickly and went to help him, but the old man waved him away angrily. "All right," he muttered. "Quite all right."

He steadied himself against the doorframe, and then got the door open and lurched out, nearly falling as he stepped down into the snow. He saved himself by his hold on the handle of the door, and the door closed suddenly and loudly.

Harold picked up the two whisky bottles, threw the empty one into the trash box under the sink, and put the other into the cabinet. Gwen began to clear the table, and he helped her, but they still didn't talk.

When the old man returned, he balanced in the doorway and peered at the table. "Where'd you put it?" he asked. He left the door open, and steered carefully across to the table. The cold air and the fresh smells of snow and pine came in behind him. He leaned on the table and looked around over its top. "Where'd you put it?" he asked again.

Then he grinned knowingly. "Is no use," he said. "Think you can hide things from me, eh?"

"I was just picking up, Dad," Harold said. "It's in the sideboard. You'd better get some sleep now, though. You look tired."

The old man was touched by this sympathy. The tears welled up over his red lids, and began to trickle down his cheeks. "Tired," he said. "Waited up all night for him. Better get some sleep."

He worked his way to the foot of the stairs, and there, holding onto the rail, drew himself up and turned to face them.

"Beg your pardon, young woman," he said to Gwen. "Inexcusable. 'Solutely inexcusable." He said inexcusable very slowly and carefully, and didn't miss a syllable. Then he turned back and began to pull himself up the stairs, using both hands on the rail and pausing on each step.

Harold came over to the foot of the stairs, and he and Gwen stood watching every move the old man made. His heavy breathing and the creak of the stairs under his weight were loud in the room. A step or two above the middle of the stairs, he stumbled and swung back on one heel. Gwen uttered a little, nervous cry and put her hands up to her cheeks quickly. Harold sprang up the stairs. The old man caught himself with the rail behind him, and hung there, his chin down hard against his chest, and his eyes closed. Harold got up to him, and steadied him above the rail. After a minute, he drew the old man's arm over his own shoulder, and, still holding him around the waist too, started him up again. They went very slowly, the father sagging and letting his head roll, but pulling with one hand on the rail. They reached the landing, and paused while Harold got a new hold to take the whole weight, and then shuffled in through the bedroom door. Gwen sighed, and let her hands down again slowly. She stood there a moment more, listening, and then turned back to the sink. She was still quiet, though, not touching the waiting dishes. She heard their voices speak briefly above, and then the old man made a long, relaxing groan. Harold said something more, and his boots sounded loudly, coming out onto the landing. The door was closed, and the boots came down the hollow stairs.

"Fell asleep the minute he hit the bed," Harold said.

He didn't say anything more about it, though. He carried in wood from the pile against the house and filled the wood-box and built up the fire. Then he brought the mother's cup and plate from the bedroom, saying softly, "She only drank the coffee again," and blew out the lamp over the table.

Gwen had Joe Sam's cup and plate ready then. She gave them to Harold and went ahead of him to open the door.

"Make him eat something this time, Hal," she said.

Harold nodded. "And you get some rest," he ordered gently. "You'll get a little peace for a while now. You let the dishes wait, and get some sleep."

Gwen took hold of his coat with both hands and raised her

face toward his. They stood in the doorway, with the idle flakes turning against them and their mouths together. Finally Gwen gave him a quick little extra kiss and let go of him. She stood in the doorway until he had gone around the corner of the house.

14 ⚬ - ⋅ - ⚬

Harold let himself into the bunk-house, saying, "Here's some breakfast for you, Joe Sam," and knew before he was done speaking that the old man wasn't there. The fire was almost out and the whisky smell and the staleness of sleep-breathing were heavy in the cooling air. Joe Sam's bunk was empty, but his clothes were still lying across the foot of it and his moccasins still stood together under the edge of the stove.

Holy cat, Harold thought, he's gone out with nothing on. I should have seen his tracks when I came up, he thought, and for a moment felt again the fear and bewilderment that had made him sweat in the clearing in his dream.

"He made tracks, all right," he told himself aloud. "You just didn't have your eyes open."

He set the plate and cup down on the box by the stove, crossed quickly to the trash keg, and tilted it so the light from the window showed the inside of it. The bottle neck wasn't there. He let the keg back and went to the door and looked down the hill toward the house. The fear took hold of him again. There were only the two lines of his own tracks, one already softened by new snow, the other still sharp-edged and clear. For a moment he wanted to run back down to the house and see with his own eyes that Gwen was all right. He wanted to touch her and hear her speak. He was briefly possessed by a superstitious notion that everybody on the place was changing toward something strange and evil, but all of them together, and so gradually that no one could see what was happening except when some little hint of the unnatural got out, like this. But then he saw the tracks, and they were real enough, only already blurred by the new snow too. They went close along the side of the bunk-house, and then straight up into the edge of timber, where he lost sight of them in the brush. Reading the tracks as far as he could see them, he could imagine the old Indian making them, advancing slowly and watchfully, and stopping often to look around, like a timid, dangerous animal stalking something or escaping. He'd be holding that bottle neck ready all the time too, like a knife.

"This is the craziest yet," he said aloud. "Have to lock the old bastard up next," and again wanted to run down to the house and be sure everything was all right before he did anything else.

"You just came from there," he told himself. "Let's not everybody start playing crazy games."

He pulled the door shut and started up the slope beside the line of prints left by the small, square feet. Where they turned into the thickets, he stopped and looked warily ahead, stooping a little to take cover in the bushes. Except for once in a while a startling fall of snow from an overburdened bough, there was only the white and shadowy quiet under the pines. There were hiding places everywhere, though: the walls of snow-drifted brush and granite boulders as tall as a man, and all the dark tree trunks. He'd have to keep his eyes open, be sure of the tracks far enough ahead so they couldn't circle back on him without his knowing it. He could feel between his shoulders the thought of the little, dark man with the bottle neck in his fist and the secret joke in his good eye, creeping out of some cover behind him.

The tracks went south across the hillside above the house. They never came down out of the woods, but zig-zagged from hiding place to hiding place up and down the slope, and deepened in each hiding place, as if Joe Sam had stood or squatted there for a long time. Where the pines had kept the tracks free of the morning snow, Harold stopped too, to stare down. It made him uneasy to see the print of a naked human foot in snow. It wasn't right there. The split-heart print of a deer, the dots and dashes of rabbits, the fine tail line and tiny forget-me-nots of wood mice, or even the big, broken flower of a panther or a bobcat, those were all as right in snow as black letters on paper. But this complicated, unique print, not even a little like any of them, was all wrong. There was too much time forgotten between. He shook himself out of the wondering, and moved faster along the trail, sometimes taking short-cuts where he could see both legs of a side trip.

South of the house the tracks curved out toward the valley along the low, descending ridge that made the ranch into a kind of little bay. They led down out of the pines and into the manzanita and then the high, feathery sage where the quail lived. The quail startled him once, breaking up out of cover with a soft, multiple thunder of wings. He caught his breath and stopped where he was. The quail all fled upslope from him, but fanning out toward the valley and the mountain. Toward the top of the ridge, they began to drop out of sight again in the brush by ones and twos, and one bunch of a dozen or so together. The silence came back, and he was ashamed, and a little worried, because he had let them startle him. He should have seen them first, and he certainly should have noticed the spidery writing of their tracks everywhere in the lanes through the brush. But he hadn't; he'd seen only the heavy, human track he was following through them. After that he was ashamed of his worry. It's still only Joe Sam, he told himself. A little, old man half your size, and full of whisky and dreams.

He was still worried about that bottle neck, though, and because he couldn't guess what Joe Sam was up to. He tried to remember something that would tell him for sure whether Joe Sam had broken that bottle on purpose or by accident. All he could find was his own dream-groggy first impression that it hadn't been an accident, and he didn't trust that now. He thought he discovered something else, though. That was what made the shot, he thought. It was too close for Curt to make it. He was still clear up at the top of that avenue through the trees. That's how I got into the bedroom and saw the hole come in Arthur's face. That was when Joe Sam broke the bottle.

What difference does it make? he thought. I didn't see him break it. He took it back out of the keg, though, and maybe that does. He wants it for something. He was saving it for something all the time, he thought suddenly. He put it down so carefully when I told him to drop it. Well, what of it? When he gets to thinking black painter—

He stopped short again, telling himself sharply, Wake up, will you? The trail had entered an open space in the brush with tracks all over it, and flecks of blood and the slaty blue feathers and tawny down of a quail. It was a mess that would show from yards off, and he'd walked right into it before he saw it.

A coyote or a bobcat got one, he thought, and Joe Sam stopped to look at the marks, like I am. But then he saw that there weren't any tracks but the quail writing and Joe Sam's, except one wandering line left by a hopping rabbit. He looked around until he saw where Joe Sam's tracks went on out of the open space. There were no blood marks going with it. He hunted around then until he saw the dead quail. It lay under a sage bush a little way above him and to the right, and there was no track going up to it, not the bird's or any other. He climbed to the place and picked up the quail. It was a valley quail, with the black top-knot curving forward like a plume on an old lady's bonnet. Its round, gray body was already cold, and it didn't weigh enough on his hand. The head, with the half-closed eye, hung away limp over his finger tips, and he could feel that the neck was nearly cut through. He turned the quail over on his hand. On the other side the feathers and down were torn away from half the breast and shoulder, and the wound showed. It was circular, with several deep punctures around the edge. Flesh had been torn out of the center of the wound till the bones showed, but there was no wet blood in it.

Not much blood, he thought. Not much dry blood, even, and then thought, quickly, The shape of that wound, and lifted his head and looked carefully all around, but saw only the motionless brush, with the light, separate flakes of snow falling silently upon it. Sucked the blood, he thought, looking down at the hole again. Ate some of the meat raw, and then sucked the blood.

He dropped the bird back beside its bush, giving it a small, pitying thought, but no more, and went down, and out of the trampled clearing along Joe Sam's trail again. He went much faster now, and kept a watch around him all the time. The tracks curved down along the north slope of the ridge, and then, where the brush thinned out and grew smaller, and the grass began, they changed. There were hand prints, and only narrow rakings of the toes, and deep pits, always two together and a little staggered.

On his hands and knees, Harold thought, watching the house. And he still has that damned bottle neck, he thought, seeing the print of its teeth several times, spreading out of the ball of the right fist.

From there only the footprints showed ahead, though, dwindling in a straight line toward the house. And running, too, Harold thought, seeing them farther apart and the snow between them only lightly marked and sometimes not at all. He broke into a run himself, peering ahead at the house all the time, now that the trail didn't need watching. There was nothing moving in sight, except the cluster of steers that had come in off the snowy range and were waiting by the fenced haystacks, and more of them coming, far off in the north.

At the corner of the house he had to stop again, because the trail divided. There were crawling tracks again, along the base of the south wall. They ended under the bunk-room window, and then came back, making a confused double trail. It thinned out into a single, clear trail along the back of the house.

Looked in at the window, Harold thought. Watching Grace?

He followed the single trail. It stopped again under the kitchen window, and then under the west window of the bedroom, beside the bed where Arthur was lying. Looking in every place, Harold thought. He didn't try to get in, though. What's he want to watch them for?

Half running, he followed the tracks around the corner and along the north side. At the northeast corner he stopped and breathed easier, and even grinned a little. The tracks didn't go to the door at all. They went out straight across the yard to the sheds and into the tunnel between them.

"What the hell is he up to now?" he asked himself softly.

He went across the yard and into the tunnel, just walking now. From the tunnel, he could see Joe Sam standing inside the corral fence with his back turned. He was naked, all right, and one of his braids had come unraveled at the end and hung in a loose brush behind his shoulder. He had the bottle neck in his right hand, but he wasn't doing anything with it, just holding

159

it as if he'd forgotten it. Harold came to the gate, where he could see the whole corral. There were mounds of hay newly thrown out along the wall of the shed, and all the horses were lined up there eating. The tiny feathers of snow clung on the tips of their velvety coats like frost, and their breathing made small clouds in the cold air. Joe Sam was just standing there watching the horses eat, for all anybody could see. Harold spoke his name.

Joe Sam didn't move, and Harold spoke again, more loudly. The horses all raised their heads together and looked at him, the hay working like big, false moustaches at the corners of their mouths. Curt's black stallion, Kentuck, was right in front of Joe Sam. He raised his head with the others and looked at Harold, but then, while the others kept watching him, their large, blue-glazed eyes only faintly curious, Kentuck looked at Joe Sam. He reached down and drew sideways at the hay, taking a new mouthful, but at once raised his head again, rolling the hay between his jaws, and looked at the old Indian.

Watching each other, Harold thought. Now what? and stooped and crawled between the bars. He stopped just out of reach of Joe Sam and spoke his name again. This time Joe Sam turned part way toward him, and turned his head farther to look at him. He moved slowly and calmly.

"Give hay," he said. "Horse eat."

He was all ready with that, Harold thought. He knew I was here all along.

"You'll freeze, standing around with nothing on," he said. "Here, give me that thing before you cut yourself."

He held his hand out, but watched the old face steadily. The life went out of it now. It aged greatly while he looked at it, and became sad and confused. After a moment Joe Sam lifted the bottle neck and looked at it.

"Bottle break," he said dully.

He held it out to Harold. When he had let go of it, his jaw began to shake, and then the shaking spread until he was jerking all over. He hunched his shoulders against the jerking, and crossed his hands in front of his crotch.

"Cold," he said.

Harold tossed the bottle neck out of the coral on the far side, toward the haystacks. "Come on in the tack room," he said, "and we'll find something for you to put on."

"Cold," the old Indian said again. "Whisky good."

"No more whisky," Harold said, wondering if it was a joke this time too. He took Joe Sam by the arm, and led him in through the open door of the hay shed.

"Your breakfast's up at the bunk-house. You get up there and get dressed and put some wood in the fire and eat your breakfast. You'll feel better then."

Like he just woke up from a bad dream, he thought. He doesn't even know what he's been doing. Or is he still playing possum?

He found an old linen dust coat of the father's in the tack room, one he'd used to make a show in, years before, in San Francisco. It was stained in big patches now, and most of the buttons were gone. He took it off the nail, and held it for Joe Sam to get into. The old man wouldn't move, though, and he had to put it on him as if he were dressing a young child who was thinking about something else.

Then he opened the door into the yard and said, "Now go on up there before you freeze to death. I'll be up as quick as I finish the chores."

"Help," Joe Sam said.

"No. You go on up and get dressed and eat your breakfast."

"Eat soon," Joe Sam said. "Help now."

Sucked enough blood to hold you? Harold thought, and after a moment shrugged his shoulders and said, "All right, then. You feed the chickens. Better get something on your feet, though. Here, take these."

From the corner under the work harnesses, he pulled out an old pair of boots with rubber feet and felt tops that were used for mucking out the corrals and the pig pen. Solemnly and slowly, hindered by spasms of jerking, Joe Sam put them on. Then he stood there, small and half asleep, lost in the huge duster, and with the boots like a solid base under him, not anything his feet could move. Harold smiled a little in his mind, remembering, already as if it had happened a long time back, how he had made a mystery to be afraid of out of this tired, little, old man, who was just holding death off with whisky

161

and legends. He rolled up the sleeves of the dust coat, so Joe Sam could get his hands out.

"All right. You feed the chickens."

Joe Sam went out slowly, dragging the big boots. Harold stood in the door and watched until he disappeared around the end of the south shed, toward the chicken run. Then he closed the door and went out to start the other chores himself.

He finished by tossing out hay from the stacks for the cattle that were waiting in the trampled snow outside the fences. Then he went back up toward the sheds in the lane between the stacks and the corral, and remembered that he'd thrown the bottle neck out there somewhere. Might as well get it out of his reach for good, he thought, but as soon as he started to look for it, saw the trenches the big boots had made in the snow. He looked for the bottle neck out where the tracks ended. He found the mark of it, but the bottle neck was gone.

Still at it, he thought patiently, but then his patience broke. But it's the last time, by God, he thought furiously, and imagined with pleasure how his hands would make the old man pay attention this time. He went on up toward the sheds, walking with stiff, quick strides.

When he came to the stake fence of the chicken run, he saw Joe Sam already inside, standing out in the middle, with the wooden, half-peck measure in the circle of his left arm. He was slowly scattering the grain for the chickens, making a kind of ceremony of it, as he always did. Harold could not hold his anger against the peaceful sight.

Don't you get like Curt, he told himself, and remembered how Curt had bullied the old man, pushing the stallion at him until he was forced to retreat, and then many other times back of that.

He stood holding two stakes of the fence in his fists, and watched Joe Sam. He thought of Arthur watching Joe Sam feed the chickens. It was like watching a kind of play, Arthur said, a small play that had more meaning than you'd think at first. It made you hunt for what it meant. If Arthur was working anywhere near, he'd always stop and come to the fence to watch Joe Sam feed the chickens, and he'd always go away afterwards slowly, and smiling to himself. It made Arthur alive again to think of him standing at the stake fence watching. It was at such times that the quiet, thinking happiness, the peace as lively as hope, was in him, making a light through his face. It was like making a prayer that worked inside to put a hand on his shoulder then, and feel his thin body warm with sun, through the blue work shirt. He always thought of Arthur as watching Joe Sam in sunlight, in the spring, really, when the sun was just warm and full of promise, and the little movements of cool wind came up from the green meadows, and the pines on the mountain stood perfectly still and glistened softly in the new light. It made the loss worse to remember what could never be dead, while you also remembered the dead face on the pillow, that already could never have been alive. It tore you in two directions; it made it impossible to get across the space between.

Harold bowed his head a little and gripped the two stakes fiercely. When the intolerable tearing was over, and the ghosts of the two parts flowed together again, he drew a deep breath and loosened his hold and looked up. In the half-aliveness that remained, he was capable only of pity among the strong feelings, but his vision was cleared like that of a man who has rid himself, for a time, of prejudice and memory, so that what he sees is all new and strange.

Joe Sam had trampled the snow down in a wide circle with the big boots. He was standing in the center of the circle, with the grain measure in his arm, and the chickens were crowding around him. They were all kinds, gray and red and black and crossed, and the harder colors of their combs and wattles, their beaks and legs, made bright flecks and spots upon the soft colors of the feathery mass. The two fierce, painted little bantams darted back and forth on the edge of the crowd, picking up the grains that fell outside. Arthur had brought the bantams all the way from the Carson Valley. They were his favorites, and they were Joe Sam's favorites too. Curt always snorted about the bantams. "No damn use at all," he'd say. "One egg a week, as big as your thumb."

Joe Sam fanned the grain out slowly and thinly, a handful at a time. It was the motion of a man sowing seed who likes to do it, and has a feeling that the act is holy and should be thought about. Only it was even slower than that, with long pauses between sweeps when Joe Sam's hand waited above the measure and he solemnly watched the chickens turning and pecking about him. He looked from one to another of them, considering each by itself. Only when they began to move uneasily, hunting and not finding anything, would he slowly fan out the next handful onto the snow. It took Joe Sam a long time to feed the chickens this way. He was nearly done now, though. He was already holding the last handful for the part of the ceremony he liked best. He squatted and set down the measure on the snow beside him. Then he divided the last handful, and holding half of it out in each hand, close to the snow, began to make a soft, continuous sound through his teeth, now clucking, now whistling. The bantams at once stopped hunting around on the edge of the flock and came running to him, forcing their way boldly among the big chickens that had shut them out before. The cock began to strike quickly at the grain in his right hand and the hen at the grain in his left. The other chickens knew better than to push into this final rite. It was just for the bantams, and all the time it went on, Joe Sam kept up the soft clucking and whistling, and at the same time grinned with a faint, malicious pleasure to feel their tiny beaks darting against his palms. When they had taken the last grains, he stood up slowly, still grinning, and stopped the coaxing sounds, and held out his hands, palms down, to show they were empty. The little cock reared and beat the air before him with his wings and crowed exultantly in his high, thin voice. Joe Sam laughed out loud. The same happy malice was in the laugh that was in the grin, and a pride like the bantam cock's as well.

"Shoo," he said finally, and waved first the bantams, and then all the rest of the flock, away from him. The small magic of the ceremony dissolved, and it was hard to tell what had made it in the first place. Joe Sam picked up the measure and went slowly out of the chicken run, dragging the big boots so they made channels in the snow. He closed the gate carefully, fastened it with its wire loop, and plodded on up to the store room at the south end of the shed.

Harold went up after him. Watching the feeding, and remembering Arthur watching it, had cleaned the last anger out of him. He had to remind himself, with an effort, that Joe Sam still had the bottle neck somewhere, and of what he had already done with it.

The store room was shadowy and cold and full of the smells of grain and of the new wood that was stacked up along the east wall. Joe Sam was standing by the grain bins, holding up the big lid that covered them all.

"We better take some boards up with us, to make the coffin, Joe Sam," Harold said. "It's too cold to work down here."

Joe Sam looked at him without expression, and waited.

"Make box for Arthur," Harold explained. "To bury him."

"Make box," Joe Sam said. He dropped the measure into a bin, and let the lid down.

Harold chose five long boards that were still white from the saw and plane. He drew them out of the pile and laid them one on top of the other on the floor. He brought the tool tray from the bench under the cobwebby front window and set it on top of the boards. Then he signed to Joe Sam to take the other end. They carried the boards out and set them down in the snow while Harold closed the store room. Then they picked them up again, and went slowly, with several stops to let Joe Sam rest or get a new hold, across the yard and up the hill to the bunk-house.

In the bunk-house, Harold built up the fire again.

"Better get your clothes on now, Joe Sam," he said, and waited until the old man had taken off the big dust coat and the boots and begun to dress beside the stove. Then he hung up the coat on the wall by the wash stand, and set the boots together under it. He stood there for a moment, watching Joe Sam, but the old Indian seemed to be away in his mind again, and not noticing anything around him, so he went outside and up to the woodpile, and came back with two sawhorses. He set the sawhorses up in the middle of the room and laid the first board across them, and a saw, a folding rule, a square and a blue pencil on the board. Then he looked at Joe Sam again. He was sitting on the box beside the stove, slowly pulling on a sock. He had set his breakfast down on the floor beside the box.

Harold crossed to the water bucket and dipped himself a glass of water. This time he looked at Joe Sam in the mirror.

The old man was very small, and way back there on his box, in the mirror, but Harold could see that he was pulling on a moccasin now, and not paying any attention to anything else. Harold raised the glass of water, and while he drank, felt quickly over the old dust coat, hiding the search with his body. There was nothing solid in the dust coat. It hung flat and limp, and was getting damp now from the snow melting on it.

Harold finished his drink, set the glass down, and went to the window, where he pretended to be looking down at the house. As he turned back, he took a quick look into the trash keg in the corner. The bottle neck was there again, lying on top of all the smaller pieces. He smiled a little at the way he was setting tricks of his own against Joe Sam's now, and took off his cap and mackinaw and hung them up. Then he went back to the board across the two sawhorses. As long as he knew where that bottle neck was, that was the thing. As long as it didn't show up where he didn't expect it. There'd be some chance to get rid of it for good when the old man didn't have to watch him do it. Or when he was sober again, if that was what made the difference.

He stood looking down at the board and thought for a minute. Then he unfolded the yellow rule along the edge of it, and began to mark off the length he wanted.

Joe Sam had finished dressing now. He crossed slowly to his bunk and sat down on the edge of it and watched the work. He followed every move with his good eye, but didn't appear to be really paying attention to any of them.

"You better eat something," Harold said.

"Maybe, soon," Joe Sam said, and didn't move.

"Well, it can't get any colder now, that's sure," Harold said.

He laid the square across the board at the end of the length he'd measured, and made a quick slash along it with the pencil. He started the saw against the square too, and when it had cut a fine groove to hold the teeth exactly on the blue line, pushed the square away. Then the rasping of the saw began, loud and rhythmical in the closed room. The sawdust fell in little, soundless spurts from the cut, and in the window behind Harold, the thinning snow fell soundlessly also, and always slower and slower. It was just floating now, as if it were being let down carefully and all together.

15 ⬤ ━ ━ ⬤

It was about one o'clock when Gwen came up with coffee and sandwiches. Harold tried to get Joe Sam to eat, but the old man just looked up at him slowly, and as if he didn't really see him, and said, "Maybe, soon," and looked back down at the curly shavings under the plank.

"No use trying to make him eat when he's like this," Harold said, and set the plate and cup down on the box beside the untouched breakfast.

Gwen turned back toward the door, and Harold asked, "How's everything going down there now?"

"All right, I guess," she said.

"You don't have to go right away, then, do you?"

"Well," Gwen said, "I could stay a little while, I guess."

She came around the planks laid out on the sawhorses and sat down on Harold's bunk. She smiled up at him quickly, and looked away again quickly. After a moment she said, "It's awfully hot in here," and stood up and took off her cloak and laid it carefully over the foot of the bunk. Then she sat down again, with her hands together in her lap. Harold sat down on one of the planks, where it crossed the sawhorse nearest to her, and began to eat his lunch. When they looked at each other at the same time, they both smiled, but they didn't try to talk. It was too quiet in the bunk-house, and both of them felt Joe Sam there too much. They kept looking at him, first one of them and then the other.

When Harold had finished eating, he got Joe Sam's breakfast and lunch and set them on the plank, and began to break the food into a little pile of scraps on one plate, crumbling the bread in with the rest.

"We might as well give it to his birds," he said. "He's even forgotten them, this time. He most generally puts grain out back for them, when it snows."

He stacked the used dishes together on the plank and picked up the plate of scraps and the cup of coffee, and they went out together. Harold emptied the coffee into the snow, and led the way around to the back corner of the bunk-house. There he gave the plate to Gwen, and with short steps going around and in, in a spiral, he stamped the snow firm over a small circle. When he was done, Gwen scattered the food onto the packed surface. Her hands worked quickly and deftly at the little task. Her yellow blouse was bright as fire against the snow and the dark edge of the woods, and the floating snow slowly laid its thin crystals on the heavy coil of her hair. Harold stood there watching her all the time. When she finished, she stood for a moment looking at the birds that were already appearing in the nearest trees, and then turned and came back to him. He took the plate from her gently, looking down at her face and smiling a little all the time, and dropped the plate and the cup into the new snow behind him. They made a small, muffled clatter against each other, but neither Gwen nor Harold heard it. He took her hands and drew her slowly against him and bent his face down to hers. After the long kiss, he pushed her off a little, and kissed her lightly on the forehead, meaning to let her go. He couldn't, though, but suddenly drew her closer again and kissed her repeatedly on the cheeks and eyelids and throat, and at last on the mouth again. He bent her back under this kiss, and their faces became fierce and bereaved. They clung to each other desperately, with their eyes closed and their hands beseeching.

The many little black caps and chickadees and the two orange towees that had been waiting fluttered down and hopped into the circle, one at a time, and then two and three together, and began to pick quickly about among the scraps. A downy woodpecker went twice around the big pine that was nearest on the other side of the circle, making a faint, rhythmical scratching on the bark. Then he walked straight down it for a few feet, launched out, and lit abruptly by the morsel he'd chosen. A big, black-crested jay came down onto the corner of the roof and stalked about in small circles, complaining stridently. Three more jays arrived in the big pine and hitched and scolded too, one on the lowest branch and the other two on the second branch above him.

It was Gwen who finally gently pushed Harold from her and shook her head at him. Harold lifted the pushing hands to his lips, pressing them together in his own, and kissed them many times. The hunger came on Gwen's face again as she looked down at his head, but after a moment she whispered, "No, no," and kissed his hair quickly and lightly and drew her hands free.

"I have to go back now, Harold."

He stood looking down at her again, with a little, one-sided smile like Arthur's. Finally he just nodded and touched her arm with his fingertips. Then he turned and dug the cup and plate up out of the snow.

"I'll get the rest of the dishes," he said huskily.

They stood looking at each other again, and then, suddenly Gwen's eyes filled with tears.

"Honey, honey," Harold said, and would have moved to her again, but she held him off, gently but stubbornly.

"No, Harold, please."

"No," he said finally, and tried to smile. He stepped back to let her go ahead of him, and the way he did it made it a big gesture, as if he were opening a way through a crowd for her. Then he turned and followed close behind her, glancing down at the house as he did so. He wasn't thinking about it at first, but after an instant he really saw what he was looking at, and something pierced swiftly and coldly into him. Small, not quite real, a puppet in the box of the closed stage down there, the mother was standing in the north window, watching them. Her face was only a tiny, blank oval, but he knew how it looked. He knew what she was thinking as if he could hear her saying it, and the knowledge separated him from Gwen. A quick, murderous fury leapt up in him, but it was partly the fury of a culprit caught in the act. He looked away from the north window at once.

Behind them, the scolding jays came down into the circle, and the blackcaps and chickadees and towees fluttered away. The downy woodpecker stayed where he was, though, and went on picking at what he wanted. The jays left a clear circle of snow around him, but they were angry because they had to do it, and squabbled loudly with each other. Two of the chickadees came back down and started to feed again. They kept close to the woodpecker, and the jays let them alone too.

"Mother's watching us," Harold said.

"Is she?" Gwen said absently. Then she said, "Oh," and that little sound coming by itself afterwards told him the cold blade had struck into her too. He didn't want to look down at the north window again, but he saw Gwen glance down, and then away again quickly, and he began to feel that he was even walking awkwardly. In spite of himself, he looked again as they went around the corner to the front of the bunk-house. The dark puppet with the white patch of face was still there in the window.

Gwen stopped outside the door and turned to face him. He halted an arm's length from her.

"Will it make her awfully angry, Hal?" she asked.

"Don't you care about it," he said. "Don't you care, no matter what she says."

After a moment, Gwen said, "It was pretty bad, wasn't it? I mean now? She'd think it was?"

"What was?" he asked angrily. "What did we do that was so awful?"

"It's what she's thinking about it," Gwen said tonelessly. "I don't think she likes me very much anyway, and now . . ."

There wasn't anything good to say to her that was true. After a time, he turned and stared down at the house. His fists were doubled, and the fury came out in his words, though quietly. "Just because she's never been anything but a whore and a slave, just because that's all it's ever meant to her, she thinks even God sees it that way now. If she even . . ." He turned back and saw Gwen standing there, perfectly still, staring at his face, and the anger turned cold in him. Gradually he knew what it was that he'd said, and heard a little how it must have sounded to her.

"Well," he said finally, "she's seen us now, and she can't pretend about it any more. The sooner we get it over with, the better. Wait'll I get the dishes."

Gwen turned her back to the house and stood there while he went in and picked up her cloak and the dishes and came back.

"If you'll take these for a minute," he said, "I'll put your cloak on."

She took the dishes without looking at him, and turned her back to him, and waited. He laid the cloak gently over her shoulders, and then, because he had to do something more, drew the hood up over her head and forward to shield her face. While he still had hold of the hood, he leaned past her shoulder until he could see her face inside, in the shadow, and smiled at her. She wouldn't smile back, though, and after a moment he couldn't smile either. He straightened and walked stiffly back and closed the door. When he turned again, Gwen was already going down toward the house, carrying the dishes. He couldn't hurry after her and try to take them from her when she had done that, so he just followed her down, feeling that he had already lost all that would matter in the trouble he was sure was coming.

When they entered the kitchen, Grace was sitting by herself at the table, holding Arthur's little carving of a sheepherder carrying a lamb over his neck. She wasn't really looking at it, though. She was staring at the edge of the table, and then she looked up at them. Before any of them could speak, the mother appeared in the bedroom door. She had the black shawl on still, and was holding it together at the throat with one hand. She looked only at Harold, and she spoke to him as if Gwen weren't there.

"I saw you up there with her."

"Did you?" Harold said.

He took the dishes from Gwen, and walked slowly over and set them down on the sink shelf. He did it carefully, so they couldn't see how he was trembling.

"How could I help it?" the mother asked, in the deep voice like a man's. "Playin' with your little whore right out in plain sight, and your brother not yet in his grave."

Harold turned around and took hold hard on the edge of the sink shelf behind him, with both hands. "You could maybe pick your words a little better," he said softly.

"You've done the pickin' for me, I'd say. Your pa called her a dirty, foreign little mucker's brat. Well, she's that, right enough, but that's the least of what she is. I never been one to mince my words, when they tell the truth. Whore is what I called her, and whore is what I meant. I'm sayin' only what has to be said, and you'll listen to me."

"Get it all said quick then."

The mother stared at him. "I'd send her packin' this minute," she said finally, "only I won't have it on my conscience she got put out in this storm by herself. And you can't take her home now. You'll have to finish the coffin, and with Curt gone, you'll have to dig the grave too. She can get her things together and take them up to the bunk-house, and wait there till you're ready. If she . . ."

"That'll do," Harold said.

Gwen said scornfully, "Never mind, Harold. I'm going, and I won't need any help, thank you."

"You'll go when the buryin's done," the mother said.

"We'll go now," Harold said. "Curt can dig the grave when he gets back, and finish the coffin too. If you think . . ."

Gwen turned away suddenly toward the door.

"You better take your things up with you," the mother said.

Gwen went on toward the door.

It was Grace's voice that stopped her. "Mother, you're making a nasty, filthy lie out of nothing. It's you that's shaming Arthur, not Gwen. And not Harold either."

They'd nearly forgotten she was there, and even Gwen stopped and turned, astonished by the sharp voice. They all stared at Grace. She was standing behind the chair now, gripping the back of it with both hands so hard her knuckles were white. Her face was white too, and her eyes were very wide, and dark and shining. She was staring at the mother.

"What's Gwen done, anyway?" she cried. "You, to be always talking as if you were God around here."

The mother slowly let go of her shawl and gripped her two hands together in front of her. "Don't blaspheme, girl."

"Me blaspheme?" Grace cried. She lifted her face for a moment at the rafters, and laughed shrilly. "Me blaspheme?" she cried again, staring at the mother, and even leaning a little toward her, as if about to spring, though still clutching the back of the chair.

"Grace," Harold said, moving toward her with his hand out.

"Don't you touch me," she cried, but still holding the mother with her staring eyes. "Don't any of you touch me. Oh, God, I've needed to say this. We all need to. Even the house needs to. It's rotten with lies and greed and bad dreams. Arthur knew; oh, how he knew. But he was too kind-hearted. He always forgave everything. All he'd do was make little jokes that told the truth if you listened to them. But you and your God don't hear little jokes. And Curt and Father don't even have a God, not any kind. Only money. Only self-importance and wanting their own way, and money, money, money. And there isn't any use for money around here, or anything to be important about. So all Father wants now is to be drunk and pretend he's not here, and Curt wants to kill everything; he wants everything in the valley dead but Curt. He was happy when he found those steers dead. Didn't you see that, you old fool? Couldn't you hear that when he talked about it? They were dead already, and it gave him an excuse to kill something else too.

"And think how happy he was when he found Arthur out there. He let him go out there alone, didn't he? He sent him out there, so he could come back here and strut around. He knew Arthur wouldn't kill anything. He knew he'd get to do that too. And that isn't all; that's just the end of it. He's been robbing Arthur for years. He's taken Arthur's share time after time, with your blessing, and your God's, and Father's too. To improve the ranch, he says. Oh, yes, but his ranch, his. You don't think he ever means it to be anything else, do you?"

"Grace," the mother said sharply.

"Oh, yes, he has," Grace cried triumphantly. "You know it, but as long as nobody says it, you can pretend you don't. Well, now I'm saying it, and you'll listen to it, too. I don't care what happens any more. What does it matter what happens now? Arthur's dead. You don't even seem to know that, any of you. Arthur's dead." She leaned forward still more at the mother. "And Curt killed him. He wanted him dead, and now he's killed him. Oh, yes, he has, just as sure as if he'd shot him. And he's glad of it, do you hear me? He's dancing for joy out there. He was afraid of Arthur; Arthur was all that kept him from selling the whole valley right out from under us. He wouldn't fight for himself, but he would for the rest of us, and Curt knew

173

it. He couldn't sell us out with Arthur alive, so he killed him. Now he can do what he wants. There's nobody he's afraid of now. Oh, he's glad. Don't you ever think he isn't. And he can kill his painter and be a hero, too. He has everything, and all with the blessing of your wicked, selfish, ugly God."

She paused, breathing hard and quickly, and none of them could speak after the sound of her flying voice. After a moment, though, the father's deep voice spoke from the landing above.

"What's going on down there?"

The others were freed a little, and even in Grace herself the frightened hatred was checked. She was about to go on, but didn't. They all looked up at the old man, the mother moving out of the doorway to see him. He appeared huge up there in the shadow. His hair was on end in the little flame shapes and his clothes were creased and twisted from his restless sleep. He was holding himself steady with his left hand on the rail, and cradling a new whisky bottle in his right arm, like a baby.

"You all deaf?" he asked. "What's going on? I want to know. All this screaming?" He stared down through narrowed eyes at Grace.

"Don't ask me," Grace cried. "Ask Mother." She pointed at the mother. "Ask her. She's the one that started it."

"Your daughter has been screaming blasphemous nonsense," the mother said stiffly. "But we've listened to about enough of it now, I think." She turned to Grace. "You get back in that bunk-room and stay there till you can keep a decent tongue in your head."

"Screaming nonsense, have I?" Grace cried at her. She looked up again at the old man on the landing. "She's sending Gwen home. And she's sending her up to the bunk-house to wait. She's sending her up there where she'll have Joe Sam for company, and he's drunk, and God only knows what he'll do. And then . . ."

The mother's voice came over hers, saying fiercely, "Grace, you get back in that bunk-room. You hear me?"

"Lettie," the father said angrily, "have you gone crazy? She can't stay up in that bunk-house with that old fool. Nobody knows what he'll do when he's got one of these idiot spells. What on earth gave you such a notion?"

Nobody answered him. Nobody could answer that question when he asked it from up there, like a chairman on a platform.

"What did she do? I asked you."

"Yes, ask her," Grace cried. "She's the eye of God. She's the one that saw it."

"Saw what?"

"Awful things," Grace cried. "She saw them from the window."

Gwen made a little, choking sound, and turned suddenly toward the door again.

"No, Gwen," Harold cried. She was already struggling blindly with the latch when he caught her. She wrestled to free herself, but kept working at the latch too, and crying, "Let go of me. Let go of me, I tell you." Finally, breaking half-free, she struck at him, so that he had to let go. She got the latch to work then, and pulled the door open and stumbled out, beginning to weep so they could hear her. Outside, on the snow, Harold caught her again, pleading, "Gwen, Gwen."

The others, watching through the open door, saw her face turned up at him furiously, her eyes blind with tears, and heard her cry, "You God-Almighty Bridges. There's nobody good enough for you, is there? To hell with you all too, then. I'll get my dirty, foreign muck out of here so fast . . ." Her voice broke, choked off by a sob, and Harold, holding her with both hands now, said something they couldn't hear, still pleading with her.

"No," Gwen cried, twisting harder to get free. "No, you won't. I'll go by myself. Let go of me, will you? Even a whore wouldn't take any help from you now, not any of you."

The mother crossed to the outside door and closed it. With her back against the door, she said, "We've heard about enough of that, I guess. What decent woman would be screaming things like that?"

Grace cried up at the father, "She was only saying what Mother called her, and you. Mother called her a whore."

"I saw them," the mother said in the deep voice.

"Eh?" the old man said. "Saw who?" he asked.

"Those two out there. That little easy woman, and your son."

The father lurched against the rail, bending dangerously far over it, but then pushed himself up again. "Easy woman?" he asked.

"That Gwendolyn Williams. You get back to bed now, Pa. You ain't fit to be up. I'll take care of this nonsense."

The old man still stood there above them, though, searching in the mist of his mind, repeating Gwen's name twice in a question to himself. At last he said happily, "Oh, the little dark one. Curt's intended." After a moment, he frowned and said heavily, like a man who is very patient but pushed near his limit, "And what's she done now?"

"There's no need to bother now," the mother said. "She's took care of it herself. You heard her. You go finish your sleep."

"What's she done? I asked you," the father said loudly.

"What would you expect a whore to do?"

"Don't you believe her," Grace cried. "She says she saw them. All right, then, make her tell you what she saw, not just keep calling her names."

"Grace," the mother said, starting away from the door, "did you hear what I told you? I ain't gonna say it again."

"Make her tell you," Grace cried.

"Yes, by God," the father said. "Hiding things from me again. Always hiding things. Well, not this time, not after all this uproar. You tell me now, you hear?"

The mother stopped by the table, and turned up at him the knife face her will made in anger. "You want to know? You want to make me talk about such things? All right, then. They was actin' up right up by the bunk-house, in broad daylight. I seen 'em myself, from the bedroom window. And Arthur lyin' right there beside me, not a day dead. Is that the kind of a woman you want in your house? Is that the kind you want your own son marryin'?"

"No, by God," the father began.

"She's lying again," Grace cried. "Can't you see she's lying? Acting like what?" she cried at the mother.

"Acting like what?" the father repeated. "Yes," he said, with sudden rage, "lying to me. All the time lying. I won't stand any more of this goddam lying, you hear me?"

"I'll get Harold," Grace cried triumphantly. "He'll tell you." But the father had come upon something sure in his own

176

mind. He chuckled. Grace and the mother both stared up at him. He leaned over the rail and grinned at the mother, blinking slowly, and shook his head three or four times.

"No, they wouldn't," he said. He chuckled again. "Not in all that snow, they wouldn't."

"If Harold hadn't seen me watching them . . ." the mother began.

"You see?" Grace cried at the father. " 'If,' she says. She didn't see anything."

"She was kissing him," the mother declared, "and the way no decent woman . . ."

"Kissing," the father said loudly. He lurched again, and again caught himself on the rail, and hung there, staring down at her. "Kissing," he said again, his head jerking from the violence with which he said the word. "Now, you listen to me, old woman." He worked himself around and started down the stairs, taking them one at a time and with the help of the rail, but as fast as he could. He was breathing hard through his nose.

"And for that she calls her a whore," Grace cried.

"Grace," the mother said, the little furies dancing behind her eyes, "I told you to keep out of this, and I ain't gonna tell you again. You've made trouble enough already."

"I've made trouble?" Grace cried.

The father didn't seem to hear either of them. His anger had already sunk into a muttering petulance against the stairs. He'd heard the words, though. At the foot of the stairs, leaning against the rail, he said, "All women are whores at heart."

He was pleased at having mastered the stairs, and now his own words pleased him too. He repeated them. "Yessir, all women are whores at heart." He chuckled.

"Harold," the mother said.

"Only," he said, "some's honest whores, and some gets religion." He made a foolish, thin little laugh. "You got a good enough price yourself, old woman," he said, grinning. "The best of them would have settled for clothes and a carriage, but what did you charge me, huh? I'll tell you what you charged me. My life, that's what you charged me, my whole damn life. And no fun for my money either."

"I ain't gonna stand here . . ." the mother began.

"Oh, yes, you are," he said. He lurched a little, and thrust his head forward. "It's a fact," he said grinning. "Most expensive whore in the whole damn world, and no damn good. A clothes-pin in bed, a goddam, 'normous, wooden clothes-pin. There." He nodded happily, and uncorked the bottle and lifted it to his lips with his head tilted back. "Gotta keep drinkin'," he burbled around the bottle, "just' to forget the goddam, 'normous wooden clothes-pin."

The mother stared at him. Her face was gray, and the grooves of time and labor and war with herself grew deeper while she stood there. Finally she spoke slowly, and almost as thickly as he had spoken.

"Is that all it means to you, a lifetime of slavin' and lookin' out for you, and bearin' you four young uns?"

The father let the bottle down a little and said cheerfully, "That's all," and lifted the bottle and drank again. Then he lowered it all the way and corked it. He cradled it in his arm once more and leaned across the rail, twisting sideways. "You think I'm too drunk to know what I'm saying. Not though. Everybody saying just what they think, so I am too. Know what I'm saying. Just what I think." He began the whinnying laugh again, but broke it off short as his head drooped and rolled toward his shoulder. He jerked it up after a moment and peered at the mother. She hadn't moved from where she'd been standing the whole time.

All at once Grace stirred herself. She crossed swiftly to the foot of the stairs and stood right below the old man.

"Father," she said, and then again, "Father."

Finally the father's head turned slowly, and he squinted to see her too. "What you want?"

"You won't let her send Gwen away, will you?"

"No," the old man said, speaking angrily, because she asked the question so urgently. "Course not. Stay if she wants to."

"And she can come down here, can't she? You won't let Mother keep her up there in the bunk-house with Joe Sam?"

"Course not," the old man said. "My house. Have who I want in it."

Still standing there on the other side of the table, the mother asked slowly, "You want a woman like that in your house?"

For a moment the old man didn't seem to understand where the question had come from. Then he let his head roll back again, and peered at the mother. "Eh?" he asked. "What's that?"

"I asked do you want that kind of a woman in your house?"

The father kept staring at her till it seemed he hadn't understood, or had already forgotten the question. Then suddenly he chuckled, and leaned over loosely and pointed at her. "Clothespin," he said. "You damn right," he said. "Gotta have whore inna house anyway, have a good whore. Only one around here does anything anyway. Not a damn clothes-pin."

"If that's the last word you have . . ." the mother began heavily.

"Father," Grace cried. She put her hand over his on the rail. "You can't just say that. She's got to apologize. Mother's got to apologize. Gwen can't . . ."

"Grace," the mother said, "ain't you heard enough . . ."

"Father," Grace said again.

"Shut up," the father said suddenly and loudly. "Both of you shut up," he said. "Clothes-pins, both of you. Not women at all. Not human. Goddam clothes-pins."

The room was very quiet for a moment, save for his loud, enraged breathing. Then the anger passed slowly from his face. He appeared to have remembered something which made him very sad.

"Man's gotta have a drink, anyway," he said finally, and balancing himself against the rail, began to struggle with the cork of his bottle. Suddenly he stopped and frowned. "Yes," he said to himself. " 'Pologize. You hear me, old woman," he said, staring at the mother. "You 'pologize. Good girl. Only one around here does anything. Got my breakfast even. Curt's intended too. Then you call her names like that. You 'pologize. Understand?"

The mother just stared back at him.

"You hear me, woman?" he yelled.

"I hear you. Anybody could hear you, up to the crick."

"All right. You better. You 'pologize. Go 'pologize now. Understand?"

"No," the mother said finally. "You can do as you please with her. From now on you can all do as you please about everything. Only I warn you," she said, her voice rising a little, and the tiny furies beginning to dance in her eyes again, "don't you bring her anywheres near me." She came quickly around the table, not looking at either of them, and stalked into the bedroom and across it, and stood in front of the north window. She stood there for a long time, with her back turned to the door, and her arms down stiffly at her sides.

The father carefully let himself down until he was seated on the second step, and got his bottle uncorked again, and drank from it. Grace waited at the foot of the stairs, still clinging to the newel post.

The old man wiped the trickling liquor from his chin with his sleeve and then corked the bottle again. "Curt's intended," he said mournfully. "Talk about her own son's intended that way. Be Curt's wife."

Grace closed her eyes and leaned her forehead against the post for a moment. In the bedroom the mother let herself down into her chair and took the big Bible into her lap, but then did not open it, but only sat staring across the bed and out the west window.

Grace opened her eyes and sighed, and came around to the foot of the stairs. She knelt below the old man, and put a hand on his knee. "Father," she said softly.

"Eh?"

"We mustn't let Mother send Gwen away. She has to apologize, or Gwen'll go, Father."

"Course," the old man agreed. "Said so, didn't I? Curt's intended."

"Harold's, Father."

"Eh?" said the old man. "What?" He thought about it. " 'Sright," he said finally, "Harold's." He seemed cheered by the discovery. "Better," he said, nodding. "Much better. Curt marry some decent American girl now, not little foreign whore."

Slowly Grace took her hand from his knee and stood up. She stood for a minute staring down at him, and then turned and started toward the bunk-room. Half way there, between the table and the stove, she stopped and began to turn around, but then changed her mind again. Very slowly, like one feeling her way, she went to the table and stood with her hands on the back of the mother's chair. Finally she leaned over and picked up Arthur's little carving of the sheepherder, but listlessly, as if it didn't matter to her. Then she turned and went on into the bunk-room and closed the door very slowly and quietly.

The old man sat alone on the stairs, cradling his bottle. A long time passed, with only the clock and the fire sounding in the room. Then he spoke.

"Not going upstairs," he said stubbornly.

He hoisted himself to his feet and worked down the last step and around the post carefully. He made his way to the table in one tack, and then, keeping a hand on the table, got around to his place and pulled out his chair. He sank into the chair suddenly, and sat there brooding and wheezing, the bottle still in his arm, his chin sunk into the folds of his neck.

A long time later, he suddenly aroused himself, and looked about as if someone had spoken. "That you, Curt?" he asked.

"Damn clock," he said finally. "Goddam clock, always tickin'."

He tried to uncork his bottle again, but gave it up this time. He lowered the bottle slowly onto the floor beside his chair. Then he let his arms slide out onto the table in front of him and pillowed his head on his right arm. Once in a while, after that, he muttered something, a protest or a lament, to the empty kitchen, but most of the time there was only his heavy breathing and the clock and the fire. Toward dusk the snow really began to come down again outside, thickly and silently, in big flakes.

16 - .- -

It was nearly dark when Harold came in. He stopped in the doorway to shake the snow from his cap and coat, and kick it gently off his boots. Then he stood there peering into the shadowy room. Only the little worms and butterflies of light from the stove moved and were distinct, but he made out the bulk of the father asleep on his arms on the table.

"Come in, Joe Sam," he said. "And close the door."

He crossed to the stove and got matches. The old Indian entered silently and closed the door and remained there against it. Harold lighted the lamp and slid it up again. Then he looked back at Joe Sam. The old man had on a coat that was much too big for him, and a black sombrero with a flat crown. There was a blue bandana tied around his head under the sombrero. His braids hung down from it, and the loose braid was all unbound now and spread over his shoulder. The new snow still clung to him, and was thick on his shoulders and hat.

Harold started to speak to him, but heard steps in the north bedroom and turned back. There was a quick scratching in there, and a white light showed through the open doorway and grew stronger and steadier. He took a deep breath and straightened himself, and crossed to the doorway. The mother was bending over the lamp, slowly bringing the wick up to where she wanted it.

"We're going now," Harold said.

The mother waited until she had the wick set. Then she drew herself slowly erect, and turned to face him.

"Going where?"

"To Williams'."

The mother just stood there, dark against the light of the lamp.

"The coffin's finished," Harold said, "and the grave's dug. We dug it up back, on the hill. But it's too late for the funeral now. I'll be back tomorrow, if I can make it."

"You'll be back?"

"For the funeral."

Finally the mother said, "You don't have to go."

"We can't stay here, that's sure."

The mother waited even longer this time, but finally said, "You can't go now, not with it snowing again."

"You didn't leave us much choice," Harold said. "Gwen'd go without me. You don't think I'd let her do that, do you?"

"You could wait till morning, anyway."

"In the bunk-house?"

The mother was silent for a long time again, but he just waited. At last she said, "You'd leave us with everything this way?"

"There's not much choice, is there?"

"No," the mother said slowly, "I guess there ain't." Then she said bitterly, "Seems like I'm always the one that's wrong."

Harold's mind flared, but he thought, No more of that, and just waited again. After a minute, the mother turned away from his stare and stood looking down at Arthur. He could see then that she was twisting her hands together.

"I'm half out of my mind," she said. "I been thinkin' all day somethin's happened to Curt too. Could be I spoke too quick."

Could be, Harold thought grimly, and still wouldn't help her.

The mother let her hands down to her sides, and turned back to face him. "I don't guess it matters much what I say now. Bring the girl down here, if that's what she wants."

Harold stared at her. At last he said softly, "It's not what she wants. All she wants is to go home. She wasn't even going to let me go with her."

"You needn't of been too much afeard of that, I guess."

When Harold spoke this time, it was even more softly. "All right, then, if that's the way you like it." He turned, and saw Grace standing by the table in the kitchen, watching them.

"Harold," the mother said.

He waited, with his back to her.

"I said more than I should of, I guess," she said. "Do you want I should go up and tell her that?"

He turned to face her again, but then Grace was beside him, saying, "You'd better let Harold go, Mother, or me."

"You'll have to beg her pardon," Harold said.

"Oh, she will," Grace said quickly. "You will, won't you. Mother?"

"I'm not the only one around here that said too much."

"I know, I know. I said terrible things, Mother, and I'm sorry. But you'll say that much to Gwen too, won't you? That you're sorry? We can't let her go like this, Mother."

"No," the mother said slowly, "seems like we can't."

"You'll tell her you're sorry, Mother?"

The mother nodded.

"I'll go get her to come down." Before either of the others

183

could speak, she ran over to the pegs by the door and took down the first coat she got hold of, and struggled into it. It was Curt's red mackinaw, and it was much too big for her. She had trouble getting her hands out of the sleeves far enough to open the door. Harold started toward her, saying, "Grace, wait," but before he could get to her, she had the door open.

"Grace," he said again.

"No, Harold, you better let me," she said, and slipped out into the snowy darkness, and closed the door.

Harold opened the door and called after her, "Grace," but she didn't answer. He went outside and called, "Grace, take it easy." She didn't answer this time either, and he couldn't see her out there. He started toward the corner of the house, but then stopped. After a moment he went on again, more slowly, and stopped at the corner, and stood there looking up at the lighted bunk-house window. He saw the angle of light when the door opened, and Grace's small, dark figure go in, and then there was only the window showing again. He waited there, staring up into the darkness, until a gust of wind full of snow blinded him. He bent his head against it, and when it eased off, turned and went back slowly. The kitchen door was still open. He went in and closed it behind him. He was startled, then, to see Joe Sam looking at him out of the shadowy corner between the bunk-room door and the stove. He had forgotten that the old Indian was in there. He was half-sitting on the wood-box, with his hands hanging limp between his knees, and he still had on the big coat and the black sombrero.

"You better take off your things, Joe Sam," Harold said. "We won't get at the chores for a while yet."

The good eye, gleaming steadily in the shadow, seemed to be looking at him, but Joe Sam just sat there, and didn't answer. Harold didn't want to say anything more, with the father asleep there under the lamp, and the white light in the door of the north bedroom, but everything quiet in there too. He went slowly over to the table, and pulled out Arthur's chair, lifting it so it wouldn't scrape, and setting it down again carefully too. He sat down in it and looked at the big, gray head in the circle of light, and the little, flame-shaped locks standing up on it.

I ought to get him up to bed, he thought. If he wakes up

when they come back, and puts in his two-bits' worth, but then put that idea aside also, at the thought of the old man's voice in the quiet, and the ridiculous struggle to get him up the stairs.

If only Grace don't go at it the way she did at mother here, he thought uneasily. Even if she gets Gwen to come down that way, it'll only set her dead against us.

The waiting became very long with only the clock ticking and the slow, heavy snoring of the father.

Well, he thought, I can see to their fire, anyway, and got up and went into the bunk-room, being as quiet as he could in his boots. The fire was out, and the room was cooling fast. There was a faint sweetness of women in the air that made the place strange, and made him feel like an intruder. The stool Gwen had sat on was still there beside Arthur's bunk, and the hollow Grace's head had made in the pillow was still there too. Arthur's little carvings lay every which way in the wrinkles of the blankets. Gwen hadn't left much mark of herself, though. She'd used his bunk, and it was made up smooth now, with the top quilt pulled up over the pillow. The only thing he could see that belonged to her was the canvas satchel with the leather handles on it, and her initials stamped on the side of it in big, broken letters, G.A.W. The satchel was sitting in the middle of the neat bunk. It looked as if she had been thinking about going away all the time, or at least ever since the father had called her names, and accused her of causing the trouble.

Harold wanted to go over and put his hands on the satchel, because it was hers, but it made him feel sneaky just to think about it, with that woman smell in the room, and Gwen so angry with him now. He stood looking at the satchel for a minute, and then went over to the stove and shook down the ashes and laid a new fire and lit it. When the small wood was burning surely, and he could begin to feel the heat working out, he put in a couple of chunks, and then went back into the kitchen. From in front of the stove, he could see that the mother was kneeling by the bed in the north room again. It made the quiet of the house more oppressive than ever to see her back at her praying, and it made him angry too.

Half an hour of that, and we'll be right back where we started from, he thought.

He moved over to the table and stood looking down at the father again, without seeing him. Finally he went into the store room and came back out with one arm full of potatoes. He closed the store-room door carefully, and almost tiptoed over to the sink board, and let the potatoes down onto it one at a time. He got out a pan and a paring knife and began to peel the potatoes slowly, taking off straight slices that were too thick, and putting the square, peeled potatoes into the pan. It got night dark in the windows while he worked, and the wind came up outside again so he could hear it roaring in the pines and slithering the snow across the panes.

Then, finally, he heard the latch of the outside door click. He turned around quickly, and saw Gwen come in, and then Grace behind her. Grace's face, looking at him over Gwen's shoulder, was still too bright eyed and triumphantly pale, in the way he didn't trust, but Gwen looked at him out of the shadow of her hood and looked away again at once. She moved into the room a couple of steps, to let Grace in behind her, and then stood there, the way Joe Sam always did.

"This is the worst yet," Grace said, in that high, happy voice. She closed the door briskly, like a person with a thousand things to do and eager to be at them. "A little more and you could get lost between here and the bunk-house," she said happily. "We could hardly see the light."

Gwen began to brush the snow, that was fine as salt now, from her cloak, and then leaned over to brush the heavier snow from the hem of her skirt. She didn't look at either of them.

"I put some more wood in the stove for Joe Sam," Grace said. "His fire'll keep till bedtime. Is she in there still?" she asked.

Harold stood there holding the paring knife in one hand and a half-peeled potato in the other, and kept looking at Gwen. He just nodded to answer Grace.

"Good heavens, Harold," Grace cried, "you're taking half the potato with the skin. You poor boy, peeling potatoes. You let them wait now. We'll get our little formalities over with, and then Gwen and I'll get supper in a couple of shakes."

While she spoke, she took off Curt's red coat and hung it on the back of the chair nearest her, and then brushed at the snow on her skirt with the same busy cheerfulness her voice had.

Harold looked at her, thinking, If she starts on Mother like that.

"She's praying again now," he said. "Maybe we'd better . . ."

"There's no use putting it off," Grace said. She came over and took the knife and the potato from him, and put them on the sink board. "Everything will go better once we get that settled, better for all of us." She started toward the bedroom, her chin lifted a little, and that hopeful half-smile on her mouth. "Mother," she called cheerfully.

The father stirred and muttered in his sleep.

Gwen said, "No, Grace, let her be."

Grace stopped in the bedroom doorway and turned around. The white, excited shining of her face was already beginning to fade. "There's no use putting it off," she said again, but not so quickly or so clearly.

Gwen moved over into the light by the table, but still with her cloak on and the hood up to conceal her face. "Let it go for now," she said. "She sent you up, and that's good enough."

Nobody sent her, really, Harold thought. She took it all on herself.

As if to speak for him, the mother's voice, the deep voice like a man's, said from the doorway, "I didn't send her. It was her own idea."

Harold turned, and Grace moved over against the stairs quickly, and they were all three looking at the mother. The light behind her was stronger than the light in the kitchen, so they could see her face only dimly, but the tall figure in distinct silhouette, the narrow body rising out of the skirt that filled the lower part of the doorway.

"I had a notion to come myself," she said clearly, "but Grace thought better not. I got a stiff tongue at the best of times, and it don't limber up none owning I'm wrong."

"It's all right, Mrs. Bridges," Gwen said.

"No, no it ain't," the mother said, almost triumphantly. "I should of come myself. I been upset kind of, but that ain't no excuse. I said more'n I meant, and I should of come myself."

"I know," Gwen said. "I understand."

"No. I made a promise, and a promise I make, I keep. I want you should hear it from me. I would of come up there myself, only it seems like I ain't to be trusted now, not even by my own children. There, I've owned I said too much. You can put your pride away now, and maybe poor Arthur will get a little peace anyway. I won't hinder you no more, anything you want to do. Seems my ways, and the Lord's too, for the matter of that, don't hold around here no more."

Now she's done it, the old bitch, Harold thought fiercely. "Gwen," he said quickly, and turned toward her.

But Gwen just stood very straight where she was, and looked back at the mother, and said, "If you want me to go, I'm sure . . ."

"It's not what I want any more," the mother said.

"As far as I'm concerned," Gwen began, but the father's voice interrupted her, asking thickly and loudly, "What's the matter? What's going on here?"

They all looked at him. He was holding his head up with difficulty, only a little off his arm, and peering across at them. But he didn't say anything else, and the mother looked at Gwen again.

"Don't talk like a fool," she said. "You couldn't go any place on a night like this if you wanted to." She turned and went back into the bedroom.

"What ails her now?" the father asked.

"It's nothing, Father," Grace said.

"Gwen, listen," Harold said, coming beside her and taking hold of her arm gently.

"It's always nothing," the father said angrily. "What's she talking about? I asked you."

"She meant it all right, at first," Harold pleaded. "It's only that she gets her pride up when she starts to talk. She knows she was wrong. And we want you to stay, we all do. You know that."

Gwen still wouldn't look at him, but she put her right hand out from under her cloak and patted his hand that was holding her arm. "She's right enough about one thing, anyway," she said. "We can't go now. So let's not talk about it, shall we?"

She turned away from him and went quickly across to the clothes pegs, and stood there in front of them, with her back to the room.

"Talk about what?" the father asked loudly, and thumped the table with his fist.

"Please, Father," Grace cried. "It's all done with."

"All done with, is it? Now, you listen to me, young lady," he said angrily, and tried to rise, but lurched to the side and kicked over the whisky bottle. He looked down at it, and said, "Oh, oh," and sat back in the chair again, and leaned over and picked up the bottle. He cradled it in his arm and began to pat it. "Almost spilled it," he murmured.

Gwen swung her cloak off suddenly and hung it up, and turned back to face them, saying, "It's time we got some supper."

The father stopped patting the bottle and looked at her, startled. He watched her cross the room and pick up the knife and the half-peeled potato from the sink board.

"There's sensible girl," he announced finally. "Glad somebody's got some sense left. Have to eat, no matter what happens." He thought about that. "Just time for one more little drink before we eat," he said finally. He set the bottle on the table and sat forward and began trying to uncork it.

Harold came to the side of his chair in two strides and took the bottle out of his hands and yanked the cork out so it popped loudly. Then he got a glass off the sideboard, poured it a third full, and set it in front of the old man. He corked the bottle again, and set it down sharply beside the glass.

The father's red, searching eyes found him then. He nodded, making it almost a sitting bow. "Thank you, my boy," he said. He raised his head heavily to look at Harold again, and then let it swing back down of its own weight. After a moment he remembered the glass of whisky and held it up and peered at it, grinning.

"One true friend of man," he declared.

He drank half the whisky, and said, "Ah," and set the glass down again.

Harold looked at Grace. "I'll get at the chores," he said. "I'll be done by the time supper's ready."

He got the lantern from behind the stove and set it on the table and lit it. He put on his coat and cap, and came back for the lantern, and went to the door. When he opened the door, the cold wind sucked in and a thin sifting of snow came with it,

189

twisting and sliding along the planks. The roaring of the pines came in loudly too.

"Come on, Joe Sam," Harold said.

The old Indian rose from his seat on the wood-box and crossed the room silently, and went out past him into the noisy darkness.

"He'll be eating with us," Harold said. "Set him a place too."

"But if Mother . . ." Grace began.

"She'll stay in there," Harold said. "She'd damn well better," he added, with sudden fierceness, and went out, closing the door so hard the window beside it rattled more than the wind was rattling it.

- - - 17

When Harold and Joe Sam came in again, the father was already eating. Grace straightened up by the table, with the coffee pot in her hand, and said, "Mother wants to see you."

"What about now?"

Grace shook her head. "I don't know. She just said she wanted to see you as soon as you came in."

Harold took off his coat and cap and hung them up.

"Did she eat any supper?" he asked.

Grace nodded. "She drank her coffee, and ate a little meat."

"Well, that's something," Harold said. "Go ahead," he said to them all, "I'll be back in a minute," and crossed to the bedroom door.

The mother was sitting in the rocker by the bed, with the black shawl around her and her hands lying one upon the other in her lap.

"Did you want to see me, Mother?" Harold asked.

The mother didn't look around, but said, "Come in here, will you? There's no use telling our troubles to the whole world."

Meaning Gwen, he thought, and went in and stood beside

her, but looked over her at Arthur on the bed. It wasn't like Arthur sleeping there now. The long, dark hair and beard looked false around the sinking face. He looks like an old man trying to be young, Harold thought. A skinny, mean, old man. With a pot belly, too, he thought, seeing how tight the black coat had become. We keep the room too warm.

"We better have the funeral tomorrow, no matter what," the mother said.

"I guess we'd better."

"If you and Joe Sam would bring the coffin down."

"All right."

"Then I could get it ready tonight," she said.

"It's all ready."

"He can't lie on the bare boards," the mother said, more in her old tone. "I want to line it with a quilt."

After a moment, he said, "Why don't you just get the lining ready, Mother, and I'll put it in, first thing in the morning."

"I'd like to do that much myself, if I'm to be allowed now."

If you're to be allowed, he thought, but finally said, "All right, then."

"If you'd just bring me down a hammer and tacks when you come."

Just what they need to listen to all night, he thought, but said, "All right," again.

"After you've had your supper."

She began to rock the chair a little.

Enjoying herself now, Harold thought. He turned toward the door.

The mother stopped rocking. "Harold."

"Yes?"

"Are there enough good boards for another?"

Jesus, he thought violently, all his anger coming up at once, the first time she doesn't have everything her own way, she wants to bury us all. He didn't trust himself to answer, and finally she looked up at him. Then he wasn't so sure. If I'm tired, he thought, think what she must be.

"It's no good trying to fool ourselves," the mother said tonelessly. "Not after two days, and all this snow."

"He's been out longer'n that, lots of times, Mother," Harold said. And if he doesn't get back, he thought, we won't need any coffin.

"It was never like this," the mother said. "I know. I can feel it. Well," she said, sighing, and looking away from him at the proud unicorn in the center of the bedspread, "it don't matter right now. It's just I keep thinkin' of things, settin' here with nothin' to keep me busy." Then suddenly she buried her face in her hands, and cried thinly, "Oh, what have I done, that the Lord should turn on me like this?"

For a moment Harold could only stare at her, his own will draining out with hers. Then he came back to her, trying to keep his boots quiet on the floor. He wanted to kneel beside her and put his arm around her, but even now he couldn't make himself do that. He put his hand on her shoulder, timidly.

"Mother, you got to get some sleep pretty quick. Why don't you go in our room right now, and try and get some sleep? There'll be plenty of time for everything in the morning." He closed the hand gently on her shoulder. "Please, Mother."

She shook her head, and then slowly sat up and leaned back, with her eyes closed and her hands in her lap, and Harold thought, That's the way she was when I came in. She wasn't taking it easy at all.

"I can't sleep," the mother said. "I'm better with something to keep me busy. If you'll just bring me those things when you come down." After a moment, she added fretfully, "If only that wind would stop blowing. It keeps blowing the snow against the window all the time."

Finally Harold said, "Well, we'll bring it down now."

"No," she said, without opening her eyes, "there's no such hurry as that about it. It's way late for your supper now. You get something to eat first."

When he still didn't go, she added, "I'm perfectly all right, I tell you. You go get your supper."

He thought, She's poisoning herself in here, but he couldn't think of any way to say that either, and finally turned and went back out as quietly as he could.

Grace and Gwen were already seated at the table, but they were waiting for him. Grace looked up at him, but saw his face and looked down again without asking the question. Joe Sam's place was still empty. Harold looked around. The old Indian was sitting cross-legged on the floor, with his back against the wood-box. He still had on the big coat and the black sombrero.

"Come on, Joe Sam," Harold said. "Take off your things and pull up a chair."

Joe Sam didn't move. Not even the faint glitter of his eyes changed. Harold went over to him and leaned down and put a hand on his shoulder. Joe Sam came back slowly from the distance he was watching, and looked up.

"Come to the table," Harold said. "Eat supper."

"Table?" Joe Sam asked.

"It's all right." He coaxed with his hand under Joe Sam's arm. Joe Sam did it easily, not using his hands, or any help from Harold, but just uncrossing his feet and rising silently, in one motion.

"Better take off your hat and coat," Harold said. "It's hot in here."

"Hot," Joe Sam said. He took his hat off and put it on the wood in the box, and then slowly took his coat off, and folded it carefully, and laid it down beside the hat. He followed Harold to the table like a sleep-walker, and sat down in the chair beside Gwen, when Harold pulled it out for him. He didn't look around at anybody, but right across the table, over Grace's shoulder, at the stairs. Harold sat down between him and the father. The father had finished already, and he was just sitting there now, hunched over his plate and breathing heavily. He wasn't paying any attention to anyone else.

Harold glanced several times, out of the corners of his eyes, at Joe Sam. It made him a stranger to see him sitting there at the table, very upright, and blinking slowly against the light. Grace and Gwen kept looking at him secretly too, staring at the blue bandana and the hair that had come unbraided as if they had never seen them before.

Finally Harold said, "You better eat something, Joe Sam."

The old Indian looked down at his plate, and after a moment, with all three of them watching him, picked up the two slices of beef that Gwen had put on it, and began to chew at them. After a couple of mouthfuls, he stopped chewing, and looked around at the others. He was smiling, and he looked

193

politely at each of them. "Good meat," he said. They all looked away from him then, and he finished the meat and sat there motionless and upright again, with his hands in his lap.

For a long time nobody else said anything. Then Harold set down his coffee cup and cleared his throat. He didn't want to speak, but they had to know about it before the hammering began.

"Mother wants the coffin down here tonight. She's going to line it."

They both looked at him, but then they looked down at their plates again. Neither of them said anything. Harold knew they didn't understand what he meant, but after that he wasn't going to say anything more. Even after they'd finished eating, though, they all sat there staring into the shadow under the lamp. Finally Harold roused himself and stood up. That motion, and the sound of his chair scraping on the floor, woke Grace and Gwen too. Gwen glanced at him quickly, but when she found him standing there watching her, she looked down again at once. Her face was awake and guarded now, but she sat as still as ever, and wouldn't look at him again.

Well, he thought finally, if she thinks I'm going to hang around here forever, like a bum waiting for handouts. Still, he thought, looking at the father, I can't leave her with that on her hands again. Where's he got to now? he thought, seeing the blind eyes and the anger in the big red face, and the heavy lips moving. Somebody's getting the best of him, anyway.

"Dad," he said.

The old man didn't turn his head, and the look in his eyes didn't change, but he began to speak so they could hear him. "The captain's a fool, I tell you," he said thickly. "Nineteen days now, and still nothing but the same goddam head wind and the snow and the goddam axes going chop, chop, chop. When you can hear anything but the wind, it's just the goddam axes. And we're frosted up like a wedding cake. 'Turn the ship around, you goddam fool,' I told him, and he just yelped at me. He's crazy, I tell you. He don't even talk like a man any more; he barks like a dog."

He paused, wheezing like a man enraged beyond speech. "Drunk too," he added. "Drunk all the time."

Clean back to the Cape, Harold thought. He's really getting away from it this time. But not out of trouble.

"Dad," he said again.

The father drew himself up and turned his head slowly and stared at the big nickel buckle of Harold's belt. "No, sir," he began, "I tell you if we don't give . . ." but then stopped, and tried to look up far enough to see who Harold was.

"Don't you want to go to bed now, Dad?"

After a moment the old man let his head swing back, and nodded. "Go to bed," he said dully. "Never get any sleep around here. Always . . ." He let it go, and then said, more clearly, "Gotta go out first." He peered around over the table. "Where's my bottle?" he asked. "Somebody took my bottle," he muttered. "Damn, thievin', female tricks. If I . . ." but then stopped again, because he had found the bottle. He poured his glass half full, spilling some over onto the table this time. He drank the whisky off in two or three gulps, and carefully let the bottle down onto the floor again, and got to his feet very slowly, and breathing ferociously. He stood there for a moment, balancing himself on his fists on the table, and then swung around and started toward the door. He moved in wide lurches, and twice he had to stop, and peer around to discover where he was, and start over again. Harold moved over and followed close behind him, but the old man reached the door by himself and leaned against it. His breathing was like snoring now, and he rested there, with his head against the doorframe. Finally, holding onto the handle of the door with one hand, he rolled around with his back to the wall and raised the other.

"Evenin' everybody," he said, "wonnerful evenin'," and swung around to the door again and got it open.

The wind leapt in, nearly wrenching the door from him, and the snow sprayed in over him, making a fine, glittering mist in the light. He peered out into the darkness, and then looked back over his shoulder, more wakeful and completely astonished.

"Snowing," he told them.

He peered out again. "Wha's a lil snow?" he asked, and let go and stepped down into the shallow drift outside the door. The door blew wide back, and the broken crest of the drift slithered

195

in across the floor. Harold caught the door, and went out, dragging it closed after him. The old man's voice, thin and small in the gale outside, sang, ". . . play jack o' diamonds and trust to my luck," and then was gone, as the deep roaring came down the mountain again.

Without looking at Gwen, Grace said, "It's the worst I've ever seen him."

Gwen didn't answer, but Joe Sam made a small, soft sound in his throat. It might have been a chuckle, and it might not. When they looked at him, his face didn't tell them anything. His good eyes was looking at them now, though, and seeing them.

Gwen rose and began to clear the table. She moved quickly and sharply, putting the plates together too hard, and letting the knives and forks clatter on them. Grace got up slowly and began to help her.

They were washing the dishes when Harold and the father came back in. The father had a new bottle of whisky. He leaned against the door and embraced the bottle while Harold brushed the snow off him. He was quiet now, though, and his face was dull and sleepy. He let Harold help him around the table and up the stairs without saying anything. Only as they were going in through the door from the landing, he said plaintively, "Curt should be back. No night to be out. Nobody be out."

Harold came down again, and began to put on his coat and cap. "He'll stay there this time, I think," he said. He went over and took the lantern down and lit it. "Joe Sam," he said. He had to speak three times, before Joe Sam looked at him and stood up, and then he had to help him into his coat and put his hat on him. They went out, letting the sound of the storm in, and a gust filled with snow, and then shutting them away again.

Grace and Gwen finished the dishes in silence. Then Gwen went into the bunk-room, though she left the door open. Grace went slowly to the mother's place at the table, and sat down. She was still there when the heavy knocking came at the bottom of the outside door. The knocking came a second time, even louder, before she slowly got up and walked across and opened the door.

196

Harold came in first, carrying the big end of the coffin, and with the lantern hanging from his belt. The coffin was black, with a new, thin coat of paint. It looked huge, coming into the small, white room, and a strong smell of tar came with it. Joe Sam stumbled up over the sill, carrying the narrow end, and blinking against the light. There was a fine powdering of blown snow clinging all over both the men, making them almost white, except for their faces, and a sifting of dry flakes stirred like sand on the lid of the coffin. Grace closed the door and stood against it, and watched Harold and Joe Sam carry the coffin slowly around the table and into the bedroom. Their feet made a soft shuffling because they were taking such short steps, and in the bedroom door, Harold had to turn around and tilt the coffin a little to get it through.

The figure on the bed was covered with a white blanket now, and there was a folded quilt on the floor by the table. The mother stood up and pushed the rocking chair back to make room by the bed.

"Set it over here," she said, "where I'll have the light to see by."

They set the coffin down beside the bed, being very careful not to make a loud sound. Then Harold took the lantern off his belt and set it down by the coffin. He lifted the lid off the coffin, and a strong smell of wet sage came out of it, stronger even than the tar smell. He carried the lid over and stood it on end beside the wardrobe. The nails were already standing up all around the edge of it, ready to be driven in. He came back and took a hammer and a box of tacks out of the coffin and put them on the table. Then he took out the two, big, twisted pieces of wet sage and stood there holding them, one in each hand.

"He liked the smell of it when it was wet like that," he said.

The mother nodded. "You could leave it on the bed," she said.

He laid the two gray branches on the bed, one on each side of the feet under the white blanket.

The mother looked down into the coffin. The inside was still white, raw wood, and there were sage leaves scattered all over the bottom.

"I thought maybe I'd put balsam in the lining," she said.

Harold nodded.

The mother looked at Joe Sam, who was standing at the foot of the bed, looking at the long shape under the blanket. His face didn't show anything.

"That's all for now, I guess," the mother said.

"Well," Harold said, "if you want me for anything, you can send Grace up for me."

The mother looked at him, but she didn't say anything, just nodded. Harold picked up the lantern, and said, "Come on, Joe Sam," and went back out into the kitchen. The old Indian followed him silently. Harold hesitated for a moment between the stove and the table. He looked at the open doorway of the bunk-room, and then back into the white bedroom. The mother was already bending over the coffin, unfolding the quilt along the edge of it. It was a patchwork quilt, with patches of all shapes and colors on it. Some of the patches shone in the light like water, and changed color when the mother moved the quilt.

Grace was still standing by the outside door.

"I'll leave the lantern," Harold told her. He blew the lantern out and set it on the table. "If she needs me for anything, you come up and call me, will you?"

"All right," Grace said.

Harold looked at the door of the bunk-room again, but it stayed empty, with only the soft light showing in it from the lamp that was out of sight.

"And you might tell Gwen good night for me."

Grace came away from the door and stood beside the table. "You better tell her yourself," she said.

"I don't guess so. You tell her for me."

"All right," Grace said. "I'll tell her."

"And you get some sleep too."

"Oh, I will."

He tried to grin at her, and patted her arm, and said, "Come on, Joe Sam."

They went out, and Harold pulled the door closed, getting a last look at Grace, still standing there against the table, looking at nothing. Then there was only a square shaft of light coming out of the window beside them. The light spread quickly against the driven snow, and didn't reach far. When they had crossed it, the darkness was thick everywhere in front of them, and when they came around the corner of the house, the wind shut them off too.

"Keep close behind me, Joe Sam," Harold yelled, and then looked ahead again and up the slope, trying to keep the bunkhouse window in sight. Sometimes it would show brightly for an instant, but most of the time it was dim and small behind the twisting veils of the blizzard, and sometimes it almost winked out. Twice he felt Joe Sam touch him on the small of the back, to make sure where he was.

18 - - -

Harold woke gently into a deep hush in the morning. For some reason he could not remember, he felt lazy and profoundly at peace, almost happy. After a minute, he turned his head on the pillow and looked at the window. There was a little wall of snow at the bottom of each pane, and beyond them he could see huge, far-separated flakes floating down through a brightening air.

It must be pretty well snowed out, he thought, and then, remembering the sweeping blizzard of the night before, he remembered everything else that had happened too. The wall of peace that sleep, and perhaps good dreams, had raised in his mind, crumbled away. It seemed to him then that he must have slept too long, and that something had happened while he slept, something he might have prevented if he'd been awake. He threw back his blankets and started to roll up onto the edge of his bunk. Then he saw Joe Sam, and froze where he was, propped up on one elbow.

The old Indian was crouched on one knee, so close to the head of the bunk that Harold could have reached out and touched his face. He was naked again, and holding the bottle neck down against his hip, like a knife ready to be driven forward and up. He was whispering rapidly and softly, like an excited breathing, and making little, quieting motions with his left hand, as if to keep someone else still. Harold glanced quickly past the old man to see who it was, but there was only the bare floor, with a little sawdust and a few shavings on it, that he had missed when he swept up after his work. Harold looked back at the bottle neck again, to be ready to jump when it started. It didn't move, though, except to tremble a little where it was.

I can't stay here all day like this, Harold thought, and turned his head very slowly to look at Joe Sam's face. Joe Sam wasn't watching him at all; he was watching something down at the foot of the bunk. He was turned a little toward the foot of the bunk, and was holding himself ready to leap at it. Harold looked quickly down where the old man was looking, but there was nothing there either, except the shape of his own legs and feet under the covers. He didn't dare to move his feet, for fear Joe Sam would pounce on them like a cat. He was watching them like a cat watching a hole where he'd seen something move.

That's it, Harold thought, the cat. He's holding the cat back, but he's ready to help it, too. They're together. The image was distinct for a moment, but then it passed, and he wasn't so sure. Or maybe he's helping Curt, he thought. Maybe it's the cat he has cornered. What's the good of making fool guesses? he asked himself more wakefully. The old man's seeing things again, that's all that's sure.

"Joe Sam," he said quietly.

The excited whispering stopped at once, but Joe Sam still crouched there, with one hand out to hold back his invisible ally. He appeared to be holding his breath now, in order to hear better.

"Joe Sam," Harold said again, and more loudly.

Moving only his eyes, the old Indian looked up Harold's length from the feet he had been watching so intently. When he saw Harold's eyes looking into his, his body slackened a little at once, and then, gradually, the excited pleasure faded from his face. His lips, which had been drawn back in a half grin, closed over the worn stumps of his teeth, and he let the bottle neck down to the floor. Then, before Harold could speak again, he stood up and padded softly across the room and let the bottle neck down into the trash keg without a sound. More slowly, all the purpose gone out of him, he drifted back to the stove and stood beside it, holding his hands out to the cold iron. The snow light from the window revealed all the bony knots of his dark body. He began to shake heavily. He hunched and tightened himself against the shaking, but that only made it worse.

Same as it was in the corral yesterday, Harold thought. He comes out of it, and he's a hundred years old again. He swung up onto the edge of the bunk, and felt much better because he had completed the motion.

"Joe Sam," he said once more.

The old Indian looked back over his shoulder. His face was sad, and his jaw was shaking like the rest of him.

"Hello," he said.

Like it was any morning, Harold thought, and asked, "What were you after with that bottle neck?"

"No got bottle neck," the old man said finally.

Harold watched him intently, but he said nothing more, and finally he looked back at the stove. Harold shrugged his shoulders and stood up.

"You better get into your bunk. The fire's out."

The old man slowly drew his hands away from the stove and held his elbows with them, hugging himself. Still hugging himself, he moved slowly across to his bunk, but then just stood there beside it, staring down at it.

"Get in, Joe Sam. Get under the blankets," Harold said.

Still the old man just stood there, staring, until Harold began to feel uneasily that it wasn't the bunk he was looking at, but something left over from the excited dream. Then, instead of getting into the bunk, he took up the red flannel underwear that lay on top of his other clothes and began to get into it very slowly. He was shaking so badly that he had trouble balancing himself when he had to stand on one leg.

He doesn't know it, though, Harold thought, watching him. It's like he woke up into a dream, not the other way round.

"You better get under the covers and warm up first," he said.

"Whisky," Joe Sam said. "Make warm." He went on trying to get into the red underwear.

"All right. I'll get you a drink when I go down. But you better stay in bed a while first. You got the shakes bad."

"Feed chickens," Joe Sam said. He got into the underwear finally, and buttoned it and reached for his shirt.

Harold stared at him, angered in spite of himself by this stubborn, sleepy defiance. But then he thought, letting the anger pass, Better keep him where I can watch him, at that, and looked down at the boot he was holding, and began to pull it on. But no more bottle necks, he thought. We're done with bottle necks.

He slowed his dressing to let Joe Sam finish first. When the old man was dressed, he said, "You go on down, Joe Sam. I'll be along in a minute."

He stood up and crossed to the wash basin and poured it full of water. The film of ice that had formed in the night clicked faintly as it broke into the basin. Harold watched Joe Sam in the piece of mirror on the wall. It was more real, some way, than looking right at him, to see the small figure standing out so distinctly in the middle of the room in the white, snow light, and behind him, much farther behind him than they really were, so that he was standing in a long hall, the bare board wall of the other end and the pile of stove wood, with a bridle hanging from a nail above it. It was Joe Sam's dress-up bridle, and the silver studding on it made tiny points of shining. The points of shining weren't attached to the bridle. They were alive in the air by themselves.

The little, dark man in the center of the hall just stood there, looking at Harold's back. He was too small for his face to show clearly. Only his eye on the side toward the window shone by itself, like one of the silver nails. Harold wanted to turn around and look at the face that was too small to show anything in the glass. He didn't, though, but doused his face quickly with the cold water, wetting his hair too, and looked into the long hall in the mirror again. The little, dark figure was still there, but water had splashed onto the mirror, and made it appear only waveringly, and then disappear. Suddenly Harold was really afraid of the figure. It became the same dangerous stranger who had come to life before, when there were no tracks in the snow.

"You go along, Joe Sam," he said sharply, and then, ashamed of the edge in his voice, added, "You're cold enough now. Get down there and get yourself warm. I'll be down directly."

He doused his face again, and cleared his eyes, and saw the little figure in the long hall turn toward the door, appearing between water streaks and vanishing behind them. Then the door opened, making a white rectangle in the dark hall. The figure appeared in the white rectangle, and vanished from it as it had behind the water on the glass. The faraway door remained open, showing only a faintly moving whiteness, like breath on the glass.

It occurred to Harold that the figure hadn't gone through the white rectangle at all, but only across it, and that it was still in the hall, creeping along the wall toward the trash keg. In spite of himself, he turned around quickly. The long hall with the shadows he couldn't see into became the small, ordinary room, with plenty of light to show everything in it, and there was nobody else in the room. He relaxed slowly. Finally he even grinned at himself a little.

"It's me I better keep the eye on, not Joe Sam," he said.

He looked through the open door and down the hill. Only the snow-covered plane of the house roof showed, and the dark, log tower at the north end of it, with its cap of thick white. They were small and faint through the falling snow. Joe Sam wasn't in sight.

Harold quickly finished washing, wiped his face and hands and combed his hair. Then he emptied the basin into the slop pail, and straightened up and looked at the door again, and then at the window. There was still only the faraway roof and the falling snow. He went to the tool box under the sawhorses and took out a hammer and went to the trash keg. He lifted out the jagged bottle neck and laid it on the floor and smashed it into small pieces with the hammer. He swept up the pieces and dumped them into the keg. Then he dropped the hammer back into the tool box, put on his cap and mackinaw, and went out.

He was just closing the door when he saw Joe Sam. He stiffened and held his breath, because the old man was standing flat against the outside wall, so close to the door that their shoulders were nearly touching. Then he let out his breath and loosened his shoulders. Joe Sam wasn't even looking at him. He was just standing there, hugging himself and staring down dreamily at the house from under the brim of the black sombrero.

After a moment, Harold said, "Come on, Joe Sam," carefully keeping the anger out of his voice, and pulled the door to, and started down the hill. The snow was nearly to his hips now, and he had to drag his way down through it. It made a quilted hush over everything, that could be felt in the body, especially after the loud noise he'd made with the hammer in the hollow bunk-house. He looked back once, and Joe Sam was coming down right behind him, stepping carefully in his tracks in the bottom of the trench his legs were plowing. Harold smiled in his mind, and thought, He hates to leave a track. Then he thought, looking at Joe Sam's face, He couldn't help hearing me break that thing, but if he cares, he's sure keeping it to himself.

He looked out toward the valley, but in this heavy snowing, it wasn't even the beginning of a plain any longer. The white world was closed in to its smallest yet.

Gwen was alone in the kitchen when they came in. She was already dressed, wearing the bright, yellow blouse again, but her hair wasn't braided yet. Instead it was hanging in a heavy mane down her back, drawn together at the nape of her neck and tied with a yellow ribbon. Harold had never seen her with her hair down before. It was just one more little difference, but suddenly everything in the familiar kitchen was strange, the way the bunk-house had been in the mirror.

Gwen half turned around from what she was doing at the stove, and looked at him. With her hair drawn back tight that way she appeared older too. She looked very tired, and her eyes were only seeing him, not saying anything or asking anything.

"Good morning," she said, and turned back. "I'll have your breakfast ready in a few minutes," she said.

So it's still that way, Harold thought, and after a moment said, "I brought Joe Sam down too."

"I see you did," she said, turning something in the pan.

"Grace up?"

"Not yet. She didn't get much sleep."

"Then you didn't either, huh?"

"Don't bother yourself about me."

Don't think I am, he thought, with sudden anger, but waited, and finally said, "I do, though. You know that."

"Thanks," she said.

He waited again, and then said softly, "All right. Have it your own way."

Gwen didn't say anything.

So he was still in a strange place when he went around the table and into the north room. The lamp in the window was out, but everything in the white room was clear with light from the snow. The shape on the bed was still covered with the white blanket, and the smell of sage and balsam was almost strong enough to cover the other smell. The coffin was still standing where they'd set it, by the bed, but the lining was all tacked into it now. It looked queer, that soft, puffy patchwork of bright colors inside the plain wooden box that had only a thin coat of black paint. Harold looked over at the lid, leaning against the wall, and saw that there was a piece of quilt tacked onto it too.

The mother was sitting in the rocking chair beside the coffin, and Harold thought at first that she was asleep, but when he didn't speak, she opened her eyes and looked up at him.

"Ain't this snow ever gonna stop?" she asked, hardly moving her lips. She wasn't really asking a question, but just protesting faintly.

"It can't last much longer at this rate," Harold said.

The mother closed her eyes again. "We'll have the buryin' as quick as it stops," she said. "I'd like we should have a preacher for it," she added.

"Not much chance of that, I guess," Harold said.

"No," she agreed, and after a moment said, "Your pa should do the talkin', by rights, but there ain't much chance of that, either."

"No," Harold said.

"Well," the mother said finally, "we'll wrap him in that blue spread, I guess. He's always been partial to that blue spread. When he was a little feller, he was always after me to get out the blue spread so he could look at it. He'd sit there and study over it an hour at a time. Run his finger around on all the birds and trees and things like he was drawin' them hisself. Tell hisself stories about 'em while he was doin' it. They was more real to him than people that come to the house. He was a queer little feller. Had a world all his own, couldn't anybody else get into, half the time."

"I know," Harold said, and thought, Not only when he was a kid, either. "We'll clear the grave off as soon as the snow lets up," he said.

"We gotta have it today, even if the snow don't stop," the mother said.

"I know, but it's going to. Has to, the way it's snowin' now, and no wind."

The mother opened her eyes again, and looked at the coffin. "We could put him in now," she said. "While we're alone."

"All right," Harold said, and without knowing it rubbed his hands hard and slowly down his thighs. "You better let me get Joe Sam, though. Why don't you go in the kitchen and get yourself some coffee? Joe Sam and I'll take care of it."

"I don't know," the mother said wearily. "I don't like too much he should do it, a last Christian duty like that."

After a moment Harold said, "Arthur thought a lot of him."

"I know that. More than he did of the rest of us, I thought sometimes."

"You better let us do it, Mother."

She sat so long, motionless and with her eyes closed, that he began to wonder if she'd fallen asleep, but finally she asked, "Is that Gwen Williams getting breakfast?"

"Yes, it is."

Again the mother waited some time before she spoke. "I'll just go in your room and lie down a while, I guess. You could bring me some coffee when it's ready."

And she's still at it too, Harold thought wearily.

"All right," he said.

The mother opened her eyes and sat up. After a moment she took firm hold upon the arms of the chair and pushed herself to her feet. She faltered when she let go of the chair, though, and Harold quickly put a hand to her arm-pit to steady her. When she was sure on her feet, she stiffened against his hold.

"I can do for myself, thanks."

Harold let go of her. She stood there looking down at the shape under the white blanket for a minute, and then turned and walked slowly into the kitchen. She went across the kitchen the same way, without looking around, and into the bunk-room, and closed the door again behind her. Harold followed her into the kitchen, and stopped by the table. Gwen was standing at the stove, where the mother had almost brushed her going by. She was holding the long fork in her hand, and looking at the bunk-room door.

"She's going to lie down for a while," Harold said.

Gwen looked down at the fork, and said, "Your breakfast's all ready."

"Could you keep it a couple of minutes?"

"Whenever you're ready," Gwen said.

"Joe Sam," Harold said.

The old Indian stood up in his place by the wood-box and started toward the outside door. He still had his coat and hat on.

"Could you give me a hand in here?" Harold said.

He went back into the bedroom. Joe Sam came in after him, and stood at the foot of the bed, where he had stood the night before.

"We have to put him in the coffin, Joe Sam."

"Put Arthur in?"

He doesn't like it, Harold thought. Doesn't want to touch it, or maybe it's the coffin that bothers him. Wants it done some other way, maybe. Right into the ground. Or even one of those crow's-nest burials. He studied the old face, but couldn't guess anything from it.

"That's the way Mother wants it."

"Not like," Joe Sam said.

"Maybe not, but that's the way we'll do it."

"Arthur not like," Joe Sam said.

What the hell does it matter, coffin or crow-bait? Harold thought, staring at him. It's not Arthur anyway, this bloated old man with a profit-counting face. When he didn't answer, Joe Sam looked at him, and the retreat took place in his good eye, the way it did when Curt bullied him.

"Woman say so, I not care," he said.

The hell you don't, Harold thought. He lifted the two branches of sage off the white blanket and laid them on the floor. He stood beside the bed for a moment then, holding his hands against his thighs again, but finally set his mouth straight and tight, and moving quicker and harder than the task needed, drew back the white blanket and let it fall over the foot of the bed. He held his eyes from looking at the face, and he was holding his breath too. Joe Sam, though, was looking down the length of the body at the face. He was seeing it, and he had thoughts about it.

"We'll wrap him in the blue spread," Harold said. "He liked the blue spread. He liked the pictures on it. Even when he was a kid he used to look at them all the time. He'll like that."

He spoke rapidly, almost chattering, while he kept his eyes nearly blind and made his hands quickly lift the head and draw the pillow from under it. He dropped the pillow on the floor and then lifted that side of the blue spread and laid it over the body as far as it would go. Then the face was covered again too.

"Good blanket," Joe Sam said. He touched the blue spread with his fingertips, where it was turned over the feet. Then he moved around to the other side of the bed, before Harold could, and lifted the other half of the spread and folded it over too. Harold waited at the foot of the bed, a little ashamed that the old man should be finishing the task for him, but relieved too. He watched the dark, gnarled hands fold the spread into itself all the way down, and then turn the corners in again over the feet and at the throat, so it would hold.

Like he was alive still, Harold thought. Like wrapping a baby or a sick man. And gentle as a woman at it. It suits him better than the coffin.

He woke himself from the thoughts, and looked across at Joe Sam. The old Indian was just standing there beside the bed, waiting for what came next. Harold went around beside the coffin again, and pushed back the rocking chair, and picked up the pillow. He laid the pillow in the big end of the coffin and smoothed it and straightened up again. Then he made a little motion toward the feet of the blue-wrapped shape. When Joe Sam had moved down there and slid his hands under the feet, Harold made his mind blank and set himself to endure the touch and the stiff weight. He pulled the body over at an angle, so he could get hold under both shoulders, and then the two of them lifted it. It wasn't as bad as he'd made himself ready for. The body sagged a little, but not enough to make trouble, and it wasn't as heavy as he'd expected, either. He breathed hard and slowly, and was afraid the head would roll off the arm he had under it, but actually they lifted the body evenly between them and let it down slowly into the coffin, until it settled into the quilt and the pillow, and nothing went wrong.

Harold straightened up at the head of the coffin, and stood there steadying his breath and wiping his hands slow and hard on his jeans again. Joe Sam waited at the foot of the coffin. Both of them were still looking at the long, narrow mummy the blue spread made.

Harold's mind took hold again, and he thought, No damn line-up, like a church. No going around it, staring in. There's no knowing what she'd think of to do. If we put the lid on now, she can't.

He leaned over and picked up the two branches of sage and pushed them down into the coffin beside the legs. Then he went around the coffin and Joe Sam and picked up the padded lid in both hands and came back with it. But then he had to stand there and hold it, because Joe Sam was kneeling beside the coffin, leaning over it so the hair of his loose braid hung inside. He was reaching in by the head with one hand. When he took the hand away, Harold saw that he'd left a little, buckskin pouch between the bulges made by the chin and the crossed hands. There was a pattern of black and white porcupine quills around the pouch, a line of little wedges, like birds flying in a row.

His medicine pouch, Harold thought. He looked at the shape of what was in the pouch, and thought, One of the black paint-ers Arthur made him.

Joe Sam took something out of his coat pocket and reached into the coffin again. He did this three times. Then there was a red tobacco tin lying on one side of the head, and on the other side there were five arrowheads in a line, like the flying quills on the pouch. One of the arrowheads was white quartz and one was a dull, hard red, like dried blood. The other three were shiny black obsidian. There was a thin band of yellow buckskin stretched across the forehead of the shrouded figure too. It had a quill pattern on it, like the one on the pouch, and a row of small, iridescent, green and black feathers sewed along one edge of it. Two little rawhide tie-thongs, with beads on them, hung down from each end of the band.

I wonder how he makes a warrior out of Arthur? Harold

thought, and then, But maybe the feathers can mean something else too. And then, looking at the feathers, he knew where they came from. They were from the neck and shoulders of the bantam cock.

Joe Sam was standing up, waiting for him to put the top on. "That's fine, Joe Sam. He'll like that," Harold said.

The old man looked at him, showing nothing in his face, only waiting, and he felt how bad his words had been.

Get it over with, he thought. Anything anybody could say would be bad, and laid the lid down carefully, and set it so the nail points were in the holes they'd started. Only then, when he stood up and looked down, and there was only the black, flat-sided shape of the coffin, did he feel how final the act was. The loss and the love came together strongly in him, making a real prayer, although he didn't bother with any words, only Arthur's name repeating itself in his mind. He looked up, and Joe Sam was holding out the hammer to him. He took it. Then he thought of Grace and the father still sleeping, and said, "Close the door, will you, Joe Sam?"

The old man went over and closed the door softly, and stayed there against it. Even then the pounding seemed to make a terrible din in the small, white room. Harold screwed up his face against the sound, and struck the first nails awkwardly, needing extra blows. After that he did better, driving each nail in with just two blows, but even so, when he had driven in the last nail, and stood up again, he felt the hammering still going on in his head. There was a fine sweat on his forehead, and his hands were shaking a little. He laid the hammer carefully on the table, not making a sound with it, and then, more to steady himself than for any other reason, straightened the bed, moulding it with his hands to take the long shape of the body out of it, folded the white blanket and draped it over the footboard, and opened the north window a crack. The cold, clean air sucked in, breaking the powdery top layer off the snow that had piled up on the sill and blowing it over the table. Then he turned back. Joe Sam opened the door, and he went out into the kitchen. Joe Sam followed him, and pulled the door closed.

Grace was standing by the stove, sipping at a mug of coffee. She had on a blue flannel dressing gown, pulled close around her throat, as if she were cold, and her hair was hanging loose down her back and in front of her shoulders. Gray hairs showed in it that were hidden when it was done up. Her face was very white, with great dark hollows under the eyes. She let the cup down, and Harold saw that her hand was shaking.

"That hammering," she said, and her mouth trembled too.

"I'm sorry," Harold said.

"It isn't just now," Grace said. "She was hammering in there all night. She'd hammer, and you could hear it echoing all over, as if there wasn't anything in the house."

"Everything's ready," Gwen said, setting the first two plates on the table. "You'd better eat something too, Grace."

"No, I couldn't," Grace said. "Is it going to be today?" she asked Harold.

Gwen put two more plates onto the table, and began to pour coffee into the mugs.

"I guess so," Harold said. "If this snow'll let up."

Grace sat down at the table and went on sipping her coffee, not looking at anybody, but only into the center of the table, where the light from the window made a faint shining.

Joe Sam sat down in his place without anybody speaking to him. He watched Gwen and Harold sit down, and glance at each other, and then quickly down at their plates. He kept on watching them from under the brim of the black sombrero, and again his presence grew until they could not speak or move easily before him. He seemed to fill the room, and to be the only real thing in it.

19 ‑ ‑ ‑

All morning, while the falling snow thinned out and the air grew colder and brighter around them, Harold and Joe Sam shoveled paths and did the chores, forking hay out of the shed for the horses and off the stacks for the cattle, and feeding the hogs and the chickens. Joe Sam worked slowly and dreamily, and often Harold, looking back in the trench they were cutting through the drifts, would see him just standing there, leaning on his shovel and staring out over the piled snow at the mountain or across the valley. He'd have to speak to him two or three times to wake him. Only while they were clearing the chicken run, and the space behind the bunk-house to feed the birds on, did he work steadily. He scattered the grain on both clearings too, but even the ritual of feeding the chickens wasn't quite the same as usual. His face remained expressionless and his vision turned inward even at the very end, while he held the grain down in his hands for the bantams to pick at. Harold stopped work for a few minutes to watch him, though, and was cheered a little because the vain bantam cock was still there with his hen.

He must have been saving up the feathers for a long time, he thought. There were fifteen or twenty of them on that bonnet, anyway.

When the chores were done, they dug a path up the hill behind the house to the woodpile, and then on up to the open grave under the pines. The wind was beginning to move on the mountain by then, and they were showered repeatedly by long, glittering veils falling away from the boughs above them. When Harold stopped to rest, and looked out over the house at the valley, he could see faint shadows racing across the open under the surface-scud, and even the solid, white shapes of the hills on the other side beginning to show here and there. By the time Gwen came out to the corner of the house and called up to them that lunch was ready, a great, formless shifting of half-light and faint shadow was going on everywhere beyond her. Harold was almost ashamed, when he thought of what they were doing now, and of Curt out there somewhere in the white sea of mountains, to feel how life and meaning came back into everything when he heard her voice calling his name, and looked, and saw her down there. The sound of that life was in his voice answering her, too, but before it was quiet, even, she had disappeared behind the house again, without replying. The world darkened and emptied again, and he set his jaw, thinking, Am I to blame for my whole damn family too? But he couldn't keep up the temper while he was swinging the shovel, and after it came the familiar despair, and he thought, Well, aren't I, as far as she's concerned?

He and Joe Sam finished clearing the grave, and a path around it, and stood their snow shovels up in the mound on the north side of the grave, with the shovels that had dug the earth, and went down to the house.

Gwen was still quiet and apart, and Joe Sam didn't eat, or even drink his coffee this time, but only sat there, straight and motionless, with his hat and coat and the blue bandana on. There were only the three of them in the kitchen, and nobody spoke. Harold and Gwen tried to eat, but mostly they poked at their food or just sat studying their plates. It was only when Harold stood up that Gwen finally broke the silence.

"Your mother said to tell you it wouldn't be till later, not till about sundown."

"Changed her mind again?"

"I don't know. She just told me to tell you."

"She's still hoping Curt will get back," Harold said finally.

"Maybe. She didn't say."

Harold felt the little anger against her rise in him once more. He waited until it sank back, and said, "I'll take the drag down on the meadows, then. The stock's coming in from everywhere now. Can't get anything through the snow. If you need me for something, just come down by the stacks and wave. I'll keep an eye out for you."

Even before he finished speaking, he was ashamed that he was saying so much, making it a kind of begging for her attention.

"We're getting along all right," Gwen said.

"Well, when she's ready, if I'm not back by then."

"I'm not helpless," Gwen said. "I'll come for you if you're wanted."

Harold stared at her, thinking, To hell with you too, then, but she wouldn't look at him, after the angry glance that went with what she said.

Harold waited until the red dancing was out of his own eyes, and he could speak to Joe Sam quietly. Then he held the door and went out after the old Indian, and closed the door again, without once looking back.

All afternoon, though, while he walked beside the drag, or

213

stood on its shallow deck astride the stones that were piled there, he kept looking back at the house. Joe Sam rode in the back of the drag, sitting down, with his arms spread along the tail-board, like a man riding in a rowboat, and every time Harold looked, he looked too, but there was nothing to see that wasn't there all the time. The wind grew steadily colder and stronger, until Harold had to make Joe Sam get out and walk behind, on the bent grass of the wake, and beat his arms across his chest to warm himself. The snow mist broke open over them, and islands of light began to glide across the meadows to the southeast, and then the islands of light became islands of shadow that fled over the white expanse and diagonally up the eastern hills, to vanish in the blue, and still nothing moved up by the stacks except the cattle that were feeding there. The drag moved on steadily through the light snow, and the wind whipped the curling snow away from the prow like spray. A long line of cattle, far behind and moving slowly, followed in the wake, heads down to the discovered grass. In the north there were more of them coming in, singly and by twos and threes, only black dots on the dazzle of the drifted range. At last the drag was so far out that the stacks and the sheds and the house were only tiny toys, already in shadow at the foot of the home mountain. The whole length of the lower range showed from there, stippled black with timber the wind had cleaned, and the main range loomed above it like a white wall, with the last dark clouds rising thinly out of it here and there.

It was Joe Sam who saw Gwen when she did come out. The wind had died down again, by then, and the white breath of the men and the big horses, laboring with arched necks, floated in slow white plumes in the frosty air.

"Woman say come," Joe Sam announced from the back of the drag, and Harold peered far across into the shadow over the ranch, and could just make out the tiny figure standing at the end of the shed. He raised his arm and waved it, to show that he saw her, and turned the drag back in a wide curve. She stood there for a long time, watching while they moved in until the big range sank slowly out of sight behind the timbered one, and then until they had come into the reaching shadow themselves. Harold began to hope that there would be a difference now, but then, when the drag was moving upslope through the feeding herd, he saw her turn and go back without a sign or a sound. He hardened himself inside again, and his face was as expressionless as Joe Sam's while they were putting the drag away, and letting the team back into the corral, and forking out the hay for them.

When they came into the house, the mother was sitting in the big chair, reading in a pocket Testament with a black leather cover. She was holding it close to her face, with her big fingers far up the back of it. The black shawl was folded the long way and draped over the chair behind her. Gwen was sitting sideways in one of the chairs by the table, with her hands in her lap, just waiting. She had on the dark skirt still, but a new blouse, a white one with puffy shoulders and a lace front and a narrow, black ribbon at the throat. Her hair was done up in the heavy braid again. The room was full of just waiting, and yet of not wanting the waiting to be done, either.

The mother was reading with her fingers and her lips now. She finished the passage she was reading and lowered the Testament into her lap and closed it.

"It's pretty near dark already," she said.

"I'll change as quick as I can," Harold told her.

"Never mind any changing now," she said. "I don't reckon there's anybody to care what you have on."

"I'll get Grace up," Gwen said, and rose, and took Grace's coat from its peg, and went into the bunk-room.

"You might light the lamp for us to come back by," the mother said, "and then go up and see is your pa fit to come with us."

Harold pulled the lamp down and lit it, and let it up again, and the little moths stirred on the white walls. Then he went up the stairs onto the landing and opened the door and looked in. The reflected light from the hills came in the east window and showed the father sprawled on the bed with the top quilt pulled half over him. A bottle with the cork out of it lay on its side under the edge of the bed. The old man's hand was hanging limp over the edge, as if it had stayed just where it had let go of the bottle. He was snoring slowly and heavily.

Every time, Harold thought. He gets out of it every time,

215

and closed the door and came back down the stairs. The mother was standing by the table now, with the shawl over her shoulders, and her hands folded together and holding the little Testament against her, like a priest's hands holding his breviary. She looked at Harold, asking the question, and he shook his head. Her mouth grew wide and thin, and curved down, but she didn't say anything.

Harold said, "Come on, Joe Sam," and started toward the north bedroom, but then he thought suddenly, We can't let it down into the grave, and was frightened at how close he had come to forgetting that. It would be terrible to have them all standing around the grave there, waiting, and then not have any way to let the coffin down. We have to have ropes, he thought, two ropes, one for each end. The words came off the top of his mind. He was acting because of words that came off the top of his mind. The lariats, he thought. They'll do, and went over into the wood-box corner. There were four lariats hanging coiled on one big wooden peg there, and he took two of them down.

Gwen and Grace came out of the bunk-room. Gwen was wearing her cloak, with the hood already up, and she had her arm around Grace. Grace was walking in a daze, with her head down, not really over on Gwen's shoulder, but just turned and bending toward it. One look at Grace made it all worse for Harold, so he could feel the same weakness taking all the stuff out of his own knees. It was funny how, just when you were getting used to it one way, you had to do something about it, like this, and it all got worse again.

You had to tip it part way to get it in, the words from the top of his mind said, so you'll have to tip it again to get it out. Only he's in it now. You don't want them in here watching it tip that way with him in it. He laid the ropes on the table.

"You take them outside and wait, Mother," he said.

The mother nodded and said, "Come along, Grace. We'll wait outside," and opened the door and went out. Gwen and Grace went slowly across after her.

When they were in the door, Harold said, "Just leave it open, will you?"

Gwen nodded so he could see the wrinkles in her hood move,

and took Grace out onto the snow. Grace went as if she couldn't have done it by herself, and maybe didn't even know for sure where she was going. Then Harold could see the three dark-skirted figures two together, and the third and tallest one apart, waiting out there on the snow, with the steep wall of the mountain snow behind them, with the black pines on it.

He went into the bedroom. Joe Sam followed him, and went to the small end of the coffin without being told, when Harold went to the big end. "All right," Harold said, and they picked it up, first the right side and then the left side, to get their fingers under it, and then all of it together and held level. Harold could feel the weight shift a little inside, but not sliding, like something rolling heavily on an axle.

"We'll turn it around in here," he said. "There isn't room in the kitchen."

They turned it around slowly, and Harold backed to the door, and then they had to do the tilting. The weight shifted inside again, this time falling clear down against the side of the coffin, and the top of Harold's mind said to him, You should have made it so he couldn't slide in it. It would have gone through the door straight then, too. You wouldn't have had to tip it at all. Then the big end was through, and they leveled the coffin between them again, and the weight slowly shifted back. After that it was better. Harold backed between the stove and the table, and around the table, so the coffin was headed for the door. Then the top of his mind said, You can't back all the way up there, and added sharply, because he had nearly forgotten again, And you've left the ropes on the table.

"Let's put it down here a minute, Joe Sam," he said, "and get a fresh hold on it."

They set it down very carefully, so that it scarcely made a sound on the floor. Harold took the ropes from the table, and stood there a minute, holding them and thinking.

"You take one over your shoulder," he said, "and I'll take the other. Then we won't drop them on the way up." He hung one coil over Joe Sam's shoulder, with his arm through it. He slipped the other on himself the same way, but then felt how it would slide down when he had to lean over, and said, "No, better put it around your neck, I guess," and changed his own.

He thought he'd have to change Joe Sam's for him too, but the old Indian did it for himself. Then the coils of the rope hung down on his chest like a huge necklace with several strands. After a moment Joe Sam slid it up so the strands were tight against his throat and the coils hung down on his back.

He's doing better than you are, at that, the voice said to Harold, and he pushed his own rope up to hang on his back too. They stood still at opposite ends of the coffin, their shadows big on the white walls among the shadow moths.

Then Harold said, "You ready?"

Joe Sam nodded.

Harold turned his back to the big end, and saw the mother standing in the door watching them, trying to hurry them without saying anything.

"We'll try and go all the way in one lift," he told Joe Sam, "but if you feel it slipping, you say so, and we'll set it down. Don't let it fall, that's all. If you feel it slipping, say so, quick."

Joe Sam made a soft sound to show he heard. Harold squatted and got his hands under the big end, first one side and then the other, and lifted slowly. When he felt the other end rising too, he stood up.

"I'll go ahead," the mother said, and Harold nodded as he advanced toward the door. "You and Gwen can follow them, Grace," the mother said, and had the little procession arranged the way it was in her mind.

Gwen said, "All right, Mrs. Bridges," and when Harold came out past her, said softly, "You go on, Harold. I'll get the door."

There was more light left outside than he'd expected, after being in the kitchen with the lamp on. There were still faint, golden edges on the clouds that were getting smaller above the mountain, and there was still color from the sun on the tops of the eastern hills, too. It reflected back, and colored the snow around them softly, and even seemed to rise up out of the snow and make a glowing in the still air.

The mother led the way around the corner of the house and up the slope, walking very straight in the deep, narrow path between the snow banks, but still holding the Testament against her in folded hands, and taking her steps slowly, so they wouldn't get too far behind her with the coffin. Harold had to kick into the snow each step he took on the hill, to be sure he didn't slip back. Once, when they were half-way up the slope, he heard a long, weak, whimpering sound behind him, and then Gwen's voice, murmuring too low for him to hear the words. He looked quickly at where his next step would go, and then glanced back over his shoulder. Grace and Gwen were standing still, back around the turn below Joe Sam. Grace had her face buried all the way in Gwen's shoulder now. Gwen was holding her with both arms and talking softly with her mouth right against the turned-up collar of Grace's coat. Seeing them like that, with the sound of the whimper still alive in him, Harold felt his knees go slack, and his fingers under the edge of the coffin getting too weak to hold.

"We better put it down a minute," he said.

The turn by the woodpile was nearly level, and the snow was shoveled off it. They set the coffin down there, and Harold straightened up and breathed deeply and looked at the mountain and the dark cloud with a pale fringe of light that was looking over it. Gradually the trembling in his knees stopped and his hands felt stronger. Joe Sam just waited for him, not moving at all, or even breathing hard. The mother went on up the path nearly to the grave before she knew they weren't following her. Then she turned and waited up there, looking down at them.

Gwen and Grace began to climb again. They moved in step and close together, with Gwen's arm still around Grace, but Grace was holding her head up now, and trying to step firmly.

"All right?" Harold asked.

The little, private joke was in Joe Sam's eye, but he only nodded and didn't say anything. They took up the coffin again, carefully, and started slowly up the last slope. The mother turned and moved ahead again, and onto the level space beside the grave. When they got up there, she was already standing at the head of the narrow pit, with her back to the mountain. They set the coffin down again on the north edge.

"You better put it in now," the mother said.

Harold glanced down and saw Gwen and Grace slowly making the turn by the woodpile, and nodded. He lifted his rope off over his head and uncoiled it. He looked across the coffin, but Joe Sam was already uncoiling his rope too. They slipped the ropes under the two ends of the coffin, but then had to wait while Gwen and Grace passed slowly behind Joe Sam, and around onto the south edge. When they were standing there, like one double figure, with Grace hiding her face in Gwen's shoulder again, Harold looked at Joe Sam and nodded. They lifted the coffin a little off the snow and shuffled sidewards with it cradled between them in the ropes. The mother moved back to let Harold in front of her. When they were standing spread-legged, one at each end of the grave, Harold nodded again. Breathing hard, more from carefulness than from the weight, they leaned over as far as they dared, and then began to let the ropes slip through their hands very slowly. Even so the coffin grated once against a stone in the side of the grave, and then a second time. The second time it swung a little too, and struck gently as it swung back, making a soft, woody, hollow sound. Grace put her hand up to her face quickly, as if to shield it from a blow, and burrowed a little into Gwen's shoulder, making the whimpering sound again.

The coffin settled onto the bottom with only a faint, sandy grating, and Harold and Joe Sam began to work their ropes out from under it. When they were free, first Harold, and then Joe Sam after him, coiled his rope and fastened it with the twist around it again. Harold took Joe Sam's rope too, and laid both of them down at the end of the piled earth. Then he came back and stood by himself in the middle of the north side. The mother moved down close to the head of the grave again, and looked across at Gwen and Grace. Gwen murmured something against Grace's face. Grace drew a deep breath, as if she meant to make it last the whole time, and lifted her head and stood up straight, though with Gwen's arm around her still. The mother looked around at them all, and then bowed her head. Harold bowed his head too, so that he was looking down at the black lid of the coffin.

But then too much time went by, and the mother didn't say anything. Finally Harold peered at her from under his brows, and she was standing there, looking right at him, and twisting the little Testament into a roll in her two fists. It was like being hit when he didn't expect it, because her look was begging him for help, and her mouth wasn't drawn out thin and tight any longer. It was a little open, as if she couldn't get enough breath, and her lips were trembling. He looked down again quickly, thinking fiercely, Oh, what does it matter what you say? Only say something. Say anything. Don't just stand there till you start to blubber. For Christ's sake don't start to blubber with Grace like she is. He closed his hands into fists and pressed them hard against his thighs.

The mother began to speak. Her breath came in the wrong places, making queer pauses, and some of the words faded away, as if maybe she wouldn't get them out at all, but she wasn't crying.

"I can't preach no proper funeral sermon for him," she said, "and it don't seem there'd be much use in it if I could. We all knowed him too well to need much talk about it."

She paused, and started again. "Still, he was a hard one to really know, at that. Seems to me I'm just learning a lot of things about him I should of knowed all along. But even if I could make out clear every last thing about him, body and soul, and had the words to tell it, I don't know as it would help. It don't make no difference to him now, that's sure, and we'd all find it out for ourselves soon enough, with him gone."

When she stopped this time, Grace made another long, trembling sob, and what it did was the worst yet. Harold bent his head farther and held himself harder, but the weakness brought innumerable hurrying thoughts and feelings that he couldn't stop, and they carried him away from Arthur, not to him.

The mother was speaking again, and her voice sounded very loud and much clearer. When he could make out the words too, she was saying, ". . . so if the Lord won't judge for me, it surely ain't my place to pass judgment myself. He was a good man, like he was always a good boy, not a mean streak in him, that I ever see, and that'll do for us, being mortal ourselves, and the best of us none too good."

But there she lost her way again, and stopped, and when she went on, she sounded as uncertain as she had at first. "Some ways it seems to me he's with us more now than he ever was before. I keep rememberin' things he said, and thinkin' . . ." Her voice trailed off. "Well," she said finally, "Harold done well pickin' this place for him. It's close to home, and still he liked it about as much as he liked any place, I guess. It was a kind of favorite spot of his. He used to come up here all the time, about now, or maybe a little earlier, about sundown, and set here and watch the light over on the other side, and do some of that whittlin' he was always at."

Once more Grace made the long, helpless whimper, and this time Harold couldn't help looking across at her either. Gwen was holding her in both arms, and crying herself, proudly and silently, with her face up. When he saw them, he couldn't hold it down in himself any longer. His tears came suddenly, and blurred the two dark figures together on the other side of the grave. He looked down again quickly, and fought against making a sound. He was astonished and ashamed because he was crying. There didn't seem to be any real reason to cry. It was more for them than it was for Arthur. Nothing anybody could say about Arthur went anywhere near as far as a lot of the things he could remember himself. They couldn't touch Arthur, any of them. Arthur was the one who was out of it; he was the quiet center of things.

"Everybody just pray accordin' to your own heart," the mother said, her voice breaking, and almost not finishing that much.

Harold tried to make a regular prayer for Arthur, but it wouldn't come, and finally the thought went through his head, all by itself, It would make more sense if it was Arthur praying for us. That was when it got hold of him big, beyond any doubt and beyond any softening it with a living memory, that Arthur wasn't there at all, and that he never would be again. It was as if all the other times had just been getting ready for this. He stood very still and tight, not making a sound, and without a thought in his mind, feeling the emptiness go down and down in him.

"Amen," the mother said out loud.

The sinking stopped, and then his mind could cry Arthur's name. He knew that his mouth was closed tight, but it seemed to him that the name, cried out like that, must be echoing all over the valley that was so still now. Arthur, Arthur, his mind cried twice. Then he got the memory that did help. It was as if Arthur had come because he'd called him. He saw Arthur's long, bearded face quite clearly for a moment. The face was very dark, burned almost the color of an old saddle, the way it got toward the end of summer. The deep-sunk eyes were looking right at him, and they were very sad, but the long, gentle mouth in the beard was making the little smile up one side that it always made when Arthur had his own reason for making secret fun of the person he was pitying.

The mother turned at the head of the grave and started toward the pile of earth with snow on it and the four shovels standing up in it. Then he wasn't seeing Arthur's face any longer, but he was feeling only a quiet, easy sadness and a great weariness. It was a queer weariness, not so much like being really tired as like being suddenly a great deal older, tired from time, not from doing anything. It wasn't a bad feeling at all. His own mouth wanted to make the same kind of an easy, crooked smile about it that Arthur's mouth had made. He believed that he was pretty close to understanding what Arthur had thought about things, close in a surer way than he'd been that strange, bright, expanding moment in the kitchen.

The mother came back to the head of the grave. In her left hand she was carrying a little pile of earth from the big mound behind him.

Harold looked down at the lid of the coffin in the pit below him and thought, making that little, crooked smile in his mind, All right, Art, I'll try and find out. I'll try and make things go the way you wanted them to.

The mother leaned over the grave, and with her right hand took some of the earth from her left, and without saying a word, sprinkled it wide and thin, with a motion like Joe Sam's when he fed the chickens, over the lid of the coffin. It made only a faint, sandy tapping, like the beginning of rain on hard ground. At the first tapping, Grace made the long, moaning sound again, but softly, half smothering it in Gwen's shoulder. The mother paid no attention to her, but sprinkled another little handful of earth onto the coffin, and then a third. Then her left hand was empty too. She straightened up, brushed her hands lightly on her skirt, and took the Testament out from under her left arm and held it in her two hands again. She stood that way for a moment, looking down into the grave. Then she raised her head and looked across at Grace and Gwen, and said clearly, "All right, you girls come on down with me now, and let Harold finish up here."

She came around the grave behind Harold and started down the path, and after a moment Gwen turned Grace and the two of them went down more slowly after her, their heads nearly together and their skirts sometimes brushing the light snow from the walls of the path.

Harold waited until they went out of sight around the corner of the house. Then he looked across the valley to the east, at the vast, deep blue darkness coming up that curve of the sky out of the white hills, and at the first stars showing in it. He shivered a little, and looked down from the stars at Joe Sam.

"All right, Joe Sam," he said.

The old Indian didn't move or answer. He was standing just where he'd been standing all the time, at the foot of the grave, and he was still staring down into it.

"Joe Sam," Harold said.

He had to speak a third time before Joe Sam raised his head. "We have to get done before it's too dark."

"Get done," Joe Sam said, and came around the grave slowly, moving in the thin, darkening air like a swimmer treading water.

Harold took the first shovelful of earth, and then paused for a moment, holding it above the open grave. Then he leaned far down and spread it quietly the length of the coffin. He kept on letting the earth down that way, instead of dropping it, until the lid of the coffin was covered and the space around it was filled. Joe Sam did the same thing at the other end. Then they both stood by the mound and just tossed the earth in. They both swung rhythmically, but their rhythms weren't quite the same, so that sometimes the two shovels swung together, and sometimes first one and then the other would swing. As the darkness increased on the hillside, the pines around them became great black columns against a white wall, and below them the small, orange window of the kitchen grew brighter, and so did the longer, yellow window it made on the snow.

224

20 ●━━ ●━

Once more there were only the three of them at the table for supper, Gwen and Harold and Joe Sam. And Joe Sam just sat there again, too, not eating anything, and with his coat and the blue bandana and the black sombrero on. The curving light of the lamp crossed his breast, showing the big wrinkles of the worn coat, and the long hair of the braid that had come undone, lying loose and flat over them. The other braid was beginning to loosen now too, so the ends of the red and blue ribbons stood out from it. In the double shadow of the lamp shade and the brim of the sombrero, both his eyes appeared to be alive and staring with horror, because the irises made single big centers with the pupils. The big centers were looking right at Harold all the time, or through him at something they saw where the stairs went up against the wall. Harold kept looking away, but every time he looked back, the two big pupils in the faintly glittering whites were still staring at him.

Staring back at them, Harold thought, For a while up there, I had a notion he was coming out of it, but I guess it just set him off again.

Then he had to look away from the eyes again. He looked at Gwen, but she was keeping her head down over her plate, and picking at her food, as if she were all by herself. In the long silence, the fluttering of the lamp and the fire and the slow ticking of the clock became voices he didn't want to listen to. Several times he started to say something to Gwen, but then, each time, thought how loud and foolish it would sound, and didn't speak.

He had become afraid of even the sound his fork made on the plate, when suddenly the father's voice spoke above, angrily and loudly. "It was Curt, I tell you. I saw his coat. I guess I know Curt's coat when I see it, don't I?"

Then the clock and the fluttering came back, and after a moment, Harold said, "Just talking in his sleep, I guess."

Gwen had looked up quickly when the loud voice spoke, but now she looked down at her plate again. "I left his door open to let some heat up," she said.

She didn't say anything more, and finally Harold asked, "How is Grace doing now?"

"I'm scared for her," Gwen said slowly. "She's quiet enough. She's too quiet. She just lies there staring. She wouldn't answer me when I spoke to her. I don't think she even heard me. I wish she'd take on some way. I wish she'd cry, or do most anything."

"Maybe now it's all over, she'll let up after a while. Maybe she's just worn out with it."

"She's not letting up any," Gwen said. She was still keeping herself away from him. She wouldn't look at him, and she might have been talking to anybody, just to answer the questions. Harold looked at her bowed head intently for a moment, and then set his jaw, and pushed back his chair and stood up.

"Well, I better get at the chores," he said. "Come on, Joe Sam."

The old Indian didn't move.

"Joe Sam."

"Why don't you let him alone?" Gwen said sharply.

He looked at her, and this time she was looking right back at him too. A little fury was dancing in her eyes, almost as wildly as it did in the mother's or Curt's sometimes.

"Why don't you let the poor old man alone?" she said. "He isn't fit to do chores, and you know it. You've had him doing everything all the time, and he hasn't slept or eaten for days."

Harold stood there looking down at her, and feeling the heat come up his throat and face so he knew it showed.

"Are you trying to work him to death?" Gwen asked.

Her voice was higher, and even with his anger finally beginning to rise through his weariness, slow and heavy, he was afraid she'd start screaming at him so she couldn't be stopped, the way Grace had at the mother.

She had only started again, though, saying, "Just because he's old, and an Indian, and doesn't know our ways, you . . ." when they heard steps in the north bedroom. Gwen stopped speaking, and they both looked at the open door. After a moment, the light of the lamp showed there, bright, and then dimmed, and then coming up again, slowly whitening, until finally it was the brightest yet and steady.

The mother's voice said, "Harold."

Gwen looked down at her plate again.

"Yes?" Harold said.

"I want to see you before you go out."

His anger turned against the mother and flared. Christ, won't you ever let me alone? he thought. Then he thought, Like Curt again, and you made a promise to Arthur. Somebody has to try around here, and you're the only candidate right now.

"All right," he said.

He looked down at Gwen again. It was so quiet they could hear the bedsprings creak as the mother lay down once more, and even the rustling of her stiff, black dress. He stood there, trying to make Gwen look up at him before he spoke, but she wouldn't and again it was the father's voice that broke the silence. It was complaining now, almost weeping. "It did, though. I saw it, big as a horse. Listening to that goddamned dreamer," it moaned, and muttered for a moment, and was silent.

Harold said slowly and distinctly, "I was just going to put him to bed up in the bunk-house, if that'll make you feel any better."

He turned and went to the door of the bedroom. For a moment he was frightened, because he thought, in his dull weariness, that it was Arthur lying there again, and had a couple of wild glimpses of an opening grave and a ghost that carried its dead flesh on it, and couldn't be kept out of the house. The mother was lying straight out on the bed, with the same white blanket pulled up to her chin. Her hands were crossed on her breast on top of the blanket, and her eyes were closed.

The wild notion passed, and he thought, though only wearily, What now? Playing dead? It's a bad joke, old woman. Or do you just forget that fast?

He went in and stood by the bed, but the mother didn't

open her eyes or speak. Finally he said, "What did you want, Mother?"

She opened her eyes then, and without moving her head, turned them slowly to look at him. "I was thinking," she began, hardly moving her lips, but then turned her eyes away from him and let them close again. "It was just a notion I had," she said.

"What was?"

"Never mind. It doesn't matter."

"If it's anything I can do," Harold said finally.

She waited for a long time, and then slowly opened her eyes and looked at him again. "I was just thinkin' we might keep a fire out front tonight, now it's clear." She looked away from him. "But it wouldn't do no good, I know that," she said. "It's just I keep feelin' we oughta do somethin'."

"Well," Harold said, "it wouldn't do any harm."

The mother rolled her head a little in the pillow to mean no. "You got more'n enough to do the way it is," she murmured. "It was just a notion."

"I'll get one going as soon as I've finished the chores."

The mother didn't move or speak, and after a moment he went back into the kitchen, and lit the lantern and roused Joe Sam. Gwen was still sitting there bowed over her plate. She let them go without saying anything.

On the way up the hill, Harold stopped once and looked up at the sky, letting Joe Sam go on up the path alone. All the stars were out sharp and small now, and the constellations weren't broken anywhere until they got down to the hills. He looked north and searched out the Great Dipper, and then the Pole Star.

He wouldn't even need the lamp, let alone a fire, he thought, and then, Well, it's not for him anyway, and felt his weariness settle down upon him full weight again. He felt the cold working into him already, through the house-warmth in his clothes. It pinched his nostrils every time he drew a breath. If he's still out there, he'd better have a fire for himself, though, he thought, and turned and went on up, climbing with his upright shadow the lantern made on the snow wall of the path.

When he came into the bunk-house, the lantern showed him

Joe Sam, already undressed down to his underwear, and barefooted, but standing by the cold stove again, with his hands out to it.

"Get in your bunk, Joe Sam," he said. "I'll make you a fire."

He set the lantern down by the stove and went over to the woodpile and began to whittle shavings for kindling. When he came back with the long, white splinters in his hand, Joe Sam was still by the stove, but now he was taking off the underclothes too.

"You better keep those on," Harold said. "It's gonna be colder than hell tonight."

The old Indian, his face dead and away by itself, went on taking off the red flannels. Harold stared at him for a moment, but then thought, Have it your own way. Everybody else is, and took an old newspaper from the box behind the stove and wadded it and thrust it down in onto the grate. Then he shook the ashes from under the paper, and tossed the light kindling in, and four bigger sticks on top of it, and lit the paper. When the kindling was burning, he closed the stove door and stood up. Joe Sam was in his bunk and under the covers. He was lying on his side, drawn up like a kid again, and his eyes were closed.

Harold waited until he could put chunks on the fire, and the old man didn't move or open his eyes. When the chunks were burning too, Harold picked up the lantern and went out. In a slow, tired walk that was still perfectly regular, so it made a monotony in his mind too, he went down the hill and past the house and out across the yard, all broken into white peaks and walls and long black shadows by the lantern moving through the work of the shovels and the drag. He did the chores in the same dull, steady way, his mind hardly taking hold on anything, and his body working by habit. He broke the ice on the corral trough and forked hay out for the horses the last thing, and then, still walking with his legs only, climbed back up to the woodpile and got his axe. Carrying the axe and the lantern in the same hand, he went down once more, and out of the yard to the south, in the track the drag had made. Where the track curved away east on the rise, he broke through the wall of snow it had left and went floundering on up through the loose snow above until he came into the big brush the quail liked. He stamped a circle firm in the snow there, and set the lantern at the side of it. Then he just stood there resting for a while, looking up at the vast dome of stars over the glimmering valley and the ghostly mountains that closed it in, and down at the brighter, yellow spark that was the bunk-room window. The cold began to work into him again, and far up in the northeast, toward the pass, a coyote cried, small and quavering and desolate. Something in him cried back to it so much in the same voice it made him uneasy. When it happened a second time, he shook himself awake.

He moved out beyond the circle and began to knock the snow out of the brush with the axe, and to kick it away from the stems. When he'd gone as far as the lantern would let him see, he began to hack at the twisted stems of the brush he had cleared. The stems sprang back from the blows, making the axe jump so that his hands tingled, and sometimes it took half a dozen strokes to cut through. He began to strike harder, and to flare with rage when a bush resisted him too long.

All right, he thought, if you want a fire, I'll make you a fire that'll show to Oregon. There's nobody to see your goddam fire, but what do we care about a little thing like that. We'll have a real fire. We'll burn every goddam bush on the hill.

"Never let it be said," he muttered, feeling the sweat beginning to come on his face, even in that sharp cold, "that a Bridges ever did anything in a small way, even if the small way would be better. Whatever it is, do it big, and do it as fast as you can."

He worked faster, grunting every time he struck. Each time a bush fell or leapt away into the snow, he caught it up and threw it fiercely back into the circle where the lantern was.

"Why not burn the damn haystacks," he glowled. "Hell, we're no pikers," he muttered. "Burn the sheds, burn the house. Think what a light that'd make for the coyotes to see."

Later, when his lips were curled back and his breath was hissing in his teeth, he gasped, "It's Curt's fire. Do it Curt's way."

Three times he worked out of the farthest reach of the light, and each time he moved the lantern to another side of the circle. When the pile of brush filled the whole circle and was as tall as he was, he rested, bent over and leaning on the axe handle. Little lights that didn't come from the lantern danced in the night where he looked, like the stars come down and whirling. He closed his eyes, and they were still there. He waited until they slowed down, and became fewer, and darkened. Then his breath was coming slower too, and not so much like sobs. He could feel the sweat starting under his armpits now, and running down over his ribs, tickling them. He opened his eyes and looked at the pile of brush.

"Even for Curt, that would do," he said.

He still rested, bent over the axe, until the pain in his side was easier and he could breathe with his mouth closed again. The temper went out of him too, while he waited.

"Jeez," he said softly. "Watch it, boy. It's in you too."

Then he saw the whole performance the way it would have looked to someone else, to Arthur, for instance, that rage of cutting in a little puddle of lantern light, and with the stars there over it all the time, and the big, cold, dark silence of the valley around it. He looked up at the stars and made a little, one-sided grin, and chuckled softly.

"All right, Art," he said. "Have it your way."

He stood the axe head down in the snow by the lantern, and began to hook the cut brush together by its branches. When he had as much in the bunch as he thought would hold, he towed it down into the track of the drag, and along the track into the yard, and across the yard into the center of the big whorl the drag had made turning around at the north end. He made eight trips that way, and then one more to collect the brush that had come loose along the track. He stacked all the brush into one big pile again, in the center of the whorl, and left the lantern beside it, and took the axe back up to the woodpile. He brought four of the cord-cut timbers down from the woodpile and leaned them on end against the brush. He kept on, stubbornly, but very slowly now, carrying down timbers and standing them against the brush until they made a close, tall tepee over it. Even then he didn't stop, though he could only carry the timbers two at a time now. He built a stack of them over against the snow wall of the circle. Orion was up over the sheds before he finally stopped to rest once more. He stood looking down at the stack.

He had no feeling about what he was doing now, and his thoughts about it came slowly and separately, and had no force.

"That'll hold it till daylight," he said.

It would start better with kerosene on it, he thought, but then thought, It's in the store room. I'd have to go in the kitchen again.

Finally he picked up the lantern and went slowly down to the sheds and around to the lumber room. In the lumber room, he broke up some light boards into kindling, and took them in his arm with a pile of old newspapers from the bench. He started to pick up a bucketful of the black oil they used to waterproof the fence posts and poles where they went into the ground. Then he thought of the lantern. He laid the papers and kindling on the bench and fastened the lantern to his belt. Then he picked up the papers and kindling again, and took the bucket of oil in his other hand, and went back to the pile of brush and timber. He thought carefully about each little act now. He wadded the paper and pushed it under the brush in one place, and pushed the kindling in on top of it. Then he poured some of the oil through the brush onto the paper and kindling. Finally he went slowly around the whole pile, splashing the oil in between the timbers until the bucket was empty. He carried the bucket to the edge of the circle, where the track went out of it that passed the house, and set it down as carefully as if it were made of glass. When he straightened up again, he caught his breath for a moment, because Gwen was standing there, so close she could have touched him. He couldn't see her face at all in the hood.

"I didn't see you there," he said.

"I haven't been here very long," she said. "I didn't know if you had any matches." She gave him the matches she was holding. "I made some fresh coffee," she said.

"That's good," he said, but then turned away from her at once, because he was afraid he was going to cry. He was so tired it made him want to cry to think of her making the coffee for him. He went back to the pile of brush and timbers, and squatted in front of the place where he'd put the paper and kindling in. He scratched a match on the nearest timber, held it in his cupped hand until the flame was steady, and then slowly put it in until the tip of the flame touched the oily paper. For an instant the flame shrank, and only tiny wisps of quick, black smoke went up from it. Then there was a sudden little gasping explosion, and a dark red flame leapt up, making a cloud of black smoke. The flame broke into many flames over the surface of the oily paper, and he stood up and moved back from the pile. The flames drew together and sucked up into the brush. The big flame began to roar, and the brush hissed where there was still snow on it. Then a thin, nervous crackling began. The flame brightened and rushed up into the peak of the tepee, and spread quickly through its base, mostly white and noisy, but breaking out in a new, small explosion and another murky red fire every time it came to oil again.

Harold picked up the lantern and moved back into the drag lane, where Gwen was. They stood there together, not looking at each other, but only watching the fire grow. After a few minutes the flames were bannering high out of the peak of the cone, and the slumping and crashing of settling began inside, where the brush was burned away to fibres like glowing wicks that curled and broke off and winked out. The banks of the snow wall began to sink a little and run in the heat. The waving, colored light spread over the snow beyond the circle, and made phantoms that danced along the walls of the house too quickly to take clear shape. For a time, while the blaze was highest, the light on the tower window made it look as if there was a raging fire inside the house too. Only the brightest stars, out around the edges, on the hills, showed beyond the glare. Turning once to look at the fire in the window, Harold saw that the kitchen door was open, and the figure of the mother was standing in it against the lamplight.

When the timbers had sunk over each other, burning separately in many places, and the column of fire in the center was slower and uncertain, he went into the circle again, and walked slowly around, prodding the timbers in with the heel of his boot. When the flame in the center was single and steady once more, he came back and picked up the lantern.

"That'll hold for a while," he said.

He waited until she had turned and gone ahead of him into the path, and then he followed her slowly.

The mother wasn't in the kitchen when they came in, but the Testament she'd carried in the afternoon was lying open at her place at the table, with an empty coffee mug beside it. Harold set the lantern on the table, and took off his cap and stuffed it into his pocket. Then he slowly turned the lantern down until it went out. The warmth of the room closed on him like first sleep, and he stood there staring at the Testament and thinking, as if he were reading a title page, The words of Christ are printed in red.

Gwen's voice said, "You'd better take your coat off, Harold," and he obeyed like one in a trance. He hung the coat over the back of Arthur's chair, and sat down in the chair. After a minute he put his elbows on the table, and rested his head in his hands.

Gwen set a mug of coffee beside him, and went around and sat down across from him with hers. She began to sip at her coffee, but Harold couldn't bring himself to move. After a few sips, Gwen set her mug down again.

"Do you have to keep it going all night?" she asked. She spoke very quietly, because of the three open doors, and because the Testament and the empty coffee mug between them made a kind of bodiless deputy there.

"What?" he asked, and lifted his head to look at her.

"The fire. Do you have to keep it going all night?"

He nodded. "I guess so."

Gwen was silent, looking at him, and thinking something she wouldn't say. Then she said, smiling a little, "You'd better drink your coffee, then, hadn't you?"

"I guess so," he said again, but didn't move to pick it up.

After a minute, Gwen said, "I'd better go see how Grace is, I guess. I'll be right back."

Harold smiled at her faintly, and nodded, and she got up and went quietly into the bunk-room. Harold sat there staring in front of him until he began to hear the clock. Then he pushed the mug of coffee aside and laid his head down on his arms on the table.

21 ‑ • ‑ •

It was morning in the kitchen, and Harold was very happy, because Arthur was sitting there across from him, whittling at one of the wooden cats, and getting ready to make another of the little jokes you had to think about too. But just when he looked up to speak, someone far away began screaming. Then Arthur wasn't smiling at all. He was leaning across the table, staring with terrible eyes that had only pupils and no irises. He was looking right through Harold at something where the stairs were. "Hal," he cried softly, "Hal." He reached across under the lamp and took hold of Harold's shoulder. "Hal," he said again, no louder, but even more urgently, and began to shake him gently.

Then suddenly there was only an empty coffee cup in his place, and the barred chair-back showing above the table. The kitchen was much smaller and darker too, and the stairs were behind the empty chair, not behind Harold, where they should have been. The shaking went on, though, and he heard his name again. He looked up, and it was Gwen standing beside him, with her hand still on his shoulder. She was saying something quick and frightened to him, but he couldn't understand it yet. Grace was there too, standing by the stove and hugging the old bathrobe around her. She was staring at him almost the way Arthur had been staring at him. He was frightened, and he didn't know what was wrong, except that Arthur had been frightened, and now he was gone.

"What?" he asked Gwen.

"Something's at the horses."

"The horses?" He struggled to his feet and looked around at the front window. Then he saw that it wasn't morning at all. The window was full of darkness, with only a faint, red light wavering across the little Alps of plowed snow outside.

"Yes, the horses," Gwen said sharply.

The mother's voice behind them said, "Harold, don't you go out there now. There's been enough . . ."

"Harold, wake up," Gwen cried.

"I'm awake," he said, "only I don't . . ."

"It's black as pitch out there," the mother said angrily, and he could tell she was coming toward them from the bedroom.

The scream came again. It was the same one he'd heard while Arthur was there. It trailed away in a long, shuddering, high cry, and then he was sure that it came from outside, and understood what Gwen had been trying to tell him. He started toward the door.

"Harold," the mother cried, to stop him, and Gwen was coming after him, crying, "Here, Harold, take the gun. If it's that painter again . . ."

Even Grace's voice cried shrilly now, "Harold, don't be a fool," and then the loud, heavy voice called down from above, "What in hell's going on down there?" He was already at the door, and had it partly open, but this voice was so different from the women's voices flocking after him like beaked birds that he stopped and looked up. The father was up there, enormous and faceless in the shadow. He leaned over the rail so that part of his face and one eye came out of the shadow of the platform, and said angrily, "What's going on? I asked you."

He wasn't real either, though. Arthur, with the knife and the carving in his hands and that horror beginning to come on his face was still what was real, and the rest of this was a bad dream he'd fallen asleep into. But Arthur had heard the screaming too, and tried to tell him something about it. He went on out the door, with someone catching at his sleeve, and saying something he didn't understand because the father's big voice was saying, "What's burning out there? Damned fire woke me up. Are you all . . ." but then he was outside and couldn't hear the rest, but only the rumbling of the voice in the house.

Still heavy with sleep, so that the fear was alive in him by itself, but he wasn't alive around it yet, he heard the horse make the shrill, sudden screams twice more, close together. The sound was much louder now, and it made something go swiftly and coldly up his back, raising the hairs on his neck. He began to run heavily in the snow, with voices still calling behind him When he got out of the light from the doorway, he missed the path somewhere. He floundered on across through the deep snow with the far-away firelight moving the shadows on it, and came into the tunnel between the sheds with snow on him up to the waist. Between the dark bars of the corral gate at the other end of the tunnel, he could see the horses all running in a shadowy bunch along the far fence. The wildest pounding was separate from them, though, and nearer, and then the terrible, sudden cry of the horse came again, and it was very near. It shook him like a blow. A horse in the bunch on the other side nickered like a whimper, and then another and another took up the sound of fear, and suddenly, piercing as a steam whistle, the scream came again. It came suddenly each time, as if struck from the lungs by sharp pain.

Harold came to the gate and crouched there, holding onto the center pole. He was filled with a murderous rage now, and at the same time he wanted to run back into the greater darkness of the tunnel and watch from there, with the wall behind him, ready to defend himself. This straining balance held him motionless at the gate through three quick screams. Then the cold man's mind said, There's no black painter. You're sunk in two dreams, that's all, Joe Sam's and the one you had in there. You fell asleep on the table.

He climbed onto the gate, not wanting to be caught between the poles if it was a cat in there after all. He knew that Gwen had somehow got there right after him, but he hardly felt her clutching at his shirt, and didn't understand anything of what she was saying so rapidly. He wished he had the lantern, though. He wanted light. From his high post astride the top bar, he could see only the great, unclear shadow of the horse plunging and turning in the darkness by the shed. He couldn't make out at all what was at it, but only a thickening and blurring of its forelegs and shoulders. The horse suddenly screamed and leaped again, and in spite of himself, a belief in the black panther took hold of him for a moment. He felt how helpless he was against it too, against any kind of a cat, without a weapon that would keep it from reaching him.

"Gwen, get back," he said fiercely, but all the time watching the dark plunging by the shed, no clearer than a cloud moving on a night sky. "Get away from here, out of the tunnel." He felt her hand leave him, but she was still talking at him. "Did

you hear me?" he said. "Get out. If it breaks . . ." Then he
didn't hear her voice any longer either. He watched the plunging, waiting, and when it came toward the gate, cried out as
loudly as he could, "Hi-ya, hi-ya, hi-ya," in the high, piercing
tone he used to harry the cattle, or turn a steer that threatened
him. With his second yelp, the tortured horse screamed again,
and the rest of his cry was small and lost, but this time the pattern of the battle was broken anyhow. The horse reared and
crashed against the shed, its weight cracking the poles, its hoofs
rattling down them, and spun suddenly back along the wall,
and out free in a long curve into the center of the corral. The
nervous bunch swung and streamed away along the far rail with
dull, numerous thunder, leaving it in lone silhouette against
the starlit snow, and Harold guessed it was Kentuck.

Then the enemy came out into the starlight after it, gliding
quickly and soundlessly, like a soft-footed dancer, stooping, and
maneuvering to keep the big stallion from getting in with the
bunch.

Harold said softly, "The damn little bastard," and let himself
down into the corral. He felt a hand clutch at his shirt again,
and heard Gwen's voice crying, "Hal, don't go in there. Hal,
take the gun; here's the gun," and then again, when she lost
her hold as he moved away, "Harold, take the gun, you fool."

He said angrily, over his shoulder, "Quit yelling, will you?
It's all right. It's only Joe Sam."

"Joe Sam," he called sharply.

The little figure still danced on the snow, cutting off the
stallion that moved slowly now, trying to run, but stumbling
each time, and only turning away in a limping trot.

"Joe Sam," he yelled again.

The little figure straightened up in the center of the corral
and stood waiting.

"Harold," Gwen said, "don't go out there. He's crazy."

"He'll be all right now," Harold said. "He heard me, and he
knows who it is."

He went out slowly, just the same, watching the old Indian
for any sudden move, stopping beyond his reach and peering,
trying to see him better. The old man was naked again, even
in this cold that was already shortening Harold's breath, but

there was something about the shape he made against the snow that wasn't right.

Behind him the horses were running again, to keep away from the black. When he slowed to a walk and turned across the open at them, they waited, moving restlessly in a small space and only nickering a little, until he was within two or three lengths of them. Then they milled suddenly, several of them rearing like a shadowy surf, and lined out again, streaming back around the fence. Kentuck stood then, blowing heavily, only turning his head to watch them.

Joe Sam turned a little too, at the sound of the running, and Harold saw it was his hair that was wrong. It hung down tentwise over his shoulders and back, so his head had no shape except in profile. The second braid must have come all undone too.

He looks like a Digger, Harold thought. Like a damn cave man. Well, no bottle neck, anyway. But he's got something, he thought suddenly. He didn't make the stud scream like that with his hands.

"What have you got there, Joe Sam?" he asked. "In your hand?"

"No got," Joe Sam muttered.

Still playing possum, Harold thought. He isn't giving up yet. "What's in your hand? I asked you."

After a moment, Joe Sam said, "Arthur give. Arthur my friend."

"Drop it," Harold said.

Still the old man kept his hands in the dark by his sides. It was hard to wait against this stubbornness, and with no way to guess, in the dark, what he was thinking, but Harold waited, only holding himself ready to move quickly, in case the old habit of his authority were broken now by some older vision, or some thwarted remnant of the strange fury. The waiting and the cold won for him. When the old Indian spoke at last, he was pleading.

"Arthur give. My friend give. Please, I keep."

"All right," Harold said. "You can keep it, but give it to me now." He held out his hand.

Joe Sam made some small movement with the object, in the

dark against his side, and then slowly reached out and laid it on Harold's hand. Harold felt the corrugated bone of the handle through the slippery, still warm wetness on it.

"Kill black painter," Joe Sam said.

Black painter, hell, Harold thought. You can't dream that hard, and felt with his forefinger along the base of the blade, where the blood was already cool and thickened. The blade was worn narrow as a dagger's with long use and much sharpening. It was Arthur's knife, all right, however Joe Sam had come by it. When they carried him out of the tunnel? No, or why all that trickery with the clumsy bottle neck? It must have been when he put his gifts into the coffin, then. The mother, knowing it was Arthur's treasure, must have put it in the black suit when she changed his clothes.

"Kill black painter," Joe Sam insisted. "Black painter kill Arthur." He was beginning to shake now. The shaking was in his voice.

Harold squatted and thrust the blade of the knife through the hoof packed snow into the dung and earth of the corral, and worked it there to clean it. Then he rubbed the handle with snow too, and cleaned his hands in it, and stood up. He wiped the knife on his jeans, closed it, and stood tossing it slowly on the palm of his hand and looking at Joe Sam.

"It was no black painter," he said finally, "and you know it. It was Kentuck. You knifed Kentuck. Why did you do it?"

"Black painter," Joe Sam said again, but now without conviction. His teeth began to chatter, and he hunched himself a little.

He knew, all right, Harold thought. Because it was Curt's horse, maybe? The one that made him dodge?

"Harold, what is it?" Gwen called.

"He was knifing the black stud. Curt's."

"Oh, the poor horse. Why?" She was coming out to them now.

"Wait a minute," Harold called. "We're coming."

"Black painter not dead," Joe Sam said mournfully. "Not kill. You stop."

Or did he know? Harold thought. How can you guess what

240

he sees? He slipped the knife into the pocket of his jeans, and took off his shirt and held it out to Joe Sam.

"Here, put this on."

The old Indian suddenly shook so violently he could hardly stand, but made no move to take the shirt. "Arthur give me," he pleaded between chattering teeth.

"All right," Harold said. "I'll give it back to you. But you have to get some sleep first. Get up in the bunk-house and get warm."

He held out the shirt again, but the old man still just stood there, his head bowed and his body jerking, and he had to put the shirt on him. Then he took his arm, feeling how thin it was in the big sleeve of the shirt, like a starving child's.

"Come on, old man," he said gently. "Get to bed now. Get warm."

Joe Sam took the first step with him, but then he made a little, whimpering sound, and sagged forward, and Harold had to take him up in his arms. He was astonishingly light.

Old bird bones, Harold thought. Dried out with age, or burned out with seeing things. His pride weighed more than he did, and I've robbed him of it. He walked toward the gate.

Gwen came to meet him quickly, peering at Joe Sam, and asking, "Is he hurt, Hal?"

"I don't think so. Worn out and half-frozen, I guess. And the fit's off him. That knocks him out sometimes. Let the bars down, would you, please?"

Gwen hurried ahead and let the poles down at one end, and Harold went through with his burden.

"By rights it's the horse I ought to look at first," he said.

Gwen, raising the bars again, asked, "Is he hurt bad?"

"I don't know yet, but it was no fun for him. The old fool had Arthur's knife."

Gwen hesitated, with the top pole still in her hands.

"Don't go in there," Harold said. "He's crazy afraid still. I'll be back as quick as I can." He started through the tunnel.

Gwen slid the last bar into its slot and followed him, carrying the rifle.

"Can I help?"

"You could get the lantern, if you would, and a halter from the harness room. And get a coat on too."

"How about some hot water and rags?"

"We'll need them, I guess. And carbolic too. It's on the window ledge in the harness room."

Where the drag lane crossed in front of the house, he turned and went up the hill to the bunk-house. Although he was shivering himself now, he had to go slowly, digging his toes in, because the cold had made the path glassy. On the level in front of the bunk-house, the snow squealed under his feet. He raised Joe Sam higher in his arms, sprung the latch with the hand that was under his shoulders, and pushed the door open with his knee. He crossed the room and laid Joe Sam down in his bunk. Then he closed the door, lighted the lamp and came back to the old man. He took the big shirt off him, worked him into his own red flannels and got him under the covers. At once Joe Sam drew himself together, hugging his knees. Harold stood looking down at him while he put on his shirt again. Joe Sam was still shivering and breathing jerkily. His eyes were closed, and his face, half veiled by his long hair, looked tight and hollowed as an old skull.

No possum this time, Harold thought. It's done, and there's not too much between him and being dead.

He built the fire up again, and brought the top quilt from his own bunk and laid it over Joe Sam too. Then he took Arthur's knife out of his pocket, and stood bouncing it a little on his hand while he looked down at the old, secret face. Finally he leaned over, turned back the covers, and pressed the knife in between Joe Sam's hands and knees. The right hand closed around the knife, and when Harold had pulled the covers up again, Joe Sam sighed, letting go of something in him, and loosened under the covers, as if he had caved in. But then his breathing began again, slow and even and quiet, and the little fear that had started in Harold thinned away to nothing. He crossed to the lamp and blew it out, and came back through the imps of firelight to the door. He looked at Joe Sam once more, and went out, and closed the door softly. From the step, he saw the lantern, like a big, soft star, going into the tunnel between the sheds, and he hurried going down, as much as he could on the slick snow.

When he came into the tunnel, he saw Gwen already inside the corral gate, but waiting there uncertainly, and when he was closer, he saw the big stallion still in the center of the corral, watching her with his head lowered. His eyes shone hollowly in the lantern light, as if from a burning inside him.

Harold crawled between the bars and took the rope halter from Gwen's hand.

"Don't get too close," he said. "He doesn't know you."

He moved out slowly toward the stallion. It waited quietly, only lifting its head higher to watch when he was close. When he was beside it, though, and raised a hand to touch the bulging shoulder, the stallion flinched away. He spoke to it softly and steadily, and after a moment, still murmuring, moved to it again. This time Kentuck bore his touch, only starting a little at first, and then trembling. Harold worked the halter on and clicked the snap shut. The rest of the horses stood in a line against the far fence, watching, and making only small movements of uneasiness, snorting their breath out white into the starlight. Gwen came up with the lantern and Harold's coat. She held the coat out to him.

"I thought you'd want this."

Harold held his hands down into the light, and saw the dark, glittering blood he had felt. He rinsed his hands in snow again, and took the coat and put it on.

"Thanks," he said. "It's not too warm out here, at that."

Gwen held the lantern up, and they could see the blood on Kentuck's neck and shoulder too then. It had no color on the black hide, but shone where it was still flowing.

"We better take him in the stall," Harold said. "The others don't like it." He put a hand on the halter, and began to coax Kentuck toward the gate.

"They look bad," Gwen said, raising a hand toward the gashed shoulder, but not touching it.

"Bad enough," Harold said, "but they're just on that one side, anyway. He's dry on the other side."

"Why would Joe Sam do a thing like that?"

"He says he thought it was the black panther."

243

"Oh, but he couldn't. How could he?"

"I don't know. But he'll never say anything different now. You can bet on that."

Gwen let down the bars, and raised them again behind Kentuck. She picked up the kettle and cloths and the bottle of carbolic she'd set down by the fence, and followed Harold and the big stallion into the tunnel.

In the one stall, which was just a corner boarded off in the hay shed, Harold tied Kentuck to the manger, and they looked at the wounds again, holding the lantern up close. There were eight cuts, like small, moving mouths, all on the shoulder and the neck just off the shoulder. One of them, high behind the shoulder, was still bleeding with a pulse, new blood squeezing out at each beat.

"The poor thing," Gwen said. Twisting her face as if the pain of the cuts were in her own body, she raised a hand toward the creeping blood again, but didn't touch it this time either.

"They could be worse, though," Harold said. "I thought out there they were worse."

He hung the lantern on a nail in the rafter above, and eased a hand onto Kentuck's shoulder, between two wounds.

"Wild with that knife, wasn't he, boy?" he murmured. "But you weren't giving him much time to pick his target, were you, boy? No, not you. And a good thing for you, you didn't, too. It has a long blade, that knife, for something just to whittle with."

Kentuck flinched, and jerked his head up until the rope checked him, and rolled his eyes till the whites showed staringly, but then let the hand explore.

"How that little, old guy ever got in that many wallops," Harold said, in the same voice for Kentuck to hear, and shook his head. "He must have hung on like a burr." Then he talked to Kentuck again, always in that one tone, low and smooth and constant, while he washed the blood off and bathed the wounds with the warm water. Finally only that one, high wound, where the knife had gone in straighter and deeper, was bleeding. The red, small lips of the cut showed clearly now, and the new blood squeezing between them in the slow rhythm of the big heart.

"Now's when it begins to get touchy," Harold said.

244

He got an old, battered grain pan out of the manger, and rinsed it and filled it with water from the kettle. He poured a little spurt of the carbolic into the water, corked the bottle, and set it in the far corner. Then he dipped a rag into the solution and stirred it slowly.

"Keep away from his hind end," he said, straightening up with the rag in his hand. He waited until Gwen had moved into the corner by the manger, and then began the quiet patter of talk again. He fingered the wounds while he talked, until Kentuck stopped flinching. Then, quickly, he put the rag to the bad wound and squeezed it and wiped along the edges of the cut. After a moment, Kentuck fought back on the rope, his head jerking up, and then suddenly, he trumpeted, an ear-splitting sound in the close stall, and jerked so the timbers of the manger creaked, and struck with his haunch, and then twice with his hoofs against the side of the stall. Harold kept a shoulder against his shoulder, though, moving with him, and still working at the wound until he was satisfied it was clean.

"Take it easy, boy," he said. "Take it easy. That's the worst of it. The rest of it's nothing to that. Just a little sting, maybe," and kept up the patter, stroking the big flank and the neck above the wounds, until Kentuck stood quiet again. Then he moved slowly away from his shoulder, and soaked the rag in the pan once more, and went back with it. This time he dabbed and squeezed at three of the cuts before the burning started, and then Kentuck only sidled a little, and rapped the boards once, trying to turn his head to see back.

Three times more Harold soaked the rag and came back, coaxing all the while in the soft, monotonous voice. Twice he was shouldered away heavily, and several times Kentuck snorted and flinched, but then the job was done, and with his hand that didn't sting, and still the soft chatter, Harold quieted him a last time.

"He'll be all right now," he said. "If he isn't bleeding inside somewhere, and I don't think he is."

He took the carbolic back to the harness room and returned with a blanket. He covered the shoulders with warm, wet rags, and laid a piece of dry sheeting over them, and then threw the blanket on over the sheeting. Then he took the pan of reddened solution out and poured it into the snow, and cleaned the pan and his hands in the snow too. Finally he forked hay down into the rack, and brought the pan full of grain and a bucket of water. Kentuck drank thirstily, draining the pail, and Harold brought it full again. Kentuck drank only a little this time, and then nuzzled the surface, blowing softly, and swung his dripping muzzle and blew in the grain. He lipped up a mouthful of the grain and raised his head and began to munch, only stirring restlessly now and then from the itch and fading sting of the cuts.

Gwen came back to his shoulder and caressed the blanket, murmuring comforts. Her face was still a little twisted at the thought of the wounds, and the hot cure that must have seemed like stabbing again, and because of the blood she had longed to touch. When Harold turned from lengthening the hitch rope, he blundered against her. She turned quickly, looking up at him, and caught his coat tightly in her two fists. Her eyes were still dark with her pity, and something else which had moved in her also because of the blood, and she cried up softly at Harold, in the voice she'd used to Kentuck, "Oh, darlin', I'm sorry, I'm sorry."

She kept tugging at his coat with one hand, but slid the other up over his shoulder and behind his head. "I've been horrible, darlin', I know. But it wasn't you; it wasn't you, really. I just couldn't, with all . . ." and finished in broken murmuring against him.

He held her tightly, and then, when she tugged at him less, the small, hard body softening in his arms, loosened his hold a little too, and lifted her chin with a big knuckle crooked under it, and put his mouth down to hers. Her head fell back, and she bent limply to him in his circling arm, letting it bear almost all her weight. Her lips parted, and her breath came quick and shallow against his mouth. Harold's mind thundered at this joining after the long weariness and the separation the mother had made. He jerked back the hood from her hair, and holding that hand under her head, hunted with his mouth along her throat and shoulder, and then back along her face until he found her mouth again. Then they clung there, under the low, burning lantern, and almost against Kentuck's shoulder. Kentuck swung his head, munching and dripping a little at the mouth, and watched them curiously.

When the wish that bound them ebbed a little, being too long denied, Harold turned Gwen, almost roughly, still holding her close in his arm, and led her, half lying against him, and both of them stumbling, into the shed beyond. The light of the lantern came in there through the cracks of the board partition, making thin lines of brightness over the mounds of hay, and a dry sweetness stirred in the cold air where they moved. They sank together against the first yielding bank of hay that blocked them, and Harold lay over against her, murmuring her name like the soft echo of a cry that would break him, and fingered her throat and cheek and temple with a trembling hand.

"Darling," she sighed, "oh, my darling," and closed her eyes again, and drew his shoulder down toward her.

"Harold," the voice called, from outside and a distance, and they lay still exactly where they were, his face close above hers, but not yet touching.

After a moment Gwen turned her face into his shoulder, pressing hard, and made a long, soft moan that was muffled by his coat. Harold's hand lay in the nape of her neck still, curved as it had been in his last caress, but not moving now, not even pressing.

"Oh, damn her," he whispered, "God damn her to hell. Will she never . . ." but stopped there, choked by the quick fury.

"Harold," the voice called again.

Gwen drew her head back quickly, whispering, "She's coming out here, Harold," and stiffened away from him. Then there was only the knowledge again, almost like hatred, of the clumsy winter garments between them, and of the mother's will. It was as if their own wills, and the sweet, savage desire that had fused out of them, were sucked away to nothing, leaving them separate and ashamed and wanting to hide, most of all from each other. Harold loosened his hold, and Gwen struggled to her feet at once and moved away two steps toward the door, and stood there with her back turned. After a moment Harold got up too and stood behind her. They waited, separated and listening, the thin bars of light from the stall across them and the motes they had stirred from the hay spinning among themselves in the narrow gleams.

"Harold," the mother's voice called again, from much nearer.

"You'll have to answer her, Harold," Gwen whispered, and moved away from him, and began hurriedly brushing the hay from her skirt and cloak.

The quick rage whirled in Harold again, and he couldn't keep it out of his voice, shouting, "Here. What do you want?" But then he began brushing the hay off himself too.

"Is Gwen out there too?" the mother called. The voice came from no closer now. She had stopped when he called.

"Yes, she's here," he called, but then couldn't help adding, "She's helping me. The black stud is hurt. Kentuck."

Gwen looked up at him, and then straightened up from her brushing, and drew the hood over her head and moved away into the lantern light in the stall. She stood in there by the outside door, with her back to him and her head bent. The lantern made her shadow like a praying nun on the door. He passed her and opened the door. The mother was standing out there in the deep path, half way across.

"You're letting the fire go out," she said.

"I can't do twenty things at once," Harold said, and again felt the guilt of a half lie, and how dirty the sweet wildness had turned now. "I'll get it in a minute," he added wearily.

"The girl had to take care of it for you once before," the mother told him. "While you caught up on your sleep."

Harold just stood there, not answering, and finally she said, "Well, you better fix it, and then come in before you freeze."

Harold came back into the stall and took down the lantern and picked up the kettle. Gwen waited for him outside, and when he had closed the door, went on slowly ahead of him, toward the house. The mother was already standing in the open kitchen door. When she saw the lantern moving away from the shed, she went in and closed the door, shutting away its light from the path.

Harold turned off in the drag lane and went out to the fire. The timbers had burned apart and there were only small, separate flames at their ends, and the great pile of shimmering embers in the center. Harold worked slowly around the circle,

248

kicking the timbers farther in. Then he set the kettle and lantern down, and brought more timbers from the pile and tossed them on. When the flames drew together again, and began to rise at the center, he picked up the lantern and kettle and turned toward the house. Gwen was waiting for him where the drag had crossed the path, but when he was nearly to her she went on ahead and into the house alone.

The father was the only one in the kitchen when they came in. He was sitting at the table, playing Black-Jack against himself. There was a pile of matches on each side of him, but the pile by his right hand was much larger than the one by his left. A new bottle of whisky and a glass full of it stood by the right pile. He lifted the glass and drank and made a long, sighing "Ah." Then he set the glass down again, and looked at them.

"No sign of Curt yet?" he asked.

Harold shook his head.

"Two o'clock in the morning," the father said angrily. "Almost two in the morning, and the young fool's not back yet."

And now he's dropped two days clean out, Harold thought. Well, if you have to lose two days, they were good days to lose. Does he know Arthur's dead? I wonder.

Gwen turned and moved off toward the bunk-room, and the father peered after her. "Little game of Black-Jack, young woman?" he asked loudly.

Without giving any sign that she'd heard him, Gwen went on slowly and turned into the dim light of the bunk-room, and disappeared, letting the light fill the door again by itself behind her shadow.

"Who in hell was that?" the father asked Harold. "Creepin' around here like a damned ghost," he muttered. "Won't even answer a civil question. To hell with her then."

He looked at Harold and held up the cards. "What about you?" he asked. "It's no fun robbing myself," he said, and snorted happily at his joke, and began to fish clumsily in his vest for a cigar.

"I guess not now, thanks," Harold said, and having spoken, could move again too. He started toward the stove.

"And what's wrong with cards, may I ask?"

"Nothing," Harold said.

249

He slid the kettle onto the stove and blew out the lantern and set it up on the shelf. Then he sat down in the mother's place, across from the father. The old man stared at him fiercely for a minute, his heavy, black brows drawn together and his breath snoring in his nose, but Harold wouldn't look at him, so finally he just snorted loudly, making a mouth of contempt, and struck a match to light his cigar. The match made a sound like another snort. When the cigar was drawing well, he clenched it between his teeth in the right corner of his mouth, half closing his right eye against the smoke, and flipped two cards out, face down, and then two more on top of them, face up, a nine of clubs on one and a queen of hearts on the other. Holding the rest of the deck ready, he looked at Harold again.

"Have a drink?"

"No, thanks."

The father stared again. "Everybody getting holier than Christ," he said. "A whole goddam houseful of preachers," he exploded, and then, after a moment, asked, "What's the matter now? You sick?"

When Harold just shook his head, he snorted again. "To hell with you too, then," he said. "To hell with the whole, sniveling, goody-goody bunch of you. What a family for a man who . . ." but took a deep, defiant drink instead of finishing. Then, just in the time it took to put his glass down, his expression became happy and calculating. He peered at his hole cards.

"Hit me easy," he said for the right-hand cards.

He turned up a four of spades and chuckled. "That's just about right, just about right," he said.

Harold watched him turning the cards for a while, though with empty, unseeing eyes. Then he folded his arms on the table in front of him, and laid his head down on them.

The father went on flipping the cards out and talking to himself. Sometimes, catching a glimpse of a card as it came off the deck, he'd say quickly, "Turn one under. House rule," and turn it onto the bottom of the deck, and flip the next one out instead. Whenever he could move another match onto the right-hand pile, he would chuckle and pause in the game and take a sip of his drink.

PART

3 _-˗-

22 -·-

Far below, Kentuck moved into the shadow of the pines again. The red coat across his saddle darkened and vanished, and did not reappear. When a minute had passed in the increasing light, in the slow settling of the flakes, and nothing else had moved, Curt drew a deep breath, let it out slowly, and looked down at his bare hand holding the sombrero, as if surprised to see it. Then he turned and climbed back up to where the cowhide parka lay on the snow, with the snow-shoes beside it, and the little pile of things he had taken out of the red coat. He laid the sombrero down carefully, like something brittle, and picked up the parka. He spread the parka in front of him between his two hands and looked at it. He moved the torn flap on the shoulder of it with his forefinger. Except for the fierce black moustache, which seemed alive by itself, his face was that of a sleep walker.

Finally he slipped the parka on over his head, knotted the belt around his waist, and drew up the hood. The coat was very heavy, but the sleek, quilted lining felt warm and kind. He didn't like the hood up though, blinding him on both sides. After a moment he pushed it back and let it hang between his shoulders. Then in the same way, slowly and dreamily, he stuffed the oilskin packet into his left pocket, slid the knife into its sheath and dropped it and the cartridges and the matches into the right pocket, slung the bear-paws onto his back, and drew on his mittens. The black sombrero with the rattlesnake band was left alone on the snow. He picked it up, bending stiffly because of the bear-paws, and stood holding it and staring at it as he had stared at the parka. Finally he rolled it until he could hold it in one hand, and turned and looked down through the stone gate again, at the edge where he had sent Kentuck over. Once the wind moved, making soft flutings in the rocks above him, and the pines down there stirred and whispered and dropped clots of snow, which broke and thinned away into little veils over the ravine. There was no other sound or motion. Once more he took a deep breath and sighed, as if reluctant to move, and then he turned and started up the trail.

He stopped under the wall of the Cathedral Rock and pushed the rolled sombrero into a crevice in the granite, thinking, from the surface of his closed mind, and without interest, I'll get it when I come back.

He went on up to where the carbine leaned against the rock, and picked it up and stood looking at it. Finally he took off his right mitten and stuffed it into the left pocket of the parka, beside the oilskin packet. Then he stood staring again, at the marks of the scuffle in the snow, with sand and brittle manzanita leaves strewn over them, and the long, bare place across the center where Arthur's body had melted through. Finally he looked slowly around at the confused circle of the big cat prints, like broken flowers.

"No matter what color you are," he said softly. "No matter what color, or how big, or how long it takes."

Once more the oath released him. He cradled the carbine in his right arm, and began to climb again. Out of old habit, for he wasn't really thinking about anything now, he climbed slowly but steadily, keeping each step short enough to be easy, and flat-footed and a trifle pigeon-toed, so that the soft pacs gripped firmly in the snow or on stone. The same habit made him walk carefully beside the tracks of the cat and not in them, and glance up ahead every now and then, to guard against ambush, and to be sure the trail made no big swing within sight. Unless the cat had been badly hurt, it would be a long hunt. He'd been sure of that as soon as he'd seen the long fork of the trail going up and north, and taking its time. The thing was to keep the bastard moving until you got a good shot; don't give him a chance to rest, don't give him a chance to hunt. Keep him feeling the pressure all the time. If he'd been hurt bad, it would be different, of course. You might come up with him in an hour or two. It all depended on how much of a head start he had. And he might have been hurt bad, at that. There were still flecks of blood showing sometimes between the flower prints. Maybe Arthur had hit him with that one shot. But you couldn't count on that. You had to count on a long hunt, and take it slow and steady, just keeping the pressure on the bastard all the time, only keeping your eyes open too, because if he was hurt so he couldn't keep running, he'd be waiting for you somewhere, up on a ledge, as he had for Arthur.

His mind didn't really consider these possibilities, which were all familiar from many hunts. It merely tabulated them, turned the tracking over to his body, and closed around the little fears and the flights about the black panther, and about finding Arthur that way, and having to send him home face down over a saddle. The slow, steady motion of his climbing lulled him, and the floating mists slowly parting above him and the diffused radiance that filtered through them, made it like climbing in a dream on a mountain that wasn't real.

Even in the upper woods, the dream persisted for a while. The light was only a half light, and the shadows of the trees were only half shadows, the moving vapors blending and transforming them. The sleep thinned out when the track of the cat disappeared among the trees up ahead, or when a sudden sound or movement near him demanded attention, but his eyes quickly found the track again, always farther up and a little farther north, or at once explained the interruption: a bough had dropped its burden of snow and sprung back higher, or a junco had launched off a chinkapin twig and flitted away downslope, and his attention withdrew from the world again. He had no sense at all of the time that was passing, either. It was transformed like the shapes of the mist, seeming now to be none at all, and now to be half a lifetime, a kind of sum of all the winter hunting he had ever done.

As he approached the crest of the first ridge, however, the timber thinned out, and the wind, drawing down at him out of the northwest, grew colder and stronger. It broke the mist open in many places, making little, spasmodic blizzards over an acre or two of the mountain, and clearing the air between them and after them. Where it had passed, the light entered in full strength, and was painfully bright on the snow. The cold and the dazzle fretted him, and after two of the small, whirling blizzards had sucked over him, nicking his face and making him close his eyes and bow his head, he drew up the hood of the parka, and that woke him still more. His eyes didn't trust themselves to watch alone in such a narrow range. He saw too that the blown snow was powdering over the cat's tracks, and felt a little alarm, and a need to climb faster. So it was that he saw the cat, where he might have missed it half an hour before.

The trail led him out to the edge of a deep ravine, and then turned almost straight up toward the crest. The trees below him in the ravine, and over on the far wall too, were larger than those about him, all old, twisted growth in an insecure rooting of sand and boulders among patches of brush. He paused on the edge, with no purpose except to look down, and the tiny movement on the far side, high up, near the head of the ravine, a movement less than that of a fly on a window rubbing its wings, caught his eye. In an instant he was wide awake. The cat was distinct in tiny, black silhouette against the snow, just below the skyline. It must have moved, for the movement was what he'd seen first, but now it was perfectly still, and broadside to him, though above him. The north wing was higher than the one he stood on, with a bald ridge, clear of timber and broken only by shapes of rock. He believed the cat was standing with its head turned at him, but he couldn't be sure. It was too far across the airy upper spread of the ravine. The sudden pain of guilt and loss his mind let out into him moved him as if his insides were being twisted, but he didn't know it. He believed the catch in his breath came from excitement, for he was trembling, as he slowly turned the carbine in his hands. The weakness angered him.

God Almighty, he thought, I'm like a kid on his first time out, and forced himself to move slowly and attentively. Even so a tiny dancing remained in his hands and his knees, and there wasn't time to wait it out.

Shaking like a goddam girl, he thought, and didn't raise the carbine to attempt a standing shot, but let himself down behind it instead, bracing his left elbow upon his raised left knee and bringing his eye over behind the sight in the same movement.

He's above me, he thought, and the wind's a little down-canyon, though mostly from him to me, and made allowance for those variations even while he was drawing the breath to hold.

The cat moved, advancing a step or two and starting to turn up. Curt held himself with difficulty, and didn't make the quick useless shot he wanted to. The cat stopped again. He was sure it was looking across at him now. He let his breath half out and held it, lifting his sight again toward the center he had chosen, just above and ahead of the shoulder, and slowly squeezing the trigger to slip home just when the least tip of the sharp front sight came there.

Only a guess how far, he thought. Hard to guess over a canyon, like this. The cat and the tip of the sight drew together.

The cat moved again, though only slightly, just as the trigger's tension broke. While Curt was still enveloped in the roar of the report, the tiny black cat on the point of the sight jerked visibly, a twin jerk, it seemed to him, with that of the butt in his shoulder.

Hit, the black bastard, he thought, like a white flash of joy in his head. But at once the flash dimmed while the report was spreading, for the tiny cat turned above the sight and went up in leaps toward the place where the north ridge became the mountain.

Moved, the bastard, he thought fiercely, while he was leaping to his feet and springing the lever of the carbine, and lifting it to his shoulder again. The echoes fired back the first shot from the far wall, twice sharply, once more slowly and thickly, and finally, just as he thought, Nearly stern on, and bobbing; high, left, and come down to meet the jump, in a final, deep, pro-longed roaring below. The carbine leapt again, but while the blow of the new report still closed his ears, and without a hitch in its smooth bounding, the cat became an instant hair upon the bald summit, and was gone. The thin receding scream of the ricochet went into the sky behind it.

Clean miss, the bastard, the goddam bastard, Curt raged, pumping a new cartridge home with the words. But then he held the carbine lowered, and the ravine returned his fire multiplied, exactly as before, two sharp, one muffled and slower, and the roaring like a rockslide down out of sight. Still hearing the ricochet, like a white rocket streak up across the black roaring, he knew there had been none after the first shot.

The thunder dimmed away among the boulders below, and he thought, more slowly, Maybe fleshed it at that. Or got sand, he warned himself.

He turned up along the edge of the ravine, walking quickly, and sometimes half running, replacing the used cartridges as he climbed, and then carrying the carbine free in his right hand to lengthen his stride. He didn't even look at the tracks now, but only quickly picked out his footing ahead. If he didn't catch sight of the cat at the summit, he could pick up the trail where it had gone over.

Gained on the bastard all the way, he exulted, and it's still going up. It's hurt. It wants to rest. No rest, you black bastard, he exulted.

The exultation sank away as he saw what he'd been thinking all this time. Not black, he corrected himself. It only looked black that far away and against snow. He was troubled, nonetheless, by a swift, superstitious passage of the black flight, and by half a notion that this cat wasn't even the one he had started to track; that this one was black, and was leading him, with a purpose like a man's, a thinking enemy's, into a trap. He didn't stop climbing, but there was a moment when he wanted to stop, when something in him wanted to turn and go back down.

"Black painter," he said loudly and scornfully, against this impulse. "Didn't you see it jump, you son of a bitch? It can feel lead, all right. And it's running. It's hurt, and it's running. Black painter, my eye."

He went on up, now striding swiftly from rock to rock under the snow, now half running where the footing was better. From up on top, with only thin timber all around, he'd be able to spot the cat a long way off. He might even get another shot. At any rate, no tricks were going to do it any good. From a lookout like that, he could see the whole map of the range. He could guess in one look what it was up to, whether he saw the cat or only its trail. Then it wouldn't be just a stern chase, a long dogging. They would begin to match wits, and that was his game, not the cat's.

You'll have to be a spook then, you bastard, he thought, exulting.

Suddenly the bright snow he climbed on was darkened. The light just faded away downward, behind him, and the whole ridge came under a shadow. He glanced up, and saw the new snow mist reaching up out of the ridge like smoke. It was coming up without a break in it. The farther west he looked, the thicker and more shapeless it was. The wind felt colder under the shadow too, and heavier.

It won't help you now, though, you black butcher, he thought savagely. It's way up still. It won't snow for hours. Maybe it won't snow at all, he thought. Just the tail end of the storm blowing over. It can't snow forever, this early.

Nevertheless, he felt hurried. He realized suddenly that he had no real idea how long he'd been out, and then it felt late under the shadow of the cloud, past the middle of the afternoon. The sun had been way west of the ridge, that was sure. The arms of the snow mist had cut it off long before they came over him. They were just coming over him now, for that matter.

When he came among the last, stunted, wind-bent trees, with all their branches reaching east like tattered banners, he went up carefully, just the same, with the carbine held ready. He let himself down onto his knees against the granite backbone of the ridge, and crawled up slowly, not to appear suddenly against the sky, and at the very top crawled on his belly. If it was really so late, if there was really snow in the new darkness, it was all the more important not to miss a shot now, and not to make himself a running target by carelessness if he had a chance for a sitting one. He eased his way up to where he could see all along that end of the ridge. There was only the long, gray stone, swept almost clean of snow by the wind, and west of him, clearly separate from here, the big range, with the snow much deeper on it, its upper fields an unbroken white, and over the big range, and west of it as far as he could see, a dark, moving sky of snow clouds. Here and there the white wall of the big range was already veiled by falling snow bent a little southward by the wind.

He stood up then, and came onto the ridge with one of the leaning trees behind him, so he wouldn't show. From there he could see the whole long blade of the ridge, clear to the sky on the north, and even farther south, two or three miles, perhaps, to where a long dragging screen of snow already falling came through a pass in the big range, and, sweeping slowly up the one he stood on; shut off everything beyond. He could see down the ridge on the west side too, clear into heavier timber and the whitened forest on the valley floor. The cat wasn't in sight anywhere, nor was there a single track that he could see anywhere in the snow below him.

For a moment the cat became more than natural again. There was no cover on the ridge, and there couldn't have been time for it to get down into timber below. With nothing there, with only the wind streaming over the rock ledges, and far across, only half seen as his eyes searched nearer him, the gigantic, slowly changing drama of the storm in the big range, it was as if the cat had turned the joke on him after all, and really vanished, dissolved, become wind itself.

Then he thought, It wouldn't go down yet. It's deep snow down there, hard going, and a deep trail behind him. It's gone north, the other side of the height of the ridge.

Leaning a little against the strong wind, feeling it fill the hood and belly it out, he went north swiftly on the good rock footing, and down toward the head of the ravine, where the cat had come up. He found the track there, already dim with blown snow, but it only led him back up onto the trackless rock. On the ridge again, he stood for a moment, looking all about quickly, and then went north once more, half running. At the skyline the granite shelved down steeply, and only a little below him the snow had banked against the ledges. There were no tracks in it. He let himself down to the edge of the snow, and then followed it around to the west and south again until he was opposite the tree he had first stood up against. The snow edge wasn't broken anywhere, except by gray rock or the curving blade shapes the wind had given it. Once again, for a moment, the cat formed and was able to vanish in his mind, and its first form was big as a horse and black. Then first the white snow showed faintly through it, and then the twisted tree, and finally even the gray ledges, before it was not there at all.

His waking mind, now angry and hurried, pressed the brief vision aside at once, as less than the enemy shapes a child makes for himself in a dark room.

"Must have gone south, then," he said aloud. "Nowhere else it could have gone."

With a moment of fear, half made up of the time he had already lost on the ridge, he thought, But the bastard must have plenty left to move that fast. He couldn't have been hurt too bad; not bad enough to do any good.

He climbed back onto the ridge, and turned south where he met his own tracks. With the wind behind him, or quartering down over his right shoulder, so he felt it finger in now and then through the tear in the parka, he was warmer, and moved faster and more easily, and saw more clearly. He pushed the hood back impatiently, so he could see all around him, and traveled quickly along the crest of the ridge, watching for any place among the ledges where the cat might have crouched to hide or to wait for him, and scanning the edge of the snow on both sides.

Twice he saw breaks in the stone where the cat might have hidden, and held the carbine ready, and worked up to them carefully. In the first there was a little slanting drift of snow the wind had dropped over the edge, but no mark in it.

The second was sheltered by an overhang, and the stone floor was bare. Standing above it, and looking south as far as he could see, without finding any break in the snow below the ridge, he thought, The bastard waited here till I went up the north end. It has to be that. Then he could of got clear down there where it's snowing before I got back around.

He went down and around and into the flat, long, shallow cave, and stooped and looked carefully at the thin scattering of sand over the granite, and the lines of sand caught in the crevices. There was nothing that was clearly a track, but in three places there were breaks, the sand spread a little and across its natural line, as wind couldn't have moved it.

Couldn't have been there long, either, he thought, or the wind would of straightened them out again. He watched them

261

for a moment, and saw the grains stirring now, moving bit by bit, a few here, a few there, back into their lines with the wind.

"It's you, you damn spook," he said aloud, eagerly, and straightened up quickly, and climbed back onto the ridge again, and turned south. He went at a dog-trot now, glancing along the edges quickly, and as far ahead as he could, and looking up and beyond that now and then too, worried by the snow cloud spreading along the ridge. Still there were no tracks.

As the first flakes of the snow began to move across him, he said aloud, "So you made it, you lucky bastard. But it won't cover for you yet."

The snow thickened, though. He couldn't see anything distinctly in it, and had to go more slowly, peering to find the white edges, sometimes waiting out the heavier flurries in order to see at all. And again, as it became suddenly darker in the blown snow, time jumped away from him, all the way to the edge of evening.

"Oh, you lucky devil," he said. "But it's not done yet, you son of a bitch," he vowed angrily. "This goddamned ledge can't go all the way to Mexico. You'll have to show some time."

Then, after all, in his anxiety, in the ever-thickening pall of the snow, he almost missed what he was looking for. It was only chance that he saw it. A gust of wind uncovered it for a moment, and before his eyes lost it again, he guessed what it must be. Standing there peering toward it, waiting for another break in the whirling of flakes about him, which had already whitened the parka, and now was beginning to hold on the rocks too, he felt the little fear again, the cold, slight thrill of being outwitted, as he realized that what he'd seen wasn't at all what he'd been watching for. He'd been watching right along the edge for the flower prints and the groove of a tail drag. These marks were far down from the edge and just holes in the snow. The wind broke the snowing open for him again, and he saw them clearly, only one group, all bunched together, and twenty feet or more below the bare granite ledge.

He went down to them, partly blinded by the snow driving against his face. It was the cat, all right. In the bottom of the little pits the legs had made, he could still see the broken flowers of the pads. He couldn't see out of the snowing in any direction now. He worked on down slowly, and found another cluster of marks, and then a third, and a fourth, each many feet farther down. Then the incline lessened, and the tracks closed a little. He drew up the hood to shelter his eyes, and followed the descending clusters, forcing himself to go slowly and carefully in spite of his impatience, and his fear of the storm and the coming darkness.

"You can't go any farther than I can in this," he said aloud, but now less as a threat than to encourage himself.

Farther down the slope, where the wind-bent timber closed in again, the tracks became single and evenly spaced, and now and then a short crescent of tail-drag showed. The cat was sure of itself again, trusting the cover of the storm, and the bare ridge and the long leaps behind it.

"Give me one look, just one," Curt said softly, half exulting again, but continued to work his way carefully down among the trees, pausing and peering, and sometimes flaring angrily inside against the snow and all the hiding places which made him go so slowly and kept him from seeing any distance around him. It was quieter down there though. The wind passed high above him, and the snow fell gently under it, making only occasional mild eddies.

Toward the bottom of the ridge, the snow grew rapidly deeper. The cat had floundered several times, leaving long, deep belly troughs, with dark holes in them where its legs had sunk.

Been snowing here all day, Curt thought. On and off, anyway.

And a little later he thought, And all night too.

The cat marks floundered on, though, going as straight down into the valley as they could among the trees.

No tricks now, he thought. Thinks it's clean away. Just traveling. It'll hole up by dark, and lick its scratches.

When the snow came almost to his hips, and it was difficult just to push through it, he stopped long enough to lace on the bear-paws. Then he went down again, clumsily, with the little side-swing of each leg the bear-paws made necessary, but even so, faster and more easily.

The trail led straight across the high valley between the two ranges, first through a reaching peninsula of timber, and then across a wide, open meadow, where the snow was blown into sharp, curving drifts over the earth humps and along the turns of the creek that meandered south through the middle of it. The creek was frozen over and then covered with snow.

By the time Curt came among trees again, on the west edge of the meadow, real darkness was spreading into the gray gloom of the snowing. The snow was the deepest yet there, and light and evenly spread. The cat had dragged badly in it, and floundered from side to side, hunting for solid footing underneath. Even in the dusk and among the trees, the big trail was still easy to follow, going up through the terraced pines in long, irregular switchbacks. Curt was encouraged, thinking how he gained here, going nearly straight up from point to point of the cat's slow zigzags. He climbed as fast as he could, but it was exhausting work. The webs sank in, and a little burden of the snow had to be lifted and shaken off at each step, and often he had to dig into the white slope to keep from slipping. He was breathing quickly and loudly, and beginning to feel shaky and a little lightheaded from the steep pitch and the height, and painfully empty from his long fast.

Also, as the darkness increased, he began to mistrust his eyes. The burdened trees loomed ominously all about him, and sometimes seemed to be closing in. He couldn't be sure of distances among them. He was high enough now, too, for broken gusts of the wind to reach down to him sometimes, whirling the snow and moving the trees jerkily, so that he stopped several times, with the carbine held ready against the shadowy jumping. The snow was falling more heavily all the time, and he had to give up cutting across the cat's long detours for fear of losing the trail altogether.

He'd hardly been thinking at all for a long time now, only watching, when all at once, like a warning from outside, as sharply as if somebody had called to him, he thought, Cats can see in the dark.

The thought stopped him at once, right where he was. Mountain lions can see in the dark, of course, he thought. They hunt at night all the time.

He was almost as much alarmed because he had gone so long

without thinking of this obvious fact as he was by the fact itself. His confidence was shaken again, as it had been shaken when he came onto the first ridge, and couldn't see the cat or any tracks. Now it was getting to where he had to be almost within reach of a tree to pick it out of the moving darkness of snow and nightfall and wind together. But the cat could see him as well as ever, if it was in the right place. The snow would blind it a little, perhaps, but hardly more than in daylight. Again he quickly remembered stories of the malice and cleverness of mountain lions, and also what the tracks had told him at first hand about this one, doubling back and waiting above the trail for Arthur, and then gaining all that time by using the granite ridge. In the darkness, his mind made very clear pictures, too. He saw Arthur's dead face, the way it had looked when he first turned him over. Then he saw Arthur coming up the trail under Cathedral Rock, alive, but not watching and not thinking about what he was doing either, and the cat crouched on the ledge above him, working its hind legs carefully, nervously under itself for the leap, the tip of its long, serpent tail slowly curling and uncurling. At once, after that, he imagined it preparing in the same way now for him, on a ledge he couldn't even see.

After a moment, though, he made himself go on up. He had sworn to get that cat. He had repeatedly made a vow to a dead brother for whom he had wept his first tears since he was a little kid that he would get that cat if he had to follow it all the way to the ocean. And he had said something to the little Welshy about a lion skin too. It had been a foolish boast, but he'd made it, and when he thought of going back without the hide now, the boast became a vow more compelling than the one to Arthur, because others had heard him make it. If he stopped here, and the snow kept falling, he wouldn't even be able to make a guess, by morning, where the cat had gone. He knew this range. He knew exactly where he was on it now. If he could just keep tracking until the cat holed up, or set a clear course from the ridge, he could guess his way back onto the track in the morning.

He had to stoop to see the trail now, and he climbed more and more slowly and guardedly. He was nearing the real timberline. The trees became smaller and smaller around him. He couldn't really see them, but he knew what they looked like, low and flat and one-sided, with loose fibred, twisted trunks, like sagebrush, the tough, misshapen little dwarfs of height and cold and wind and rocky rootholds. The darkness seemed to be holding off, to be giving him a little more time up in the open among them, but the wind was constant and icy, and the snow it carried pelted him like fine shot.

At last he came up onto the dark rock ledges of the crest. The wind was so strong he had to stoop against it, and sometimes hold onto the rock to steady himself. It blew the snow at him like weapons, in long spear lines out of the dark northwest. He couldn't see the tracks at all now, but only make out the long, black fish shape of the wind-swept rock in the snow. This was where he had to quit. The long rock would have to do as a starting point in the morning.

Standing still for a moment to think about that, he felt the sweat in the hollows of his knees and running slowly from his arm pits down along his ribs, although his face and his trigger hand were numb. Also he realized for the first time how tightly he was holding the carbine, and the tiny, dancing tricks of their own his tired eyes were playing on him.

When his breath was evener, he moved slowly along the edge of the dark rock, feeling with his bare hand for the tracks his eyes kept making in the snow when they weren't really there. Sometimes he got down on his hands and knees and put his face close to the snow because he couldn't trust the numb hand either. He was luckier on this rock, though. He'd started south along the edge, because he couldn't see at all going north, with the blizzard in his face, and the cat must have made its choice the same way. He found the tracks going off the south point of the rock. He made sure of them, taking off his left mitten and trying them with the fingertips of his warmer hand. There was no question about them. Through the thin sifting of new snow, he could feel the little pattern of hollows and ridges made by the pads.

You weren't far ahead, you cocky bastard, he thought, to leave them that fresh. And sure you'd done it, too, just walking off, like taking a Sunday stroll.

266

He stood up and put on his mittens, both of them now, and leaning over, bracing his back against the wind, peered south down the funnel of the streaming darkness. He could see nothing but the ghostly, slanting spears of the snow.

"We're not done yet, you murdering bastard," he said aloud, addressing the enviable panther his mind made, which was curled up, its nose buried in its own warmth, in some sheltered crevice not very far south.

He went slowly back down among the tough little trees. He fell several times, because it was impossible to judge the pitch and because of his trembling knees. When the trees were bigger and closer together, and the wind was more a roaring overhead than a power, he hunted, almost by touch, and with the dogged overcarefulness of exhaustion, for just the kind of tree he wanted. He hunted all in one direction, south, and he counted his steps. He had taken forty-eight deep, dragging steps which he hoped would still show in the morning, when he found the tree. It was a fir tree, tall and thick for that altitude, and it stood flat sided against a low cliff. The snow had drifted deeply below the rock, burying the tree far up. It had drifted into a firm wall too, where the wind had sucked down around the rock, a curved wall with the tree inside it.

He worked his way into the fir until he could hold its main stem. Clinging there, he laid the carbine across two branches, took off his mittens and stuffed them into his pocket, and slowly, because his fingers were stiff and cold and tired, unharnessed the bear-paws and strapped them together, and bound them to the joint of a branch. Then, pulling the hood far forward over his face, and holding the carbine, muzzle up, against his shoulder, one hand covering the trigger guard against twigs, he let himself slowly, spirally, down through the branches onto the bed of old needles. No wind at all got down there, and no snow. The needles and twigs at the foot of the rock had only a thin powdering of snow on them. It was very good to be down there, and able to give up until daylight came again. It was as good as a homecoming after a long time away.

He leaned the carbine carefully against the rock, memorizing where it was by hand. Lying there on one elbow, under the lowest branches, he drew the knife and the container of matches out of his right pocket, and took the knife out of its sheath.

Holding them, he carefully went over in his mind the turns he had made coming down through the branches. Then he lit a match and began to scratch with the point of the knife on the rock wall beside the carbine. The rock was granite, and made a fine tinsel glittering in the light of the match. It was so hard that only a faint scratch appeared on it, no matter how he dug at it. He burned six matches while he scratched an arrow pointing north that he could really see, and eight more matches to make a little 48 above it.

In the thick darkness again, he closed the match container and put it back in his pocket, and pulled the oilskin packet out of his other pocket, and unfolded it carefully on the needles between him and the rock. There were six slices of bread in the packet, his fingers told him, and a roll of stripped jerky as long as the packet and as solid as a cut off a side of bacon.

Three meals at least, he thought. Maybe four. And I'll need it more by tomorrow night than I do now.

He allowed himself one slice of the bread, and three of the thin strips of jerky. There was butter on the bread, and the butter tasted wonderful. He was very grateful to Grace for putting butter on the bread. He ate the buttered bread slowly, a small bite at a time. Then he chewed the jerky even more slowly, not swallowing it until it practically ran down by itself. The chewiness of it was pleasing, and the juice it made in his mouth was very good. It was salty, though. He'd only chewed a little of it before he was very thirsty, and realized that he'd been thirsty for a long time.

When he'd finished the jerky, he carefully rolled up the rest of the food in the oilskin again, and pushed it well down into the left pocket of the parka. He returned the knife to its sheath, and slid it back into the other pocket. Then he began to draw snow, a handful at a time, in from under the edge of the branches, and press it together. He worked at it patiently until he had a dripping ice ball that nearly filled his hand. He stretched out on his back, letting his body feel its weariness completely for the first time, smiling a little at its twitching, which once or twice even jerked his heels on the slick needles, and sucked the ice ball slowly down to nothing. The snow water had a faint, stinging taste of granite and dead needles, but it washed down the saltiness of the jerky, and slaked his thirst enough to let his body rest better. He wiped his hands dry on his pants, and reached inside the parka and got the pad of cigarette papers and the little sack of tobacco out of his shirt pocket. He had trouble rolling the cigarette by touch, and it came out nearly empty at one end and limp in the middle. Holding it between his lips by the empty end, he returned the papers and tobacco to his shirt pocket, and got out one match, and put the match container back too. Then he lit the cigarette, defending the flame of the match with both hands, although there was not a breath of air to move it, and carefully pinched the match out, and lay back again, drawing slowly and deeply on the cigarette. Its glow made a surprising amount of light in the closed darkness. The shining points of the granite appeared faintly at each drag, and he could see every needle of the bough above him. He blew the smoke out against the base of the rock, and held the cigarette there too, when he wasn't drawing on it. The smoke thinned out to nothing before it rose very far along the granite. He was sure that not the least whiff of it could get all the way up through the tree and the snow. He considered that carefully. He was so tired that he had to consider with care and determination every detail of each act he performed.

When the cigarette burned his thumb, he extinguished the limp butt of it against the rock, put on his mittens, rolled onto his side, with his back in the shallow cave at the base of the cliff, and drew his knees up into the long shirt of the parka. Lying so, he pillowed his head on one arm, and almost at once fell deeply asleep.

23 ‑ ‑ ‑

He was kneeling beside a small fire, with his hands held close over it. He was trying to warm himself, and at the same time trying hard to remember something. It disturbed him greatly that he could not remember, because he was alone in the middle of a darkness in which not a single star or mountain shape could be seen. He was lost, and he believed that what he couldn't remember had to do with where he was, or with some danger which threatened him there.

Then he saw that he wasn't alone. Arthur was standing on the other

269

side of the fire, looking down across it at him. It comforted him enormously, after the first start of fear at seeing him so unexpectedly, to have Arthur there too.

"It's Joe Sam. You know that, don't you?" Arthur said.

Curt didn't understand this remark, but he knew it was important. Arthur spoke loudly for him, and very seriously, even urgently, as if he intended the remark to be a warning. Curt looked at him intently, trying to understand what he meant, and then he was no longer comforted by his presence. There was something bad the matter with Arthur. His eyes weren't open at all. Curt had mistaken the blue, shadowy lids in the deep sockets for open eyes looking at him. Also, his face was too hollow and still, and there were four long, deep scratches across it, diagonally from the left temple to his mouth, and his beard was full of twigs and clots of earth and yellow willow leaves.

He was surprised to hear himself asking, in a worried voice, "Where is the wooden Indian?" He hadn't intended to ask any such foolish question. Joe Sam wasn't wooden.

"No," Arthur said. "I killed him. I had to," and opened his eyes. They were enormous and frightened. He stared down at Curt, and said, "Years ago," and held out his hands for Curt to look at, as if that would explain what he meant. Curt saw that his hands were red to the wrists, and that the red was fresh, and dripped between his fingers.

"It was the painter," Arthur said unhappily.

That's it, Curt thought. The painter's wooden, and that's just paint on his hands too.

"Don't say that, Curt," Arthur cried, so suddenly, and in such a terrified voice, that Curt leapt up. Then he was alone, and in complete darkness. Even the little fire was gone.

"What?" he cried anxiously, but his voice was all alone, and closed in against him, and thick. But he knew what the danger was now. It was himself, not Arthur, the panther was going to kill. Arthur had somehow escaped after all, but he, Curt, was lying down there against the fir tree, under the boulder, and the black panther was waiting for him on the snow above. It couldn't get down to him, but it knew he was there, and it knew he'd have to come out sooner or later. It was going to wait for him. He could hear it sniffing up there, at the edge of the snow around the tree.

Then, all at once, he was greatly relieved.

"Not black, the son-of-a-bitch," he said aloud, and remembered everything clearly.

He lit a match just the same, and felt much better to see the fir bough over him, and the carbine leaning against the rock, and the arrow and the 48 scratched beside it, just as they had appeared by the last glow of the cigarette the night before. To see the whole little hollow just as it had been, completely separated the dream from what had really happened. He still couldn't entirely free himself of the feeling that the cat was waiting for him above, but he knew better than to believe it. There wasn't a sound up there, when he really listened, and besides, the snow wouldn't hold the bastard up.

"I'll really put something in the old belly this morning," he said aloud. "I'll have to chase the son-of-a-bitch again, God knows how far."

He stretched himself, and worked his shoulders inside the parka and his feet inside the pacs, doing everything he could in that low, narrow space, to break the cold that had hold of him, and to reduce his stale weariness. He didn't spend long at it, though. He had a feeling that it might be hours after daybreak already, up there on top of the snow, and if it was, the cat would have a long start on him. As soon as his body felt usable again, he got out the food packet and ate two slices of the bread and butter and six of the strips of jerky. After that he packed two snowballs and sucked them down to nothing. He considered making and smoking a cigarette, thinking, Take your time and feel right; gets there fastest in the end, but decided against it after all.

Waste too much time, he thought. Gotta get up there and take a look around.

He didn't admit to himself his other objection, that he didn't want to make a smell of tobacco smoke down there in his hole.

He rolled the food packet up again, stuffed it into the left pocket of the parka, and took the carbine, covering the trigger with his hand again, and started slowly up through the branches. At first he began to repeat to himself, "Forty-eight steps north," but shortly he couldn't spare the breath for it, and then he wasn't even thinking it. It was much harder going up than it had been coming down. The limber branches wouldn't support

271

him very well, and the ones above kept pressing him down, so that he had to squirm among them at each whorl to discover an opening through which he could get up to the next level. He didn't allow himself to curse or thrash in his irritation, however, because he wanted to hear anything there was to hear, and he didn't want to make any loud sound himself, in case there should be something up there listening. When the trunk of the fir became noticeably smaller, and he began, vaguely, to see the shapes of the branches around him, he went still more slowly, and stopped after every gain to listen. He also worried a little now, about how he could get the carbine free in all that limber tangle, if he had to use it.

He bumped his head on the snowshoes before he saw them, and was briefly alarmed because they were so much harder than the branches, and yet were dangling free. Then he was alarmed because he had found them there, so far down under cover. A lot of new snow must have fallen in the night. He wondered if the tree would support him far enough up its tapering trunk to get out of the snow. He worked the webs free of their branch and slung them around his neck.

I'll be breakin' out any time now, he thought. Gotta keep around against the rock as much as I can. Have one side of me covered anyway.

He worked his way around and up through one more whorl, and then, suddenly, a shower of snow poured down on him, a lot of it falling coldly inside the hood. When it stopped falling, his head was up out of the snow, and he could see clearly. For a moment he clung there, motionless with alarm because he had been exposed so suddenly, and without time to prepare himself. There was nothing in sight, however, except the slope of deep snow and the terraces of snow-laden trees, and the new snow falling, but in big, quiet flakes now, coming straight down. He was relieved about time, too, for there was only a blue, very early daylight among the trees.

It was impossible to get his bear-paws on in the tree, and when he reached a foot out into the bastion of snow, it broke up and fell away through the branches below him in little, whispering showers. Finally, furious after struggling against something like that, something with no weight and no solidity, which crumbled away at every touch, he scrambled recklessly up on the boulder side until he could get a hold on the edge of the rock, under the snow. He flailed some of the snow off the top with the stock of the carbine, and threw the carbine up, well back from the edge, and scrambled up himself, pitching forward into the snow. The short fury, and the little triumph that came with getting off the tree onto the solid granite, did him good, washing out the last of the closed-in dream notions, and leaving him wide awake and out free in the daylight.

He crawled up safely away from the edge, knelt in the snow his body had packed, and laced on the bear-paws. Then he put on his mittens, recovered the carbine from the bottom of the deep, carbine-shaped well it had made in the snow, and brushed it off, and cradled it in his arm, and turned north. Going as straight as the trees would let him, and making his steps short, to match the tired, plowing steps he had taken the night before, he counted the forty-eight, and stopped and looked around. There were no signs of tracks. The new snow and the wind had smoothed the mountainside perfectly, save for the curving dykes around the trees. This didn't matter too much for his start, but it worried him about the chances of the cat having left any kind of a trace. His only hope was that it had holed up for the night, and broken a fresh trail out this morning, a trail he could get to before any wind came up, or the new snow filled it.

He turned upslope, and climbed as rapidly as he could with the webs sinking a foot into the snow at every step. He couldn't see far through the heavy, floating snowfall, and everything within the circle of his vision was changed by daylight and the new depth of the snow. The dwarf trees at timberline, when he came among them, were only a field of small, white domes, and some of them didn't even make domes, but had vanished completely under wind-flattened drifts. It was easy to tell when he reached the fish-shaped ridge, though. There was snow on it too, now, but the wind had kept it shallow, and he could kick through to the dark rock anywhere on it.

He turned south and began to move faster, the shallow snow supporting him at once, and the light, steady, southeastward suck of the summit wind helping him along. He still moved in a small, snowed-in circle by himself, though. The trees below him faded down quickly into a white blank, and when he looked out straight above them, there was only the gray-streaked curtain of falling snow. He could barely make out the constant, gray wall of shadow above him on the right, that told him that he hadn't got quite to the top of the ridge the night before. He watched the snow in front of the webs attentively, until he felt sure he'd gone well past the place where he'd found the tracks in the evening, and after that he watched all around him, the best he could, for any remnant of a mark in the snow that the wind hadn't made.

It was hard, though, in that small, all white world, to keep his mind working with his eyes. The whiteness everywhere made as good a screen for his memory to work on as the darkness of night or of his shelter under the fir tree, and the steady drifting away before him of the falling flakes was hypnotic. He almost missed the retreat in the ledge above him because his eyes saw it inattentively through Gwen in the yellow blouse sitting across the kitchen table from him, and coffee and hash-brown potatoes and ham in front of him. He had gone several yards beyond it before his mind, changing to show him Arthur's body in the red coat going down over the edge across the saddle, let him know for a moment what his eyes had just seen.

"Geez," he said aloud. "Now who's dreamin'?" and the little fears stirred in him again.

"Keep your eyes open, stupid," he warned himself. "The bastard could of had you any time the last half hour."

And then the fears stirred once more because he realized that he had no trustworthy impression of the passage of time either. It might have been a half hour, but it might just as well have been ten minutes, or two hours.

"We'll take a look," he said aloud and boldly, and turned up toward the cave, watching it attentively, and holding the carbine ready. It showed at first only as a long, narrow, blue shadow in the snowing, almost at the end of his vision. As he came closer, it darkened, and he could see that it was larger than he'd thought, because he'd seen only the higher south end of it. The drifting snow had made a long, curving dyke in front of the north end. He couldn't tell how deep the cave was, and he climbed at it slowly, stopping every few feet and trying to peer into the shadow behind the dyke. When he could see clear to the back of the open end, and knew it was empty, he circled a little to the south to make his final approach at an angle that would let him see in behind the drift. There was nothing in the cave.

When he had made sure of this, he climbed over the drift and knelt and worked in under the ledge. There was a sifting of sand on the stone floor, and again he believed that the sand had been disturbed as the wind couldn't have disturbed it.

"He was here, all right, damn him," he said aloud and cheerfully.

He laid the carbine down and took off the bear-paws, and used one of them to shovel out the snow fill and let more light into the low, sheltered, north end. Then he crept in on his belly and peered very closely at the wall and the floor, and even took off his right mitten and searched them with his hand. Finally he found it, more with his fingers than with his eyes, a little tuft of hairs caught on the rock at the back. He crawled around into the light with them, and examined them closely. They were short hairs, just the right length, and properly coarse and wiry too, but they were very dark. They could have been called black without stretching things much. The swift, numerous flight started across his mind again, but he cut it off by grinning and speaking aloud.

"Real hair, and it came off," he said. "He's a dark one, all right. Maybe Joe Sam brought his old friend south with him after all, but he sheds, and he bleeds, the bastard."

And, he thought, standing up and letting the little tuft of hairs go out of his fingers into the wind, After eighteen years, he must be a son, or even a grandson. Spook stock must be shrinking some these days, too. He was a good deal short of the size of a horse, that one, to get in there at all.

He picked up the webs and the carbine, and scrambled back over the drift onto the open ledge, and stood there looking at the snow all around him. The swift, chittering flight went over his mind unchecked, this time, for he was thinking about what he saw. There were no tracks anywhere in the snow except his own. He stood the bear-paws on edge in the drift and circled the cave, crossing the overhang that made its roof, and coming back around the north end. There were no tracks anywhere, but only the wind-smooth snow.

He stopped the birds this time, by saying aloud, with a little chuckle, "Must be light enough on his feet to see through, for a fact." It was not a successful joke.

"Hell," he said, arguing boldly against the stone and the snow and the easy wind, "he just got off too early for me, that's all. They been rubbed out."

He laced on the webs again, and took the carbine and stood up with it cradled in his arm, and peered all around, thinking, But if he waited for daylight, there hasn't been much wind. It wouldn't cover up for him, anywhere but up here. And he didn't double back, or I'd of met him, or seen where he went down. He could of gone over the top, but it's ten to one against it, or he'd of done it last night. This must be about the end of his territory. So it has to be south again.

"But you're chasin' spooks for a fact now, Bridges," he told himself aloud. "And there's gotta be a strict time limit to that sorta fun. Let's see where we are."

He went carefully over the course of the hunt so far, and tried to estimate the distances roughly by the over-all time. He couldn't be very sure of his guess, because his pace had changed so often, and because he was so uncertain about the time he'd left Cathedral Rock and about what time it was now. He believed, however, that he must have come back south along the two ridges even farther than he'd gone north on the first tack.

"Hell," he said cheerfully, "the bastard's practically leadin' me home."

And less than half my grub gone, he thought. Half the bread, and less than half the jerky.

"You're not out of this yet, brother," he announced. "You gotta start back down somewhere," he went on, commencing to shuffle south again, and down the ledge to keep an eye on the deeper snow below it. "And when you start down this time," he said happily, "you'll leave a track like a flash-flood."

Snow's lettin' up some too, he thought, a little later. He was seeing farther and more easily, and with the shadowy shapes of the trees and ledges to hunt among, his mind was resisting the moving whiteness better. He watched all about him, pushing the hood part way back on his head to increase the span of his vision.

Nevertheless, the notion persisted in his mind, though he didn't allow it to become more than a notion, that the cat had outguessed him, that some time before daylight, so the wind and snow had erased its trail, it had circled back north and waited for him, and that now it was trailing him. Several times he stopped and turned all the way around, to take a good look behind him, but there was never anything but the long spears of snow floating at him across snow.

As time went on, and he did nothing but drag along at the same slow, steady pace, even the opening mountainside could not prevent the monotony from lulling him. He was still tired from yesterday's run, and from the cold sleep. Several times he came to suddenly, and realized that he had been moving for a long time, how long he couldn't guess, without really seeing anything around him. Then the little fears would stir again, though now they seemed to move less within him than at some distance behind him, and either above him, among the ledges of the summit rock, or below him, in the edge of timber. After each startled waking, he would stop and look all around him, but particularly north, and when he went on again, he would move in a shuffling, spread-legged trot for a while, to get warm and to wake himself up.

The most alarming of these starts came when he woke to realize that it wasn't even snowing around him any longer. The heights were still shadowy dark, and the wind was up again, so that at times the flurries of ground snow around him were thicker than the real snowing had been, but there was no new snow falling where he was. The effect wasn't encouraging, however. The wind had divided the storm for a while, that was all, and the ridge he stood on was aloft and clear between two forces, with only a thin veil of gray high above it, torn here and there so the blue showed faintly through. On his left the lower range and the valley between the two ranges were completely hidden by the base of a great wall of cloud, which rose until its paler, billowing top towered into the sky far above the ridge. On the other side, separate reaches of cloud, like rolling smoke, were already advancing obliquely down the slope, and behind them, though at some distance still, came the dark main body of the new storm of which they were the scouting columns.

Once he had clearly seen that storm upon the west, Curt, though he continued to go south along the ridge, and to watch below him on the left, went much more quickly, often breaking into that shuffling trot, and he watched at least as much for some opening in the cloud below him that would let him guess where he was, as he did for tracks.

The break didn't come. The front storm remained trapped in the valley, only drifting southward and changing shape within itself, while the dark storm above him in the west continued to advance, though sliding mostly along the blade of the ridge, and only slowly working over it.

Trotting almost constantly now, until he was panting with his hurry, and glancing up more and more often at the near, moving darkness, he came to a place where the ridge began to slope gradually downward ahead of him. Here and there the ragged tops of dwarf trees showed through the snow again, and as he descended, they became more numerous. The wind lost its full force behind him, too, and turned gusty, so that instead of moving with his feet invisible in the long tide-rip of surface snow, he was repeatedly caught in whirling clouds of it that forced him to stand for several seconds with his head bent and his arm across his face, until they had passed on over him and were skirmishing and twisting a hundred feet in the air out over the hollow.

It didn't look like a true pass he was coming down into, but only a wide, shallow depression, a scoop at the south end of the long col he had been following. If he knew the place, he didn't recognize it now, in his hurry and confusion, and under all the snow that had drifted into it, and with the first, long scouting tendril of the storm sucking darkly down into it from the west. He had never hunted this high when there was anywhere near so much snow, and he could remember a lot of hollows that might have come to look like this one when they got drifted in. If it was the one he thought most likely, though, he was still way north of the ranch. He must have gone much farther north from Cathedral Rock than he'd realized.

He hurried on down the slope, finally no longer even pausing for the most blinding of the snow dervishes that whirled across him, but only putting his head down, and holding the hood across the right side of his face. Even so, the new snow caught him in the bottom of the hollow. Then he was forced to stop. The air darkened around him and the snow drove thickly at him, seeming to come from every direction. He meant only to wait out the first blast, but it didn't let up. It even seemed to be getting thicker and wilder. Coming down into the hollow, he had only been thinly frosted over by snow crystals, but now, in a moment, the parka was so thickly plastered that its red patches vanished.

And this is only the first of it, he thought slowly, the words coming separately and far apart in his mind. He didn't dare wait for a lull, but began to push forward, dragging the webs, bracing himself in one direction or another at every step, and half the time with his eyes nearly closed against the black whirl of the snow. He kept twisting his body away from the storm, trying to get it to ride up off him on the blade of the hood. It didn't work, though, for whenever he got set in one direction, the snow would suddenly be coming from another. The hollow seemed a mile across at least, and it was only by the slower laboring of his legs, and the need to bend forward a little to keep his balance, that he knew when he began to climb out of it on the other side.

As he climbed, the darkness decreased swiftly. He had worked up into the top and south edge of the shadowy advance guard, and soon he could see the tall whirlwinds of snow dancing up the slope ahead of him again. Finally the gray reach of the storm was entirely behind him and below him, pouring on down to reinforce the high cloud that was trapped in the valley. He was on a ridge still, but lower than before. He could make out the near, ghostly spires of evergreen timber in the edge of the valley cloud. The ground snow kept racing across him as he hurried south, and then, after perhaps an hour—it seemed a long time, anyhow—the first thin veils of the new front came down over him, often broken by the gale, so that at one moment he could see only faint, hardly distinguishable shapes, and the next he could see clearly a long way down or ahead. He kept telling himself then, only that he must get farther south and that if the main storm caught him solidly before he found a familiar way out, he could always turn straight down into the lower storm and find shelter under a tree again.

At this lowest ebb of his confidence, however, when he had nearly forgotten that he had started out to hunt, he was suddenly encouraged by an accident of the storm. The mingled ground snow and mist of the new storm, sweeping southeast across him, and very high, was rent, like the parting of gigantic theatre drapes, and in the sharp perspective distance took on through that frame, he saw a tiny movement, against the wind, and high on the white wall of a mountain or pass ahead of him. He couldn't tell whether it was the wall of a mountain or of a pass, for there was only that one region of it revealed, without a top, and without an end in either direction. He didn't try to guess which it was at that moment, either. He just stood still, shocked out of his numbness, and watched for that tiny movement against the wind to come again. He believed he saw it again, too, but almost at once it vanished. That could be because of snow blowing over it where it was, though, as it had been blowing over him here. He kept peering, blinking frequently to rest his eyes, and tilting his head back to look out narrowly from under the lids, as Joe Sam had taught him to do when he had to look a long distance and for a long time. He believed that he saw the movement twice more, each time a little farther west upon the white wall.

The bastard's still running, he thought. I've really got him going; running hungry, and right into the storm. He's trying to get over on the other side, clear out of his territory. He's pretty near done, then. He must be pretty near done to be tryin' that.

He didn't, however, feel altogether confident of the truth of these silent and aggressive words. He couldn't be sure that what he had seen was the cat, or even, to tell the truth, that he had seen anything at all. Men often saw queer things at high altitudes in snow. They made them up out of nothing, with their eyes. He admitted these reasons for doubt, but the very fact that he perceived them so clearly, that he was still measuring his chances with such calm, was encouraging in itself. He didn't really believe he was just seeing things. He believed that what he had seen was the cat, still retreating before him. The feeling that he was in undirected flight himself, and with a personal and malignant doom imminent, abated within him. He was wonderfully restored, as if the discovery that the cat was still retreating from him would in some way enable him to master storm and distance too.

"Right on your tail still, you son-of-a-bitch," he said aloud, and thought, I can stretch the food another day easy, if I have to. And maybe I can even pick me off a rabbit or a buck, if he goes down far enough on the other side. The thought of fresh meat filled his mouth with saliva. It seemed to him that he could happily eat the fresh meat raw; that it might even be better raw, still hot and bloody and with the strong, salty, wild taste in it. He might even eat the cat, if it came to that.

He was already advancing again, and at the same time keeping watch for that tiny movement into the wind on the high, white wall.

"You'll still get your blanket, you little Welsh bitch," he said aloud, and gleefully. "And I'll charge you for it, too; don't you ever think I won't. My own price, and no tricks."

Then the long chain dance of the wind snow came over him again, and the white wall he had been watching was closed away. He kept peering ahead for it, prepared to use the least instant of its appearance to pick out the tiny movement again. Several times the snow dancers broke their lines before him, or sank away, subsiding along the lower slope in final, spreading curtsies, and he saw the white wall again, the last time astonishingly closer, so that he seemed to be approaching it with the speed and ease of a bird, but he didn't catch sight of anything moving on it again.

All at once, and quite surprisingly, so completely had his attention been fixed ahead, he was enveloped again in the darkening, blinding whirl of flakes that was not ground snow. Everything else vanished. He was shut in entirely by himself in a motion like a tremendous and infinitely various noise.

In an instant his optimism was gone, and not only because of his present danger. He had been taken unawares again, and not by any little, narrow advance column of the snow either, but by the dark main body of the enemy, which he had been watching for hours as it hung upon the ridge. It was a mile high, and God only knew how deep, yet it had caught him napping, blind with a little, no-account fancy of his own.

After this first panic, which he endured standing still and bowed against the storm, he began to advance across the blast again.

I've got to hole up, he thought. That's all that matters now; hole up and wait this out.

"All the same," he muttered stubbornly, inside the hood, "I saw something, and it wouldn't be anything else, up this high, in a blizzard like this. The damned cat wouldn't be up here, even, if I hadn't chased him up. And if I have to dig in, so does he. And I'll know that wall he was on, the first good look I get at it."

He was encouraged by the fact that he was still able to argue in this way, but the argument itself was not convincing in that whirling half-darkness. On the contrary he felt, profoundly and unreasonably, that the storm and the panther were now in alliance against him. Shortly, also, it began to grow darker around him in a way he didn't believe was caused by an increase of the snowing. Once again time leapt ahead in him. He guessed, as soon as he noticed the change, that he must already have overrun his mark badly, that he must be way south of the ranch, as much as ten miles south, maybe. With the growth of this first impression into a belief, all the latter part of the ridge he had followed became increasingly strange in his memory. He had never, until today, seen the white regions he'd caught glimpses of through the curtains of storm, or the shallow pass where the first skirmishers of the new snow had caught him.

Before the darkness had settled much more about him, he was no longer certain, in the tangled whirling of the flakes, of any direction except up and down. Then even that last safeguard was weakened because he felt himself to be going down steeply. The webs slipped a little sometimes, and the force of the wind was lessened, and the whirling around him was slower. He must have got switched around to the east without knowing it, and be going down between the ranges. Well, there was nothing to do but go on down, and hole up as soon as he could. Not only was he lost, but a new, fierce cold had come down with the second army of the snow, and even in the heavy parka, he was already shivering from it. He had to get cover, and get it quick. Since he was already south of the ranch, it was all to the good, so far as getting home was concerned. It was the end of the last pretense of keeping up the hunt, though, and what was a lot worse, it proved that his sense of direction, that infallible guide that was just in him and to be obeyed, was no more to be trusted now than his deliberate calculations of time and distance, if as much.

Gradually, with the barrier of the slope behind him, it became possible to see a few yards into the dusk around him. He had come among twisted, timberline trees once more, but much bigger ones than those in the shallow pass, standing well up, blue and ghostly, out of the deepening snow. He felt a more wakeful hope that shelter was near, and began to increase his pace. He fell several times, but struggled and floundered to his feet again each time, and hardly gave the falls a thought.

It was only a last-moment glimpse, a something he felt to be wrong, though he couldn't have said what, that saved him from tumbling over the cliff. He checked himself so close to the edge of it that his left web broke off a block of snow, which vanished with startling suddenness, leaving a faint, shadowy break in the snow line, like the place where a tooth is missing. Perhaps it was only that break that warned him, for the sloping snow at the bottom of the ravine had appeared perfectly continuous with the slope he was coming down. Nothing had trustworthy shape or distance any longer, but only a scarcely distinguishable difference of pallor and shadow.

After the first moment of shock, however, he felt much better. He wasn't going down into the valley after all. He was going down into a ravine, a pass, a cut of some sort through the range. He had been going south all the time, after all. The compass of his reasoning swung back to agree with the compass of his body, which had never stopped insisting that he was going south, and he felt wonderfully relieved. It was like being joined again, without a flaw, after having been cut in half.

The edge of the cliff seemed to slope downward to his left, to the east, that was, and he turned that way, climbing upslope a little first, to be safely above that too vague falling-off place, and followed it down. He felt the wind growing steadily stronger as he descended, but it seemed to him that it kept shifting also, coming at him straight from the north sometimes, and at other times from as far around as the southwest.

- - - 24

When a slow, step-by-step testing with the webs finally told him he was off the cliff, it was so nearly dark he could no longer guess at the mountain shapes around him. It seemed to him, from what the webs told him, and from the fury of the wind, that he must have come out into an open and almost level space beyond the mouth of the pass. He wanted to keep going east, down the slope of the big range, and take shelter as soon as the trees were tall enough and deeply enough sunk in the snow, but the wind whirled about him so continuously now, enclosing him with blinding spirals of snow, that he was mortally afraid to venture any farther into the open.

"Got to work back under the cliff," he muttered in the hood. "Can't miss that. And find a cave or something; get out of this goddam wind."

He turned right once more and began to shuffle ahead. He kept expecting the wind to ease off, broken by the cliff rising beside him, or to come more directly at him, funneled through from the west by the pass or the ravine, or whatever it was, but it didn't. It continued to buffet him from every side, and to whirl the snow so that sometimes it struck him unexpectedly in the face, bringing him to a halt, and sometimes there would be a dark quiet before him, while the snow struck its hundreds of tiny blows against the back of the parka. He drew the hood nearly closed over his face, leaving only a little opening to peer through, and held it that way.

Gradually he began to believe that the wind was blowing more against his back than against his front, and again his inner compass fell into disagreement with the compass of his reason. It became an expensive effort of will to continue his advance with this argument going on, and after a time, he turned sleepy and inattentive as well as weary. Twice he almost blundered into one of the haunting trees, unable to see it until it loomed sudden and monstrous right before him. Each time the tree became, for an instant, a leaping black panther, but each time he forced the terrible fear down again, and told himself doggedly, "Right; go around it to the right," speaking aloud to make himself listen, and as a challenge to the tree. The third time, he actually struck against a springy, reaching branch. He was almost knocked over, and a little bleat of dread was squeezed out of him by the contraction of his belly. He was very near to weeping from exhaustion and bafflement, when at last the wind did begin to ease off, and the snow to fall more slowly and more evenly around him.

"About time," he said angrily. "Goddamit, it's about time."

He could make out the trees a little sooner now, their goblin shadows against the glimmer of the fallen snow, and though he was stopped by them several times, believing he saw them move, even lifting the carbine against them, yet each start of fear was milder than the last, and each time, before he moved on, he remembered to warn himself, "Around to the right; keep going around to the right."

Gradually the trees became fewer and smaller and farther apart around him, until at last he seemed to have come into a region where there were no trees at all, but only the light, deep snow he shuffled through, and the thick, falling snow slanting across him. He had been worried before about losing his direction as he steered around the trees, and now, unreasonably, he was much more worried about circling in the pale emptiness.

He was about to risk making a complete right turn, to go straight at the north cliff, when the falling snow was twisted by the wind, and opened before him, and he saw the white wall looming up there, and the dark band of cliff under it, close ahead of him. In the moment he was allowed to stare at them, he was sure that he'd seen that shape of whiteness before, that, from far north, in the afternoon, he had seen that tiny, dark movement across it and against the wind. The uneasy needles of his compasses spun wildly against each other, and he stood still, and the white slope that looked like a wall in the darkness was closed away from him again. He waited, feeling every least turn of the wind now, as something he must judge, and staring at the place where the wall had vanished. Finally there came another gust that was strong enough, and from the proper quarter, and he saw the white wall again, or enough of it to make him feel that its top might rise through the storm, and into the clear darkness and the light of stars.

Until then, he had most nearly believed himself to be going west, but now it became evident that he must already have got turned either north or south, unless he was in a box canyon, instead of a pass, and this was the end of it, and that didn't seem likely, so high in the mountains, and with the storm sucking through the way it was. He brooded half-attentively upon the problem until his mind stirred resentfully against the waste of time.

You know damn well it's no box canyon, and north cliff or south cliff, the thing now is to get to it and find a hole of some sort in it, before you fall asleep or fall over.

He began to move forward again, more quickly than before, though he didn't know it.

Now that he'd actually seen the white wall, seen something with a real direction to it, instead of just snow and trees, his inner compass steadied, but it insisted, perversely, that he was still going west, and that couldn't be right. The needle of his reason, because of the memory of the white wall he had seen from afar, began to swing to a north behind him. He had gone to the right around each tree, but that didn't matter, because it was most likely between trees, or on this empty canyon floor beyond them, that he'd started to circle. The way a man always turned was the way any animal would turn when it was blind lost, away from the wind. Well, he knew that the true direction of the wind, whatever the pass and the shapes of the mountains did to it, was from the northwest, but mostly north, didn't he? And it had seemed to him that the wind was working around to come mostly from behind him, hadn't it? So, if this was a pass he was in, it was most likely the south wall of the pass he was heading for.

The dark band of the cliff appeared before him again, and through the falling snow this time. It had been farther away than he'd thought when he'd seen it before, but now it was really close. It became a visible confirmation of his reasoning. His inner compass swung the quarter circle to put north behind him too, and for the first time since he'd entered the cut, the two needles lay exactly and steadily together.

This time the coincidence brought him no peace, however, for in the instant it assured him that this was the south wall looming above him, he remembered also that he'd seen the cat on the south wall, and going the same way along it that he'd been going along the floor of the pass. And surely it wouldn't have gone all the way through the pass against a blizzard like this. It must have been caught by the snow, and holed up, pretty close to where he was now. And cats could see in the dark. His fear of the cat became for the first time as constant as his fear of the storm, and almost as strong. Even as the joining of the compasses made him one man, he was divided again by his fears.

He turned left under the wall, which would be east, the way he wanted to go out in the morning, and slogged along, breathing hard and shakily, and peering around him constantly, but also glancing up often at the dark band of the cliff above the steep snow that covered the talus slope.

He hadn't gone more than a hundred steps along the cliff, when he believed he saw what he wanted, a narrow, elliptical rift of gloom, right at the top of the snowbank. He went up sidewards toward it, knocking steps in the snow with the edge of his right web. When he was close enough under it to be sure that it was a cave, and not an illusion, he stopped suddenly. It came over him that the cat might be curled up in that very niche. Then he could imagine it not curled up at all, but crouched at the edge, peering down at him. The wish to weep returned upon him strongly.

"Oh, Jesus," he whispered despairingly.

After a long minute of standing there listening, he slowly took off his right mitten and stuffed it into his pocket, and moved along the snow bank toward the east end of the cave, watching the black opening unwinkingly, and holding the carbine ready. Nothing stirred in there that he could be sure of.

At the end of the cave, he faced about and climbed up until he was at the top of the slope. He squatted there, still peering into the rift, and dug into the snow beside him with his bare hand, and brought up a big piece of the fallen shale. He held it poised at arm's length for a moment, and then hurled it into the cave, and at once brought the carbine up, with his finger on the trigger. The shale struck much sooner than he'd expected, and made only the briefest of small, dry echoes. Nothing else happened. He threw two more pieces, one into each end of the little cave. Each time there was only the prompt, shallow echo, and then the silence in which nothing moved but the falling snow. He thought of reaching in with the carbine and prodding, to make completely sure, but realized at once that such a process would put him much too close, if there were really anything in there.

He thought of lighting a match. The idea alarmed him. The cat probably wasn't in here, and if he just crawled in, daring the darkness, it wouldn't even know he was in the pass. The flame of the match would show up like a railroad headlight. If the cat didn't know where he was now, it certainly would after that. Again the wish to weep swelled terribly within him. No effort of his will, however, could bring him to crawl into that cave without seeing in first. At last he got the match container out of his pocket, and took one match from it, and closed the container and returned it to the pocket. He took a deep breath, and held the carbine in his left hand, ready to lift it quickly, and then, with an effort so desperate as to blind him for an instant, scratched the match at the edge of the cave, and held it in just under the corner of the roof. He more than half expected to see the two yellow eyes staring back at him like lights themselves. The match made a small, shadowy, moving light, but it was enough to show him, after a moment, that there was no cat in there, and no opening at the back big enough to let anything through that mattered. It was a very low, shallow cave, almost crescent-shaped, and he could see, mostly because of the shadows they made, the three pieces of shale he'd thrown, and the rough, down-shelving roof and back, and the litter of twigs and small bones and tiny droppings on the sand. He took only one good look, and then shook the match out and drew a deep breath of relief in the dark. It was a poor shelter, hardly more than big enough to let him lie down, but it was dry, and it was his, and it could be easily defended, with that steep, snow-covered slope coming up to it. It would get him in out of the wind and the snow, too, and that was the most important thing.

He peered all around below him, over the snow shimmer under the darkness, and then laid the carbine on the edge of the cave floor and crawled up and sat beside it. There he took off his other mitten, and slowly, with difficulty, unlaced the webs and laid them in together against the back of the cave. All the time he kept peering down into the populous darkness he had stirred up with the match. At last, still watching, he lay over on his elbow, with his head to the west end, and drew his legs up into the other, more tapered end, and took the carbine into his hands. Many dark shapes formed and dissolved below, but none of them ventured onto the snowy slope, and gradually he became indifferent to them. It no longer seemed so important that he had lighted a match. He must keep watch, of course, but he needn't torture himself to do it. He held the carbine then only with his left hand, and pillowed his head upon his right arm. After a little while, his eyes closed.

He started up abruptly, striking his head on the low roof of the cave, but paid no attention to the blow. It seemed to him he'd been dozing for some time, a half hour at least, exposed in his cave as upon a shelf. He glanced swiftly down over the white slope, and then more slowly studied the darkness below it. When he had reassured himself, only wondering a little what might have climbed up out of his sight beyond the ends of the cave, he realized that there was another reason why he didn't dare sleep. He was shaking ridiculously from the cold, and there was no feeling at all in the hand that held the carbine. He lay there, working the hand until the pin jabs began in it, and working his toes inside the pacs too, and slowly, laboriously, considered his position.

Finally he pushed back the hood, rolled out of the cave, looking quickly to each side as his head emerged, and let himself down onto the snow, and began to dig through it. He worked quickly, pulling up slabs of shale from under the snow and laying them, layer by layer, to make a front wall for the cave, and pausing frequently to peer around below him. He walled the lower end of the cave clear to the top, and then began to pack snow over it. He constructed a regular buttress of the snow, till finally it became like the top of the slope. Then, after thinking for a moment, he drew the carbine out through the open end and stood it against the cliff, just beyond the head of the cave, and within easy reach, and resumed his building. He was working very rapidly by now, breathing quickly and jerkily, and pausing briefly, each time he lifted a stone, to examine the moving but uncommunicative darkness of the pass. He left only a narrow opening at the head of the cave. Through this he tossed slabs of shale down toward the lower end, until he believed he had enough material inside to finish the job. He banked snow against the outside until only the opening remained dark, and then, after a last inspection of the regions below, worked into the little cave feet first, and drew the carbine in after him. At once he felt happier, less exposed and much better able to defend himself. Despite this new confidence, and his extreme weariness, however, he set to work promptly to complete the wall from the inside. The loose stone of this last portion of the defenses, without any snow packed over it, would let in all the air he needed.

When every stone inside, including the three he'd thrown in when he first came up, had been set in place, there remained only a narrow gap at the top, no wider than his hand.

Then, the most important matter taken care of, he entered into the condition of careful attention to detail. He felt of the snowshoes, back under the ledge, to make sure they were in place, and laid the carbine upon them. He searched back under the ledges with his hand, in order to know everything that was in there with him. He found no openings of any sort, but in one place, far under, he came upon a whole stock of twigs and small bits of dry wood and chips of stone.

Must of been a pack rat in here some time, he thought. Didn't know the little bastards ever got up this high. Or do those little chitterers, chipmunks, or whatever they are, collect stuff too?

While he was still searching out the bits of wood with his hand, he remembered the litter of stuff the match had shown him on the floor, and it occurred to him, like a stroke of genius, that he could make a little fire. It would give him light to eat by, and it would warm him up before he went to sleep. After that his body should do well enough in that small, closed space. At once he felt an even greater appetite for fire, for light and warmth, than he did for food, or even sleep. If the light was seen in the cracks of his wall, what of it? Nothing could get at him now until he chose to come out.

He scooped out the sticks and twigs, and also gathered everything he could feel on the sand under him and around him, even the little bones. Lying back against the ledges as far as he could get, he assembled all his findings into a pile between him and the front wall, and then chose from them to make a little pyramid on the sand, a miniature Indian fire. He lay still for some time, debating how to light the twigs without wasting too many matches. At last he grunted with satisfaction, and even chuckled a little, and drew the carbine out from behind him. He rubbed two fingers over the oily metal of the carbine, and then rubbed the oil off on a twig. When he had three oiled twigs, he laid the carbine back of him again, and fished out the matches, and lit one, and set the flame to the oiled twigs. They caught fire almost at once, even making a tiny, preliminary wisp of black smoke. He enjoyed another brief thrill of self-congratulation.

Very carefully, so as not to smother out the flame, he inserted the burning twigs and match into the base of the little cone of scraps. When the flame shrank, the beautiful light in his cell diminishing with it, he leaned his face down close to the cone and breathed gently upon it. The flame rose again inside it. It finally rose between two twigs, and danced naked, single and lovely above them, and the little cave was lighted once more. He rubbed his hands together in glee.

Lying on his side, facing the tiny fire and the new wall, he drew out his packet of food, unrolled it, and began to eat. He ate slowly and speculatively, his eyes dreaming upon the fire all the time, and at intervals he held his hands out to the flame, first one and then the other. He didn't allow this triumph of comfort to destroy his judgment, however. Although his stomach, after the first mouthful of food, rumbled and begged for more, at times paining him sharply, like a cramp, he ate only one slice of the bread and butter, and four strips of the jerky. While he was eating, he went over his directions three times like a man saying a rote prayer, in order that he shouldn't forget them while he slept.

The third time, having reduced them to a simple and memorable formula, he spoke them softly aloud, "Turn right out of the cave, go to the end of the pass, turn left and follow the ridge half a day, turn right and keep going till you see it."

While he ate and prayed, he fed the little fire now and then, from the reserve of twigs beside it.

Once more the salt jerky taught him that he was thirsty. He remembered that he hadn't even sucked a handful of snow since breakfast under the fir tree. He cursed himself for not having thought of this need before he finished the wall. Now he'd have to sleep thirsty, or put out the fire and lose all his stored warmth when he opened the wall, or allow a great deal of light to show in the opening, and lose most of his heat anyway. It was a complex problem, and he lay there for some time, debating it to no conclusion. His thirst increased greatly while he thought, and finally became so insistent that it drove him to act upon a compromise plan which would also be the quickest and least troublesome solution. He drew the carbine up into the head of the cave where it could be reached from the entrance, and lifted down the two top slabs of shale and quickly set them on edge before the fire, to cut off the light from the opening. Then, with one hand on the carbine, he rose to a stooping position on his knees and peered out of the slot he had made. He remained there until his eyes were used to the darkness outside, and then removed two more slabs and poked his face into the hole and studied the white slope under him and the dark and moving bottom of the pass. At last he lowered the wall still further, thrust the carbine forward, and slowly leaned out of his shelter behind its defending barrel. He was startled into swinging the carbine around, and nearly into firing, by a dark projection from the face of the cliff beside him, but he held himself, and then it hadn't moved after all, and finally it became only rock.

Balancing the carbine on the remaining slabs of the wall, he began to scoop up snow from below and from the side with both hands. He couldn't take time there to warm it into a more

292

profitable ice-ball, so he decided to make three snowballs, and melt them down when he was safely walled in again. When the three snow-balls had been made and set inside without incident, success led him on to an act of bravado. He continued to lie there on his belly on the wall making snow-balls, until he had a dozen of them piled up inside, like a pyramid of small, white cannon balls. Then, restored even more by his daring than by his success, he drew back into his hole, and brought the carbine in after him, and set the slabs of shale in place once more. Still huddled on his knees, he surveyed the repaired defenses, and spoke aloud and happily.

"Now, you stinking black bastard, I could last you out a week, if I had to."

He set the snow-balls in a row around the fire, to hasten their melting. He wanted to suck and chew at one immediately, light and unpromising though they were, but now, all snug and supplied in his shelter, he took pride in denying himself. It seemed a gain against all the difficulties of his situation that he should act without haste and only for the best result.

"Lots of time, all the time in the world," he told himself, and put a few more fragments of wood from his reserve into the little fire, and lay watching the snow-balls darken.

The cave was very cold again, though, and his hands were wet and cold from the snow. The violent shivering, even jerking, returned, and his cheerfulness was almost extinguished. It was alarming, with a long night in the cave ahead of him still, and another whole day of hard, watchful slogging, that he should exhibit such weakness. At last it occurred to him that he would get warm much faster with his mittens on.

As he reached into his pocket to draw out the second mitten, his fingertips felt something hard and edged below it.

Now what the hell did I put in there? he thought, and drew the object out. As he did so, he heard others rattling faintly below it. He held the first object down into the light of the fire. It was a little, crouching, wooden panther, not quite finished, but with the planes of the body blocked out enough to show the crouch all right, and the flat, serpent head, thrust forward in fixed attention, completed in detail.

"Joe Sam's medicine, by golly," he said, and then, after a

moment of consideration, "Late is right, old dreamer." Finally he said, "Well, I'm the one can use it now, that's a cinch."

He set the panther up on one of the narrow ledges in the higher end of the cave, moving it about until it lay so that head and shoulders appeared in the light. It crouched there at the edge of its ledge, staring down at him, and the moving shadows gave it life and color.

It was just like that, he thought, and was obscurely moved that his arrangement had taken on such on uncomfortable meaning.

"The hell you say," he told the wooden panther, and added, "And you're the only one will ever get in here, too, believe you me."

He removed the other two carvings from the pocket of the parka, and held them down to the light as he had the panther. One was heavier and darker than the other, and the whittling only started on it. He could make nothing of it at first glance, and gave his attention to the other. It was unfinished also, not even so far along as the panther, but it had emerged from the block enough to show itself on the way to being a kneeling Indian, a thin, young-bodied man, wearing only a breech-clout, and bending over an indistinguishable victim which he had begun to skin with a tiny, rough knife, meant to be flint, perhaps.

"A buck, maybe," Curt said, studying the uncertain victim. "No, by God," he corrected himself. "That damned cat again."

He held the carving farther out, and viewed it whole. "Yessir," he said, "and he's skinning the bastard." He chuckled softly.

"The real big medicine," he said. "The medicine to end all medicine.

"And that makes you Joe Sam, don't it?" he asked the kneeling Indian. He chuckled again, as he surveyed the smooth, lean limbs, and the square face.

"Only about ninety-seven years younger," he said.

He set the Indian up on the ledge beside the panther, and viewed them both.

"Much medicine," he said, grinning. "A regular, damn Joe Sam's Holy Family." He was pleased by the wit of this definition.

294

"Old whiskers sure could whittle, I'll say that much," he announced. "Only, like with everything else," he added, "more dreaming than work. He didn't get it finished."

He remembered Arthur lying on the trail after he had rolled him over, so that he was face up, with his beard thrusting ridiculous defiance at the mist of snow and light above him. He was moved nearly to tears by the recollection, and rebuked himself without words for his previous censure, and then added aloud, "Well, what was the hurry? He had plenty of time, as far as he knew."

The thought of Arthur's tranquil future so abruptly cut off actually brought the tears to his eyes.

"Poor bastard," he said. "Poor goddam bastard. Not a chance in the world."

His sympathy seemed about to overwhelm him, and even, possibly, to produce an uncomfortable return of his own feeling of guilt.

"Just never could learn to keep his eyes open, poor devil," he said, and was satisfied.

He began to study the piece he was still holding. He turned it this way and that, and held it closer to the fire, but still he could make nothing of it. There were only the first tiny, smooth cuts visible, like ripples on a wave, which did nothing but follow the natural shape of the piece.

"Hardly started," he said. He tossed the shapeless piece upon his hand. "Heavy damn stuff. Mountain mahogany, or something. Well, old whiskers must of had some idea about you. Get up there with the rest of the family."

He set the shapeless piece into an upright crevice above the other two, and regarded the completed arrangement.

"A regular blamed art gallery," he said. "Damned if I ain't even got a regular blamed art gallery. I got everything; the luxuries with the comforts."

His shelter had already warmed up again a good deal. He laid the last twigs on the fire, tucked the mittens back into his pocket, and began to pack the snow-balls together with his bare hands. At last he had four dark, dripping ice-balls.

"Yessir," he said, "the luxuries with the comforts. Damned if I won't have a smoke with my drink."

He wiped his hands on his pants and got out his tobacco and pad of papers. This time, with the light to work by, he made a good cigarette. He returned the makings to his shirt pocket, and rolled over and lighted the cigarette from the fire. Then he lay back and inhaled deeply, and blew the smoke out slowly, and watched it spread and disappear under the low ceiling of rock. After the third draw, he blew the smoke in a long, narrow jet toward the unsealed portion of the wall, and watched it eddy out at the top.

"Snuff that, you black bastard," he said happily. "And that's all the good it will do you, too."

At once he felt that he had gone too far, that he had foolishly laid himself open to the malicious god.

"Says you," he added quickly.

After that he lay there, alternately drawing at the cigarette and sucking and chewing at the ice-balls. Twice he twisted over and gazed up at the three little carvings in their niches. He was pleased to have them there in his refuge. He felt a fondness for them that he had never felt for any of Arthur's finished pieces.

"Yessir," he said, after the second look, "like a regular damn millionaire or a duke or something. Private statue collection and everything."

The cigarette lasted through two of the ice-balls, and then he dropped the butt into the fire and consumed the other two ice-balls slowly, even holding a portion of the last in his cupped hand until it melted completely, so that he was able to finish with a real sip of water.

The warmth was making him drowsy again, and the memory of his bewilderment and fear down in the darkness of the canyon made his weariness pleasant. He lay there staring dreamily at the fire. It was almost down to embers by now, and he regretted this. It would have been nice to keep it going. It would have made his sleep a lot more restful.

"By golly," he said suddenly and wakefully. He reached back over his head and took down the heavy, dark whittling that had only been started.

"Lord only knows what you were meant to be," he told it, "but I know what you're going to be now."

He set it against the best burning side of the embers. It lay there darkly resistant, not even a wisp of smoke rising from under it.

Curt took down the Indian, and used him as a scraper to heap the coals together under the dark piece. Still it wouldn't take. He was profoundly disturbed. It became more important than anything else in the world to him that the stubborn mahogany should catch fire."

"Stuff's harder than coal," he muttered. "Burn all night, if I could once get it started."

He regarded the unfinished Indian in his hand. "Well," he said finally, "can't be too finicky in a pinch," and laid the Indian beside the formless piece.

After a little, the Indian began to smoke on the inside, but it wasn't lighting fast enough to suit him. The embers beneath it were dying already.

"Shoot the works," he said, and took down the panther and laid it beside the Indian, and leaning to the fire, blew cautiously between them into the embers. Smoke began to curl up around both sides of the cat. He squinted his eyes against the smoke, and continued to blow. At last a little flame leaped up between the cat and the Indian, and he transferred his blowing to the space between the Indian and the mahogany. Shortly the cat and the Indian were both wrapped in flame, but the dark piece still lay there, solid and impregnable.

"Goddam stuff," he muttered, and thought about the problem for a moment.

Then, saying, "I'll get you this time, damn you," he took the knife out of his pocket and pushed the cat and the Indian closer together and then quickly lifted the dark piece and laid it upon them. He pushed the embers together under the three with the knife. The mahogany began to smoke.

"Ah," he said. "Now you're talking."

He made another cigarette and lay smoking it and admiring his new fire. It made more light than the twig fire had, and gave off more heat. The low, closed cave became really warm, and his drowsiness returned upon him heavily. He dropped the second cigarette into the fire before it was even finished, rolled up the food packet and stuffed it into the crevice above his head where the panther and the Indian had stood, and pulled up the hood of the parka. Thus prepared, he lay propped on his elbow and considered his fire once more. Despite weariness and drowsiness, he was reluctant to go as completely off guard as sleep would put him. Also, he wished to savor every moment of the light and warmth.

At last, however, he drew on the mittens and carefully pushed the fire together and back against the wall, and, when it was settled and burning steadily again, stretched out and pillowed his head on his left arm. He continued to watch the fire for a while, but each time he blinked, his eyes stayed closed a little longer. The fire was all right. The mahogany was burning now too, with tiny, insecure red flames along its sides and, in one place underneath, a glow beginning, like that of burning coal.

"Dandy fire," Curt murmured. "Lucky I had 'em."

At this expression of satisfaction, something within him again made a propitiatory gesture toward Arthur.

"He'd of said so, himself," Curt protested. "In the same fix, he'd of burned them himself."

Nevertheless, he opened his eyes wide again, and looked at the wall of brown shale, with the firelight moving on it, and listened to the breathing of the dark ravine into the cracks. After a moment, he felt behind him, to make sure the carbine was there, and then picked up the knife, drew it out of its sheath, and laid it handy between him and the wall. Then he closed his eyes, and began to recite softly.

"Turn right out of the cave, left at the end of the pass, north half a day, right, and go till you see it," he murmured, and repeated the incantation five times, and sighed and began to breathe deeply and slowly.

There were actually two winds blowing outside. One of them was very big, and made a continual, hollow roaring high above the pass. That wind belonged to the realm of immeasurable mountain chains and the whole advancing storm, and did not, at present, concern him. The other was the little, occasional wind that came sniffing and snuffling at the chinks in the wall beside his head, and his ears continued to listen to that one a long time after he was asleep.

25 - - -

He was sitting at the table in the warm, brightly lighted kitchen of the ranch house; at least the room appeared to be the ranch-house kitchen. The table, the stove and all the doors were where they should be. At the same time he was reminded of other rooms, though not entirely of any one he could remember. There were five big chandeliers hanging from the ceiling, chandeliers of the kind he had seen in the bars and hotels in Virginia City and San Francisco, made up of circular tiers of gas flames and reflectors, and all hung about with glittering crystal pendants. The walls increased the light. They were white, like the kitchen walls, and had a stairway up the north side, too, but they were made in panels instead of wide, rough-hewn boards, and they were painted with a shining lacquer instead of the powdery whitewash. The stairway was also different. It was carpeted in crimson with brass edges and had a turned mahogany rail. There was a crimson carpet with a big, leafy, black pattern on the floor, a thick carpet, that made the room quiet. In spite of these differences, however, he continued to feel that he was in the kitchen of the ranch house, and that the ranch house was standing under a timbered mountain in the south end of the Aspen Creek Valley. Part of his pleasure in being there came from the certainty that he was in the ranch-house kitchen.

On the table in front of him was a thick, elliptical white platter, on which lay the bone and fat scraps remaining from a huge steak. He was still holding in his right fist the very sharp knife which had made it as easy to cut the steak as to cut butter. For that matter, the steak had been almost as tender as butter. He could still feel the way each piece had melted in his mouth, filling it with savory, hot, salty juice. There were also so many side dishes that they almost covered the table, and there was a big, silver coffee pot at his right hand, which was vaguely familiar, but had certainly never been in the ranch house before. The spout of the silver coffee pot was sending up a delicate tendril of steam.

He wasn't alone, either, and the attitude of his company encouraged him to believe that the enormous dinner wouldn't be the last of his pleasures that evening. The door of the north bedroom was open. The room beyond *it was dark, and Gwen Williams was leaning against the doorframe in a pose of deliberate and interested indolence, with one hip high and her hand upon it, and the other hand playing with a locket which hung down between her breasts. She was smiling at him, and watching him with an amused curiosity which had only a small remnant in it of her former guarded withdrawal. She was wearing a gown made of the same shiny, yellow stuff as the blouse she had worn before, but it was trimmed with black lace, and it didn't cover her arms or her shoulders or the round bases of her breasts. He noticed this particularly, because her warm, brown skin, like a Mexican's or an Indian's, was amusingly wrong, rising out of that dress, so that he felt a comfortable sense of superiority in her presence, and at the same time believed that he would benefit from the freshness of her body and the wiry independence, even slight antagonism, of her spirit. There was no one else in the ranch house with them. The place was perfectly silent, and he could feel the emptiness of the other rooms. In such freedom, the idea of a slight hostility, of chase and resistance, intrigued him. He'd take his time about this game, make the most of the preliminaries too.*

Yet, in the midst of all this comfort and promise, he wasn't wholly at ease. He felt that he had to play the part of being at ease, in order not to lose his useful superiority over Gwen, but at the same time he kept listening to the roaring wind outside, and for something else, perhaps inside after all, that the wind made it hard to hear, and that might shorten his time, and even rob him of this desirable conquest.

He tilted back in his chair slowly, steadily returning Gwen's look, fencing masterfully with it, and set down the glass of liqueur which had appeared in his hand instead of the steak knife, and drew long and deliberately upon the cigar which was between his thumb and fingers the instant he let go of the glass, and hooked the thumb of his left hand into the arm-hole of his brocaded vest, which was exactly like the father's. He blew out a long, slow cloud of smoke at Gwen, and continued to stare at her through it, hoping to make her look down, or in some other way be the first to lower her guard.

Gwen surprised him, however, by refusing to continue the contest. It appeared to him that behind the curtain of smoke she became a much larger woman, tall even in that doorway, which was much higher than any in the ranch house. She had much heavier, rounder, arms and shoulders and breasts than Gwen had, too. She was still Gwen, however, with the same thick wreath of hair and brown skin and wide-apart, slanting eyes. In one way she was even more like Gwen than before. The withdrawn, appraising look was back full strength in her eyes, and her smile, increasing slightly behind the thinning smoke, became entirely a smile of amusement. He felt at once that in some way he had played into her hands, and his apprehensions concerning time and the sound he couldn't hear became much stronger.

Gwen turned and walked out of sight into the bedroom. He jumped to his feet, but then stood there, because the instant she disappeared, the bedroom became as brilliantly lighted as the kitchen. The bed, and the table and lamp by the window, were all he could see from where he stood, but they weren't the bed and lamp and table that belonged in the north bedroom. The table was an ornate, gilded one, with a marble top, and the lamp on it had a big, glass shade, painted with roses and hung about the edge with tear-drop pendants of crystal. The bed was a vast, brass bed, as wide as it was long, and there were two big, yellow satin pillows, trimmed with black lace, propped up against the head of it. The only thing he recognized in the bedroom was the cover on the bed, and he liked that even less than the unfamiliar objects. He was afraid when he saw it. It was the rough, blue bedspread the mother was so fond of, the one with all the twisting vines and tropical birds and fruits and beasts on it, and in the center, the horse with a horn on his forehead, the one Arthur had studied over so much when he was a kid. Well, he would go in there now, and remove that bedspread first thing, and put it out of sight. The moment he decided to do that, he saw that it had already been done. There was a yellow spread like the pillow slips on the bed now. Yet he wasn't relieved. Instead he become suspicious as well as apprehensive. Gwen, or the big woman who was so much like Gwen, wanted to lure him into that room, and not for what he wanted, either. He didn't want to go into the bedroom at all now, yet he couldn't stop himself from advancing toward it. The best he could do was to go cautiously, being careful that the floor didn't creak under his feet, and listening all the time.

He had his hand on the doorframe when the light in the bedroom went out as suddenly as it had gone on. In almost the same instant, he realized that the lights were out in the kitchen too, and then he believed that the room was shrinking around him, that it meant to crush him. Also, he heard what he had been listening for under the loud wind all this time. It was a sound of heavy breathing, of sniffing. It was going on in the bedroom. The loud wind was still blowing over the roof of the house, but he could hear the breathing sound in the bedroom as if the place were perfectly quiet. Then he knew that it wasn't Gwen waiting for him in the dark in there, or any other woman either. His fear became a paralyzing terror. He was standing in an open doorway, where he couldn't see anything, and that heavy, snuffling breathing was coming closer and closer to him from the other side.

He was lying perfectly still, on his side, facing the wall. He couldn't see the wall in the absolute darkness which had closed in when the lights went out in the bedroom and the kitchen, but he knew it was there, so close he could have reached out and touched it. He didn't, though. He had to lie perfectly still. Not only his ears, but his entire body, was concerned with detecting every least whisper of that breathing and snuffling in the cracks of the wall. He knew now that it was the panther out there, and that it had been out there for a long time already, that it had gained over him a considerable advantage of preparation while he'd sat in there letting Gwen make a fool of him. Even in his present predicament, he felt extremely bitter that Gwen had betrayed him to such a terrible extent as this. He couldn't afford to think about that now, though. He had to know exactly what the cat was doing outside, and the sniffing was all he had to guess by.

The cave was smaller than he remembered. He had to lie with his legs drawn up, like those of a child sleeping cold, because there wasn't room for him to stretch them out, and the shelving roof pressed down on his shoulder. When he imagined the cat breaking in through the loose stones in front of him, he was terrified anew because he was so tightly trapped. He felt that his position would be much improved if he could only get the carbine over in front of him, but that would be impossible without a good deal of contortion, and he didn't dare try. If he made the least sound for those attentive ears out there to pick up, the delicate balance of doubt that was preserving him would be broken. That cat was cleverer than any man about all the signs of fear and helplessness, and it would know at once how he was fixed. He could only lie perfectly still and curse himself inwardly for having gone to sleep with the carbine behind him. He even had to control his fretfulness about that, for he knew that if he were to let himself go only a little, he would be swept by brainless panic, and that would be even worse than trying to reach the carbine. It would give him away at once. Even if he managed to hold himself absolutely quiet, not a single muscle moving, not the faintest whimper escaping him—and that whimpering could begin only too easily—even then the cat would know. Those busy, intelligent black nostrils couldn't possibly miss the scent of such an overwhelming fear, and the smell of fear would set it off even more promptly than the sound of struggle. No, there was nothing to do but lie perfectly still and concentrate upon keeping his fear imprisoned in that small, round cell in his middle where it was now huddled, waiting like a dangerous internal ally of the enemy outside.

The worst of it was that he could think of no good end to this cornered-rabbit strategy. His fire had gone out some time since; just when, he didn't know, and the cave was getting cold. He was almost as much afraid of jerking from the cold as of jerking because the fear broke out of his middle. And time meant nothing to the panther out there, warm in its thick, black coat, and free to move about, and fascinated by the man smell it breathed in at every crack of the loose stone wall. Time was as much in its favor as position was, and that was another thought which couldn't be allowed to repeat itself too often or dig in too deeply.

He couldn't help imagining the panther, suddenly moved by some failure in secrecy inside, rearing against the loose stones beside his head, and pushing them in. He could see, as if it were happening, the huge, flat, whiskered head thrust into the breach, the mouth slightly open to pant, and the great yellow eyes shining at him as if there were a fire inside the cat that showed out through them. He could feel its hot breath on his face, and even smell the carnivorous reek of it.

Then, all at once, he really was seeing the panther. This wasn't because the wall had been broken in, though. He was terribly alarmed for an instant, because he thought the wall had vanished, and the cat could see him too. Then he realized, with great relief, that the wall was still there and that, although he had developed the ability to see through it, the cat had not. It was crouched just the other side of the wall, with its sniffing, snuffling nose down to the lowest cracks. It came to him only slowly, like the growth of a horror too vast to be comprehended all at once, that the beast, in order to loom up as far as it did out there, in order to stand on the top of the slope of snow and crouch down to snuff at that crack, must be enormous. All his previous notions, the lost dream of pleasure, everything, vanished from his mind at the overwhelming impression of the cat's size and nearness. He held his breath, no longer able to trust the wall between them at all.

Then he understood also, that in his complete absorption in the presence of the cat, he had overlooked another danger. Joe Sam was out there too. He was helping the cat in its hunt, and it was his mind and his unrelenting purpose which had all this time made the cat seem so humanly dangerous.

He had come up the canyon silently from the east, from the ranch, and joined the cat in its waiting on the delta of snow. Curt could see him too now, and was shaken to think that he had lain there so long, blind to the very most dangerous quality of his enemy. Joe Sam was dressed only in a breach clout, but he did not seem to notice the bitter cold at all. He had a knife in one hand, an ancient, chipped flint knife, and with the other hand, he was feeling over the uncovered rocks at the head of the cave. The great cat lifted its head eagerly, its tongue lolling out one corner of its mouth as it panted, to watch Joe Sam's hand trying the loose rocks. There was no question that the two were working together. The panther was only waiting for Joe Sam to select the best slabs of the shale, and silently, one at a time, remove them until it could reach in.

Joe Sam took hold of the top rock, and a queer, whimpering noise occurred in the little cave. It sounded very loud to Curt. Joe Sam and the cat heard it too. Joe Sam became motionless, with his hand on the rock. The cat lowered its head again, and tightened its shoulders. Joe Sam was looking down where the cat was looking. They were both looking right at him. Curt could see the thin, wicked, restrained pleasure in Joe Sam's face, with its narrowed eyes, one of them half lidded, and looking away dead, but the other looking right at him with its wicked joke. Then he saw that the cat had only one good eye too. The one eye was fixed upon him, and it winked very slowly without ever closing, as if the fire inside the cat rose and fell in response to some slow pulsing of its strong and unpleasant desire.

The courage-breaking whimper occurred again in the cave, so that the cat settled its shoulders down further, working them a little in preparation for a leap, and Curt realized that he was making the whimper himself, and probably couldn't help making it again. A sudden, tangible fear ran out all through him, but especially up his spine to spread among the roots of his hair. At the same time, he saw Joe Sam spring back, grinning, and vanish at the head of the niche, and the cat sink down still farther, till only its one burning eye was visible against the darkness of the canyon. They knew he had come to the end of bearing his confinement, and they were preparing for his break. The whimper broke out of him again, more loudly.

There was a change in his situation which he couldn't explain for a moment. Finally he understood that the wall had become solid again. It closed him in, almost as if it pressed upon him, and he was unable to see out into the pass at all. He could see only one thing still, the cat's attentive, slowly blinking, single eye. It was actually inside the little cave with him now. He raised an arm to shield himself from the expected blow, and knew that something else had changed. The arm rose quite freely. He was still lying like a cold child, with his knees drawn up, but he believed that he could stretch out if he chose to, and that there was some space between the shelving rock roof and his shoulder. It was a great relief to know that he had that much freedom of action.

Never looking away from the blinking eye, holding it with his own gaze, as if he could thus keep the cat from pouncing, he began to calculate his chances. It felt good to be able to calculate them, to be able to think, to be able to make his mind test this and that possibility as he directed, after his will had been so long extinct in terror. The impulse to whimper grew weaker. He lay silent, watchful, and tense for action, while he thought.

A second hopeful impulse, one that approached triumph, so little does it require once despair is broken, took place in him when his liberated mind informed him, at the joining of a number of faint, encouraging doubts, that the winking, which observed him from so near he could have touched it, wasn't an eye at all, but only a coal of his fire, in the last stages of burning itself out.

He was sure, then, that he was awake, although he couldn't be sure at just what point in the events he had awakened, or what, of all that had happened, was dream and what reality. The lambent eye or coal was still there; it had existed on both sides of a border he was unable to locate. The big dinner, the warmth, the glittering light, and the contest with Gwen, had receded to an unquestionable and regrettable unreality, but this was not true of Joe Sam and the panther, waiting outside. He believed that their actual presence there, particularly Joe Sam's, was to be doubted, but at the same time a more credulous and forceful part of his being insisted that he consider them real, and act accordingly, that only a fool would do otherwise.

He lay very still, listening intently all the time, and thought about how to get out. There was no wind out there now; he was quickly sure of that. Instead there was a thick, oppressive silence of snow. His breath stopped occasionally, as he believed he heard the soft snuffling against the stones, but it was very faint, perhaps not there at all, perhaps just vagrant movements of the canyon air.

He made up his mind definitely about three things: he must wait for daylight; he must trust to the carbine, not the knife, despite the dangerously crowded quarters; and he must make a rush for it, prepare in complete silence, and then move all of a sudden. That was his only chance to catch the huge cat off guard, perhaps to frighten it into a momentary retreat, at least to get time for a shot, maybe even two shots, before it could jump him. There was no possible way to get out by stealth. He was enclosed, as if by a dozen enemies, by his conception of the cat's superior senses and powers.

Despite this desperate conclusion, he felt much better when he had thought the problem out to a decision. The process restored his strength and his will considerably, as if it were a kind of act itself. He settled himself, almost with a secure tactician's enjoyment, to watch in the cracks among the stones for daylight, and to plan the rush that was forced upon him. At the same time, in order that he shouldn't betray himself by clumsiness when the moment came, he began to work against the cold which stiffened him now, continuously flexing and relaxing all the parts of his body he could without making a sound, his feet and the calves of his legs with them, his thighs separately, his buttocks and his belly, his chest and shoulder muscles together, his biceps, his forearms, his hands, even his neck, turning his head cautiously within the hood. It worked well enough to help. His whole body was stiff and sore and slow to begin with, and so rigid from cold that he had trouble commencing the exercises, but as he persisted, he gained noticeably in warmth and flexibility, and his confidence grew in proportion. The discipline interrupted his planning at times, but by jerks and single conclusions, he got ahead with it too.

By the time there was surely daylight between the stones, enough of it filtering through in pale, narrow beams to let him see dimly what he was doing, his plan and his body were ready. He had even reached the point of looking forward to the break, and had to divert a portion of his will to restraining himself, so that he wouldn't move carelessly and give himself away.

Very slowly, an inch at a time, he rolled over and got hold of the carbine, and rolled back with it. He drew off his right mitten and laid it down as if it were fragile and of great value, and felt lightly of the trigger of the carbine, to make sure it was set. He picked up the knife and took it, pirate style, between his teeth, in case something went wrong and he had no choice but in-fighting. Then, with the greatest care yet, taking minutes to accomplish the small change, he worked himself down into the narrower end of the cave as far as he could and still assume the position necessary to the surprise. The cat, naturally, would be giving its attention to the other end of the cave, where the smell of the man and his belongings, and the last little smoke of his fire, came out.

Drawing his legs up against his chest as closely as he could, he worked himself around sideways in the cave, and lay back, hunched against the sloping roof and held the carbine aimed at the point on the wall toward which he was slowly raising his feet. In the final position, his feet directly before the portion of the wall he intended to kick out, his legs and his body coiled back like a spring before release, he lay still again, and made a last check and a last exhortation to his courage. He had forgotten nothing that could be of any use. He listened intently, and believed that twice he heard the faint snuffling at the unsealed end. He grinned tightly.

Distinctly, and in a cheerfully encouraging tone, though only in his head, he said, All set, Bridges, and then, very quickly, Here goes.

His legs shot out so that he grunted with the effort. His heels, hitting the stones through the soft pacs, were bruised, and the blow jarred him all up his spine, but he didn't notice. In an instant a wide gap appeared almost soundlessly in the wall before him, and he caught a darkly framed glimpse of huge, white flakes falling softly and thickly, and through them, dimly, of the opposite wall of the canyon, astonishingly close. In the same instant that the opening appeared, and in exact accord with his plan, he drew his legs back again against his chest, bowed himself over them, rolled forward onto his knees, and thrust himself, carbine lifting, into the break, with his back toward the shallow end, in order to aim toward the deep end, outside.

So complete was his preparation that only the slight reservations he had maintained as to the exact position of the panther, and a sudden and tremendous effort of will, enabled him to check his eager forefinger. There was nothing out there; nothing at all. He could see the whole sloping buttress of snow up to the uncovered rocks, and there was nothing on it but the new, light, perfectly untracked whiteness, except, right below him, the short sliding trenches and wells made by the shale he had kicked out, and the scattering pock marks of the snow that had fallen with it.

The absolute silence and the perfect motionlessness of everything in sight save the slowly falling snow were shocking to him, so completely had he prepared for a roaring report and a scream, and some wild, confused fury of action. He was stunned, for a moment. It was as if he had been smothered, mind and body, in a thick blanket of white. Then it came to him, desperately, because of the delay, that he was the one who had been tricked, that they had heard and understood his every cautious movement in there, and were leaping at him from behind. He swung violently around in the aperture, striking his head and scraping one knee and one shoulder, and, with sickening clumsiness, managed to get the carbine around and aimed again.

There was nothing there either, only the slow, thick, sifting down through silence of snow onto unbroken snow.

Slowly he relaxed, and as he relaxed, an unthinking, still faintly incredulous dreaminess settled upon him. Finally he leaned forward and thrust his head and shoulders through the opening. He could see along that whole side of the canyon then, as far as the falling snow would let him, and there was still nothing, not even the faintest trace of a dark movement or a track on the whole tranquil, derisive whiteness. It wasn't like waking from a dream. It was like entering one.

Finally, moving slowly, with a faint, chagrined smile upon his face, and a feeling that he had been observed by a multitude while behaving like a frightened fool, he pushed more of the wall out and let himself down into the snow. He sank into it almost to his hips, and stood there, with the carbine cradled in his arm, staring across at the other wall, which was much too near, and then one way along the canyon, and then the other. Without knowing it, he still held the knife between his teeth.

26 ‑ ‑ ‑

It occurred to him finally that he couldn't stand there indefinitely, staring into the falling snow. He must get started for home. It would be uncomfortable to face Gwen without a panther skin, and to face Harold and Joe Sam when the cat had been black after all, and he had been compelled to run from it. But by now such considerations of pride had no power over him as compared with his desire to get home, to be safe, to eat hot food and enough of it, to sleep warm, and to reassure his mind and steady his will with real, limited and familiar problems. The desire to get home, in fact, was the only positive force left in him. In all other matters, the strong, unanchored logic of the cave continued more powerful than white reality.

He took the first step down, and sank still deeper into the loose snow, and remembered that he hadn't put on the bearpaws. At the same time he realized that he still had the knife between his teeth. He removed it, dropped it into his pocket and slowly broke his way back up to the little cave. There he drew the webs out, and sat down in the gap in the wall and laced them on. He had to take off his left mitten too, in order to do this, and so was reminded that the other mitten was still in the cave. He reached it out, feeling a little disturbed, as he did so, to find the red eye of the mahogany coal still winking at him. As he pulled on the mittens, however, he put the nameless eye into its place in the practical scheme of things.

"Even if there was something to burn," he said aloud, "it couldn't start a fire with all this snow down."

He took the carbine into the crook of his right arm, and slowly descended the steep snow bank sideways, leaving a flight of fluffy steps behind him. On the bottom of the pass, with his back to the cave, he hesitated again, and stood peering through the falling snow, first to his right and then to his left. There was nothing more to see than there had been from above. He resorted to his formula for salvation, only remembering it. His mind refused the effort of testing it over again, with nothing to choose between the two walls of the pass or between left or right into the one-colored wilderness of snow.

"Right out of the cave," he recited, "left at the end of the pass, half a day north, turn down and keep going till you see it."

He turned right, and began to drag slowly and steadily forward along the floor of the pass, falling almost at once into the pace his weary but experienced body believed it could maintain.

"Right, then left, then right," he summarized aloud; "Right, left, right," and was encouraged to have reduced his directions to something so brief and memorable. He continued to move forward slowly and steadily into the hypnotic falling of the snow, and to repeat aloud, at intervals, "Right, left, right."

Then, all at once, he realized that he was beginning to say right, left, right without it's meaning anything at all to him, just the way a drill sergeant might count for a marching squad, and he was a little awakened by a fear that he would forget which came first, right or left.

"Right comes first," he said aloud. "You're right-handed. You can remember it that way."

No, he thought, with a touch of panic because he was so slow to recognize this obvious objection, No, you've already turned right. It's just left and right, now. Just like the drill sergeant, Left, right; left, right. But he was stirred again by the increased danger of monotony in this even simpler count.

Gotta make it real, he thought.

He discussed it aloud, as with a companion who must be convinced.

"Call Cathedral Rock six or seven miles north of the ranch. Say some short of half a day, if I'd done it on these damn webs. That's close enough; there's no way to get this down to how many miles. Then there was about another half day to the top of that first range, only I was taking my time, and then some,

310

and it was only partly north, so that's considerable less than half a day too. Say it was about a half day all told, at a good clip. Then I come south a day and some extra, faster, but I side-tracked and stopped quite a bit. Call it a day south. And there you are; it makes me only about a half a day south of the ranch now. Half a day north, just going steady, and I oughta be right about due west of the ranch. Then I got half a day left to get across to it. Call it three or four hours, anyway," he amended, and was pleased to find his judgment sound enough to leave a margin for error.

"Three or four hours good daylight, anyway, just to get across to the valley. That's time and to spare. I might miss the ranch a little, one way or t'other, but there'll still be plenty of time to get in before dark. Another good three or four hours."

He was elated, not only by his conclusion, but because he had arrived at that conclusion so promptly, and with each figure of the calculation based upon substantial memories of his route.

"Mr. Mountain, Mr. Pass-I-never-saw-before," he declaimed happily, "and you too, Mr. Goddam Blizzard-in-October, I got you outfigured. Thought you had me, didn't you? Well, you ain't. That's where the little old brain comes in. That's the only thing you ain't got, and it's gonna be enough.

"And you too, Mr. son-of-a-bitchin' black painter," he added ecstatically.

The moment he ceased speaking, however, he was sharply reprimanded by that internal monitor who disliked prediction in vital matters, and at once he did penance aloud.

"Only you're not out of this yet, by a long shot," he told himself, in a tone of foreboding. "And all that's going to get you out is slow and steady and keep your eyes peeled. Don't you get to day-dreaming too, right under some goddam rock the goddam black bastard is waiting for you on."

Having thus insured himself against the doom of the proud, he allowed another little burst of elation within him, but even that seemed too much like making a dare.

"And don't you go to getting all steamed up either," he warned himself. "Left out of the pass, north half a day, right, and keep going," he recited, and was pleased to discover that the directions seemed beyond any danger of becoming a drill count now. He repeated them once more, aloud, still avoiding a cadence by saying, "Left, north about three or four hours, right," and was confident he had them for good.

And if it keeps up like this, he permitted himself to think, looking up into the silent snowing, so that the nearer flakes became black, like a vast swarming of flies, against the untold depth of the white ones above them, if it keeps up like this, it's gonna get snowed out and give me a look around.

"It's gonna look mighty different with all this snow down," he warned himself.

"Yeah," he replied, "but if it really opens up, so I can see any distance at all, see just one big peak, for instance, I'll have a pretty fair notion where I'm at. And if I get a look at the sun," he added.

"Take it slow and easy, just the same," the cautious self insisted. "You're wore down plenty now, boy, plenty. Take it slow and steady." He understood that the warning referred to the little, sudden elations as well as to weariness.

"Left, right, and in," he said.

The formula began to repeat itself after all, slowly and monotonously, to the slow swinging of the bear-paws. "Left, right, in; left, right, in; left, right, in." Finally he checked it by a direct, wordless effort of his slumberous will, and then he was advancing in that same dogged, unchanging pace, with a mind very nearly as blank as the world around him.

The floor of the pass began to slope downward before him, and the white domes, of the timberline trees with here and there the dark, agonized branches breaking out through them, appeared around him and grew more numerous as he advanced.

Here's them damn spook trees again, he thought mildly, and then thought, And I'm going down some, and experienced a faint revival of his elation because his reasoning had been sustained.

The wings of the canyon mouth appeared, vast and insubstantial through the falling snow, their tops invisible. He felt that the trees were watching his retreat as neutrals, approving of it as the performance of the cleverer contestant, although perhaps mocking him a little too, in the dry, silent way of old inhabitants, because it was a retreat. It seemed they had some-how been informed of his boast and of his vow. They wouldn't harbor the cat, however, as they had the night before. The snow in the pass was too deep and too light. The bear-paws had become a great advantage. The cat would have to stick to the wind-swept heights and ledges now, and could be kept at a distance by the simple expedient of staying where the snow was deep. It might even be shaken off behind the screen of flakes, during one of its extended detours. It wouldn't do to trust to such a hope, however. He continued to feel that the cat was not far from him, and this made it impossible to believe that it wasn't being guided by a sense of neighborhood at least as strong as his, and probably much stronger. It was likely, indeed, if he was able to maintain this vague but constant sensation of its presence somewhere above him, and on the left, that it knew exactly where he was all the time. This was no cause for alarm, or wasteful caution. The storm in its third day had become his ally in retreat, as, in its first day, it had been his ally in pursuit. Only he mustn't get careless or absent-minded; he mustn't trust too much to its protection. He must remember to avoid overhangs of any kind, and slopes where the snow was shallow.

When he came between the great wings of the canyon mouth, where the slope became wider and went down more steeply in front of him, he stopped and peered all around, and then stared for some time downslope and then, finally, straight out before him into the falling snow. He believed that he could make out the ghostly, whitened spires of big trees below, but looking straight out, he could see nothing at all but curtain behind curtain of the falling snow. There was a choice to be made here. The alternative had occurred to him almost every time he had repeated his set directions knowingly, and now he had to choose. Slowly he brought his ponderous mind to bear upon the problem. Here he might either turn north, and go back the way he had come, or he might venture straight ahead, crossing whatever was there, and do a good part of his distance north in the security of the Aspen Creek itself.

There was something to be said each way. If he went north along the ridge again, there would be many stretches of shallow snow, which would allow the cat to draw nearer, and to charge if it got within range. Down below there, where the big trees had broken the wind, the snow must be very deep by now. The cat would almost certainly have to stay well above him, and follow him by wide circlings.

On the other hand, he could see a reassuring distance around him up here, as long as no wind came up, fifty yards or more, while down there he'd be shut in by the trees, and if any cliff or boulder or close line of trees did let the cat get near him, or over him, he might never even see it, and certainly he wouldn't see it in time to do much good.

Also, he had come so far south that he couldn't trust his summer memories of what the region was like. He was probably clear south of the lower end of the Aspen Creek Valley by now, and it was a confusing country down there, full of little, broken hills, all alike, and the timber thick on them. It was easy to get lost down in there, even without a blizzard. For that matter, the upper valley, between the two ranges, didn't go nearly as far south as the Aspen Creek Valley did, and the section south of it was pretty well tangled itself, ridges and canyons slanting every direction. He found that he couldn't even make a general map of them in his mind, and knew that unless he had the sun to go by, he might never get out of them before dark. His margin of time was enough, if he knew where he was going, but there wasn't any to spare for just running in circles.

No, back by the ridge was surer, just as he'd thought all the time. Even if the storm increased instead of breaking, or the wind began to blow again, he couldn't lose his general direction up there. He had only to remember to keep the downslope on his right, and he could hardly fail to do that. There'd be no mistaking the top of the ridge if he got up too high, and there'd be timber to stop him below. The ridge and the timber would keep him pretty near straight between them. The simple pattern of the mountains up north, just the one open meadow between the two ridges and the one lower range, would make a lot safer crossing too, one he could do in the dark, if he had to. More than that, if he stuck to the upper ridge, and the storm did thin out, he'd stand a much better chance to spot landmarks even the snow couldn't disguise. There was maybe a little to be said for going down to get away from the cat, but there was a lot to be said for sticking to the heights to beat the storm and the darkness. If he kept his eyes open, the balance was all for the ridge.

Again he was elated by the soundness of his decision, and because it agreed with what he'd felt all along, but this time, with the stability of a good start already made, he was able to resist voicing his triumph. He said aloud only, "Turn left, go half a day, and keep your eyes peeled."

He swung left out of the pass, climbed the gentle incline to the side of the ridge, and began to shuffle steadily forward between the gray shadow-wall of the ridge above him and the timber he couldn't quite see, but knew must be below him.

After a little, his mind began to repeat, in rhythm with the webs again, the only advice immediately necessary: "Keep your eyes peeled." He had gone a good way comfortably to that count, before he realized, with a little, frightened start, that he hadn't been keeping his eyes peeled at all, but rather had been entranced by the advice itself. He stopped and looked quickly up the gray shadow, and then more slowly the rest of the way around him. There was only the slow, uniform downpouring of the snow. He went ahead again, but now drove his floating mind to seek a method of preventing such lapses.

Say I can see seventy-five yards, he thought. I'd guess it's more than that, but say seventy-five to stay on the safe side. It would take, say, five seconds for him to cover that much in this snow. It takes me, say, he thought, counting the steps he took and judging their rate, five seconds to take five steps. I'm giving myself margin on both those counts too.

"Take a look around you every five steps," he concluded aloud, "and he can't catch you napping."

The counting will keep you awake, too, he thought.

He began to count the slow, outswinging shuffles of the bear-paws, and to look upslope and behind him after every fifth step. He had only done this four times, however, when it occurred to him that each time he looked around that way, he left a blind spot behind the other shoulder. He began trying to look each way each time, and found that it broke his gait badly, practically stopped him, in fact. It was a process more tiring and more irritating than he could afford. His body warned him that it must work smoothly and steadily if it were to finish this job at all. He settled for looking over his left shoulder after the first five steps of every ten he counted, and over his right shoulder after the second five. It wasn't much help, he had to turn so far to see out of the hood. He tried it with the hood back a couple of times, but the snow on his uncovered face blinded him more than the easier turning helped. Finally it occurred to him that there was practically no chance of an attack from below anyway, because the snow was too deep under the ledges and the slope so steep he didn't think the cat would try it. After that he looked only over his left shoulder, and only every ten steps, and just once in a guessed-at while, about every hundred yards, he thought, stopped and looked carefully all around.

The step counting gradually became as dreamy as the repeated directions had been. Sometimes he counted to fifteen or twenty before he realized that he hadn't looked over his shoulder. Twice he forced himself back into the pattern of count-and-look and kept it up for a while, but each time it finally got away from him again. When he brought himself back the third time, it came to his mind that with no sun, and nothing but a guess to go on as to what time he'd left the canyon, the only way he could estimate his half day north was by steps too.

"Two feet to a step," he said aloud, and stopped and looked back at his tracks. "Less," he said. He moved forward again.

"Say three thousand steps to the mile, and say fifteen miles before I turn down. That's forty-five thousand steps. Make it forty thousand from now, for an even figure. I've done anyway a mile already."

He began to count his steps. He had counted, with a happy sense of progress, to three thousand and nineteen, before he was touched by panic because he had forgotten to look around at all.

"Geez," he said sharply, "wake up," and stopped, and turned completely around once, peering attentively into the falling snow. There was still nothing else moving, and he relaxed again.

Then he believed that he'd been able to see farther than when he'd last looked around. He peered part way around again, and became sure of the improvement.

Yessir, he thought exultantly, yessir, it's thinning out.

He began his rhythmical advance again, privately enjoying, down out of hearing of the jealous god, his certainty that the snow was thinning out. He had been moving for some time before he remembered that he should have been counting. Then he discovered that he couldn't remember where he had dropped the count. He was flooded by angry despair.

"Oh, God damn this snow," he cried aloud.

The monitor pointed out at once that this burst of temper was extremely foolish.

It could've heard you a mile, it declared severely, and then added that the emotion had also cost him good strength. He could feel how it had cost him strength. His knees were even jumping a little.

"Take it easy, boy," he said aloud, but quietly, and shook his head at himself.

He moved forward again, saying, "Call it another mile; that's close enough," and resumed his counting.

From then on, he looked around only when the monitor spoke. His progress became almost entirely the rhythmical shuffle and count. Yet, for some reason, an independent uneasiness began to develop in him. It increased until he had to pay attention to it, and had trouble keeping his mind on the count. Still he couldn't discover the cause of the uneasiness, and finally he tried to dismiss it.

"Now you've started fussing about nothing at all," he said loudly and scornfully. "Take it easy, will you?"

The uneasiness, however, refused to be dismissed by any such casual wave of the mind. It continued to nag at him increasingly as he shuffled and counted his way along.

The moment came, some ten thousand steps later, when the uneasiness gained his complete attention, and in a manner against which he could mount no defense. It came to his eyes first, and then quickly to his mind, that there was a faint color in the light upon the fallen snow ahead of him. At first he thought exultantly, right in with his count, Breaking up sure, but in almost the same moment he understood that there was something wrong about the light, and the uneasiness rose swiftly from the dark animal region in which he had imprisoned it, and moved about swiftly in his middle and in his mind. He dropped his counting and came to a halt on the webs.

The trouble was that the light was coming down from the ridge.

He looked up, and could see the sun up there on his left. It was only a small, silver disc, with a wide, confused aura of pale light about it. The high fogs of the snow blew half-formed across it, and the closer flakes swarmed blackly before it, but it was nevertheless, and beyond any question, the sun. Even then he didn't at once perceive what was wrong, but only knew that for some reason or other, the sight of the sun up there above the ridge was terrifying. It required what seemed like a long time of just standing there staring at the pale, emerging sun, for his mind to gather its forces and construct an explanation.

It turned out to be very simple, really. The sun just shouldn't be up there, that was all; the sun just shouldn't be up there on his left. There were only two possible explanations for a sun up there on his left. Either he had slept all morning in the cave, and it was afternoon now, and time running out on him fast, or he wasn't going north at all; he was going south.

The whole of the orderly schedule by which he had steadied himself fell apart. He was unable to move in any direction because of the terrible doubts which arose to confront him whichever way he turned in his mind. He stared about him through the thinning snowfall. He could see much farther now. He could see that it was timber below him, all right; in fact he could see far down the slope of brightening, motionless spires. And he could make out distinctly the skyline of the ridge above him. This didn't help, though; the place was entirely strange, and it might have been on either side of the ridge, all depending on which way he was facing, and whether it was morning or afternoon now. He was disastrously weakened by his inability to answer either of these large, simple questions, questions which just didn't come up for a man, any more than he'd have to stop and think which hand was his right hand. Is it morning or afternoon? Am I facing north or south? Who'd ever think of arguing such things? He wished to burst into tears where he stood. He endured the first movement of that helplessness which at last leads men in a blizzard to lie down and go to sleep where they are, rather than to keep struggling on, perhaps in circles, and perhaps in exactly the wrong direction.

He protested against this desire to surrender. "Use your head, boy; use your head," he said aloud.

His voice was hasty and worried, but, even so, the sound of it in that pale, silent wilderness helped. The despair receded a little. It occurred to him that he really had only one answer to find; the answer to either of those big, simple questions would be the answer to both. Then he saw that he couldn't guess which side of the ridge he was on, or which way he was headed, unless he knew whether that was a morning or an afternoon sun. That was the question then: What time is it?

The sun was nearly above the ridge. Say, roughly, then, very roughly, he thought, with another seizure of panic, about the same length of time one side or the other of noon. Say ten or eleven in the morning, or one or two in the afternoon.

"Two or three hours difference," he said aloud. "Not more than four, anyway."

He remembered how he had lain so carefully silent for so long in the little cave, waiting to be sure he saw daylight in the cracks of the wall before he broke out. It must have been early, then. His calculations of times and distances, his little, repeated plan of retreat, was no longer worth considering. There was not, there never had been, he felt now, a trustworthy figure or direction in the lot. There had been too many lapses and too many blind spots, and at least one enormous, tragic error which was enough all by itself to render the rest of his laborious thinking useless. But loosely, in a big general way that he could depend on even now, it had been early when he broke out of the cave. Even with the darkness of snow, it couldn't have been much after six o'clock at the latest. And little as he could now trust all that counting of steps, even allowing for the fact that he hadn't begun to count until he was out of the pass, he couldn't have been moving the seven hours it would take to make it one o'clock. He'd have come at least twenty or twenty-five miles in seven hours, and he certainly hadn't come that far.

"It's morning," he declared, challenging the sun. "It's still morning. It's gotta be morning, goddam you."

The monitor at once added the awful corollary. You've been heading south all morning, then. The morning's nearly gone, and you've got all that to make up. You've already used up your half a day, and you'll need another half just to get back to where you started from.

The compass of his body was spinning wildly by now, but the compass of his mind, as if locked where it was, still insisted that north was ahead of him.

"How the hell could I be?" he asked aloud.

Once he dragged his attention from the whirling needle, it became evident that there was only one possible answer to that question too. He hadn't got turned south, in the dark, among the spook trees in the pass, he'd got turned north. He believed he knew now just how it had happened too. He'd kept feeling he'd be turned south by the wind, when he wanted to get under the north wall, and he'd been stubbornly working against that happening all the time. So the cave had been in the north wall after all, not in the south, and that meant he'd come out of the west end of the pass, not the east. So he'd been going south on the west side of the range all this time. It was that simple. One mistake, and everything he'd done for hours had been exactly wrong.

Still he couldn't bring himself to believe it. He'd seen the cat moving, small as a fly, across the south wall at a time when there wasn't a chance that he'd mixed his directions yet, and with all the power of the night behind him, he remained convinced it had been the south wall he'd seen looming before him when the snow drapes parted in the dark.

"Only it couldn't of been," he complained. "By God, you ain't seen nothing for sure," he wailed.

The monitor promptly called his attention again to the bodily weakness which accompanied such despair, and spoke sternly against it.

"You gotta do something, and you gotta do it now," he declared. "You can't just stand here and let time run out on you. You can't last another night and have anything left to go on. Your damn knees are caving in now."

320

At the thought of a third night in the mountains, he thought also of the oilskin packet of food, and was invaded by another doubt which brought panic with it. He felt in his left pocket. It was empty. He hurriedly shifted the carbine to his left arm and pulled off his right mitten and felt in the right pocket. The knife was there, though without its sheath, which produced another but very minor shock, and the extra cartridges were there under it, and the match container, but there was no food packet. He remembered, then, quite distinctly, stuffing the food packet up into the niche he'd taken the Indian and the panther out of to burn them. To save him, he couldn't remember having taken it down again. No, and he hadn't eaten this morning either. That was part of what ailed him right now, of course, this fuzzy thinking and easy scaring. And the packet was still back there in that niche in the cave.

"Oh, Jesus," he cried, despairing as much because he'd forgotten the packet as because he didn't have it.

The fact that the food packet was still back there in the cave, however, made a decision possible despite the conflict of the compasses.

"Gotta have food," he declared. "Damn little chance I'll make it home tonight, with all that time down the flume. I gotta have something to eat."

It occurred to him that he might even have to spend another night in the same cave. The idea was repulsive beyond all reason, yet the cave remained, dark, narrow and haunted though it was, "Like layin' myself in my own coffin," he lamented, the only refuge his memory could produce out of the whole two days of white emptiness that alternately stretched and shrank like a concertina.

He turned and started back along the soft furrow of his own track. The pale sunlight then cast his own shadow faintly and downhill before him. He had gone only a few steps when his eyes began to watch the shadow sliding along there, and then suddenly his mind saw it too.

The sun's behind me, he thought. It's October, and the sun's way south already in October. So it's south behind me.

"Geez," he cried softly and wildly, "don't I know nothing no more?"

The needle of his mind settled and the needle of his body turned and lay with it, and the two pointed north unquestionably ahead of him.

He didn't feel much better for their agreement, though. There was no doubt now about the time he had to make up, and his confidence, already so often tried and shaken, was nearly extinguished when he remembered himself standing back there, arguing so elaborately with the sun, while all the time it was shining right in his face with the only answer he needed. The self-doubts crowded upon him in great numbers, whispering all the time, and many of the little fears mingled with them unrecognized. Before he had gone a hundred steps, he was shuffling along at a half-run and breathing quickly through his mouth. He had practically forgotten the panther, so much closer were his other enemies pressing him, time and distance and the entrancing snow.

— — — 27

The storm had thinned away everywhere over the mountains into a final, passive settling out of flakes. Now the wind began to move among them, making long, sweeping rents in many places, through which the light reached the snowy trees below, and even, here and there, the steep snow fields of the next range to the west. The snow fields turned back the light with such an intolerable shining that Curt couldn't look at them except by squinting and peering briefly through the shadowy flickering of his lashes. He didn't try to look very often. If there was anything to be learned from that range, it wouldn't be until he could see whole peaks and ridges at once. His own plowed track in the snow was all he needed for now. Just watching it, he was enough aware of the increasing light around him to be encouraged too. If the storm had really given up, even time and darkness might be outwitted. He was careful not to declare to himself, even silently, that the storm had given up. It was always "if" it had given up.

Gradually the wind drew together out of its first faint gustiness, and blew against him all the time. It was a very cold wind, and sometimes it stung his face inside the hood with crystals of snow, but it felt good anyway. It seemed to give him more air to breathe, and the stitch in his side, which had been growing into a real pain, began to thin away again. He didn't even notice so much the alarming weakness in his knees, or the cramped emptiness of his stomach. He began to feel that he might—the mentor would not allow him to put it more boldly —that he might make up all the time he had lost.

The last mists of the snow were breaking and thinning out faster, too, as the wind increased. The brilliant light was coming through everywhere. Finally it lay single and blinding upon the slope of the ridge above him, and sprang at him in golden arrows from every angle of the mountains, so that he had to squint just to watch the trail ahead of him.

He slowed down occasionally to get his breath and steady his knees, and then he would try to rest his eyes by looking up into the deep blue of the sky that was showing through in many places. Even that didn't always help, though, for often rising planes of light from the snow fields angled across between his eyes and the blue, and sometimes the waving and folding of a snow veil in the wind would make it glitter, high in the air there, almost as painfully as the mountain slopes. Even so, the light remained encouraging. The lengthening, widening vistas released his mind as well as his eyes. He felt a little airy-headed, even really dizzy at times, as if the light and the wind were making him drunk, but it was a pleasing drunkenness, a kind of champagne elation.

Still the fear of time remained nagging faintly within his growing hope. It was that small nagging which made him keep looking west, as the world opened up, to see if he could locate himself yet. He never could. Even when he was able, finally, to see clear to the western skyline, over one wave beyond another of dazzling, angular whiteness, it might as well have been the winter roof of Asia he was looking across. The first whispering doubts, and the little fears that had come out again to join them, had been dispelled with the mists, but now there came moments when a single, active, quickly moving fear ran out through him, escaped from the small, dark core in his middle. The monitor set it off each time, by suggesting that perhaps none of his calculations had been even close to right, that perhaps the lapses into inattention had been much longer than he believed, and that first eagerness and then fear had made him travel much faster than he thought he was traveling.

Maybe, the monitor would keep suggesting, you're way to hell and gone west and south, in mountains you've never even seen before.

Maybe, it would say, you might just as well be looking across the winter roof of Asia, for all the good it's ever going to do you.

These spells of fear were short and well separated, though. Most of the time he was hopeful. When he had the food packet again, and was out the other end of the pass, and going north on the east slope, he kept telling himself, he'd know where he was.

You'll be able to see then, insisted the monitor's optimistic antagonist.

You'll see something you know for sure from there, it said again, almost gaily.

Even if it gets dark on you now, it added, a couple of minutes later, there'll be stars out. They can't get you tangled with stars out; you can keep right on going all night, if you have to.

He continued to plow rapidly north, slowing to rest now and then, but always resuming the hurried shuffle again as soon as his knees and his lungs would permit, and always peering ahead, or across at the gleaming sea of mountains in the west, through the little, protective clouds of his lashes. Gradually the monitor began to speak up, if at all, only to suggest his confidence was approaching insolence again. He was getting so warm that, in spite of the light, he pushed the hood back to let the wind work on his head.

He had to pull the hood forward a few minutes later, though, and across his face from the left as much as he could and still see. He had come around a sharply drifted buttress of the mountain, and the wind was suddenly much stronger against him, and much colder, and full of a twisting, glittering scud of ground-snow. It blinded him, for the moment he was pulling the hood up, and he stopped until it slacked off and he could see again. Then his growing confidence received its first serious setback. The wide, crooked wake of the bear-paws, which he'd been trusting all this time to the point of not even giving it a thought, was barely visible, and not as a distinct, broken track at all, but only as a narrow, shallow depression, as smooth as the slope on both sides of it.

"Goddam," he muttered violently. "Everything, even the goddam wind."

The spur of time struck into him deeply again. He hurried forward faster than ever along the faint depression, keeping up the bent-kneed running without a break, until he was breathing all the time in gasps through his mouth and the champagne dizziness was constant and produced no elation whatever. Yet he didn't go fast enough. Before he was off that buttress of the range, the trace had vanished completely. There was only the smooth, trackless snow, with the glittering serpents of scud slithering up and across it at him. He let his pace slack off a little. There was no use hurrying that much any longer.

What the hell, he challenged the fear. It can't be far to the pass now. I've come back most of the way, that's a cinch. And nobody could miss a pass like that.

Actually he was not at all sure that nobody, himself in particular, could miss a pass like that. He was watching the slope and the skyline above him anxiously, peering ahead along them again and again, and they were no more familiar anywhere than the shining sea of mountains in the west. At the first break in the skyline, a wide but shallow dip, with a shallow, drifted draw going up to it, he paused and studied it uncertainly.

"Not deep enough," he declared finally. "It's no real pass. It ain't it."

He really wasn't that sure, though. The snow was deep and light, and it drifted fast in a wind like this. Also, he discovered that he wasn't at all sure what the mouth of the pass had looked like in the falling snow, let alone what it would look like now. He went on after a minute, watching constantly ahead again, scanning the ridge as far north as he could see it, each time the clouds of windy crystals broke or subsided. It began to seem possible to him that he had already gone by the mouth of the pass.

Twice more great dents in the snow wall halted him. He didn't believe he'd ever seen them before, but he knew now that he hadn't really seen anything around him that morning, only the snow. He believed, trying to think back, that he hadn't even turned around, when he came out of the pass, to take a good look at the mouth of it. It worried him that he had been capable of such incredible carelessness.

The fourth of these troublesome depressions of the ridge particularly disturbed him. It could quite justly be called a pass. It was very high and not very deep but it went all the way through, there wasn't a doubt of that. He finally decided against it, though. The mouth of the pass he'd come through couldn't be that high above him, even allowing for a lot of heavy drifting, and maybe for his being a little farther down now. The white domes of the timberline trees had been more numerous in the mouth of it, too.

Nevertheless, he began to be troubled, as he went on, by all four breaks he had passed. They pulled back upon something within him, as if he were a spider simultaneously reeling out four lines behind him. The farther he went, the more strongly the four threads tugged at him, until at last he was forced to stop and turn around and look back as far as he could. He couldn't make out, for sure, any of the notches he'd passed.

What he did make out, beyond any question, however, was the fact that the sun had already gone far past the height of its arc. He felt that it had taken a great, curving leap while his back was turned, and that made it seem likely that he'd gone by the pass long since, maybe even before he'd started to watch for it. If so, however, there was nothing to do but give it up, and the food packet with it. He was profoundly alarmed by that leaping sun. He turned north again, and began to hurry on, the four threads dragging at him as heavily as cables now. He even began to debate, as his belief grew stronger and stronger that the pass was behind him, whether he hadn't better go up over the ridge any time now. He didn't want to overshoot the ranch to the north, and waste the increasingly precious daylight on that end too.

He worked his way swiftly out around one more great bastion of the range, and at the first look beyond it, the four cables let go. There, not far ahead, was the mouth of the real pass, the unquestionable pass. Now that he saw it, he was amazed that he'd ever been troubled by those four shallow fakes. The end of the ridge he was on sloped down northward toward the pass, and then broke off steeply into it. The north wing of the V shone blindingly in the sun, but its height and its slant were unmistakable.

He hailed it joyfully. "That's you, you son-of-a-bitch."

The joy, however, died quickly, squeezed out under the terrible burden of the time that had already passed. The shadows of the evergreen spires below him were now clearly pointing uphill as well as north, and each of them pointed toward coming darkness. He hurried on along the side of the ridge and up into the mouth of the pass. The wind, blowing fiercely now, along the spine of the range, was repeatedly hurling the snow in great clouds off the edge of the north wall and out over the hollow. It sank in long shimmering curtains into the cut and around him. A little way into the pass, he salvaged another moment of certainty. There was the wake of his webs, going right up the middle ahead of him. He followed it as fast as he could among the watching trees, and through the shining, soundless rain of crystals from above.

The pass seemed much longer to him now than it had in the morning. Twice he stopped and looked attentively along the dark rock cliffs of the north side, thinking he must have gone as far as the cave, even though he could see the half-erased track meandering on ahead of him. And once he even stopped to study the south wall, being assailed by a brief doubt as to which he had stayed in after all. In this matter, as in the case of the pass, however, there was no mistaking the right cave when he saw it. The break he'd made coming out and the buttress of hand-packed snow, and the little section of uncovered wall in the upper, far corner, tiny as they were in the base of the great wall, like the work of some improbable survivor of cliff dwellers, did not for a moment appear to be an accident of nature. He was dismayed to remember the faith he had put in that flimsy and trivial shelter. He was fascinated by it too, as if it were a long-deserted home in which some family tragedy had taken place.

When he came right under it, he stared up at it and said softly, "God, a blind cat with no nose could of picked it out. And knocked it in, too," he added, "knocked it in like nothing."

He went straight up toward it as far as he could, and then climbed sideways in what was left of the steps he had made that morning. When he reached the top of the talus slope he went across at once to the corner of the wall that had no snow on it. There was no time to waste mooning over the strange hold the cave had on him. He would knock in a few slabs of the shale and reach out the oilskin packet without taking off the webs, and get going again as fast as he could.

At the thought of having the packet, of opening it and finding the buttered bread and the salt jerky, his mouth filled with saliva so that he had to spit. He would eat it all, and go the rest of the way tonight, wherever he was when it got dark. That's the way he would do it; no more dallying, no more silly notions.

He pushed, and the loose shale fell, clattering with short, thick echoes inside, and let in enough light so he could see the ledges he wanted to see. There was no sign of the yellow oilskin of the packet. He reached in as far as he could, and felt to the back of one ledge after another, but couldn't find it. Everything else—time, distance, darkness, the now only half-believable cat—vanished from his mind. Nothing mattered except to get hold of that packet. His watering mouth and the growling hollow of his stomach demanded it fiercely.

He leaned the carbine against the cliff, and tore away the rest of the wall, throwing it down the slope behind him, shale and snow together. When the opening was large enough, he crawled up into the cave and searched in the crevices, at first carefully, but then, before he would be convinced, with his mittens off and frantically. There was nothing in any crevice.

After a moment of kneeling there, blank with despair, he unlaced the webs and let them fall outside, by the carbine, and then crawled along over the stones he'd pushed in, and searched the other end. He found the sheath of the knife, and slipped the knife into it, and dropped it back into his pocket, but the oilskin wasn't there either, on the floor or in any of the crevices. He thought wildly, for an instant, that he must have taken it with him after all, and lost it somewhere along the side of the mountain in the snow.

He corrected the notion savagely. "No, by God," he declared, "I left it here. I didn't eat this morning. I never touched it this morning. It's gotta be here."

There was only one chance left. He began to hurl the slabs of shale from the floor out the opening onto the slope. He had thrown out only four or five of them when he saw the yellow patch between two stones on the bottom, and exulted. Furiously he tossed away the last slabs that kept it from him, and then, suddenly, with his hands out in the air, ready to grasp another slab, he knelt there motionless, staring down at it. The oilskin itself had been clumsily unrolled and then ripped, in places practically shredded, and there was not a single visible crumb of bread or scrap of jerky in it.

At first it seemed to him that the mountain itself must have developed a malignant spirit, an evil, trivial, crumb-eating thing that delighted in tormenting him. Then it crossed his mind that the cougar might have entered the cave after he was gone. A moment more, however, during which his disappointment and revived despair brought tears to his eyes, and he knew that it must have been the work of some of the little rock mice or chipmunks of the heights. They must live in there under those back ledges, farther than he had been able to see or feel. This guess did nothing but embody the malice he had imputed in general to the mountain. He continued to kneel there for some time, staring blindly down at the empty, shredded oilskin.

At last, slowly, almost as dazed as when he had left that morning, he crawled out onto the edge again, and laced on the bear-paws and drew on his mittens. He lifted the carbine into the crook of his right arm, where it felt now like part of himself restored, and stepped slowly, both feet upon each step, down the slope of snow into the bottom of the pass again.

"Even the mice now," he muttered. "Even the durned, stinking, little tiny bits of mice now. Everything. Every goddam thing in the world."

It was a dispirited summary, however. He didn't feel very

329

strongly about anything, even the mice. Half asleep he went on through the pass to its east end, and out of it to the north, and up onto the high ledges in the sun. There the cold wind struck him fiercely once more, full of the dancing, glittering particles of snow, like faults of his vision, and the dagger of time struck into him again, and woke him a little. He began to hurry but he felt his weakness all the time now, and knew it for what it was.

"That's done it," he muttered. "Oh, the goddam, stinking, little bits of mice, damned if they haven't done it."

He kept on trying to hurry, just the same. The fact that he was already up to his knees in the shadow of the ridge made him feel that he had to hurry. It was a constant reminder, almost as if he were wading in icy water. Also, in spite of the fact that it would take a long time, two or three hours anyway, to change what he could see from up there enough to help him, he kept glancing anxiously into the northwest, and even more often downslope to his right. There were four big mountains up there in the northwest, with snow plumes streaming straight off their peaks. One of them had to be Pinto Peak, but he couldn't tell from here which one. The ridge swelled and wandered ahead of him so that he couldn't guess yet which peak it was leading to, and none of them, seen from this angle, and in their heavy new snow, had a shape he could be sure of.

It was even worse below him, a jumble of snow-covered ridges and ravines he didn't know at all, and then, over beyond them, on the east, what looked from this side like a broken range of separate mountains, miles across, and some of them nearly as high as the ridge he was on. There was nothing to do but keep going north as fast as he could, get far enough north before dark to be among mountains he knew, or to see over into the northeast. What he wanted to see more than anything else was the pass that went out of the Aspen Creek to the northeast, the opening through the low hills, with the dark, desert mountain across the far end of it like a wall. That, at least, was something he couldn't possibly make a mistake about. But so far, all he could see in the northeast was the long, flat line of clouds, with sunlight on it, that was the rear guard of the departing storm. It would be bad if he didn't find something he knew before dark. The stars would do to tell north by, but they wouldn't help much with anything smaller, and mountains became even stranger in darkness than under snow. He didn't have enough left in him to trust to just big directions, North and East, with their indifference to a few miles of error.

So he kept on hurrying, even though the weakness stayed in his knees all the time now, and the wind was so strong against him he could practically lean on it, and getting colder fast. Even half running, as he was, and with the hood of the parka pulled around from the left to shield his face from the little blizzards of ground-snow, he was no longer warm. His right hand, holding the carbine in the crook of his arm, was growing numb inside its heavy mitten, and his feet in the pacs were beginning to feel dead and lumpy too. It hurt his throat and chest to suck the cold wind in through his mouth, but he had to, or slow down.

Just after the shadow of the ridge had reached the skirt of the parka, he failed to see before him a knife-edge drift of snow curving down from a ledge above him. The drift was packed hard by the wind, and his right snow-shoe swung straight into it. His knees gave way at once, as if only the habitual rhythm of their movement and the lack of any obstacle had kept them working, and he fell across the drift, pushed over onto his right shoulder by the wind. The carbine leapt out of his arm, slid across the sharp crest of the drift, and vanished down the other side. For several seconds he lay still where he'd fallen, unable even to muster up any anger about the accident. He felt only weak and ready to weep. It didn't seem to him, while he lay there, that there was the slightest chance left for a man who was so far gone he could be knocked down by a snowdrift.

Then suddenly his body granted him the saving anger. "Goddam snow," he yelled. "Nothing but goddam snow, snow, snow," and he struck fiercely into the drift with his left fist, as if it were a human being who had played a practical joke on him. He struck the drift three times, to match the "snow, snow, snow," he was yelling. At the third blow, his fist slid upward and broke the blade-shaped crest of the drift. The loosened snow, torn off by the wind, struck him full in the face, blinding him, and blew down inside the hood in big clots.

At once his anger was transformed into caution. He became

331

greatly alarmed that he should be lying there, still miles of deep snow from home, and with daylight nearly gone, pounding a snowdrift as if it had tripped him on purpose. Part of his alarm, indeed, arose from the fact that the drift had struck back so promptly and effectively. The sudden caution was that of a man who has unexpectedly encountered a superior foe.

"Geez, boy," he admonished himself, "use your head. You got nothing to spare for that kind of nonsense."

With difficulty, he got himself upright on the webs again, and then he had to stand there, leaning against the wind with his head bowed and his eyes closed, because he was so dizzy. His knees were jumping too. After a moment the dizziness passed, but his knees kept right on trembling. His whole legs were trembling. He opened his eyes. The mountains to the northeast, where he was looking, swayed and flowed together, and tiny black spots, like the swarming flakes, only there were no flakes swarming, circled rapidly and flew back and forth across one another at a great distance. The mountains soon drew apart and became firm again, but the swarming slowed down and thinned out very slowly.

Like damn bats, he thought, like damn bats hunting.

He closed his eyes again, and waited until the bats stopped flying on the whiteness inside his lids, after becoming, during the last instant, white bats upon black snow fields. Then he opened his eyes again, and there were only the fixed black points of timber in the distant snow.

"Take it easy, boy," he advised himself. "Slow and steady is what gets there."

His mind went on by itself, Left out of the pass, half a day north, right, and go till you see it; left out of the pass, half a day north . . .

At that point he managed to stop its jabbering.

He worked his way carefully up over the drift, and started north again, saying, "Slow and steady," and carefully refusing to let the advice become another chant. He had shuffled perhaps twenty steps before he understood that he felt queer because there was nothing in his right arm, which was nonetheless crooked as if the carbine still lay across it. He was badly frightened by this lapse. For the first time since he'd left the pass that morning, the real flight of the small dark birds swept over him.

"Jesus," he yelled at himself, "wake up," and then promptly, because he felt how his strength was drained by the anger, he whispered, "Take it easy."

And don't cuss, the monitor said. Now, of all times, don't take the name of the Lord in vain.

He returned almost to the drift, and then saw where the carbine was lying, the groove of its descent, and the well it had made a few yards below. He went down and picked it up, and dusted the snow off it with his mittens, and climbed back up until he could start north again in his own tracks. He went slowly now, lifting each foot as little as possible, sliding it around and forward through the loose top-snow. He took the steps slowly too, trying to stay within the bounds demanded by his failing energy and to lessen the light-headedness, which wouldn't leave him, and prevent its maturing into another swarm of bats.

This careful husbandry of his remaining powers did not last long. He couldn't keep his thoughts or his will upon maintaining it, and the dark, internal traitor of time gained power over him steadily as the shadow of the ridge came higher. Gradually he began to increase his pace again, and at the end of half an hour, he was once more shuffling along as fast as he could, bent forward into the wind, and making little bleating noises when he breathed.

Caught in a sudden and unusually vindictive spray of snow, he faltered, and stepped with one web onto the other, and fell again, half burying himself. No rage came to his rescue this time. He lay there for a minute or two, weeping a little, but easily, not even with desperation. It was finally only the slow return and growth of fear which drove him to undertake the labor of struggling to his feet, and picking up the carbine, and moving on.

He had gone only a short way, when he realized that he was entirely in the shadow of the ridge now, and that the wind, although it seemed to be slacking off a little, was very much colder. He had to get into the light again. He didn't reason about it. It was simply that the shadow and the cold in the shadow were intolerable. Slowly, on a gradual slant, he climbed to the crest of the ridge and into full sunlight again. It wasn't much help, though. It was only light now, a deepening, end-of-the-day kind of light, without any warmth in it whatever, and the wind up there was even worse. The sun stood far down on the west, gilding a low and infinitely distant horizon of clouds into a city of domes and enormous banners that extended as far as he could see into the north and into the south. Everywhere the light of that low sun struck, it frightened him with the sense of lateness. There were many more shadows than lights on the sea of mountains, and where high, angled snow fields took the light it was no longer dazzling, but only softly glowing.

After a very few minutes he was desperately half-running again, each lift of a web throwing behind him a short snow plume like the long ones that reached south from the peaks. He kept no watch at all around him. He didn't even look west again, but only marked his steps with the short bleatings of his breath, and turned all himself to the one business of getting north as fast as he could.

So he was again surprised, this time by the sudden fading of the light. He turned his body to look west, like a man startled awake, and saw the sun more than half sunk in the city of clouds. Great spokes of light and shadow went up from the domes and towers and banners of the city, and reached high over him into the east, and the domes and towers and banners themselves shone along their upper edges as from a golden fire behind them. Everywhere over the sea of mountains, snow fields that only an instant before, it seemed to him, had been glowing, were now in blue shadow. Mountains lay under the shadows of mountains west of them, and only on the highest peaks were there a few small, darkening remnants of the glow. Those last peaks stood out clearly, like small islands far apart on the darkened billows of the ranges. Even the ridge he was on had sunk into the shadow, so that only his head and shoulders were in the light. He looked the other way quickly, hunting for that place in the northeast corner where the pass went out of Aspen Creek. He could see over the lower range now, but everything out there in the northeast, except one very distant, lighted rim, which could have been either clouds or snowy mountains too far away to matter, was already shadowy and indistinct. Queerly, since it had been tormenting him for hours, he was most disturbed because the wind had fallen away with the light. The quiet about him seemed as ominous as the awful distances and the slowly rising darkness.

The careful planning of the cave came back to him a last time. "Half a day north," he said aloud, and then quickly, with something near a waking of his mind after the waking of his body, "Half a day or no half a day, boy, you gotta get down offa here while you can still see."

He glanced at the nearest of the big peaks north of him and not too far west, and believed it was the Pinto, but didn't give it very much thought, for he had started down already, and he saw now what must have been true for some time, for hours perhaps, that there was no longer a jumble of unknown hills below him, but a single, long, snow-floored valley between two ridges. Despite fear and weariness, his hopes rose again.

"Not too far off at that, boy," he told himself softly and quickly. "Not too far off, at that."

28

He went down as quickly as he could, but it wasn't easy going. The snow grew deeper all the way, so that even on the webs he began to sink and flounder, and the downhill stepping made his legs shake badly and give at the knees. When he came among the bigger trees, where the wind had piled up steep, curving drifts, he stumbled constantly, and fell a good many times. Each time he fell, he was a little slower getting the webs back under him and rising out of the foam-light snow, and each time he rose he swore to be more careful, to go slowly and save himself this costly and exasperating effort, but he couldn't. It was much darker in the hollow than it had been on the ridge, and his eyes, untrustworthy from hunger and bad sleep and the long brilliance of the heights, often blended the drifts into a smooth slope going down before him. Even worse, he couldn't seem to keep it in his mind for more than a minute or two at a time that he would do better to go slowly. He couldn't seem to keep anything in his mind for more than a minute or two at a time, except his fear of the closing darkness, and that was constantly urging him to go faster and faster. His breath no longer labored and bleated as it had when he was running on the ridge, but he began to make small, uncontrollable moaning sounds, like the beginning of helpless weeping, each time he fell and while he was struggling to get up again.

It was almost dark when he finally came out of the edge of timber onto the open meadow. The going was easier there, for the wind had swept the length of the valley, smoothing it and packing the snow a little, so that he didn't sink into it so far or have so much to lift on the webs. But now he was plagued by imaginary drifts, which kept him testing the white glimmer before him, and also he was delayed by the need to stop often and peer around him.

All day the black panther had remained far off and scarcely more real than the creature of last night's bad dream. For half an hour at a time he'd forgotten it entirely. Now, with the approach of night, it was back again. Several times he believed he saw it moving silently and with disturbing ease and speed among the black pyramids of trees the wind had cleared of snow. It was going around the north end of the meadow, gliding from tree to tree and keeping always opposite him or even a little ahead of him, despite the much greater distance it had to go. He could never quite catch sight of it when he looked directly at a place where it had moved, but always saw it out of the corner of his eye and just as it was completing its swift passage between trees, and merging with some black fir or cedar.

"You're seein' things; you're just seein' things, like those damn bats," he told himself, but knew that he couldn't afford to believe what he said.

"Just keep your eyes peeled," he said later. "It can't get at you across all that snow, if you just keep your eyes peeled."

Four times on the way across the meadow, he turned when one of the shadowy flittings occurred, and raised the carbine to cover the next open space the cat would have to cross. It never moved out in front of the carbine though, and after the fourth attempt, a movement several trees ahead of where he was aiming told him that the cat had even made use of his halts to gain on him. It would be waiting for him among the trees on the other side, where there was no such guardian expanse of snow. He told himself again that he was just seeing things. He reminded himself that he hadn't seen the cat, to be sure of, since the first day, when he'd missed it twice across the ravine in the lower range, and that he hadn't even seen a sign of the cat since he'd found those few dark hairs in the shallow cave on the ridge. When the fearful mentor spoke of the tiny crawling against the wind across the white wall of the pass, he replied aloud and scornfully, "Yeah, and I saw a million bats in broad daylight too," but the retort was hollow. Too much of him refused to be convinced. The mentor continued to insist that the cat, or at least something he couldn't afford to ignore, was already around in the trees on the other side and waiting for him. It was waiting in that thick cluster, like a black patch on a black and white pinto, a little way up the slope and just to the left of where his course would take him if he held to it.

When he finally came among the trees, therefore, he increased his precautions. He took off his right mitten and stuffed it into his pocket and held the carbine ready all the time, with his forefinger touching the trigger. He watched intently each tree that he approached, particularly any tree above him and to his left, and in every space that was open enough he stopped and looked quickly around him. He was having no trouble going slowly now. Darkness was as good as on him already, and time and distance and even the night cold were nothing compared to the necessity of never, in the least or for even the fraction of a moment, relaxing his guard. One such lapse, however brief, was all the cat was waiting for. It wouldn't do to fall, either. That airy snow would render him completely helpless. So he made his way up among the trees, stopping every few steps to peer and listen, and testing the treacherous snow before each step, though never looking down at it, but only trying it with a bear-paw, feeling his way around or up over one drift after another.

By the time he was half way up the ridge the stars were out.

Rocks and the spires of the fir trees broke the constellations with small towers of darkness above him. It was impossible to guess an irregularity or judge a distance up the glimmering slope. Sometimes the snow stood like a wall before him, and then all at once it would lie down and become a plain of infinite extent.

The cat was in no hurry. It simply matched its pace and watchfulness to his and went up stealthily, always just out of sight and hearing and always to his left and a little above him. He went more and more slowly, and spent longer and longer in each of his watchful pauses, but he never saw anything but the last, illusive flicker of a movement, and he never heard anything but his own strained breathing. Before he finished the climb, nonetheless, he was crouching every time he stopped, almost sitting on his heels, with the carbine held ready across his knee, while he studied each tree to the left of his course and stopped his breathing in order to be able to hear any sound, however small and whispery, in the now perfectly silent and motionless air. The most important single fact in the world was again the fact that cats can see in the dark. He resented bitterly the fact that cats could see in the dark. It seemed to him that the malicious and chancy god of things had enabled cats to see in the dark for the sole purpose of rendering this already unequal hunt even more unequal. Often, as he crouched, he felt very sorry for himself, and wondered at the enormous indifference of a universe which could permit a tragedy of these proportions to be enacted before no audience but trees and stars.

When at last he came up into the open on the long, firmer drifts of the ridge, almost solid under the webs, he came up stooping, in order not to make a shadow in the patterns of the stars himself, and crouched once more under the overhanging eave of a summit ledge. He crouched there for a long time, watching the ridge both ways, though mostly north, but couldn't be sure that he saw anything moving on it. He couldn't be absolutely sure that he didn't, though. Half a dozen times he thought he detected a faint, shadowy passage over the star glimmer, but always, as on the meadow below, it began just in the extreme corner of his vision and much farther up the ridge than he'd expected, and each time he looked directly at it, blinking his eyes quickly to cure them of the spooks that came from staring, he could make out nothing certain.

There was no doubt about one thing, though. It was bitterly cold now, a still, eating-in kind of cold that was two or three months ahead of itself. The cold worked into him even through the parka and the heavy underclothes. He was shaking all over and had to clench his jaws to keep his teeth from chattering, and his moustache was growing heavy and crusty as the steam of his breathing froze in it. At the same time, the tightening of his muscles against the cold gave him a new, false strength and cleared his mind a little.

"Hell," he said finally, through this star rift in his dark belief, "no painter'd hang around this long, not even a black one."

A moment later he said, even more loudly, "Black, hell. A few black hairs on his back, maybe."

He forced himself to stand upright. "You're seein' things this time for sure," he remarked scornfully. "And who the hell's gonna hear me?" he asked that greater part of him which was outraged by his loud voice in the open silence of the ridge and by the foolishness of exposing himself, and wished to crouch again immediately and resume the vigil.

"If I can spot a light now, I'm as good as in," he declared.

He went around the sheltering drift and climbed up and stood boldly against the stars on the very top of the ridge, and looked down to the east. There were only the terraces of shadow trees going down the snow out of sight. He was seized by a momentary fear that he had got his directions mixed after all. He looked up into what he believed to be the north. He was very little off. He had only to search the sky a trifle to the left of where he first looked and there he found the Dipper, wheeling slowly upon its invisible tether, and out the line of its pointing lip, the tiny, reassuring pole star.

"It's too close under the mountain still," he explained to himself, looking down again and north and south for the light he couldn't find. Everything down there was as if no man had ever been in it; as if it had been covered with snow and lit only by stars since the beginning of time.

339

"Geez, you'd think they'd have a signal out, or somebody lookin' for me, by this time," he complained.

It occurred to him that on the contrary it might have been too long, that they might have given him up, and he was embittered by the notion, as if help had been about to reach him and then had been suddenly, perhaps even deliberately, withdrawn. For a moment, as he had approached the crest, expecting to see the light below him and not far to the north, he had been nearly home. Now he felt as far away as he had been that morning, or farther. The hollowness caused by his hunger was enlarged by a hollowness of another kind, and despite the clenching of his jaws his teeth began to chatter audibly.

"Well, there's no use my freezin' to death while I think about it, even if they have given me up," he said.

The boastful ease of his words was not present in his voice. Tears of self-pity stung his eyelids. Here he was, three days out and alone and still lost, and all his family, and that little Welshy in her yellow blouse too, fed and warm and careless in their well-lighted room, were as indifferent to his plight as the god of stars and snow and cats that could see in the dark. He wished to die to avenge himself upon them.

"Not even keepin' a light," he said tearfully.

He imagined himself found dead right where he was on the ridge. He saw himself lying half drifted over with blown snow which wouldn't melt against his face or upon his long-closed eyes. He imagined in particular, so that the other members of the searching expedition became only her accompanying shadows, Gwen in her blue cloak with the red lining, being suddenly overcome with remorse because she had been so unkind to him while he was alive and casting herself upon him in the snow, weeping and calling his name over and over in a choked voice, like the heroines of the plays he had seen in Piper's Opera House and San Francisco.

In the midst of this satisfying vision, he was seized by a chill that shook his whole body. When it had passed he was once more possessed by the fear that had come with him up the mountain.

"And don't think you won't be," he said, "if you just start dreamin' now."

His powers, so convincingly restored for a time as he held himself against the cold, were used up again by this little orgy of emotion after the long, attentive climb. The brief rift in his darkness was clouded over, and once he had moved north along the ridge a way and selected himself a downward course, the last guards of his will dozed off and the citadel of his mind was freely ransacked by the multitude of fears, doubts and credulities he had held so long at bay.

He was well down among the trees, descending slowly, almost limply, and whimpering a little every now and then at the weakness in his knees, when suddenly he knew that the panther was traveling beside him again and closer to him than it had dared to come at any time before. He caught his breath in the midst of a whimper, shocked at the plaintive, tell-tale sound he was making. His brief drama of defiance and disappointment on the ridge came back to him now as if enacted by another, and that other a suicidal madman, beyond self-control and lacking the last vestige of a sense of reality. The cat had been up there watching him all the time, waiting only for a better chance to pick him off, and he had revealed to it every secret of his weakness. Now, contemptuous and confident, it was going down with him, taking its time, perhaps even enjoying the delay, since he had entered timber again and so afforded it an endless choice of opportunities. What's more, it was on his right now. All this time, blindly, stupidly, weakly, he had been coming down under the impression that it was on his left, when it had been on his right. Only its desire to play him could explain the fact that it had not jumped him long since.

For a time he managed to hold himself to descending the ridge as he had climbed it, a few steps at a time and then a long crouch to search the darkness and the snow glimmer and to select the clearest avenue for his next retreat.

"Take it easy," he advised himself. "There's nothing'll start a cat as quick as running."

Gradually, however, he began to increase his pace and shorten the intervals of watching. Then the guarded retreat became to him a flight and he gave way increasingly to the blind desire to run. At last he actually broke into a lumbering, sliding trot, and almost at once he stumbled and pitched headlong down the slope into a loose drift. In the moment he swam there helpless, struggling to get the bear-paws under him, the last thin rind around the fears within him split open and he was flooded by panic. Diving forward, uttering a series of small, crying, animal sounds which he did not hear himself, he managed to break out of the drift on the lower side and gain enough balance to carry him, and went on down the slope plunging and stumbling.

When he fell again, this time to the side and into the sharp, springy boughs of a fir tree, he distinctly saw the cat leap from its cover on the slope above. He wrenched over among the boughs and brought the carbine up and fired. The flash and the report stunned him and he realized, without caring in the least, that his boldest declaration on the ridge must after all have been little more than a murmur. The first echoes of the shot came from nearby and were short and close together and muffled by snow. They made a new thing, a near, attentive thing, out of the silence which came back almost at once behind them. The cat had vanished when the shadow of smoke allowed him to see the snow again. Then, from somewhere far below, like the booming of someone else's shot, came a delayed echo, deep, softly thunderous and prolonged.

The brilliance of the carbine's flash, which for a tiny part of an instant had let him see quite clearly the bough above the muzzle and a little area of the snow beneath it, told him at once what he needed.

Light, he thought. Jesus, if I only had a light. A fire; I gotta make me a fire.

He worked himself free of the hampering fir and lay at the edge of its snow basin, holding the carbine ready and searching the forest around him with his eyes and ears. It didn't occur to him until he had risen and climbed out of the basin and started cautiously down again that he had been lying there all that time with an unloaded gun.

"Oh, Kee-rist, wake up, wake up," he whispered violently.

He stood still with one foot braced against a drift, looking around him more than he worked, and sprung a new cartridge into the breech and replaced the used one in the chamber. Then he started down again. Twice more he believed he saw

342

the great cat move among the trees quite near him, and raised the carbine at it, but then had no target. Before long he was plunging recklessly again. He fell several times and swam and scrambled back onto the webs and lurched on down. He glanced back often, but moving as he was, and among the ever-closing trees, he couldn't be sure of anything he saw. When he wasn't looking back, however, his mind showed him the cat clearly, a huge, elongated beast with yellow eyes that burned and flickered, slipping down from tree to tree behind his right shoulder. It glided with that unnatural ease across the surface of the snow, scarcely sinking into it at all, and every motion of its effortless pursuit mocked his heavy, staggering descent and filled him with despair. The chase seemed to him to be going on forever and to be prolonged only because the panther didn't choose to end it.

When the trees opened about a small clearing below him, and he could see that the clearing continued far below and even grew wider, he made a decision at once, not by reason or by choice, but only because he could no longer bear to play mouse. He plowed as fast as he could into the clearing and across to the trees on the north side. From there he looked back, but there was nothing moving on the glimmer of the open snow, or in the lane above it from which he had just emerged, and he felt that he had achieved an important tactical success, a success which might even justify hopes of a final escape. His movements at once became more restrained and purposeful. Still holding the carbine across his arm, he drew the skinning knife out of the pocket of the parka and then out of its sheath, and slipped the sheath back into the pocket. After a last crafty survey of the dark row of trees on the other side of the clearing, he slowly stood the carbine into the snow and moved in against the nearest fir, pressing his way into the boughs until he could get hold of them where they joined the trunk. Still watching the clearing over his shoulder, he laid hold of one bough and began to hack at the base of it with the knife. After four cuts it came loose in his mittened hand and he tossed it out onto the snow beside the carbine and leaned in again and began to cut another.

As the boughs piled up out on the snow, he cut with increasing fury and haste and kept his watch less carefully. His breath began to catch in his chest and break up into his throat in little sobs. By the time he had cut a dozen boughs, he was no longer watching the clearing at all. He felt a brief and particular triumph each time a bough came loose in the mittened hand and could be tossed out onto the growing pile. Stubborn boughs he abandoned in a rage that lasted no longer than the triumphs.

It was when he turned to move on to the next tree that he caught a glimpse of the shadowy gliding again. It wasn't on the south side of the clearing at all now, but on the upper edge and moving north. It had just crossed the snow lane by which he himself had entered the clearing. He was shocked because he had believed all this time that the cat was just waiting over on the other side, watching him curiously and giving him precious time because it hadn't yet guessed what he was up to. Now he realized that once more, and, again nearly fatally, he had underestimated his enemy. He didn't even toss out the last bough he had cut, but stood there, crouching a little, with the rough stem still clasped in his mitten and the knife in his numb, bare hand and stared up across the pale open until he was convinced that the sly motion along its edge was nearly continuous.

Yessir, he thought, with foreboding and self-condemnation, it's circling. It's working around here to where I'm cutting 'em. Geez, he thought with an instant's wildness, a minute more, just one minute more, and he'd of had me.

"Take it easy, will you?" he said aloud.

Watching the upper edge all the time, he crept out to the pile of boughs and dropped the last bough onto it and drew the carbine up out of the snow. He felt much better then. The margin of white clearing all around him, which a moment before had appeared so uselessly narrow, became a nearly adequate defense. He could no longer see the movement along the edge of the clearing either, and he understood that the cat had again settled down to watch him and to wait for another lapse, whether into dreaminess or into blind activity.

"Not this time, you murderin' black bastard," he said softly through his teeth. "No sleep-walkers this time, by God."

He had been warmed by the furious cutting, and now he was

344

encouraged by his defiance as well, and by the way his luck was holding up, even against such gross errors of inattention or bravado as some of his had been. He kept the watch for several minutes, but he really understood that the cat wouldn't attack while he was waiting for it. There was to be no short and easy ending to this game, unless he himself was the victim.

It knows, he thought. It knows, the ugly black bastard. Not a wiggle out of it when I got the gun.

Finally he slowly eased the carbine, stock down, into the snow again, so that its disappearance from his hands was concealed against his body, and squatted and began to cut small twigs from the boughs onto the snow. Every few seconds he would hold the knife still and study the edge of the woods up there. When he had a little pyramid of twigs on the snow before him, he slowly got out the match container, and after the longest pause he had yet made, quickly drew the carbine up out of the snow, rested it across his trembling knees with the muzzle toward the upper end of the clearing, brushed the snow from the scarred butt-plate and scratched a match quickly down the curve of it. The little flame made an astounding, blinding light. It required all his courage and hope to keep him from shaking it out at once. He thrust it in under the twigs, and, with its light that much dimmed, peered anxiously across it at the edge of the clearing again.

The flame didn't catch in the twigs. It broke and sputtered among them, and crept back along the match itself, and winked out, letting back the safer darkness that gradually became the glimmer of the clearing under the frosty stars.

In exactly the same manner he lit and applied seven matches, though he was beginning to sweat with anxiety by the time he struck the seventh. None of them produced anything more than a brief sputtering and tiny flash-flames among the needles. He felt with a stiff finger in the tube of the container. There were not more than four or five matches left. It was then, while he was trying to think, despite his tremulous vexation, what to do to make the next match work, that he saw the shadow stir again. It was way around on the north side of the clearing now, nearly down to where he'd cut the boughs. He was terrified because it had got so far around without his once seeing it move.

It was impossible to escape the conclusion that he no longer even knew when his attention was failing.

He slowly laid the match container down against the pyramid of twigs and even more slowly raised the carbine to ready. There was no visible target, but he carefully led the tree into which the last movement had merged, and lowered his right knee onto the bear-paw so that his left knee came up to support his left elbow, and waited. Nothing moved. The clearing and the edge of the clearing were so motionless and silent that at last the twinkling of the stars became a distracting movement and a hint of sound. He lowered the carbine and let it rest across his lifted knee.

After that, however, he worked hastily. Snatching off his left mitten, he turned up the long skirt of the parka and began to rip at the quilted lining with the knife. When he had slit it several times, he tore out the rags of the cloth and made a loose ball of them and poked the ball in under the pile of twigs. He lit another match on the butt-plate of the carbine and held it in carefully cupped hands down against the bits of red cloth. At first they took only minutely, like tiny sparks in the end of a dry wick, and he pressed the flame in more deeply under them. A threadlike crescent of sparks began to eat into one strip of the cloth. After a quick glance at the north edge of the clearing, he bent over and blew gently upon the smoldering crescent. A portion of it instantly winked out into blackness. The other side glowed intensely for a moment and then burst into a small and sooty flame.

He didn't pause even to taste this significant triumph, but, alternately working and watching, blew upon the little flame until it had come up whiter through several spaces in the ball of lining, and then busily rearranged the twigs to lie above the center of fire. This time the twigs took suddenly and brightly, and there arose a noisy fire as big as his hand. He drew a bough to him from the pile and hastily cut more twigs onto the fire. There was still snow on the bough and the new twigs sputtered and the flames sank as the snow melted and dripped into them. Frantically he stooped and blew into the fire. He continued to blow until he was so dizzy that the clearing was swinging in uneven circles. The fire saved itself. He straightened up, sighing with relief, and reached for another bough. He shook this one free of snow and when he judged the fire could stand it, laid it on whole. At last he stood up and began to lay more boughs on, first carefully shaking each bough free of snow. The blaze grew with a hostile crackling and spitting until its jumping light reached all the way across the clearing to the trees.

"There, goddam you," Curt said to the trees.

He was shaking from the long time he had squatted there denying his fear in order to nurse the fire, and from the cold which had worked back into him, but he was also triumphant. In his triumph he stood guard boldly erect beside the fire, with the carbine in the crook of his arm and gazed scornfully about the clearing. When the fire began to weaken, he fed it with the generosity of a victor. The new blaze rose higher than the first and cast its light farther, even into the alleys of snow among the trees. He grinned at the trees along the north edge.

"Black or not black," he told them, "you're as scared of a fire as any of 'em, ain't you, you murderin' black bastard."

He continued to stand with the carbine in the crook of his arm and the belittling grin upon his face, and to congratulate himself with silent bursts of satisfaction, for it was clear to him now that the fire was an ally who would see him through the night.

"And once I got daylight to see by again . . ." he said, and grinned even more widely.

It wasn't until the fire began to shrink once more, and the shadows to advance slowly from the edge of the woods, that it came to him, like a blow in his middle, that there were only a few boughs left of the pile he had cut.

"Geez," he whispered, dismayed anew that his fatuous relief should have make him overlook this first essential. He whirled and counted his reserve. "Four," he said desperately, "four measly little branches. For God's sake, man," he prodded himself, "wake up, will you? Wake up. And it's sinkin' into the snow too. The goddam snow'll put it out if you don't."

He looked all around the clearing, but saw no movement that didn't, after a second look, resolve itself into a trick of the fire. He crossed hastily to the trees along the south edge and stood the carbine up in the snow and began to hack at boughs once more. When he had a good armload, he got hold of the carbine and went back to the failing fire at a bent-kneed half run. He tossed the boughs onto the snow and fed half a dozen of them into the fire one at a time, and when they had taken well and the clearing was lighted to the trees and even up among them again, he stood the carbine up and knelt and cross-wove half a dozen boughs flat upon the snow and carefully, using two of the larger boughs for tongs, lifted the fire onto them and poked it back together again.

"There," he said. "That'll hold you for a while."

He fed the bright ally as fully as he dared and returned to the south edge with the carbine and the knife. He kept up the cutting for a long while this time, resting only when his trembling hand and wrist refused the work entirely, and now and then to trudge hastily back to the fire and throw more fuel on it and dump all the extra boughs onto his new reserve pile on the downhill side. He carried the carbine back and forth with him on every trip.

At last, when his hand was bleeding and his shoulder cramped and there wasn't much to choose between the blade and the back of the knife except for the nicks, he carried his final armload out and threw it all onto the reserve pile. It made a very impressive pile then, low compared to its length and width, yet taller than he was, fir and cedar and spruce and pine, and the biggest boughs he could cut, so the real burning would go on a long time after the needles had flared off. He surveyed the magnificent pile from his bloodshot eyes and grinned. He wasn't steady on the webs, even with the carbine as a prop, but there was in that grin the confidence of one who sees his way clear to the end of a difficult problem.

"There, goddam you," he said softly, addressing the patient, invisible cat. "And I won't move again till it's daylight; so help me, I won't."

He counted boughs into the fire until it was talking steadily and sharply and casting its bright looks on every tree around the clearing, and then laid another floor of boughs between it and the reserve pile. He leaned the carbine against the pile and squatted on the floor of boughs and unlaced the webs and stood them up together beside the carbine. He sat down and leaned back against the cushiony pile and stretched his feet to the blaze. Laying the carbine handy across his lap, he made and lit a cigarette and then let his head fall back into the boughs too, and smoked slowly. The smoke in his long freshened lungs and on his empty belly made him very dizzy at first, but it tasted good and it helped to ease his hunger. He was too tired, too cramped, dull, shaking tired to be very hungry any more anyway. After the third drag at his cigarette, he said once more, but very softly this time, "Not till it's daylight, by God; not till it's daylight, so help me."

29 ⸺ ⸺

He could not, at first, maintain a confidence which justified this little boast. He didn't feel safe sitting down and in that open place with the firelight on him. The movements of the light in the edge of the woods alarmed him repeatedly and made him long to jump to his feet and raise the carbine against some shadowy threat. His long laboring muscles jerked independently when he relaxed and grew tense at each alarm. His sore and tired eyes moved with independent fearfulness in his head, trying to keep guard all around the edge of the clearing, but particularly along the north edge, opposite the fire. They went back to the north edge after each glance elsewhere. Without knowing it, he even shifted his position a little at a time until he was half facing the north edge. Occasionally his eyes more than doubled an alarm by detecting a fleeting, shadowy passage in the very place they were watching, a movement just beyond the reach of the light and out of rhythm with the flickering of the fire, so that he put both hands to the carbine and even began to lift it. He wished to smoke his cigarette slowly and deeply, but unless he kept his mind on doing so, he sucked on it quickly and blew out the smoke quickly too, and hard, so that it wouldn't screen his vision. When an alarming shadow moved, he stopped smoking altogether and let the cigarette hang

349

motionless from the corner of his mouth, smoking only by itself, at the tip.

Gradually, however, the warmth and the light reassured him.
The small, inclined world of the clearing, which was all he
could see and all his weariness would allow him to consider,
became more and more a sufficient margin of safety, a wide and
blessed nakedness into which the enemy dared not venture
so long as there was light. He gained faith in the power of the
fire itself to hold the cat off.

"Scared of a little fire, ain't you, you black son-of-a-bitch,"
he murmured, and a little later, "I could go to sleep right here,
and you still wouldn't dare make a try."

In his mind he commented, It's all his game in the dark, the
sneaky, black bastard, but while I got a fire and this—he
patted the stock of the carbine with his mittened hand—it's
all mine.

"I'll wait you out, all right," he told the cat.

He didn't wholly believe in the truth of any of these daring
remarks, but the monitor protested each of them a trifle less
vehemently than the one before it, and he felt that he was
gaining an internal victory, a success in home politics, as it
were, that was a further guarantee of the ultimate triumph of
his strategy. Several times he repeated, either aloud or silently
in exactly the same words, "Not till daylight, by God," and with
each repetition the promise became less a boast and more a
simple reminder of the immediate tactics necessary to sustain
the greater plan. The shadowy alarms came farther apart and
with decreasing force until an occasional glance around or just
at the critical salient on the north edge seemed enough to maintain his defenses.

The heat of the fire was doubled where he sat by the pile of
boughs behind him. The ice on his moustache melted and
began to drip. He threw the wet butt of the cigarette into the
flames and pressed the ice out of the bristles of the moustache
with short, quick flips of his forefinger, and there was another
minor irritation gone. He hadn't noticed it at all, being busy
with much bigger troubles, but now he was relieved by its
absence. His body relaxed as the warmth worked into his garments, and then through them. The knot the branch-cutting

350

had tied in his shoulder was loosened and the ache in his hand and wrist diminished. The unpredictable jerkings of his arms and legs became only twitchings and finally ceased, and much of his apprehension departed with them. Even the busy chewing of his stomach on itself eased off, and that was where every fear began. His feet suffered a period of excruciating tingling as the feeling came back into them, but he flexed them slowly and steadily inside the steaming pacs until he knew all their parts again and each toe could move by itself, and actually gained a small, perverse pleasure from the tingling. It gave him something to work the feet against, and afforded him a minor but certain triumph within the great triumph of fire and clearing and rest which he could not yet permit himself to celebrate without reservation.

He took off his left mitten too, and with his warmed hands dug up snow from around the edge of the platform of boughs and pressed it slowly into ice-balls. When he had set four of the wet, gray balls in a row beside him, he reached back, congratulating himself on the arrangement which made all these tasks so easy, and pulled down five boughs, and leaned forward and laid them on the fire one by one, taking care that their solid stems should cross so they'd keep burning after the flare of the needles. Then he made another cigarette and lit it with a twig from the fire, and picked up an ice-ball and leaned back again. He meant just to suck slowly at the ice-ball but the first wet in his mouth made him so eager that he bit off chunks and chewed them to get the water faster. With the second ball, however, he took his time, alternately sucking it and drawing at the cigarette, and the third ball was an indulgence. He breathed out a thin plume of smoke insultingly, in the manner of one who is secure before a detested enemy, and turned his eyes slowly to look at the north edge of the clearing.

"I hope you freeze out there, you bastard," he said. "I hope you're drooling for a taste of me."

He chuckled at the picture his mind made of the panther crouching in the shadow of a spruce tree and staring with great flickering eyes at the savory man at ease between his support of boughs and his sentry fire. He was amused by the indecision of its gaze, the torment it was enduring between fear of the fire and the urge to get at him. He made it slaver a little and then gulp its spittle, and chuckled again. He saw this against the fire, and without concern, as he might have looked at a colored illustration in a child's book. Indeed he was beginning to find it difficult to look beyond the happily moving fire at all, and almost as soon as he had created it, the picture of the great cat lost the power to hold his full attention. It began to change shape and dilate and blur, so that the head of the cat became much too large and bright and, to his faint, departing amusement, assumed the iridescent halo of the fire as its own before it disappeared.

"Thinks it's a damned saint now," he murmured. "Damned cat thinks it's a saint."

He was standing on the paving blocks of the Embarcadero in San Francisco. It was the middle of the morning and the sunlight was warm and clear and full of the curving, arrowy flights and scattered settlings, like fruit blossoms falling, of hundreds of pigeons. He was dressed expensively in clothes that he must have put on for the evening before, and wore a gray derby and carried a cane. With his head back, like a man for whom there is neither hurry nor care, he was breathing out the smoke of a very large and costly cigar. In fact the cigar was so remarkably large as to amuse him. He was watching, with wakeful eyes under indolent lids, the passage of three hurrying women, all laughing alarms and sudden scurryings, across the wide plaza full of drays and carriages, clatter and calling, from the Ferry Building to the safety of a Market Street sidewalk. He had divined as they passed, in the quick, laughing glance of the woman nearest him, that it might be worth his while to follow them. Certainly the glance had been more than accidental, and its brightness not entirely the result of her adventure in the traffic. She had observed him quite completely for so short a look, and had ended by gazing directly, even with a kind of boldness, into his own eyes, before her companion in the center had drawn her by. Also there was something about the woman that was familiar, and he believed the familiarity to be promising in itself. He had seen her before somewhere, and their relationship, whatever it had been, gave her look a significance that could not be mistaken. The other two women wore long coats and great, flowered hats upon high-piled hair, but the half-remembered one was wearing a yellow suit with a pleasingly snug jacket, and no hat at all, but only the coppery wreath of her own braided hair.

*While he was watching them out into the center of the plaza's confusion,
she lifted the yellow skirt and folded it forward over her thigh while making a graceful, curving escape from the path of a huge, black dray horse
with little plumes, like the plume of a band leader's shako, on its harness,
and large, yellow and peculiarly human eyes. Her escape was both more
fearful and more revealing than the danger warranted, for although the
horse was large, upon second thought unnaturally large, as arresting as a
gigantic statue in the midst of the life-sized turmoil around it, it was
advancing slowly and was not near enough to threaten her. He took the
pleasant little exaggeration to himself.*

*He was given a final encouragement when the three women were safely
beyond the black horse by one more quick and laughing glance over the
yellow shoulder. He promised himself, still watching, that he wouldn't
neglect the invitation, but also that he wouldn't put himself at a dis-
advantage by acting with undue eagerness. Hurry of any sort and for any
reason was against his natural inclination this morning anyway. He was
full of lazy well-being, heavy and at ease and also, for some reason, he
was finding the familiar uproar and motion and color of the Embarcadero
unusually satisfying. Smoking and smiling, he watched from beneath his
drooping lids the three women growing smaller among carts and horses,
street cars and hurrying men, and was about to turn after them and com-
mence his leisurely pursuit when they vanished, perhaps behind the great
brewery wagon, piled high with barrels, which was just then slowly
passing.*

*The effect of their disappearance upon him was not that of anything
so natural, however. He was astonished. His idleness and contentment
were gone in an instant, and he became alarmed because his body was so
unmanageably slow in answering his desire to hurry after the three women.
It seemed to him now that the last glance of the woman in yellow had not
been the signature of the invitation after all, but an urgent, a terrified
warning. He became certain that her eyes had been staring at him in
horror, because of some danger which threatened him. She hadn't been
laughing at all; she had been gasping, or even screaming; it was impossible
in the complex uproar of the waterfront to tell which. Nor was there any
question that the mock flight of the three women had at that very instant
become an actual flight. He believed also that there had been, at the last
moment, something familiar about the backs of the two women, with the
woman in yellow, the tall, long-striding one in the center, and the short,
quick one on the other side. Their likeness to women he knew disturbed*

him even more than that of the woman in yellow, but he hadn't even glanced at them as they passed him, more than to make sure the woman in yellow was the one worth watching, and now there was no time to consult with his memory. He had first to discover what the danger was. He believed it to be almost upon him now, and he groaned at his own unwieldiness, but managed at last to turn his head, and then knew at once that he had been expecting this attack from the moment he had seen the human, yellow eyes of the horse and the unnecessary little hurry of escape by the woman in yellow.

The black horse was nearly upon him, looming twice his height above him, and over its head, between its ears, he beheld the driver, whom he hadn't noticed before, a man unbelievably tall and narrow, with yellow, inhuman eyes full of a deadly delight. He had a long, dark beard, which flowed back upon the wind of his approach, and his left arm was lifted threateningly against the sky, which was suddenly gray and foggy and filled, as with streaming lower clouds, with the drifting smokes of the city. In his upraised fist, the bearded man was brandishing a great, black bull-whip.

Curt cried out and raised an arm across his face to cover it from the expected cut of the lash, but astonishingly he was flicked only lightly and not across the face at all, but upon his right leg just above the knee. Then he realized that it hadn't been such a light blow after all, for the pain increased until it stung almost unendurably. As he was telling himself that the whip must have cut him like a knife, it became very dark on the Embarcadero, much darker than fog alone could make it, so he knew he had been wrong about the time of day. It wasn't morning at all, but the beginning of night. He became dreadfully confused, and the most confusing thing was that he knew now, the instant the pain had begun he had known, that the vengeful, bearded man was Arthur. The pain, however, became much more important than the impending threat of Arthur and the intelligent horse, which had now begun to shine like red gold and to develop an iridescent halo, as if it were coming through a flaming circus hoop.

He moved his hand quickly to brush away the pain.

At once he was sitting, half-lying, really, in front of a small fire with nothing but empty snow around it. For a moment this transformation brought him tremendous relief, because he'd expected to have to dodge Arthur and the horse again, and now they weren't there. Then he saw that what he'd brushed off his leg was a cigarette butt. It was lying on cedar boughs beside him, not on gray paving blocks, and the end of it, with the ash newly knocked off, was glowing brightly. He came back into the waking world completely. He looked quickly up across the clearing. Certainly he had done no more than partly close his eyes for an instant, yet the shadows had advanced dangerously toward him from every quarter. He could hardly make out the trees at the edge of the clearing. His mind cried, "Jump," but the best he could do was to bring his body lumberingly to its knees and get the carbine, with maddening slowness, turned toward the north edge. After a moment of scrutiny, he relaxed, still studying the vague woods, but letting himself back onto his heels and condemning himself aloud.

"Geez," he said bitterly, "fallin' asleep."

When he felt that he could risk a look away from the edge of the woods, he glanced at the fire. It was burned down to less than half what it had been when he'd watched the panther with a halo staring out of it. Also it was falling into separate elements that would have left him no light at all in a very short time longer.

"You gotta keep awake," he told himself urgently. "You gotta keep awake and keep that fire up. That's all that bastard's waitin' for, you asleep and the fire down. Geez, boy," he exploded in the first full comprehension of what a few minutes more of sleep would have meant.

He got to his feet laboriously and, turning the carbine as he turned, peered all around the shadowy border of the clearing. When he had decided, moving his thoughts with almost as much difficulty as he had in moving his body, that he could afford another look away from the woods, he threw five more boughs from the pile onto the fire. At first slowly, and then with a rush, the flames came up through them and the clearing was once more defensible. He stood attentively at guard for some time, but then, since only the firelight and the shadows it made had moved, decided that he could risk some action against the threat of returning drowsiness. He vigorously rubbed the spot on his leg where the cigarette had burned him and then stretched himself, holding the carbine aloft and arching his back, urging every muscle of his body to return to usefulness.

He relaxed with a sigh and began to walk about in small circles and figures of eight on the sinking couch of boughs, stretching his legs one at a time, straining his head down and shaking it. But even after that he felt dull. He made another examination of the outer line of his defenses and knelt, with the carbine across his thighs, and scrubbed his face fiercely with one handful of snow after another. After that it seemed to him that his mind was nearly to be trusted, although his body still refused to be completely aroused. Kneeling there with the snow-wet on his face, he considered the problem, moving each idea separately, as if it were a large and almost square stone. Suddenly he raised his head.

"Smoke," he said with satisfaction. "Keep smokin'."

He seated himself cross-legged upon the boughs, the carbine ready across his lap, and drew his papers and sack of tobacco out from under the parka and began to make cigarettes.

"Last about ten minutes apiece," he decided. "Mostly longer, but say ten. Then ten minutes between cigarettes. That's three an hour. There'll be daylight enough to get going by six o'clock. It's about . . ."

He squinted up at the sky, trying to see the stars through the imprisoning aura of the fire. Only a few of them were visible, and they were such faint points and so far apart that he couldn't recognize any constellation. He thought of getting up and going beyond the light for a look, but he wasn't sure he could make a good guess even then. He'd never paid much attention to stars. Lethargy and the thought of standing out there in the darkness and staring up instead of keeping his gaze upon a useful worldly level decided him against the effort.

"You can figure it close enough," he said, working at the cigarettes again. "Say it was dark about six. Not any earlier, anyway, and that'll make it an even twelve hours. I must of been up in the valley about then."

He began to estimate the time it had taken him to climb the lower ridge, play his ridiculous little drama on top of it and then get down into the clearing, and start the fire and cut the big pile of boughs. For the first time he realized how spasmodically he had moved, here waiting on guard for a long while, there advancing with the utmost caution, and finally descending in a series of blind, panic-stricken rushes. In review the whole journey since dark was a dream in which action is without sequence and there is no dependable sense of time or place. The clear, even-paced dream of the Embarcadero was daylit reality compared to it, except for the final, murderous rush of the man-eyed horse and the animal-eyed driver. Yet as he reviewed his progress and at the same time remembered the dream, it was the clear and amusing passage of the three women which receded and dwindled and became transparent, while curiosity and lingering fear allied the monstrous assault of the horse and the teamster with his actual retreat from the cat.

"Holy God," he muttered, "didn't I know what I was doin' at all?" and resigned himself to calculating the time it would have taken him to get across the ridge in daylight at a steady pace, such as he might have maintained in the course of an ordinary hunt.

"That'll be close enough for this cigarette business," he assured the monitor, who had been weakened by sleep and made terribly uneasy by this last wrestling with the mingled experiences of the sleep world and the waking.

"Three hours," he admitted finally. "It couldn't have been less, that's a cinch. Call it nine o'clock now then."

At that conclusion the monitor promptly lost his self-control, and cried out wildly within, Only nine o'clock. I thought it was midnight anyway. Nine o'clock. That's nine hours to wait. You can't last nine hours, you fool. You can't keep awake nine hours. You aren't even really awake right now. Nine hours. Oh, my God.

Curt experienced a frantic urge to get up and make a run for it right now, and at the same time he underwent a great rising, dilating, tremulous motion of the spirit, a wordless prayer in extremity. The "Oh, my God," of the monitor was not merely a profane exclamation, by any means. All of the three days' need of help, of someone to talk to, of lapses into unaccustomed panic, and self-doubt, and dreaminess, came together in him, and the monitor cried it out in those three words.

In his present heaviness, and in the security of the firelit clearing, however, even despair had only the power it might have in a borderline dream which part of him refused to believe, remaining aloof and critical.

"Take it easy, will you?" he told the cringing monitor. "Nine hours? What the hell's nine hours? You can take anything for nine hours."

"What was it I figured?" he asked himself, and finally found it. "Three cigarettes an hour," he said. "That's twenty-seven cigarettes."

There were papers enough to make only fourteen cigarettes, however. When the last paper had been used, he counted the cigarettes, laid out in a row on the bough beside him, and there were only fourteen.

"All right," he said quickly, before the monitor could wail again. "You'll have to wait a little longer between smokes, that's all. It'll be . . ."

He labored slowly at the problem, helping himself with figures written into the snow with a twig, and making several errors, each of which caused a raging despair almost equal to that which had followed the attempt to review his retreat. After four tries, he arrived at the conclusion that there were five hundred and sixty minutes in nine hours. But then he brooded for some time, and finally bent his head down and pummeled the back of it with both fists, and cried softly, "Geez, can't you think at all?" because he couldn't make up his mind what calculation was required to discover the number of minutes between cigarettes. At last, however, he decided that he should divide five hundred and sixty by fourteen. He got the answer to this on only the second try, and was encouraged because it was so probable that it seemed to justify his selection of division.

"Forty minutes," he announced happily. "One cigarette every forty minutes."

He was about to settle himself in the unthinking ease of one who has only to observe a completed table of answers in order to know what to do and when to do it, when it occurred to him that he hadn't allowed for the time required to smoke the cigarettes.

"Oh, dammit to hell," he groaned, and suddenly and furiously wiped out all the figures he had drawn in the snow.

"No," he retorted, after a minute, "you gotta know. Ten minutes to a cigarette, I figured. Times fourteen, that's . . ."

He paused, and then declared happily, because he hadn't even had to write it, "One hundred and forty minutes. Take that from five hundred and sixty, and you got . . ."

He performed the subtraction in the snow.

"Four hundred and twenty minutes left," he decided. "Then . . ." but discovered that once more he wasn't sure what his problem was.

After a long, unhappy time, he decided that it was division again. He performed the division in the snow also.

"Thirty," he announced. He was much cheered because the answer had come out even. "Thirty minutes," he announced.

At those words, he made another happy discovery. "That's half an hour; an even half hour between smokes."

He drew a deep breath and smiled upon the figures in the snow. He was enjoying fully the satisfaction of the scientist who has reduced disorderly nature to a quotable mathematical certainty.

When his pleasure began to diminish of itself, he turned to applying his findings to the actual problem in hand, and the whole beautiful, painfully erected structure collapsed.

"I light the first cigarette," he began, and at once saw that there were only thirteen intervals included by fourteen cigarettes, not fourteen, so that he was at least a full half hour off, and . . .

"Oh, the hell with it," he said violently.

It came to him then, like enlightenment from an entirely different realm of knowledge, that in getting things down to exact minutes, he was perhaps going to impractical lengths, since he had no way of keeping time. He felt reassured to be back in a practical realm, and a little ashamed of having gone to such academic lengths in order to get there.

"Call it half an hour, roughly," he said.

He made himself wait for the first of the fourteen cigarettes, thinking, It'll be easier to wait now than later.

He fed the fire again during the wait, and discovered in that act a final, useful, common-sense device.

"Make it one cigarette every time you fix the fire," he said. "That'll give you margin."

He maintained this system of vigil through five cigarettes, rising to throw the boughs upon the fire each time, and then forcing his reluctant body to move about against its drowsiness. Only when the flames were high again, and he'd examined the edge of the clearing until he could see it with his eyes closed, every tree and every half-lighted avenue through the trees, would he sit down once more and light the next cigarette.

30

Even so, the sixth cigarette burned him again, and when he started awake he saw with horror that the fire had burned down to a dull pyramid of embers that gave scarcely enough light to reveal the carbine across his lap. The darkness had closed in to within a few feet of him, not one good leap for a cat like that, and the stars he hadn't been able to find when he wanted them were brilliant overhead, their every pattern filled to the least member. He sprang up clumsily, and swung the carbine against the north edge of the woods.

Only after a long, hard-breathing, peering attentiveness, during which the cold began to shake him again, did he dare turn to get another bough to put on the fire. Then he had to kneel and nurse the fire alive under it, and half a dozen times, as he knelt there, he became rigid, and brought the carbine to ready against a cat which wasn't in the edge of the woods at all, but slinking along far out on the open snow.

When at last the brightening light had driven these phantoms back toward the trees again, far enough so that he dared undertake a longer task, he experienced a great revulsion against darkness itself, and heaped new boughs on in a spendthrift frenzy. They caught with hissing bursts among the needles, and then, as the heat sucked them ever more strongly upward, the flames joined and rose, with a great roar and crackling, until the light showed him even the motionless and watchful trees way up the side of the mountain. The heat backed him into the pile of boughs as far as he could go, and then he had to turn his face aside from it, and shield it with his arm. When he turned aside, he really saw his reserve pile for the first time since he'd cut it. Immediately he was alarmed by the shrinkage of the pile and denounced himself for prodigal expenditure.

Six hours to go, he thought, six hours anyway, and I've burnt up half the goddam stuff; more'n half.

"I gotta get more," he insisted aloud. "I gotta get a lot more."

He turned to start toward the south edge of the clearing, where he could see plainly now the ravages of his last cutting, but when he stepped off the woven cedar boughs, he sank into the snow above his knees, and nearly fell.

"Geez, will you wake up?" he cried plaintively.

The monitor was shocked by the cry. The monitor warned him tremulously but fiercely that he must not again, not once, so far forget himself as to utter such a sound of fear.

They can hear it just as easy as they can smell it, the monitor insisted, with quiet, hissing violence.

He crawled back onto the boughs, now hollowed and sunk by his weight, and slowly, for his fingers were as clumsy with sleep as they had been with cold, laced on the bear-paws.

Better keep 'em on, too, he told himself silently.

He struggled to his feet, and making sure that he had the knife, cradled the carbine in his arm, and dragged his way across the brightly dancing snow, behind the wavering shadow, to the trees.

He made another great pile of boughs, right where he was working, this time, returning only once to build up the sentinel fire as big as before. It required six trips to bring the pile back and stack it beside the fire, and this time he felt no triumph. He was nearly weeping from exhaustion, and frightened by all the signs of error and improvidence in his conduct which had come back to him magnified while he worked.

"What the hell you want to make a fire like that for?" he asked himself.

"You tryin' to warm the goddam cat up too?" he asked himself tearfully. "You tryin' to light up the whole damn mountain or something?"

He decided to stand up, as a guarantee against falling asleep again, but in a very few minutes he became unable to hold the position, and when he sat down, he took the bear-paws off again

361

after all, because it was impossible to let his legs out flat with them on, and because he couldn't get over feeling that if he had to move quickly they would be more a hindrance than a help.

He lit another cigarette, and made himself smoke it slowly, and after a little he was calmer again. He reflected that it must be midnight by now, even if he hadn't kept time very well, at least midnight, and probably a lot later. If he just didn't get into another brainless hurry, there was fuel enough to last till daylight this time, and no mistake. His body, which had protested every move of the last fuel-gathering with cramps and jerks and limp failures which he'd had to wait out, surrendered itself rapidly to the warmth and the return of his confidence.

He had taken only a drag or two on the eighth cigarette, when it suddenly became evident that he had failed again in his watch, and this time once too often.

He was warned by a man's voice calling, "Curt, Curt, look out," and thought at first that it was Arthur calling, from somewhere down the slope behind him. Then he saw the eyes turned upon him from beyond the fire. At first he believed, seeing only the great black shape through the bright screen of fire, that it was the black horse from the Embarcadero, because the eyes had that same partly human look. The eyes stared out of the great dark shape exactly the way the charging horse had looked down on him before. But then he saw how it was creeping, and he knew. It was the cat all right, only it was as big as that infernal black horse. It must have crept up on him in the full light, making use of his negligence, and now it wasn't a leap away from him.

It saw that he was awake and staring back at it, and it ceased crawling, and crouched on the snow, trembling with preparatory excitement, its enormous, glowing eyes fixed on his face, and its mouth a little open, so he could see the curving sabre tusks and the lolling tip of its tongue. Silently and flexibly, scarcely changing the level of its back, it gathered the great springs of its hind legs under it. The tip of its tail was curling and uncurling in little twitches. He could see the curling tip first on one side of it and then on the other. He couldn't look away from its eyes, and so long as his own eyes were fixed by them, he couldn't move from where he sat either. He felt horribly exposed and helpless, and the carbine, which he couldn't move to lay hold of, became a millstone weight upon his thighs. He struggled frantically to bring about the internal change, the escape from those eyes, that would allow him to put his body in motion, but it was as if he had lost any direct connection with the body, as if his terrified self were anchored there immovably by the weight of another man's body, over which he had no control at all, a great, iron-heavy, feeble-nerved, settled body. He knew this paralysis was largely a result of the cat's stare. It wasn't the feelingless, gilded stare of a cat about to leap. There was that in it, all right, the barely controlled eagerness to kill him, but there was something else too, that didn't belong in a cat's eyes at all. The eyes were not only intent upon him; they were at the same time mocking his helplessness. The mind behind them knew perfectly well the cause of his fettered condition and was making a little joke of its own about this ignominious conclusion to the boastful pursuit and the laborious defense. It was the same look he'd seen in the black horse's eyes that had made him think they were human.

Then he knew what he should have known the moment he saw the eyes. The cat wasn't alone. Joe Sam was here, just the way he'd been there at the cave. The cat was thinking about him with the mind of Joe Sam, only he'd been slow to recognize the look because it was in two eyes instead of just one. Joe Sam was on the south side of the clearing, right in the edge of the woods. It was impossible to look away from the eager and mocking gaze of the cat, but he knew as certainly as if he could see through the back of his head that Joe Sam was there, the same queerly young, smooth Joe Sam in a breech-clout, with a stone knife held ready in his hand. Joe Sam was there to block his retreat, to make sure the panther got a good open chance at him.

The voice called from below again, though from much nearer, and it wasn't Arthur's at all. It wasn't even alarmed. It called with thick, stupid cheerfulness, "Curtis, where are you?" It was the father, and he was drunk. The father had got drunk and come up here to look for him. He was walking right into the same playful trap Curt himself was caught in.

At the sound of the voice, Joe Sam faded back among the trees and waited there, just out of sight. The cat was distracted by the new presence too. It looked away from Curt's eyes and past him, and held its tail still and fixed itself in exactly the stage of preparation it had reached when the thick voice called. Its monstrous intention seemed to weaken with the division of attention; Curt could feel the concentration go out of the creature, as if it were partially deflated.

His body became his own, and he leaped to his feet, bringing up the carbine even as the cat, startled by his quick motion, looked back at him and recoiled into a lower crouch. He fired directly into the forehead interval of darkness between the two great burning eyes.

The report was shocking beyond any report the carbine had ever made before. A moment earlier he had been standing in front of a big fire that lighted the clearing all the way out to the trees. Now he was standing in blind darkness, with the carbine still at his shoulder, and he could still hear the last, flat echoes of the shot on the mountain above and a deep, thunderous echo rolling downhill behind him. He could still smell the stinging powder. Yet he was as astonished by the report as if someone else, the heavy-bodied man who'd held him down, had fired the shot, and bewildered because the shot had blown out the light in the clearing like that. The shot had missed too. The cat had leapt aside from a shot right in its face; or worse, the shot had gone right through its head and done it no harm. It was crouching there again, just beyond the fire hollow and a little to one side of where it had been before. It was still staring at him with the great, lambent, knowing eyes, and the pleasure of mockery which had restrained it before had almost completely given way, because of the voice and the shot, to that murderous urge. At any instant it would leap.

And I shot right through it, he thought wildly. I shot right through it.

The monitor abdicated with a long, internal wail, and he dropped the useless carbine and turned to run. He fell into the sharp, resilient wall of the boughs and crawled up over it on all fours, yelling, "Dad, go back, go back," and fell into the snow on the other side. He scrambled forward and up to his feet again without a pause. Someone near him was making tremulous, unceasing whimpers of terror and the sound made his hair crawl and weakened his knees. He could think only to run as fast as he could down across the star-glimmering open. The snow was nearly to his hips and he plowed down through it clumsily, falling when he stepped into hollows or onto unexpected rises, but always swimming back up to his feet and downhill, with that crazy whimpering going on around him. He expected at any instant to feel the great, hurtling weight of the cat strike him across the back, raking at the torn shoulder of the parka, through which he was vulnerable, and the great curving teeth, with the hot wetness between them, close upon his narrow neck.

"Dad," he yelled again, and once more, "Dad," as loudly as he could, not warning the old man now, but begging for his help. He didn't yell a third time, though he was about to, because he suddenly realized that it wasn't his father down there at all, and that it never had been. It was Joe Sam down there, ahead of him and just to his right, in the edge of timber. Joe Sam had called in the father's voice to fool him, to get him to start running, or to jump up, as he had, and yell. He had done it to make the cat leap. He was waiting down there with that knife in his hand in order to finish the job himself in case the cat should miss.

He veered in his flight to avoid the place where Joe Sam was waiting, and went straight down the white strip of the clearing. He knew now that the cat wasn't about to jump him. It wasn't in that much of a hurry; it was only Joe Sam, really, who was in such a terrible hurry. He could feel how easily the cat was loping down behind him. He could hear it panting and making little nervous, whining noises closer and closer to him. He fell again, and rolled to one side to escape the cat's leap, and continued without a pause to scramble down on all fours through a yard of the drift before he could get to his feet.

He could see the pale, open highway of the snow reaching far down ahead, perhaps all the way into the valley, and even in his terror he knew that he was lost, really lost, and just hadn't known it before. There was no such long, open strip down any mountain all the way around the Aspen Creek Valley. He'd been wrong about everything. He was in entirely strange mountains; they might as well have been the Andes or the Himalayas or the mountains on the moon. The cat whimpered louder than ever behind him.

He stepped down unexpectedly again and fell. For a small portion of an instant he tried to scramble back onto his feet, because he could feel the cat breathing on him now. Then he knew, because he couldn't find even the loose snow with either hand or either foot, that this fall was not the same as the others. He felt himself helplessly turning a cartwheel he didn't want to turn in nothing at all. Something sharp, and set in the whole weight of earth, struck his back and threw him over faster and farther out and almost at the same instant struck his right ankle and turned him over so that he was falling head down, and then, as if it had been started by the first blow, but had been a little delayed by the shock, there was a wild, long scream going down with him. It grew around him. It multiplied and became as twenty despairing voices through whose wailing chorus he fell headlong.

PART

4

PART

A

31 — —

The hand continued to move Harold's shoulder gently, and now he was sure it was Gwen's hand, because it couldn't be Arthur's, and Curt wasn't even there, whatever Arthur had said. He realized suddenly that Arthur wasn't there either, now, and he was frightened.

"Harold," Gwen said, softly, but with the utmost urgency.

"Arthur's gone," he told her. "Arthur's lost in there. We've got to find him."

His voice sounded too loud, dangerously loud, now that the blue jungle had stopped moving and there was no waterfall. He knew that he shouldn't have spoken, and that there hadn't been any need of speaking, because that was what Gwen had been trying to tell him. She already knew.

"Darling, wake up," Gwen said, which was ridiculous, because he wasn't asleep, and he hadn't been asleep. Perhaps she only meant his confusion. He was certainly confused. He didn't know what to do. He must answer her. She had known the truth all the time, and perhaps she could tell him what to do. That was why she wanted him to listen to her.

"Yes?" he said, sitting up and turning his head quickly to look at her. "What is it? What's the matter?"

It was Gwen beside him, all right, but everything became more confused than ever for a moment, because she didn't have on the blue cloak, with the hood up over her head. She was wearing the yellow blouse, and her head was uncovered. That blue darkness wasn't around her, either. A melancholy, faraway sunlight was shining on her braided hair, showing the little gold and copper glints in it.

"It's no use," he told her sadly, and when he spoke, and heard his own voice quite distinctly, he realized at once why it was no use.

"It was just that bedspread," he explained. "The blue one we put around Arthur."

"What was?" Gwen asked, and he was confused again. He was going to say, "Arthur's dead. It was just the bedspread, the blue one with the unicorn in the middle," when Gwen took his face in her hands and kissed him.

"Darling, wake up," she said. "You're still dreaming."

He knew then that she was really there, and the blue jungle wasn't, and Arthur hadn't been with them, because he was dead, and they had buried him up by the pines. It wasn't sunlight on her hair, either, but the light from the kitchen lamp.

"Yes," he said, "I guess I was just dreaming."

The roaring of the waterfall became a new fire in the stove behind him, and the cold wind was blowing because the outside door was standing wide open. He saw that it was still dark outside. Through the open door, he could see the stars over the shed, and the soft, colored flickering of the fire on the snow in the yard. He was afraid something more had happened because the door had been left open like that.

"What's the door doing open?" he asked.

He started to get up and go and look out the door, but Gwen came back from the stove and put a cup of coffee down beside him.

"Your father had to go out," she said.

He saw the cards still spread out across the table from him, and the glass and whisky bottle and saucer full of cigar butts and ash. He must have been asleep a long time, because there were many more cigar butts in the saucer than there had been when he'd last seen it. At first he'd thought he'd only been asleep a few minutes, because the fire was still throwing its light so far out there. Even with the door open, the cigar smoke was still strong in the kitchen.

"I left it open to get some of the smoke out," Gwen said.

She had her arm around his head, and was stroking his forehead gently with her hard, warm hand.

"Drink your coffee, darling," she said. "I had to wake you up. I didn't want to, but you were having a nightmare. You were talking in your sleep, and you sounded terribly unhappy."

"Yes, I guess it was a kind of nightmare," Harold said. "It was all right at first, but then it changed."

He began to sip the hot coffee. The whole place is getting full of dreams, he thought. Half our life is dreams, and they all keep turning bad. I wonder if Arthur's dreams kept turning bad on him too. That last one did, anyway, from what he said.

Gwen went over to the door, and made a fan of it between her two hands, to get more of the cigar smoke out, and then closed it and came back.

"It's nearly morning, anyway," she said. "Your mother wants to see you. She heard you talking in your sleep, I guess, and thought you were awake. You better finish your coffee first, though."

There was something else she wasn't saying. She wanted to say it, but she thought maybe she shouldn't. He could guess that from the factual way she spoke, and went back to her work at the stove, holding herself apart from him again, after she'd been so gentle about waking him up. He couldn't ask her what it was, though, with the bedroom door open. Probably that was why she wouldn't tell him. It was probably something about why the mother wanted to talk to him.

He began to sip slowly at the very hot coffee. The dream still wouldn't let go of him. It was funny how a dream as impossible as that could go on seeming real when you were awake. Probably that was just because Arthur had been in it.

Gwen returned to the table with a cup of coffee, and sat down where he usually sat himself, with her back to the stairs. She sipped her coffee and watched him over the top of her mug. When she let the mug down, she was smiling at him a little, and not the quick, polite smile, either. She looked very tired, and the smile, which was slow and gentle, the kind she didn't give anybody else, seemed ready to turn into crying any time. He reached out his hand and touched her hand that was holding the coffee mug on the table.

"Didn't you get any sleep at all, honey?"

Gwen let go of the coffee mug and took hold of his hand quickly and pressed it hard, and the tears he'd thought were so close to coming, really came, and blurred her eyes and made drops on her lashes. She blinked them away hard, and they fell onto her cheeks. She let go of his hand and took a handkerchief out of the cuff of her blouse and rubbed at the tears almost angrily.

"Certainly I did," she said. "Never mind me. I'm just all mushy and leaky this morning."

He wanted very much then to say right out that he loved her, and to beg her pardon for all the things he felt guilty about, but it was difficult to talk of himself, and while he was fumbling for a way to begin, Gwen spoke again, smiling at him the same slow, gentle way, but trying to speak lightly, and speaking at all, mostly so he wouldn't, he thought.

"What on earth were you dreaming about, darling, that was so bad?"

"Oh, nothing much."

"Yes, you were. You frightened me, you sounded so scared. I was so glad you were getting a little rest, even if it was only sitting up at the table, and then you began to talk, and you sounded so unhappy."

"Did I say something I shouldn't have?" he asked, trying to grin.

"No," Gwen said. "There was nothing bad. I just had to wake you up because you were in some kind of awful trouble."

"What did I say?"

"Mostly you were just sort of mumbling. It was more the way you sounded. You said something about Arthur, like you were going to cry, and something about a jungle, too. And you spoke to me, like you wanted me to help you. You said, 'Gwen, he's gone,' and then you just said my name, like you were really talking to me, only you were scared. I couldn't let you stay scared when you wanted me to help you."

Harold smiled at her a little. "Poor Gwen, you can't get away from it, can you? Even in my sleep, you have to take care of me."

She shook her head at him. "You can't get around me like that. I was in your dream, and I want to know what I was doing. Or was it really so bad you don't dare tell me?"

Harold flushed. "It wasn't anything like that. It just doesn't make much sense, that's all."

"You were still talking about it after you woke up," Gwen

said. "You told me it was just the blue bedspread. What was just the blue bedspread?"

"Well," Harold said, "I was dreaming we were up there looking at this valley together, you and Arthur and me."

"You're getting me all mixed up," Gwen said, shaking her head at him. "What valley?"

"I'm kind of mixed up myself now."

He sipped at his coffee, and then Gwen began to sip at hers too, and watch him, so he had to go on.

"Well," he said, setting his mug down again, "it seemed kind of like a valley in the mountains here, only way up somewhere, and I'd never seen it before. It was this kind of country, though."

He thought about it for a minute.

"I tell you," he said. "Did you ever see Yosemite?"

Gwen shook her head.

"Well, neither did I, but Arthur used to have a big photograph of it, and I guess I made up this valley from that. It looked a lot like it, with high cliffs all around, and big mountains with snow on them going up at one end, and a big waterfall coming over the cliff from them. We were on a cliff a mile or so down the side of the valley, so the waterfall hardly made a sound you could tell from the wind in the trees. There were trees, big pines, down in the valley, and a kind of open meadow place right below us, with the river going through it."

"It sounds like a wonderful place," Gwen said.

Harold sat looking at his coffee and trying to remember.

"Yes, it was," he said finally. "That's why Arthur took us up there to see it. I know I felt pretty happy just looking at it, and because you and Arthur were there too."

It was Gwen who looked down at her coffee cup now.

"Arthur took us up there because it was so peaceful," Harold said. "There hadn't ever been anything in there but the animals that lived there. No people had ever been in there. I was sure about that in the dream. Arthur told us so, I guess. I knew some way, anyhow. And I was kind of all excited because Arthur was going to tell us something about it that would mean a lot to us. I don't know just what, because he never got a chance to tell us, but it seemed as if I was pretty sure it would fix everything up for us. You know, as if we could live there, and there'd never be any trouble."

Gwen nodded without looking at him.

"Only I was a little afraid all the time that something was going to happen, because I'd never seen any animals like that before, and even in the dream I couldn't quite believe they were real, so I was afraid the whole valley wasn't real. As if I halfway knew all the time it was just a dream."

Gwen nodded again, and looked at him. "What were the animals like?"

"They were all white, was the main trouble, I guess," Harold said. He made a soft chuckle of embarrassment. "There were a lot of white deer down in the meadow, and they all had gold hoofs, and the bucks had gold horns too. And there was a white panther lying there on the meadow too, with gold eyes. He wasn't after the deer, just watching them as if he was their best friend."

"The lion and the lamb," Gwen said.

"Something like that. Only they all looked like just pretty little toys. The grass in the meadow was so green it didn't look real either, green as the cloth on a billiard table, and they showed up on it so tiny and white. There were white birds flying around in the trees too, and white snakes, with gold eyes like the panther had, sliding around on the branches. But they all got along together."

"Only then something happened?" Gwen asked, when he didn't go on.

"Yes, but I can't remember just how it was. It was something about Curt, I think. Oh, it was just a fool dream," he said suddenly, as if he meant to drop it because he had remembered something he didn't want to talk about.

"But what made you feel so bad?" Gwen asked.

"Well, all of a sudden it just all changed. The valley got all dark, and all the animals and birds and things began to run around, scared to death, and then it wasn't even the same place. It was a kind of jungle, full of animals and flowers and trees I'd never even seen—nobody ever saw such things, for that matter—and they were all blue, dark blue. That's what I meant about the bedspread. At first, when I woke up, I could remember all that as if I was still seeing it, and I remembered there was a unicorn right in the middle of it, so I knew I must have been just dreaming about that bedspread.

"I guess," he said slowly, "that's what I meant talking to you about Arthur, because when the valley turned into that blue jungle, like the one on the bedspread, Arthur changed too. He was still standing up there on the cliff with us, but his eyes were closed, and he had his hands crossed on his chest, and he couldn't talk to us any more. It was just because mother had that spread on the bed in there all the time, I guess."

Gwen nodded again, without looking at him.

"Well, that's all there was to it," Harold said. "I got scared because Arthur looked so different, and then he just wasn't there at all. You know how things change in dreams? That must have been when I said your name, and you woke me up."

Gwen looked at him, and made the quick smile, and blinked quickly, and put her hand over his on the table for a moment. Then she stood up and said, "Well, I'm glad I did."

She came around beside him, holding her coffee cup, and put her arm around his neck and kissed him on the forehead.

"I'm glad I was there too, anyway," she said softly. "I'm glad it didn't all happen to you alone. It's worse in dreams than if it was real, sometimes.

"You want some more coffee now?" she asked.

"I guess I'd better go see what Mother wants, first."

Gwen went back to the stove, and he finished his coffee and stood up and came behind her. He thought of the open door, but defiantly, and took both her shoulders in his hands.

"I'm glad you were there too," he said.

Gwen pressed her head back against him and rolled it slowly, but didn't say anything. They stood that way, close together, for a moment, and then Harold kissed the top of her head, just a soft touch, but leaving his lips there a long time, and released her and turned away.

Without turning her head, and speaking very low, Gwen asked, "It was Curt that made it all change?"

"Well," Harold said, after a moment, "I guess it was. I can't remember that part. I never saw him in it anywhere, I don't think, just you and Arthur. But it seems as if it was just after

Arthur said something about him, and I thought he must be down in the valley there somewhere."

"And that was when it all changed?"

"I guess it was," Harold said. "Well, it was just a fool dream," he said uneasily.

Gwen still didn't look around at him, but she reached a hand back and found his belt, and slipped two fingers over it, and gave it the little tug that meant they were together.

"I'm glad I was in it, anyway," she said, and let go of him.

Harold stood undecided. At the little tug on his belt, he wanted very much to turn around and take her in his arms, but then she'd let go of him too soon. Now his arms felt empty, and the front of him felt useless and exposed, as if he'd lost part of his own strength because he hadn't done it. But the north door was open, and that made a difference again, now, and he felt a little ashamed and apart from her because he'd talked about the dream. Finally he just took hold of her shoulder with one hand, and pressed it hard for a moment, and let go of her and went on into the dark north room.

He could see the light of the fire still flickering in the window, making moving tongues of light across the ceiling and across the snow outside. He thought of when he had last mended the fire, and felt guilty because somebody else must have tended it since, and Gwen was the only one who could have done it.

He came to the side of the bed and stood there. He could just see, by the light from the kitchen door and the firelight on the ceiling, the mother's face rising out of the pillow like a mask with no head behind it. Her eyes were closed, and there was a white blanket pulled up to her chin.

"You want to see me, Mother?" he asked finally.

The mother lay quiet, and with her eyes closed, for so long he thought she had fallen asleep again. He had started to turn away when she asked, "What was it got the horses stirred up so?" Her voice was toneless, and the words hardly shaped, as if both her mind and her tongue found them difficult.

That's not what she wanted, Harold thought. She's putting it off.

"Oh, Joe Sam was pestering them," he said.

"That old fool Indian," the mother said more strongly. She

turned her head slowly in the pillow and opened her eyes and looked up at him. He could see the faint glittering in the hollow sockets. "You said Kentuck was hurt?"

"Joe Sam was after him, I guess."

"How do you mean after him? What's he want to bother the horses for, let alone that time of the night?"

"He had a knife. He said he thought it was the black painter. Kentuck will be all right. It isn't too bad."

"The black painter," the mother said. "A likely story." She lay there thinking about it for a moment. "What did you think it was? Some notion about getting even with Curt?"

"I don't know, Mother. It might be. But he could have been seeing things, I guess. He was out there without a stitch on."

"I've told your father a hundred times . . ." the mother began, but then closed her eyes and let her head roll back again, and didn't finish.

"He still ain't straightened out then?" she asked at last.

"He'll probably be all right in the morning," Harold said. "It's done snowing, and when I got him into his bunk, he went right off to sleep."

"If he ain't shammin' again."

"No, I don't think so. He's really asleep."

Once more he blamed himself silently because he had gone to sleep himself. He should have tended to the fire, and then gone up to the bunk-house and made sure Joe Sam was there and that he was all right.

They heard the outside door slam, and heavy steps in the kitchen, and the father's voice, thick and cheerful, asking, "Getting breakfast already, young woman?"

Gwen said something they couldn't understand, and the father answered, "That's fine, fine. I could do with a good breakfast. A man needs extra food to keep him going when he loses sleep." And then, "Where's Harold disappeared to? Go out to look for Curt?"

Once more they could hear Gwen's voice, but not her words.

"Well, he'd better be getting out there," the father said. "That young fool's been gone all night now. He must have got into some trouble. Somebody ought to take a horse out to him anyway. That was his horse came in last night; the black one."

The mother said, "You'd better go, I guess, Harold. Your father isn't going to give us any peace till you do."

That's what she really wanted, Harold thought. The old man just gave her a good lead.

Thinking again about the hopelessness of looking, after all that wind and snow, seeing in his mind how the mountains and the upper valleys would be covered and blown smooth now, he didn't answer.

"He's your born brother, Harold, if he does take a lot on himself sometimes."

"It isn't that," Harold said.

"You think it's no good looking for him now?"

"There wouldn't be much to go on," he said.

After a time, the mother said, "No, I don't guess there would. Only it does seem like we oughta do something. Not just leave him in his trouble."

She's got herself around to thinking there's still a chance, Harold thought.

"All right," he said. "I'll go."

"I been thinkin'," the mother said quickly. "Curt's not one to let himself get caught bad by no storm. He's too old a hand, Curt is. He'd find a way to wait it out. Only if he's got hurt. That's what I fret about, and then he'd think up a signal of some kind."

She's got it all figured out now, Harold thought. She's rubbing out three days almost as easy as the old man does. He uses whisky and she uses hope. He didn't say anything.

"It does seem like we oughta do something," the mother said again.

"Sure," Harold said. "I wouldn't feel right not to."

"For the peace of our souls," the mother said.

Never mind our souls, Harold thought sharply. For Curt's body. But that's what she means, he rebuked himself, that we couldn't stand not to know.

"Only how're you ever going to get a start after all that snow?" the mother asked.

"There's only one chance, as far as I can see," Harold said slowly. "Go up to the creek canyon and try and find something to go on."

"And if there ain't?"

"Well, I could take a look from up top. The cat would head up with somebody after him, anyway."

"You got to believe it, though, Harold," the mother said, nearly begging him. "You got to believe he's out there somewhere. If you don't, you won't half look. He's alive, I tell you. A mother's got a feelin' for those things. A bit ago I didn't think so, but now I do, strong. I been thinkin' pretty near the whole night, and I got a strong feelin' he's alive, only hurt. He'll think of some way to make a sign for you."

She pushed herself up to a sitting position as she spoke, and threw back the blanket and swung herself around until she was sitting on the edge of the bed, and he could see how her hair had been loosened again by the restless night. She clung to the edge of the bed with a hand on each side of her, and bowed her head and sat still for a moment. Then she raised her head very slowly.

"I don't know what ails me," she said. "I get so dizzy when I set up. Seems like I can't even think straight."

A reluctant pity moved in him then, not so much for his mother as for so strong a woman forced into complaining. He said what he didn't believe to reassure her.

"I'll find him. Don't you worry, Mother," and then, having spoken, came near to sharing her faith for a moment.

"You just lie back there now," he said, "and get yourself a rest. Gwen'll bring you some breakfast. No wonder you don't feel good. You've hardly slept or eaten anything for three days."

"I keep wonderin'," the mother said, scarcely more than whispering. "Seems to me sometimes like I ain't seen a single thing clear for what it really was. Your Dad didn't want to come out here, clear into the middle of no place. It was all my doing. I seen him gettin' like all the others there, with his big talk and his godlessness and his fine clothes, and money the only thing that mattered to him, and every cheap little whore and thievin' flatterer in town emptyin' his pockets when he had it. But I guess it was my good I was lookin' after more'n his. Now all he does is remember them times for a lot bigger'n they was, and get to drinkin' for any little thing comes up. And it ain't

been much better for the rest of you. Curt's a fine man, a man
to do big things, but out here he's got nothin' to put himself
against. It all turns mean and hard inside him. He ain't a man
can be by himself and think straight. He's gotta be doing somethin' all the time to be happy."

She propped her elbows on her knees and buried her face in
her hands.

"Sometimes I think it's worst of all for Grace, maybe. A
woman's made to have a man and children. Without she's got
'em, she ain't able to come to herself rightly. But it was me made
her quit her teachin' and come home here because she was
talkin' too much about that assayer fellow, talkin' just like
him, and him a foreigner and full of queer notions. But she's
just got so she talks like Arthur all the time instead, only she's
so wild about it. Arthur was never wild about it. And with
Arthur gone . . ." She didn't finish but sat there silently, still
with her face buried in her hands. Harold waited uneasily,
shifting his weight from foot to foot. This was worse than the
time before, and worse trying to think of something to say to
her.

Finally the mother went on. "Seems to me like I been talkin'
to Arthur all the blessed night long, rememberin' things he said
I didn't give no mind to then, no more than if they was the wind
in the chimney. It was like he was settin' right here in the dark,
sayin' 'em all over again. I could hear just the way he used to
say 'em, like it was his own voice speakin', and I could of
reached out and touched him settin' there, and most likely
whittlin' away while he talked. Only now it seems like everything he said kind of come together in the middle somewhere,
like he was talkin' about God all the time, in his own way, and
I'd never knowed it. Like I'd been so set in my own judgment
I'd never rightly even heard what he was sayin' before. Most
attention I'd ever give it was to tell him to stop his foolishness."

She lifted her head and peered up at Harold, searching his
face in the shadows for something she needed to know.

"But he wasn't hardly ever meanin' to mock, was he?"

"No," Harold said uneasily. "No, I don't think he ever was."

"No," the mother said, and then, "Seems like I might of seen
that before . . ."

The father raised his voice angrily out of the conversation that had been going on in the kitchen, and she stopped.

"Why don't he get out there, then?" the father demanded. "His own brother lost, and he sleeps all night on the table, like some drunk in a back room. I'm the only one cares enough even to stay awake for him. My God, what did I ever do to deserve such children? Curt's the only child of mine in the lot of 'em, I tell you. If anything happens to Curt, this place will go to pieces like a house of cards; like a house of cards, I tell you." They heard his fist thump on the table, making the dishes leap and rattle, and then the heavy voice died away into a thick and ominous mumbling.

The mother buried her face in her hands again, and cried softly, "Oh, my God, my God, why have you deserted me in this hour?" and even in those words, the lament pierced Harold. His grudging pity for the strong woman knowing her first doubt swelled into a great and personal pity. He put out one hand, awkwardly, to take her shoulder, but then couldn't. The old habit of being apart from her, even with his mind, was still too strong.

"Don't you take it on yourself so, Mother," he said. "You've done all anybody could. We're a pig-headed lot, all of us."

The mother didn't move or make any reply for a long time. He could feel how she was struggling against the tears of weakness that wanted to come, and against the long, falling despair he was getting to know so well himself.

When at last she spoke, her voice was not steady, but the words her mind had decided on were dry and self-mocking. "Well, it ain't helpin' anything much for you to stand here listenin' to an old fool cry in her bib, that's one sure thing. You get your girl there to feed you your breakfast, and then you get on up to the creek. I'll see your father don't keep at her."

She stood up slowly, helping herself with her hands, but then bent her head, and after a moment let herself down again, saying with a little, shaking laugh, a very strange sound, coming from her, "Only I guess I'll have to rest me a while first. I'm a fine one, I am. First time there's real trouble on us, I'm no more use than if I was at the bottle too, and not even able to tell the day of the week."

She lay back on the bed on her side, and let her head down into the pillow slowly, and closed her eyes. "Don't you dally here frettin' about me," she murmured. "You get on out there."

Harold drew the blanket up over her with unsteady hands. For years there had been nothing in her strength that was any use to him, but he was frightened, just the same, to see it so far gone.

"You let me get you something to eat first," he said.

She rolled her head a little in the pillow to mean no, and murmured, "I ain't hungry yet. You just ask your girl to bring me a cup of coffee after you've had your breakfast."

"You'll have to try to eat something, Mother, or . . ."

"I will, I will. Now you go along and let me be."

He stood there, trying to think of a way to get at her that would help, but couldn't, and finally turned toward the kitchen door.

"You better get Dad up to bed, out of her way," the mother said.

Harold turned back, and saw that her eyes were open again and looking at him. He nodded.

"And then you get on out there," she said again.

He nodded. "As quick as the chores are done."

"The chores can wait," she said. "Don't you waste good daylight on chores."

"All right," he said.

When he was in the doorway, she spoke again, and he waited.

"You better take that old fool Indian with you," she said.

Harold turned. "He'll be more'n half dead, Mother. You know how he is after one of these spells."

"You take him along, just the same," she said, "if he knows what he's doin'. He can read signs where nobody else would see a thing, I'll say that for him. You take him, Harold."

She doesn't want him around while I'm gone, he thought, and answered, "All right. I'll take him."

"I'll rest quieter in my mind if you will," the mother apologized. "A man shouldn't be out on such work alone. And you take some extry rations with you."

Harold nodded, and started to turn again, but she stopped him once more.

382

"And Harold."

"Yes."

"You start yourself back with daylight to get here. Don't you get led on past sense. If you ain't done no good by noon, you head on back here. There's no good to risk yourself for . . ." She hesitated. "For what can't be helped," she concluded.

"I'll watch it."

"No, you promise me. If you ain't come on a good sure sign by noon, you head back. Will you?"

"All right," he said.

He waited because he heard himself how faint a promise that answer made, and believed she would press for more. She didn't speak again though, and when the silence had lasted long enough, he felt the promise bind on him after all, and turned and went on into the kitchen.

The father had fallen asleep slumped down in his chair, with part of his breakfast still on the plate, and the cards pushed aside into a heap beside the bottle and glass and saucer full of butts and ash. His chin was down on his breast, and he was snoring softly, with a little bubbling at the lips on every out-breath. Grace was sitting there at the table too now, in Arthur's chair, with a mug of coffee in front of her. She was staring at the coffee, but not touching it. Her hands were out of sight in her lap.

Gwen stood up from the table when he came in, but he said, "I better go wake Joe Sam up first. I'm taking him along, if he's fit to move, and he'll want some breakfast too."

"All right," Gwen said. "I'll get something on for both of you. Will your mother eat anything yet?"

He shook his head. "You could take her a cup of coffee pretty quick. Then maybe you could try her again, after we get started."

He could tell by the way Gwen looked at him that she wanted to ask something more, but then she just nodded and sat down again.

"If we don't pick up something to go on by noon, we'll start back," he told her, hoping that was what she wanted him to say.

She started to nod again, as if that was all right, but didn't matter, but then her eyes filled with tears, and she looked down at her plate to hide them, and kept nodding too quickly. He pressed her shoulder with his hand, and she reached up quickly and put her hand over his, hard, and then laid it back on the edge of the table again.

Harold saw that Grace was watching them. He wasn't sure at first that she really saw them, but then knew she did, because she glanced up at his eyes, and then down again, and brought her hands up out of her lap and looked at something she was holding in them. He saw that it was that same carving of Arthur's, the old sheepherder with a long, thin beard and a partly bald head with long hair at the sides, carrying a lamb over the back of his neck, holding two of its legs in each hand. The wood was dark and smooth with long handling. Grace felt of it with her thumb, and then stood it out on the table and picked up her mug of coffee and began to sip at it. She kept looking at the stocky old sheepherder and the shadow the lamp gave him, over the rim of her mug, and her eyes were quiet, and really seeing him.

Harold took his hand from Gwen's shoulder, and brushed the knuckles of it gently along her cheek. Then he went around to the pegs and took down his coat. He stood for a moment looking at the father, and went out. When he had the door closed, he could see the first faint light in the east, giving the mountains shape. He put on his coat and went around the corner of the house, through the failing reach of the signal fire. Up ahead, over the mountain behind the bunk-house, the stars were still as bright as they had been at midnight. From down behind the sheds, though, thin, but clear and prolonged and wakeful, sounded the shrill crowing of the little bantam cock.

- - - 32

The sun was up clear of the eastern hills when Harold came onto the crest of the reach that hid the Aspen Creek. He drew rein to let the buckskin blow and steady its legs, saying, "Easy,

Kit; easy boy," and patting the sweating shoulder twice under the stock of the carbine he held against the horn.

He turned and squinted back across the glare of the snow to watch Joe Sam coming up behind him on Smudge. The little mare was making hard work of it, even in the wake Kit had left. Joe Sam sat huddled down in his saddle, moving only as the mare moved, as if his body were still asleep, but the old Sharp's buffalo rifle lay straight across his thighs.

Harold looked out over the valley. It shone blindingly, with the sun coming across it, and it was only here and there that the eye could rest in the blue shadows of drifts. Out beyond the brush-line of the creek, even the familiar, dark map of the marshes had vanished, frozen over and then covered with snow. Their shapes could only be guessed at by the curves and mounds of shadow, and little patches of black hairlines where the tules stood out of the snow. A light, broken wind had come up with the sun, and snow ghosts ran on brief, aimless excursions over the level, rising from nowhere and vanishing into nothing. One of the ghosts came glittering down about him from the ridge, and then swung away behind him and back onto the slope.

Joe Sam came up, and drew out into the unmarked snow beside him. The horses nosed at each other, mouthing their bits with a gentle clinking and blowing the steam of their breathing into one cloud, and making the girths creak. Harold looked at the old man's face, turned up to him. It was very tired, aged by the short sleep with the vision gone out of him, but the good eye was seeing things as they were, all right, and he was resting even while he sat in the saddle. He was slack as a cat in the sun.

"Hard going for the horses," Harold said.

"Much snow," the old man agreed. He looked down, and moved his leg to make Harold see the snow on it where it had dragged through the drifts. Harold grinned, because that lively, private joke was in Joe Sam's eye again, something he was keeping to himself, something quite sane and malicious, and then nodded and looked up the spine of the ridge above them.

"Should we take a look first?" he asked, motioning up with his mittened hand.

Joe Sam lifted his shoulders a very little, to show he wouldn't make a choice. "Much time go," he said, and motioned to the east and up to show how long the sun had been up.

Harold studied his face. "You think that painter's in there, don't you?"

"Snow not come now," Joe Sam said. "Maybe come back. Sleep all snow. Hungry now." The good eye was twinkling, the joke growing in it.

He means more than that, Harold thought, but knew better than to ask what.

"He could be, at that," he admitted. "It would be something to get him anyhow," he said grimly. "We'll go up by the creek then," and he pressed Kit to start down.

They came around into the canyon mouth with the glare at their backs and the shadow of the big cut ahead of them, and could look with open eyes. The snow deepened rapidly as they climbed and the sides of the ravine drew in. The horses warned them before Harold had any other sign, by beginning to snort and try to turn against the reins, first to one side and then to the other. Harold read the snow before them quickly, and then looked along the willows on their right for anything moving, but saw nothing, and looked at Joe Sam. The old man, letting Smudge wheel a little to ease her, but never as much as half way, pointed up to the north wall, above the dazzle of the sloping shoulder, at a deep line where something had come down, heading up canyon and floundering. He nodded.

"We'll leave the horses here," he said. "Too much snow, and they're spooky already."

He swung off, and Joe Sam let himself down more slowly. They led the horses into the willows and tied them by ropes around the bases of two clumps, and took their snowshoes off the saddles and laced them on, Joe Sam the small home-made bear-paws, and Harold the longer, narrow webs.

"I go that side, huh?" Joe Sam asked, pointing across the creek.

Harold nodded. "Keep where I can see you."

Joe Sam worked along the willows, until they thinned at a shallows, and went through and across the creek and up on the other side until Harold could see his head and shoulders against the snow. Then they went up canyon slowly, keeping abreast of

386

each other and alternately scanning the snow close before them and looking up ahead into the heavy shadow between the cliffs that were too steep to hold snow except in their scars.

It was Joe Sam, perhaps instructed by the tracks that came down on his side, who pointed across toward the south wall, and held his hand there, pointing, until Harold saw the dark, anonymous bulk under a shelving drift, with the rim of the drift partly fallen over it. Then he could pick out the broken trail that led from it down to the willows too. He nodded, and they moved up again. Harold didn't stop at the track, but only read it with a tightening of the chest at what it promised. The great pad marks, like broken flowers, were in the furrow on top of the sharper, split hearts of the hoofs, and only thinly covered with snow the wind had blown in. He took off the mitten from his trigger hand, and watched scrupulously from the willows to the south wall ahead of him, and more often up into the shadow.

When he saw the next tracks way ahead, but going up along the willows, so they showed plainly, he guessed, and looked almost as soon as Joe Sam pointed across, and saw where the cat had gone up diagonally toward the new trail from its kill under the south wall.

Curt was right, he thought. Not even for fresh meat. A killer for fun, and pumped the first cartridge into the barrel, slowly, to be as quiet as he could.

And not only of cows, he thought grimly. Just let me get one crack at you, just one good crack, that's all I ask, he practically prayed, even moving his lips a little, but then warned himself off, feeling the excitement hurry his thoughts and tighten his body.

He came into the deep rut he'd seen ahead, and found it made by three steers, two lumbering so close together they'd jostled each other, and one running alone, ahead of them. Where the two trails came together, just above the first aspens, the flurry of marks was too wild to read quickly, but following the heavier marks, he saw the two red hulks down among the aspens, and then went on up, the blue canyon shadow coming over him coldly, because the flower prints went up too, and sometimes blurred the last hoof prints.

He found the fourth one, a young brindled heifer, above the

387

next bend, where the canyon on his side began to rise steeply from the creek, so the aspens were gold bushes below him, only their tops standing out of the snow caught against the slope. The heifer had started down there, and lost her footing in the drift at the edge, and the cat had caught up with her. Her head was stretched into the snow and half covered by it. The hide had been ripped away raggedly from her shoulder, and the flesh chewed out deeply and widely, so the white joint showed, and the first ribs behind it. The blood was still liquid and bright in small pools in the wound, and short comets of it still flecked the snow red in many directions out from where the heifer lay, like the pattern of a little, scarlet bomb-burst.

The panther's tracks still went up beyond this last kill, along the ledge above the creek, where the wind had kept the snow shallower, and then Harold thought, peering, not quite certain in the blue gloom under the high walls, zig-zag up the high fall of boulders, smoothed almost into the canyon slope by the snow, and out of sight onto the shelf at the head.

Right into the trap, he thought. And not minutes ago, not minutes, he added silently, glancing again at the blood in the great wound in the heifer's shoulder.

Once more he checked the dangerous excitement. If Joe Sam hasn't found where he came out, he thought. He looked down across the creek, and after a moment found Joe Sam's brown face, much lower than he'd expected, looking up at him through the yellow leaves and the pale snakes of branches. The old man saw him, all right, but he only waited down there, making no sign.

So it's in there still, he thought, and felt himself tighten again in spite of all he could do.

He nodded largely to Joe Sam, and made a fierce woodpecker signal in the air toward the head of the canyon to warn him. When he started up again, the motion easing him a little, he rebuked himself for his officious gesture.

Don't waste your time worrying about him, he thought. His one old eye's better than your two young ones. And there's something else works in him, he thought, remembering the halt on the south ridge. He was sure of this before he saw a track.

Thinking that, he remembered what Curt had said about the

steers and the bull that had been killed up there on the platform ahead. Back to the scene of the old crime? he wondered, smiling a little, tightly, in his mind, but his eyes searching carefully before him, all along the curving fort of the platform.

At the foot of the rock slide, where the cat had begun to make the switch-backs going up, he paused and hunted with his eyes down among the aspen tops for Joe Sam again, and this time found him farther in than he was himself, and higher than he expected, already above the level of the aspens and working up the slanting base of the north wall still farther to see onto the platform before he exposed himself. The old man wasn't looking over at him at all now. He wasn't looking where he was going either, but feeling his way up and watching the edge of the platform all the time. He was carrying the old Sharp's ready across his body.

You'll worry yourself to death yet, my friend, Harold told himself, and made the thin smile in his mind at this joke too, wondering a little that he should be making any jokes right then, and above all, jokes of that kind, but pleased that he did.

He turned toward the south wall, where the tilt of the canyon floor rose into the platform more gradually. That was where the tracks said the cat had gone up also. He paused after each two shuffling steps to look all along the rim of the platform and to listen, he didn't know what for, just anything that shouldn't be heard there. But there was only the wind once in a while, beating hollowly over the canyon head, and always the subdued conversation of the creek in the snow and ice.

In the corner where the platform of rock joined the cliff, he squatted on his heels to stay hidden, and prepared the last step of the attack. The carbine was ready, and he was holding it ready, and he was far enough back from the platform to swing it where he had to. He must raise himself slowly, with his head against the dark cliff, and he must make the first shot count; the first shot must be at least seriously crippling. If a panther like this one ever reached him, if it ever got inside the muzzle of the carbine with even one second of life left in it, it would take him apart like tearing paper; it would break his neck like snapping a dry splinter.

There were two considerations which worried him. The

panther might be so close to him when he saw it that he couldn't get even the one precious shot, and the snowshoes, when he thought of such a sudden attack, seemed dangerously clumsy. He could discover no remedy for either trouble, though. There was no way to know where the cat was except to look, and in these drifts, he'd be even more helpless without snowshoes than with them.

He experienced a brief loathing for close quarters, blind spots, and the airiness of new snow, which surpassed any natural loathing he'd ever known before. Then it occurred to him that if he waited too long, it might be Joe Sam that the panther would be tearing like paper, and snapping like a dry splinter. He was compelled to act promptly, and there were only two things he could afford to think of; he must see the panther first glance, and if possible, before it saw him, and he must keep himself perfectly steady in order that the all-important first shot should be neither too hasty to do its work nor too slow to do that work in time.

This tactical conference was actually more a matter of feeling than of thought, and was concluded in a few seconds. As he began to inch up against the cliff, however, his mind, quite by itself, and without distracting his attention at all, made another unexpectedly humorous comment.

Darned if I think there's any cat there at all, it declared. Darned if I don't think it's Joe Sam's cat after all, and there'll be nothing to see in there except snow and three dead steers. The critter's killed seven in all, now, and never been seen. Why on earth, then, should you expect it to show itself in broad daylight, and in the one place it couldn't get out of? It won't, of course; it simply won't be there, and you're making a fool of yourself with all this caution.

The panther was there, though, and in spite of trying to ready himself for anything, Harold was surprised. In part he was expecting to find it way over by Joe Sam's edge with its back turned; and in part not to find it at all, but only empty snow and the grinning black cliffs. Actually, as his eyes and the muzzle of the carbine came above the snow, he saw the panther only at third glance, and then farther away than he had thought of, back under the cliff and over near the falls. And in spite of his care, it had taken warning in some way. It was looking right at him. Also, he'd forgotten about the snow. He was prepared to see the whole huge, clever, dark cat at once. Actually only its head and shoulders showed and the curling tip of its tail above them.

Arranged that way, dark upon a platter of snow, the head appeared black and impossibly large, and for a moment Joe Sam was the one wise man among many fools and the carbine became a useless toy against the cold panther will that was measuring him out of the yellow eyes.

Yet even then, his independent mind repeated its first joke. Beside the cat he saw, without looking away from the fascinating eyes, a red and white bulge of steer's hide, and he thought, Yes sir, back to the scene of the crime.

That small humor of disbelief freed him to raise the carbine, but at the same instant the watchful trance was also broken by some sound or movement Joe Sam made on the other side. The cat turned its head and saw the old Indian on the north slope raising the Sharp's as he came up into sight. The two threats so far apart made up its mind for it, and it moved at once. Baring its great fangs in a snarl of fear, it swung away toward the back corner upon its right, but saw at once that it couldn't climb out there, and swung clear around again toward the other corner, where the cliff sloped a little in the narrow creek chimney bearded with ice and snow. It cleared the drifts on the platform in two great bounds, crashed through the ice that covered the basin, screaming wildly at this sudden failure of its footing, and leapt into the chimney. It clawed its way up unbelievably on the ice and stone to three times its own length above the basin. While its scream still beat back and forth between the cliffs above him, like enraged eagles, putting his teeth on edge and raising his back hair, Harold forced the muzzle of the carbine up after the climbing cat. Its scrambling stiffened and slowed, the talons of the forepaws scraping desperately, and failing. It glared down over its right shoulder, the long snarl rattling in its throat, and braced its left hind foot high to drive it out over the pool when it fell. It hung there for an instant, motionless, clinging dark and spread-armed against the mottled crevice of rock and ice. In that instant, Harold fixed the blade of the front sight in the notch of the rear, and just under the straining shoulder, and jerked the trigger home. Dimly through the jet and the drift of the smoke, while the blast still closed his ears, he saw the panther launch out and drop away, like a great bat, toward the narrow snow under the north cliff. Its second scream pierced the deep echoes of the report that rolled among themselves around him, yet he saw that the fall was not helpless, but had the tense line of purpose, and thought, even as he quickly lowered the carbine and sprung the lever again, God Almighty, missed, and felt a fleet return through his body of his loathing for the snowshoes and encumbering drifts.

The cat struck, snarling continuously now, floundered for an instant in the drifts, and bounded away down canyon and toward the creek. The snow dragged heavily at it, but even so it had raced below the platform before he could sight on it again.

Jesus, right at Joe Sam, he thought, and yelled, "Look out, Joe Sam," so that his voice and the last of the cat's scream and the rocky thunder of the report fought all together for a moment in the shadowy air.

The turmoil had scarcely begun to diminish, when it was renewed. The Sharp's boomed somewhere below the ledge, and the cat suddenly broke its snarl with half a scream, and at once the cliffs again multiplied and deepened the report and gave wings to the scream. Joe Sam yelled below, but excited, not wailing. Shuffling half-around to watch the lower slope, cursing, in his mind, the screen of aspens, Harold saw the cat going down, making the dark, serpent-curving leaps, but more slowly, he thought, staggering a little at each drop and fumbling the take-offs more than the snow explained.

One of us got him, he thought, while he raised the carbine again, leading the bounding shadow to an opening in the small, dancing leaves. It came there, black between the gold and against the white, and he fired again, and again heard the sudden scream through ghosts of the report.

Hit that time, by God, he thought exultantly. He shuffled at a half-run, dragging and teetering down across the snow-bank, treacherous with broken rock beneath, toward the little yellow trees. He struggled to pump the carbine again as he went.

The echoes died, and there was no sound from the lower

canyon. Harold reached the creek, where he could cross, and saw Joe Sam coming down very slowly on the other side, carrying the Sharp's idly in his right hand and looking intently into the aspens below him. The old man's sombrero was pushed half off his head and he was covered with light, clinging snow.

"You all right?" Harold called, alarmed by the old man's slowness and the proof he had fallen.

Joe Sam looked up at him and grinned. "Good," he said, clearly enough, but with the effect, after Harold's voice, of advising quiet. Still grinning, he shook his head and made a quick motion along his side to show how fast and how closely the cat had passed him. Then he pointed down into the little dancing trees.

Harold realized the old man must have seen the whole flight from his side.

"He's down there?" he asked.

Joe Sam nodded. "Much shoot," he said, grinning.

Harold took his time then, and stood at the edge of the creek and reloaded the carbine. Joe Sam waited across from him, ankle-deep in the drift, and watched him, and once or twice looked down into the aspens again.

"You loaded, Joe Sam?"

Joe Sam shook his head, grinning. "He wait," he said. "You shoot."

"I'll have to go down this side, so he won't get across. You better load up."

Joe Sam made the little shrug, but took another cartridge from his pocket and reloaded the old Sharp's.

Harold was going to warn him not to be so sure it was all over, but checked himself, thinking, he knows what he sees. He played this game before I was ever thought of.

"Well, let's finish the poor devil off," he said and started down his side.

It was all over though. The big cat lay tangled in the first willows, his head and shoulder raised against the red stems, his legs reaching and his back arched downward, in the caricature of a leap, but loose and motionless. The great, yellow eyes glared balefully up through the willows at the rock fort on top of the south wall. The mouth was a little open, the tongue

393

hanging down from it behind the fangs. The blood was still dripping from the tongue into the red stain it had already made in the snow. High behind the shoulder, the black pelt was wet too, and one place farther down, on the ribs. Standing there, looking at it, Harold felt compassion for the long, wicked beauty rendered motionless, and even a little shame that it should have passed so hard.

Like Arthur, he thought, smiling to himself in his mind. A big price for a few stupid steers. But there was Arthur too, he told the dead cat silently. You had it coming, several times over.

The wind turned high on the wall of the canyon, and reached down in gently, setting the aspen leaves shimmering and talking around the two of them standing there, and stirring the soft, cream-colored belly fur of the cat.

"A big one, sure enough," Harold said.

"Big," Joe Sam agreed solemnly. "Devil."

"The black painter?" Harold asked, looking at him.

Joe Sam's good eye studied him, guarding against ridicule. It found no smile, and the little jest danced behind it again.

"Not black painter," the old man said, shaking his head vigorously. "Black painter," and he made a wide gesture with his arm, which might have meant it was in the mountains above, or that it was everywhere and not confined to one place, but certainly meant that it was not to be talked over dead and empty in a willow thicket. But while it was still thus formless as air in Harold's mind, Joe Sam gave it body again by kicking the dead cat's belly gently with the rim of one snowshoe.

"Not black painter," he said.

"No, that's white enough," Harold agreed. He kept watching the old Indian. He missed something he'd expected in him, some triumph, some little inflation of success. But the old man was solemn again after the small half joke of kicking the pale belly. He was waiting for something, that was it. He didn't act as if the thing was finished. And whatever he was thinking, he didn't want to be the one to speak about it first.

I don't know what he wants, Harold thought. Some ceremony? he wondered, remembering the wooden cats Arthur had made.

To make a lead, he said, "It was a killer, though, pretty near as good as your black one," and then thought of the steer he'd seen on the rock. There hadn't been time to notice it then, but now, remembering the red and white bulge beside the great head of the cat, he knew that it hadn't been an old kill. There hadn't been any snow over it.

"Kill all time," Joe Sam agreed.

"It had another steer up on the rock there. Five this time."

Joe Sam didn't say anything for a moment, and then, still looking down at the dead lion, he said, "Not steer, maybe."

"I saw it," Harold said.

"Not steer," Joe Sam said stubbornly, but now with a rising inflection that put both the steer and the cat out of Harold's mind. He waited, watching Joe Sam's face. Joe Sam still didn't want to say it, or at least he wanted a direct question to make it easier for him. Harold just waited though, and the wait became too long.

"Coat, maybe," he said.

After a moment Harold asked, "Arthur's coat, you mean?"

"Curt wear," Joe Sam said. "Arthur have red coat."

"Sure. I know," Harold said quickly. "Well," he began, but then asked, "You sure?"

"See good," Joe Sam said. "Coat." He wouldn't look up from the dead lion.

Harold took a deep breath, and it wasn't steady. "Well," he said again, "we'd better go back and see, I guess."

Joe Sam nodded, and turned away from the cat, but still without looking at Harold.

Harold worked out of the willows up onto the higher south bank, with Joe Sam behind him, and climbed slowly toward the shadowed head of the canyon again. When he came onto the platform, with the tall, black walls over him, he paused to get himself ready. Then he went on in, seeing but not noticing the deep trail the cat had left. Even before he was close to the huddle of red and white hide, he knew that Joe Sam was right, because he could see the twisted legs reaching from it toward the falls.

And dead for sure, he thought, the unnatural position of the legs hurting him, and a little darkness of guilt stirring in him because he hadn't come here at once, and just let the cat go, after the first shot. The first shot got him, anyway, he thought, and excused himself, but I didn't know that, or what this was.

He came beside the body and stopped and stood looking down at it. The head, and the hood of the coat with it, was buried in the snow, but the bare trigger hand was half showing, blue and clutching into the snow, and the body was humped up, shaped over the rocks it had fallen on like a sack only loosely filled and tossed down.

Seeing the torn shoulder of the coat, and the raking scars in the leather farther down, Harold thought, By God, it was that black devil again, and the small, quick anger relieved him a little of the dread he felt about moving Curt.

His memory, though like someone else quietly and unconcernedly setting him right, reminded him of Arthur's torn shirt and wounded shoulder, and he saw that Curt's shirt, where it showed in the rip in the coat, wasn't torn.

Joe Sam came beside him, and because he didn't want to hesitate in the old man's presence, he gathered himself toward what he had to do, and then it was his own mind thinking, No cat ever did that to him. Not like that.

He knelt and took a deep breath, and pulled at Curt's shoulder to turn him over. At first the body wouldn't move at all, but stuck closely to the rocks under it. Then it broke loose abruptly, with a little tearing of the hairs of the parka, but moved all in one piece, the legs with the shoulder, and wouldn't turn over against its reaching arm. Harold let it back down on its face and stood up. His stomach knotted in him, and a fine sweat broke out on his face. After a moment, making it a single convulsive act, he stepped astride of the body and lifted it whole and turned it over. Then he quickly straightened again and closed his eyes against what the rocks had done to the face and tried to close his mind against what his hands had felt through the parka. When he believed he wouldn't vomit after all, he lifted his right snowshoe back over the body, taking great care not to touch it, and stood beside it.

"Not painter," Joe Sam said.

"No."

"Him fall there," Joe Sam said, and pointed up. Harold

looked where he was pointing, and saw the snow eave of the cliff broken, and then, when Joe Sam pointed there too, saw where the chunks of ice had sunk into the drift like little meteors, and the rain holes of pebbles and sand among them. He nodded.

"Well," he said finally, "we can't take him home like that."

"Bury," Joe Sam said.

Harold shook his head. "We have to take him home."

"Make fire," Joe Sam suggested. "Get warm. Fix."

Slowly Harold understood, and nodded. "Down below, I guess," he said. "There's some old dry stuff in the willows."

He took off his snowshoes and lashed them side by side, over-lapping a little, and together they lifted the body onto this poor sled. Harold straightened and stood there thinking, and finally understood what was wrong, and looked around the platform, and even went back and hunted closer under the cliff and at the head of the creek. He found nothing, and there were no other breaks in the snow at the back. He returned to where Joe Sam was waiting beside the hooded body on the webs, that lay with the one arm raised still in a grotesque gesture of greeting.

"I can't find the gun," he said. "He had the other carbine, the Winchester. And no snowshoes either."

Joe Sam pointed up at the cliff again.

"Must be, I guess," Harold said. "Well, we'll take him down and get the fire started, and then I'll go take a look."

"Night. Make fall," Joe Sam said.

Harold nodded. "However he got there," he said.

Joe Sam was careful with his voice, making it flat, with no feeling at all, but the tiny, malicious light was there behind the good eye again. "Him know," he said.

Harold looked at him, asking the question silently.

Joe Sam pointed to his head, and then shook it, and then tapped himself on the chest, on the wrinkles of the too big coat.

"Know here," he said. "Not lose plenty times. Come back."

Slowly he drew a circle in the air in front of him, parallel with the snow.

"Maybe," Harold said, and thought, Maybe you have that

kind of a compass under the ribs, old man, and then wasn't sure that was what Joe Sam had meant, and looked at him again, and saw the little dancing malice in the good eye.

Celebrating it, you little heathen, he thought angrily, but the anger shrank quickly in the mind closed by handling Curt and seeing his face, and he thought wearily, Well, why wouldn't you?

"Lost in the snow, you mean?" he asked.

"Not snow," Joe Sam said. He pointed at the parka, and Harold remembered there had been no snow on it.

Since the snow stopped, he thought. Since yesterday afternoon.

"Night," Joe Sam said. "Dark. Run away."

"Run away?"

"Lose gun," Joe Sam said. "No shoe."

Harold thought about it. "What would he be running away from?"

Joe Sam raised his shoulders that inch which unburdened them. "Not know," he said. "Not see."

Harold thought, seeing the lively eye watching him out of the impassive face, You think you know, though.

"Well," he said, "let's get him down there, and get that fire started."

Between them, tugging carefully, Harold struggling in the deep snow without his webs, they drew the body on the joined snowshoes across the platform and down the rock fall and past the brindled heifer on the edge, and then the two red steers among the aspens and then the stretched cat in the willows, and on down to where the horses waited in the sun. There they gathered the long, bow-shaped dead wood from among the larger willows, the breaking of the dry sticks bringing faint, crackling echoes from the rim-rock above them. It took them more than an hour to gather enough. They made two fire piles, and lifting the body from the snowshoes, laid it between them, with the head up canyon. Already the sun had softened the stiff hide of the parka, and Harold drew the hood over the head, and closed it over the face. Joe Sam brought dry dead leaves from under the pack of past autumns in the thickets and made kindling wads of them under each heap of gray willow sticks.

"He had matches himself," Harold said. He felt in the pockets of the parka, and found the match container, and the knife too.

He put the knife in his pocket. Then he took one of the four matches from the container, and ran it quickly along his thigh, and set the flame to one and then another of the wads of dry leaves, and then to one on the other side too before he had to drop the match in. The leaves made a slow, heavy smoke, and then with soft explosions, one at a time, the three wads burst into flame. After a little, the dried willow began to crackle sharply. The wind, sucking down canyon, drew the flames east and strengthened them. The two men stood silently, one at each side, watching the flames gain and rise, and to see they didn't burn too close.

"Sun help," Joe Sam said.

Harold nodded.

The heat was making a watery dancing in the air over the body, and they had to move back from the fires.

"Skin painter," Joe Sam said. "Get skin."

Harold nodded. "Go ahead. You want his knife?" he asked, reaching into his pocket.

Joe Sam shook his head. "Got good knife," he said, grinning a little, and turned and went back up the canyon, carrying the old Sharp's.

Harold squatted where he was, watching the fires, and the still figure between them, until there were only red shimmering coals left, hissing as they sank into the snow. Then he dared try the body, and it answered to his hands enough for what he had to do. He lifted it onto the snowshoe sled again, setting his jaw when he felt the broken bones grate under the parka and the flesh. He drew the arms down the sides, and straightened the legs as well as he could. He pulled the hood back and washed the broken face with snow and covered it with a blue bandana from his hip pocket, and closed the hood over it again. Finally he took the rope from Joe Sam's saddle and bound the body securely to the webs, and it lay ready in the golden sunlight, between the two heaps of red embers.

Feeling almost impersonal about it then, the worst being over, he stood for a minute or two looking down at the body.

He wished to make a prayer, or at least some ceremonial gesture of the spirit which would move him as a prayer should, but nothing stirred any deeper than the word-making surface of his mind except a weak, nagging worry about how he should tell the mother, and even, since it was Curt, the father, and how he could manage the burial without letting them see what the rocks had done.

Finally he thought, Well, we got the painter for you, anyway, fellow, and at once was swept by a terrible loneliness. It was more for Arthur than for Curt, but Curt was in it too, a sense of real loss that his powerful body and angry will would never move anything at the ranch again.

The surge of loneliness drained slowly out of him and left only an autumnal sadness in the sunlight around him and on the bound and straightened body, and he let that do.

He went down into the willows, untied Kit, swung into the saddle and turned him down into the trail they had made coming up. When the slope was easy enough, he put the buckskin across through the unbroken snow toward the south wing, and then, by switchbacks, up onto the ridge. There he let him stand till his breathing was steadier, when he reined him toward the mountain and pressed him up once more, keeping on the spine of the ridge, where the wind had blown the snow shallower, so that sometimes brush or rock stood up out of it. Before they came to the first scattered pines, he could see Joe Sam, a tiny figure squatting in the red willows below. The sun had reached into the canyon almost to the rock platform at the head now, and the busy knife made quick, blinding flashes in the light. Once Joe Sam looked up and raised an arm to show he saw him. Harold answered the same way, and the knife began to flash again.

When the drifts grew too deep among the conical trees where the ridge joined the mountain, Harold dismounted and tied Kit, and worked his way on up on foot, leaning and floundering, and stopping often to rest and breathe. When he stopped he always looked at the figure lying way down toward the mouth of the canyon, between the two black patches on the snow, and the wispy columns of smoke that still rose from them or flawed suddenly in the canyon wind. He looked down at

Joe Sam each time too. He could always find Joe Sam in the shadow screen of the willows, because sooner or later the knife would take the right angle and flash.

At last he came onto the treeless strip of snow that went up the mountain from the end of the canyon. He found the tracks that led to the gap at the edge of the cliff, and worked up them, guessing the wild running and the wallowing falls into the drifts, till he came to a pile of cut boughs and the deep black hollow of a burnt-out fire with a few woven-together boughs laid on the snow between them and sagging from a weight that wasn't on them now. The Winchester lay on the corner of this platform of boughs, and along its edge, toward the fire hole, was a neat row of six cigarettes. The missing bear-paws stood neatly together against the pile of boughs. He picked up the carbine and tried the trigger. It gave limply, and he pumped the lever, and holding the muzzle uphill at the open snow, tried again. The carbine roared and leapt in his hands, and instantly a little spurt of snow jumped in the clearing, and a deep, tumultuous echo rolled in the canyon below. He shook his head, and laid the Winchester down on the boughs again, and looked all around the clearing.

Finally he sat down and laced on the bear-paws and rose and worked slowly, very tired now, and sleepy from the dazzle of sun on the snow, along the marks he could see. Still he found only the flat, round prints of the bear-paws, in a single, dragging trail down from the mountain, and in deep, unclear ruts from the black remains of the fire to the slashed trees on both sides of the clearing. It made a queer, lonely puzzle, a little foolish in the bright sunlight on the snow, but a little terrifying too, when you knew the end of it.

He stopped finally by the cut trees on the north edge, and looked along the single trail that went up the mountain out of sight into the timber. It went by itself as far as he could see it, and he shook his head again, and came back to the pile of boughs. He stood there looking down at the six cigarettes laid neatly side by side upon the edge of the platform of boughs.

He had himself set for a long time, he thought dreamily, and then, looking at the black fire hole again, And he was here a good part of it.

Finally he looked around the clearing once more seeing his own tracks going beside Curt's now, and thought drowsily, the whole pattern of what he had found becoming unreal, It might as well have been your black painter at that, Joe Sam.

He picked up the Winchester and laid it with his own over his right shoulder. He stood looking at the cigarettes again, but at last shook his head a little and left them there just as they were. He went back down to where Kit was waiting, and untied him and led him on down below the last trees. There he took off the bear-paws and tied them to the saddle and mounted. Laying the carbines together across his thighs, he rode the rest of the way down slowly, going almost to the end of the reach this time before he reined Kit over into the canyon.

When he got back to the body and the faintly smoking funeral fires, he took Kit down and tied him beside Smudge in the willows once more, and standing the rifles up against the brush, put on the bear-paws, and climbed on up the canyon. He found Joe Sam still squatted over his red work, but the great hide free to the shoulders. Joe Sam stopped the knife where it was and looked up. Harold saw it was Arthur's knife he was using.

He shook his head. "He had a big fire up there, but I couldn't find any tracks except his."

"You shoot," Joe Sam said.

"Oh, I was only trying his gun. It was still loaded. Something scared him, though. He was running when he fell over the edge."

"No track?"

"Only his."

Joe Sam made one short sound, a kind of soft grunt, and then suddenly, as if waking from some thought of his own he wished not to show, looked down again and began to tug at the hide and flick under the edge of it with the bloody point.

That was answer enough for him, Harold thought, A proof as good as seeing it.

He took off the bear-paws and knelt to help the old man, drawing with both hands at the slippery hide, while the bright knife flicked and flicked, severing the thin, clinging membranes.

The sun had gone out of the canyon to the southwest, and the blue shadows and the wind were in the aspens again, when at last Joe Sam rose with the freed hide in his hands, and held it up for a moment to show its great length, and then laid it on clean snow and rolled it, fur side in. The thin, marbled carcass, appearing much smaller than when the pelt had covered it, lay naked in the bushes. Joe Sam, grinning a little, held the roll of hide up, the tail flap and one claw-weighted paw dangling out of it.

"Good blanket for bed now," he said. "You get marry, huh?"

Harold thought again, You can't blame him, and said, forcing a little grin himself, "Maybe. That's up to her."

Joe Sam shook his head, grinning widely now. "She come," he said confidently. "You boss now. No trouble."

Harold looked at him, and finally said slowly, "I guess I am at that," seeing for the first time the enormous difference this could make.

"Well," he said quickly, "we'd better get moving. It'll be pretty near dark before we get back now."

Joe Sam looked at him, with the joke in his eye, but then only nodded and laid the rolled hide on the snow and knelt and began to lace on his snowshoes. Only when Harold was knotting the rawhide of his second web, the old man said, without looking up, "Not black painter."

Harold finished the tie, and knelt there, looking at the small old figure in the coat too big for it, and at the dark, square old hands, splashed with the dried blood of the cat, working awkwardly at the laces.

Going to sic it on me now? he wondered, but answered, "No. I guess we'll never get that one."

"Not get," Joe Sam agreed, and Harold didn't think he was joking now, but that he meant it for himself too.

They went back to the horses, Harold ahead, with the heavy Sharp's rifle, and Joe Sam behind him with the rolled skin in his arms. By the horses, Joe Sam bound the roll with the laces of his webs, and after a long, patient trying, got Smudge to accept it, and tied it on behind the saddle.

Harold turned the snowshoe sled so its prow was headed down canyon, and then led Kit up out of the willows, and hitched him to it by his lasso. Seeing Joe Sam already mounted and waiting, he brought the two carbines up and mounted himself, and led the way slowly down, looking back often to make sure the clumsy sled with its hooded burden was following him safely. Each time he looked back he saw Joe Sam coming down behind the sled, hunched stolidly in the saddle, the Sharp's straight across his legs, the black sombrero set perfectly straight on his head, on top of the blue bandana around his face.

A queer guard for your last ride, he thought once, addressing the dead Curt between them.

They went clear out onto the flat of the meadow, into the sunlight, before Harold turned south toward the ranch. The wind was stronger out there, and sometimes they moved in shadowy file, the leader, and the low, crude sled, and the guard, through a spinning, glittering mist of blown snow they couldn't see out of, the living any better than the dead. When the snow swept lower past them, though, or at a shift of the wind fled away east in three smoky columns, Harold could see the ranch, still tiny with distance, and already in the shadow of the mountain. Once in a while it showed clearly, so he could see even the smoke lining out from the chimney of the house, but more often it grew faint or even disappeared behind the running snow.